Rag-and-Bone Christmas

Dilly Court is the No.1 *Sunday Times* bestselling author of forty novels. She grew up in North-East London and began her career in television, writing scripts for commercials. She is married with two grown-up children, four grandchildren and a beautiful great-granddaughter. Dilly now lives in Dorset on the Jurassic Coast with her husband.

To find out more about Dilly, please visit her website and her Facebook page:

www.dillycourt.com
f /DillyCourtAuthor

Also by Dilly Court

Mermaids Singing
The Dollmaker's Daughters
Tilly True
The Best of Sisters
The Cockney Sparrow
A Mother's Courage
The Constant Heart
A Mother's Promise
The Cockney Angel
A Mother's Wish
The Ragged Heiress
A Mother's Secret
Cinderella Sister
A Mother's Trust
The Lady's Maid
The Best of Daughters
The Workhouse Girl
A Loving Family
The Beggar Maid
A Place Called Home
The Orphan's Dream
Ragged Rose
The Swan Maid
The Christmas Card
The Button Box
The Mistletoe Seller
Nettie's Secret

THE RIVER MAID SERIES

The River Maid
The Summer Maiden
The Christmas Rose

THE VILLAGE GIRLS SERIES

The Christmas Wedding
A Village Scandal
The Country Bride

Dilly Court

Rag-and-Bone Christmas

HarperCollins*Publishers*

HarperCollins*Publishers* Ltd
1 London Bridge Street,
London SE1 9GF

www.harpercollins.co.uk

First published by HarperCollins*Publishers* 2020
1

A catalogue record for this book is available from the British Library

ISBN: 978-0-00-828786-3 (HB)
ISBN: 978-0-00-828787-0 (B)

This novel is entirely a work of fiction.
The names, characters and incidents portrayed in it are
the work of the author's imagination. Any resemblance to
actual persons, living or dead, events or localities is
entirely coincidental.

Typeset in Sabon LT Std by Palimpsest Book Production Ltd, Falkirk,
Stirlingshire

Printed and bound in the UK by CPI Group (UK) Ltd, Croydon CR0 4YY

This book is produced from independently certified FSC™ paper
to ensure responsible forest management.

For more information visit: www.harpercollins.co.uk/green

In fond memory of Pippy and Beasley,
two canine best friends.

Chapter One

Paradise Row, Pentonville, London. December 1865

Snow was falling fast, but even before it floated to the ground its pristine whiteness was tainted by pollution from the black-lead works, and soot from the factory chimneys. The thunderous sounds from the iron foundry, situated a little further along Old St Pancras Road, added to the general hubbub, and steam engines roared in and out of King's Cross railway station.

Away from all this, as though in a different world, it was quiet and peaceful inside the stable, and comparatively warm. Sally Suggs worked tirelessly to keep the stalls spotlessly clean, and the two animals stabled there were fed only the best hay, with plenty of fresh water to drink. Pa always teased

Sally and said it was because she had been born in the stable that she had such an affinity with horses, but she was convinced that she had inherited her talent as a horsewoman from her late mother. Emily Tranter had been a famous equestrienne, who had delighted audiences at Astley's Amphitheatre until she met and fell in love with young Edward Suggs, the rag-and-bone man.

'Ain't you done here yet, girl?' Ted hobbled in from the yard and took off his cap, sending a dusting of snow onto the floor.

'Nearly finished, Pa. Then I'll go to the shop and get us something for our supper.'

'It'll be dark soon, love. You know I don't like you walking out on your own at night, and it's snowing harder than ever.'

Sally turned to him with a chuckle. 'Pa, I'm nearly twenty. I'm not a little girl any longer.'

'You are to me, my duck. You always will be, and I ain't as fit and healthy as I used to be. My old pins ache something chronic, especially when it's bitter cold like this.'

'You should be in the parlour sitting by the fire,' Sally said severely. 'You've done your bit for today. I won't be long, I promise.' She reached up to pat Flower's sleek neck as the horse nuzzled her shoulder.

'You'd bring that blooming animal upstairs if she could manage them.' Ted grumbled but his grey eyes were twinkling. 'You wrap up warm if you're going out,' he added as he opened the door that led to a narrow flight of stairs. His heavy footsteps echoed round the stable, and then there was silence.

'I would stay with you all night, Flower,' Sally said, kissing the horse's soft muzzle. 'But I have Pa to look after as well as you.'

Flower whickered gently as if in reply, and with a loving pat, Sally turned her attention to Boney, the ageing heavy horse who had pulled their cart through the London streets for the last fifteen years. He was still eager to work, but age was catching up on him and sometimes his joints were stiff, causing him to lumber over the cobblestones as if each step caused him pain. Sally had tried all manner of remedies, including poultices and doses of celery seeds, but in reality she knew that Boney's working days were numbered, and in a year or two he ought to be put out to pasture – the alternative was the knacker's yard, and that was unthinkable. Her dream would be a country cottage where her father could enjoy a long retirement, and Boney could end his days in peace.

Sally finished her work in the stable and went outside to make sure that the gates were locked and bolted. Although the items in the yard had been discarded by the former owners they still had a market value, and there were always those who preferred to steal rather than earn their living by honest toil. She hurried back to the comparative warmth of the stable and extinguished the candles. Fires were all too common in places such as this, and everything had to be kept out of reach of the horses. A lamp left burning might easily be overturned by a frisky horse, and the whole place would go up in flames.

Sally gave Flower a last affectionate pat on the head before slipping on her well-worn tweed jacket, and tucking her hair into one of her father's old caps. Fashion had little or no place in Paradise Row, especially when working in the scrap yard or the stable. Ever practical, Sally wore a pair of patched breeches that she had come across in one of the sacks, and a pair of lace-up boots that had also seen better days, but were still reasonably wearable. She picked up a wicker basket and let herself out into the street, locking the door behind her. A cold wind sent wisps of hay, rotting cabbage leaves and scraps of paper scudding down the road, adding sharp teeth to the swirling snow, and she pulled up her collar, wrapping her arms around her thin body.

'I was hoping I'd be in time to catch you, Sal.'

A cheery voice made her stop and turn her head. 'Oh, it's you, Josie. Is it your half day?'

Josie's wide mouth curved in a mischievous grin. 'I slipped out when Cook fell asleep after drinking half a bottle of gin.'

'She'll get caught one day and you'll be in trouble for keeping the truth from Mrs Grindle.'

'I don't care. I'm looking for another position anyway. I'm fed up with working all hours for less than eight pounds a year, and only one half day off a month. The Grindles treat us servants like slaves.'

'What else could you do, Josie? You might end up worse off with a master who beats you, or . . .' Sally lowered her voice as they passed a group of workmen, all of whom were ogling them and whistling. 'You know what I mean, and they're a fine example of what men think of girls like us.'

Josie tossed her head. 'I spit on their kind. One day I'm going to marry a decent man who'll treat me like a lady, not a common slut. I got me pride, Sally.' She poked her tongue out at a man who had loitered behind his mates to proposition her, but he laughed and slapped her on the buttocks.

'Come home with me and have a bit of supper,' Sally suggested hastily. 'Ignore him, Josie. His sort aren't worth bothering about.' She turned her head to glare at the man, who was laughing uproariously. 'I know your wife, Sidney Jones. She won't find it funny when I tell her what you just did to my friend.'

His answer was lost in the loud blare of a factory hooter in the region of the railway station.

'I don't care about the likes of him,' Josie said, wrinkling her snub nose. 'Ta for the invite to supper, love, but I'm meeting Ned when he comes off his shift at the gas works.'

'You do know that he's married, don't you, Josie?' Sally came to a halt, grasping her friend's hand. 'I'm not judging you, but I don't want to see you get hurt.'

Josie laughed and squeezed Sally's fingers. 'You worry too much. It's just a bit of fun. We'll shelter under the railway arches and have a kiss and a cuddle, and then he'll go home to his missis a much happier man, and I'll go back to Grindles' hell.' Josie's smile faded. 'I like him a lot, Sally. He's the best thing that's happened to me in years.'

'And that's what worries me. Don't get too involved – you're the one who'll suffer when it ends.'

'Ta for the advice, but I'm a big girl now. He's good for a laugh.' Josie pulled her shawl round her head and hurried off in the direction of the gas works, leaving Sally to make her way to the grocer's shop on the corner. Old man Jarvis was behind the counter as usual, and his gloomy expression seemed to have been painted indelibly on his wrinkled features. His bald pate gleamed in the lamplight as did the tip of his red nose. Sally had always suspected that he kept a bottle of spirits hidden beneath the counter, taking a nip or two when he thought no one was watching. The smell of gin hung in the cloud above his head, mingling with the aroma of roast coffee beans and the sawdust that was scattered over the bare floorboards.

Sally purchased a loaf of bread and two meat pies.

'Will that be all?' Jarvis demanded testily. 'Got some fresh eggs brought in from a farm today. You won't get none tastier than these.'

Sally hesitated. Pa was always partial to a boiled egg for his breakfast and that justified the extra expenditure. 'I'll take two, please.'

Jarvis wrapped the eggs in a page torn from yesterday's copy of *The Times* and placed them in Sally's basket. 'That'll be elevenpence ha'penny.'

Sally placed a shilling on the counter and waited for the halfpenny change. It was the last of the money that Pa had given her from the profit he made selling the last lot of rags to Rags Roper, the cloth merchant. She put the halfpenny in her purse.

'Good evening, Mr Jarvis.'

'Good evening, Miss Suggs.'

She left the shop and pulled her cap down over her forehead in an attempt to shield her eyes from the driving snow. The horse-drawn traffic rumbled past and the clock on the St Pancras Church was booming out the hour. It was no wonder she failed to hear the approaching footsteps. She cannoned into the man who was struggling to open his umbrella, and the force of the encounter sent her purchases flying out of the basket onto the snowy pavement.

'Look where you're going!' Sally cried angrily. 'That's my supper lying on the ground.'

'You barged into me, you stupid boy.' The man lowered his umbrella, staring at her in the flickering light of the street lamp. 'Oh, I'm sorry, miss. Are you hurt?'

'No,' Sally said reluctantly. 'But the eggs are smashed and the pies are covered in slush. That's our supper you've ruined and my pa will be furious.' She tilted her head back to glare at the man, who was dressed like a country gentleman, which was decidedly out of place in this part of London. He was younger than she had supposed, and his rugged features were creased in a worried frown.

'I am truly sorry.' He held out his hand. 'I was also at fault. You must allow me to reimburse you for the groceries.'

Sally looked down at the shattered eggs and pies; even if she had wanted to rescue them, she was too late. Two half-feral dogs sprang from seemingly nowhere and pounced on the food, growling ferociously as they vanished into the shadows with their bounty. She had eaten very little that day and the temptation to accept his offer was overwhelming.

'Thank you,' she said reluctantly. 'It cost me elevenpence ha'penny.'

He put his hand in his pocket and took out a handful of small change. 'Here's a shilling, with my apologies.'

She took the halfpenny from her purse and exchanged it for the shiny silver coin. 'Normally I wouldn't accept,' she said gruffly. 'But as it happens I'm a bit short of the readies at the moment, so thanks again.' She turned away in case he changed his mind and she hurried back to the shop to repeat her order to a surprised Mr Jarvis.

'You've taken your time.' Ted looked up from the crumpled newspaper he had been attempting to read by the light of a candle stub and the glow from the coal fire. 'I'm starving. What kept you?'

Sally placed her basket on the table and unpacked the contents. 'I had a slight mishap on the way home from old Jarvis's shop, so I had to go back and get two more pies and a couple of eggs.' She took out a small cob loaf. 'And he must have felt sorry for me because he threw in the bread for nuppence.'

'It's probably stale then. Frank Jarvis never gives anything away, the old skinflint.' Ted smoothed the creased newspaper, peering short-sightedly at the print. 'One day I'll make enough money to buy a paper every day, instead of reading what other folks have thrown out.'

'Yes, that would be nice, Pa.' Sally took off her sodden jacket and cap, shaking out her long, dark hair.

Ted eyed her curiously. 'You still haven't told me what happened between here and Jarvis's shop.'

'It was snowing so hard that we didn't see each other until it was too late and he nearly knocked me over – well, to be fair I wasn't looking either. Anyway, the food went flying and landed on the pavement, and then, to cap it all, a couple of stray dogs wolfed the pies.'

'But you wasn't hurt, love?'

'Only my pride, Pa. And the fellow paid up, so I went back to the shop and we have supper after all.'

'You was lucky to meet a gentleman, that's all I can say. There's many who wouldn't be so generous.'

Sally took two plates from the dresser that her father had constructed from an old chest of drawers and some wooden shelving. 'Here you are. Enjoy the pie and I'll put the kettle on.'

'You're a good girl, Sal. I don't know what I'd do without you.'

She smiled and placed the kettle on the trivet in front of the fire. 'You'll never have to find out, Pa. We're a team, you and me, not forgetting Boney and Flower, of course.'

'Sit down and eat your supper.' Ted shifted uneasily in his chair. 'I think you'll have to take the cart out on your own tomorrow, love. My joints are playing up something terrible tonight. I doubt if I'll be able to get downstairs in the morning, let alone do me rounds.'

'It won't be the first time, Pa. I know the route like the back of my hand.'

'Just leave the heaviest things for Kelly. He'll love that,' Ted added grudgingly. 'He's always trying to get one up on me.'

'Don't worry. I can handle Kelly. He won't get the better of me. That's a promise.'

Next morning Sally was up before dawn. It was cold and dark in her tiny bedroom, with space only for a narrow iron bedstead and a single chest of drawers, which doubled up as a washstand. She dressed hastily in her working clothes and went downstairs to the back yard to use the privy and draw water from the pump. It had stopped snowing, and a hard frost had turned the surface into a sheet of ice.

Her first task was to clean the stable, and then she fed and watered the horses. Flower always greeted Sally with affectionate nuzzling of her hand, and Boney pawed the ground, waiting for his food. When she was satisfied that the animals wanted for nothing, she went upstairs to do her chores before starting the day's work. Having cleared the ashes from the grate she lit the fire and put the eggs on to boil while she toasted slices of stale bread. There was a scraping of butter left in the dish, and she spread it on a piece of toast, cutting it into fingers as her father had done for her when she was a child.

The back room where Ted slept in a truckle bed below the eaves was little bigger than a cupboard. The accommodation over the stable was not spacious, but it had been the only home Sally had ever known, and she had done her best to make it as comfortable as limited means would allow. The gaily coloured patchwork coverlet was all her own work, and had taken many hours of cutting squares from the clothes discarded by the wealthier people in the neighbourhood, and even more hours spent patiently sewing them together. Sally was proud of her efforts and the quilt brightened the small room.

'How are you today, Pa?' Sally asked anxiously as she placed the tray on the floor beside his bed.

Ted heaved himself to a semi-sitting position. 'You know how it is, love. I'd get up if I could but me joints are playing up something chronic in this cold weather.'

Sally helped him to a sitting position and placed a couple of pillows behind him. Despite having hung them out last summer for days on end in the fresh air, there was still a lingering odour of the sickroom in the fabric and feather stuffing. It was fortunate that her father had lost his sense of smell after many years of handling noxious substances when he had worked on the great dust heap at Battle Bridge before its eventual removal.

'There, is that better?' She placed a tray on his lap. 'I'm afraid that's the last of the butter, but I'll get some this evening on my way home. Let's hope I have a good day.'

'Don't let anyone take advantage of you, love. I'll try to get down to the yard later on. If I can just sort out the white material from the coloured rags it'll be a help. You get more money if the stuff isn't dyed.'

'Yes, Pa. I know that, but you ought to stay indoors in weather like this. We don't want you having a fall and breaking your leg or worse.'

'But I don't like leaving everything to you, love.'

'Don't worry about me, Pa. I know what I'm doing and I'll be fine.'

'You're a good girl, Sal. I'm lucky to have you for a daughter.'

She leaned over to drop a kiss on his grey head. 'I love you, too, Pa. Now eat up and I'll bring you a nice hot cup of tea before I go out.'

* * *

Half an hour later Sally had Boney harnessed to the cart and she drove out onto Paradise Row. It was still early but the night-shift workers were shuffling home to their beds, barely acknowledging their neighbours, who were hurrying to their place of employment to begin their twelve- or fourteen-hour day. The street was lined with tenements, housing countless numbers of lodgers. There were large families crowded into one small room, single working men, who came off the night shift and climbed into a bed recently vacated by the workers who had left for the day's toil in the manufactories. Mothers with babies in their arms and toddlers clinging to their skirts packed their older children off to work anywhere they could earn a few pennies a day. There was little money to go round in Paradise Row and many women, whether married or single, were forced out onto the streets at night in sheer desperation, selling themselves to anyone with a few coppers to spare. Others were addicted to drink or opium, but Sally had seen too much poverty to be judgemental. She raised her hand in acknowledgement to those who had the time or the energy to greet her as she drove past. It would soon be Christmas, but there was little likelihood of much celebration in this street.

She encouraged Boney to walk a little faster than his customary plodding, but the old horse merely flicked his ears and continued to move at his own speed. Sally guided him towards the more affluent areas south of Tavistock Square. Each day she and her father took different routes, having worked out where they might miss their rival totters. Finn Kelly was the one who gave them most trouble. His family had escaped the great famine in Ireland of 1845 and Finn had arrived in London as a child of eight – that was the extent of Sally's knowledge about his background. What she did know was that he was a rival to be reckoned with, and he used his innate Irish charm and blarney to wheedle goods out of householders where Ted might have failed miserably. Sally was determined to do better than her father, and to beat Kelly at his own game.

When the cart entered the residential area, Sally cleared her throat and sang out, 'Any old rag and bones?' Unfortunately her voice was drowned out by the sound of horses' hoofs and the rumble of wheels. Hansom cabs and Hackney carriages vied with tradesmen's vehicles and brewers' drays. Street sellers cried their wares and they had more powerful voices than Sally, but she persevered, ringing the large hand bell that her father kept for the purpose of attracting attention.

After three hours Sally was beginning to get dispirited. The cart was less than a quarter full and it was mainly rags and sacks filled with cinders and ash from coal fires. Although these items had a small commercial value, she was not going to make more than a few pennies from the entire collection. She decided on a change of tactic and steered Boney away from the residential area, heading towards the factories that had grown up around the Regent's Canal. She was doing a little better, having managed to persuade the owner of the knacker's yard to give her several sacks of old bones, but when she approached the sawmill she was dismayed to see the tall figure of her archrival standing by his cart, smoking a cheroot while he chatted to the foreman.

She made a wide sweep, guiding Boney to amble in the opposite direction, but Kelly had turned his head and he had seen her. He tipped his battered top hat, and Sally was amused to see a sprig of holly and one of mistletoe tucked into the hatband. That, together with a multi-coloured striped muffler wound round his neck, gave him a raffish look, and he was grinning widely. He tossed the stub of his cigar onto the ground and stamped on it.

'You're too late, Sally Suggs. I beat you to it, as usual.'

Sally was about to retaliate when a small dog raced towards Boney, barking excitedly. Normally placid and slightly deaf after years of working in almost ceaseless noise, Boney reared in the shafts almost unseating Sally. The fluffy-haired mongrel seemed to think that this was a game, and continued to harass the startled horse so that the cart was in real danger of overturning. She was on her feet, struggling to keep hold of the reins in an attempt to calm Boney, when Kelly appeared at the horse's head and seized the reins.

'Whoa, boy. Steady, old fellow.' Still holding the

reins, Kelly bent down and scooped the dog up in one arm. 'And you can shut up, little miss. Take on someone your own size.'

Sally sank down on the seat, watching in amazement as the dog licked Kelly's tanned cheek. 'Thanks, Kelly,' she said reluctantly. 'But I could have handled my horse.'

'Sure you could, and you'd have ended up on the cobblestones with a broken collarbone,' Kelly said, chuckling. He released Boney and thrust the wriggling dog into Sally's arms. 'I think this little lady is your problem.'

'I don't want her,' Sally protested, turning her head as the little animal tried to lick her face. 'She must belong to someone.'

Kelly put his head on one side, his periwinkle-blue eyes twinkling. He was obviously enjoying her discomfort. 'Well now, I doubt that. Look at her, Sal. She's all skin and bone and I daresay she's running with vermin, but I'll put her on the ground if you wish, although I can't guarantee she won't frighten your old nag again.'

'Don't you dare.' Sally scowled at him, but she kept a tight hold on the dog. Kelly was right; she could feel the small terrier-type mongrel's ribs through her matted fur, and her big brown eyes were enough to melt the hardest heart.

'Where's Ted?' Kelly's smile faded. 'He must be off colour if he's let you go out on your own.'

'He's all right,' Sally said defensively. 'Well, his

rheumatics are playing him up, but he'll be back on his rounds tomorrow.'

Kelly eyed her speculatively. 'Tell you what, I'll throw in some of the wood chippings that I don't need.'

'Why would you do that? You never do anything for nothing.'

He clasped his hands to his heart. 'You do me a great wrong, mavourneen. Haven't I always been a good friend to you and your respected pa?'

'No, you haven't. And stop calling me mavourneen, whatever that means. You would sell your own grandmother if you thought it would make you some money.'

He threw back his head and laughed. 'I'd have to dig the poor old soul up first, and I doubt if she'd make much money in that state.'

'You're disgusting.' Sally tried to sound angry but it was difficult with the dog writhing around in her arms and doing her best to lick her face.

'Perhaps, but you want to laugh, I know you do. Anyway, your dada helped me out once when I was young and green, so call this repayment for his kindness.' Kelly doffed his top hat and brushed a strand of dark hair back from his forehead. He put his hat on at a jaunty angle and strolled off to have a word with the foreman, who had emerged from the mill followed by two burly men hefting sacks of wood shavings.

Sally was tempted to refuse his generous offer, but

the thought of returning home with little to show for a day's work was even worse than accepting charity from Finn Kelly. She eyed him warily as he approached with a sack slung casually over his shoulder.

'Wait here, mavourneen.' He hefted the sack onto the cart as easily as if it had been filled with feathers. 'There are a few more to come. You'll thank me for this one day, you know you will.' He winked and beckoned to the workmen, leaving Sally speechless for once. She quite literally had her hands full while the men loaded the sacks onto the cart as her new friend kept wriggling and trying to lick her face. In the end Sally set her down on a pile of rags.

'Walk on, Boney.' Sally did not look back to see if Kelly was watching her drive away, and she did not know whether to feel annoyed or grateful for his help. One thing was certain, he had added to her problems. What Pa would say when she arrived home with a flea-bitten mongrel was another matter.

Chapter Two

'Are you out of your mind, girl?' Ted glared at the small dog as it explored the small parlour, sniffing in corners and scratching at holes in the skirting board. 'Take that little brute back to where you found it.'

'I can't do that, Pa. She's obviously a stray and unwanted. She'll end up at the bottom of the canal if I don't look after her.'

'Well take it down to the yard and give it a bath or we'll be infested with fleas.'

'Does that mean I can keep her?'

Ted shrugged and turned his head to stare into the fire. 'Would it make any difference if I said no?'

Sally leaned over to drop a kiss on his grizzled hair. 'Thanks, Pa. I'll give her a bath and then I'll go out and get us some hot pea soup and some fried fish as a treat.'

'Where'd you get the money for such luxuries?' Ted asked suspiciously.

Sally smiled triumphantly. 'I sold five sacks of wood chippings to the factory where they specialise in fake raspberry pips to add to jam, and they make wooden seeds to boost the profits of the seed merchants.'

'I don't know if I hold with such practices.' Ted sighed. 'But we all have to get by, so well done, Sal. I could do with some hot soup, and I have a yearning for some fried fish.'

Sally picked up the dog. 'It was all because of her. If she hadn't startled Boney and made him rear up, I doubt if Kelly would have been so keen to help.' She held the dog at arm's length. 'Raspberry pips earned us our supper and all because of you – Pippy. That's a good name, Pa. We'll call her Pippy because she's brought us good luck.'

'I've got several names for the mongrel and none of 'em repeatable in front of a young lady. Get the blooming animal bathed and then fetch my supper, girl. I'm starving.'

With a gleeful chuckle, Sally scooped up Pippy and took her downstairs to the stable, where she bathed her and rinsed her in diluted vinegar to kill the fleas. She left Pippy to shake and race round while she sorted the rags into their different piles, finally storing them in sacks beneath a tarpaulin in the back yard. When she had enough she would take them to the Rags Roper, and he would pay two to three pence a pound for the white rag, the coloured material being a little cheaper. The same price applied to the bones, some of which would be used in the manufacture of cutlery handles, while others were sold to the glue or soap factories. Rags would doubtless make twice as much, but that was the way business worked.

'Come, Pippy,' Sally called hopefully, having lost sight of the small dog amongst the crates, sacks and barrels in the yard. With a sharp bark Pippy emerged from behind a pile of snow-covered wood and bounded over to Sally, her pink tongue lolling out of the corner of her mouth as if she were laughing. Sally picked her up and gave her a cuddle, even though the dog's fur was still damp. 'You and I are going to be the best of friends, Pippy. But I'd better leave you with Pa while I go out to buy food, and I'll bring back something for you, too.'

Next day Sally did the rounds with only Pippy for company. After her bath the previous evening, the little dog was now white and fluffy with brown ears and what seemed to be a permanent grin on her face. She sat upright on the seat next to Sally, and every time they stopped and were approached by a man, whether he was young or old, a foreman or a labourer, Pippy's hackles rose and she growled deep in the back of her throat. Sally laughed it off, giving the dog a casual pat, but secretly she was pleased to have a protector. Pippy was small but she had needle-sharp teeth, and Sally was convinced that she would see off anyone who posed a threat. She had already proved her worth as a ratter and had found a nest in the yard, which she disposed of straight away. Pippy seemed intent on earning her living and Sally was delighted with her new friend.

Sally guided Boney through the crowded streets. People were rushing about concentrating on their preparations for Christmas Day and trade was poor, and no matter how loudly Sally shouted or how hard she rang her hand bell, there was little response from either householders or the businesses on her route. There was another reason for this, which became clear when she caught up with Kelly, whose cart was piled high with items he had collected.

Sally drew Boney to a halt. 'What are you doing, Kelly? This is Pa's round, not yours.'

He hefted a sack onto the cart. 'First come, first served, mavourneen. You know that.'

'No, I don't. I thought you and Pa had a gentleman's agreement.' Sally bit her lip. She could tell by the smirk on Kelly's face that he was going to make fun of her.

'But, as you've often pointed out – I'm no gentleman.' Kelly reached up to stroke Pippy, and to Sally's chagrin, the small dog wagged her tail and licked Kelly's hand.

'She's obviously a poor judge of character,' Sally said crossly. 'You're not playing fair, Kelly. Pa's done this round for years.'

'Didn't I help you out yesterday, mavourneen?

You'll have earned a few shillings from the sacks of wood chippings, I'll be bound.'

'You did help me yesterday, but that doesn't excuse what you've done today.' Sally glanced over her shoulder at the few things scattered on the bottom of the cart. 'It's getting late and that's all I have to show for a day's work.'

But Kelly did not appear to be listening. He was studying Sally's horse and a frown creased his brow as he ran his hands over Boney's body. 'You'll be lucky to get this fellow back to the stable tonight.'

'Why? What's the matter with him?' Sally climbed down from the driver's seat and went to stand beside Kelly. 'He's panting a bit, but he's an old boy.'

Kelly gave her a pitying glance. 'I've been handling horses all my life, girl. I know when a heavy horse like him needs to be put out to pasture, or sent to the knacker's yard.'

'Never!' Sally cried angrily. 'I couldn't do that to him.'

'Tell your da what I said, Sally. He's had enough experience of horseflesh to know that I'm telling the truth.'

'But without Boney we have no way of earning a living.'

'I'm sorry. I really am, but this is no business for a young woman like you. It's a rough old world and there aren't too many gents like me around.'

Sally knew he was mocking himself, but she was too upset to appreciate his sense of humour. 'Thanks,

Kelly. I mustn't keep you, and I need to get on. Tell me where you're going and I'll drive in the opposite direction.'

He shrugged. 'I'm finishing for the day, mavourneen. There's a Christmas bowl of rum punch waiting for me at the Nag's Head, so you can have the rest of the round, but take my advice and don't push the old horse too far.' Kelly patted Boney on the neck before heading back to his cart. He climbed nimbly onto the driver's seat. 'Remember what I said.' He drove off before Sally had a chance to respond.

She stroked Boney's nose. 'You'll be all right, won't you, old chap? I wouldn't do anything to hurt you.' She bent down and picked up Pippy, placing the small dog in the footwell before resuming her seat and taking the reins. 'Walk on, Boney.'

Sally was careful not to push the aged horse too far, and she did manage to pick up several sacks of rags and some scrap iron, but as she drove homewards along a snowy Great College Street she became aware that Boney was flagging. He stumbled a couple of times and eventually came to a halt, his head down and his breathing laboured. Sally leaped to the ground and went round to hold the reins, talking to him softly, as she had always done, but he seemed oblivious to everything. They were only a few yards away from the Veterinary College and Sally walked very slowly, leading Boney by the head. Traffic thundered past them, some of the drivers shouting impatiently, while others whipped their horses to a dangerously brisk pace in order to get past them.

'Ignore them, Boney,' Sally whispered, stroking his soft muzzle. 'I'll get help and you'll be as right as rain.' She was not sure whether she believed her own words, but it kept her spirits up until they were inside the gates of the college. She left Boney, safe in the knowledge that he would wait patiently for her return, but his breathing was even more laboured than before and she feared the worst. She hurried across the courtyard and entered the main building, gazing around in near panic. Pippy had followed her and she growled menacingly as the doorman approached. His expression was not encouraging. 'What do you want, lad? This here is a college for gentleman veterinarians. I think you're in the wrong place. You'd best go and take that mongrel with you.'

'Pippy, sit,' Sally commanded, and to her surprise the dog obeyed, although she kept eyeing the doorman and growling deep in her throat. Sally cleared her throat 'I'm not a boy, and I need help, mister. My horse is very sick and it's snowing. He'll freeze to death in these conditions.'

'Like I said, miss. This is a teaching institution, the best in Europe, so I'm reliably told.'

'I'm sure it is, but this is an emergency. Isn't there someone who could take a look at my animal? I think he might die and then what would you do. He's in the courtyard.'

'Very irregular, miss.' The doorman shook his head, clicking his tongue against his teeth. He turned his head at the sound of footsteps. 'Ah. This gentleman might set you right. Mr Lawrence, sir. This young lady says her sick horse is in the courtyard. I've told her this ain't no animal hospital, but she won't budge and she's got that ferocious animal with her.'

Sally spun round and stared at the young man. His tweed jacket and country-style clothes were familiar, and when he came closer she remembered where she had seen him. 'It's you,' she said lamely.

'The young lady with the basket of pies.'

'Yes, thank you for reimbursing me,' Sally said politely.

He held out his hand. 'Gideon Lawrence. What can I do for you?'

'I'm Sally Suggs and my horse is sick. I think he's dying and I don't know what to do for him.'

'I told her this is a teaching institution, sir.' The doorman pursed his lips, glaring at Sally in open disapproval. 'No dogs allowed.'

'Nevertheless, Hopkins, I am a qualified veterinary surgeon, and I will do my best for the poor animal. Come with me, Miss Suggs.'

More relieved than she cared to admit, Sally followed him outside into the courtyard, with Pippy gambolling at her heels. She stood back watching in awe as Gideon examined Boney, talking softly to calm the frightened horse.

'What's wrong with him?' Sally asked anxiously. 'I've never seen him like this.'

'How old is he?'

'Nearly twenty, so I was told.'

'That explains it then.' Gideon glanced at the goods in the cart and shook his head. 'I'm afraid his days of working the city streets are at an end, Miss Suggs.'

Sally stared at him in dismay. 'But he's well looked after, Mr Lawrence. Can't you make him better?'

'I can do nothing to combat old age. This old chap needs to be put out to pasture or . . .'

'No,' Sally cried passionately. 'Not the knacker's yard. I'll find somewhere for him, although I don't know how I'll go about it.'

Gideon eyed her thoughtfully. 'Where is he stabled at present?'

'My pa rents a scrap yard in Paradise Row. We live there, so there's always someone to look after the horses.'

'Well, this old chap needs a good rest, but I don't think he's going to make it back to Paradise Row this afternoon.'

Sally threw her arms around Boney's neck and hugged him. 'It will break Pa's heart.'

'You say you have another horse. Will you be able to continue your business?'

'With Flower?' Sally chuckled in spite of her heavy heart. 'My Flower is a thoroughbred Andalusian. She's a delicate creature and she couldn't pull a cart to save her life.'

'I'm sorry.'

Sally met his puzzled gaze with a smile. 'You're wondering why a rag-and-bone man would own a valuable animal like Flower.'

'I wouldn't have put it quite like that, but I suppose I was thinking along those lines.'

'My mother was a performer at Astley's Amphitheatre. She taught me to ride before I could walk, but a bad fall put paid to her career.'

'Again, I'm very sorry to hear that.'

'She died a couple of years later.' Sally stared down at her booted feet. Talking about her loss always brought tears to her eyes. She sniffed and took a deep breath. 'I was just fourteen at the time, and I've looked after Pa ever since.'

'Was Flower your mother's horse?'

Sally shook her head. 'Ma's horse Gaia was sold to the owner of Astley's, and he allowed us to keep her foal in part payment, as he owned the sire – another Andalusian. Pa wanted to take the money instead, but he saw how much it meant to me, and he allowed me to keep Flower.'

'She must be a very special horse. Andalusians are almost impossible to come by these days.'

'She means so much to me. I used to dream of following in Ma's footsteps and riding Flower in front of adoring crowds at Astley's, but I have to be practical and look after Pa.' Sally looked away. 'I don't know why I'm telling you all this. It's just a childish fantasy.'

'I can't say I've ever felt so strongly about anything.' Gideon gave her a searching look. 'But perhaps I can help you, after all.'

'Really? Can you give Boney something to make him strong again?'

A smile crinkled the corners of Gideon's warm brown eyes. 'I wish that were possible. But what I can do is to keep Boney here for a while. He'll have every care taken of him, and he'll be good practice for my students.'

'That's kind of you,' Sally said doubtfully. 'But I have to get the cart home. I can't pull it myself.'

'I should think not.' Gideon frowned thoughtfully. 'We have several horses in the stables here. If you promise to return him tomorrow, I'll let you have Major. He's a heavy horse like Boney, and he'll get you and the cart back to Paradise Row, but he belongs to the college so I'm afraid you won't be able to use him on your rounds.'

'I understand.' Sally was torn between wanting to take Boney home and the practicality of returning the heavy cart to the stable.

'Boney might well have a heart attack and die, if you make him pull that cart back to Paradise Row. He'll be well cared for here, but he really needs to spend the rest of his days at pasture.'

Sally sighed and shook her head. 'That's not possible. I wish it were.'

'I might have somewhere in mind.'

'It's very kind of you but we can't afford to pay.'

'That wouldn't be a problem, but you don't want to leave Boney here, I can see that; however, I give you my word that he will have the best attention. We can't turn back time, but we can ensure that the old fellow has a chance to recover.'

'Yes, I suppose so. I don't want to sound ungrateful, but he'll be scared without me. I've slept in the stable with him before now, if he's been poorly.'

'If you try to take him home now, I doubt if he'll make it to the end of the street. It's up to you.'

'Pa will be very upset.'

'Would you like me to come with you? I could explain things in detail to your father.'

'No, thank you. I'm the best one to break the news to him. We'll manage somehow.'

'Then let's unharness the poor old chap and I'll take him to the stable. If you'd like to come with me, I'll introduce you to Major. He's a docile animal, used to being the centre of attention, so he won't give you any trouble, which is more than I can say for your dog.' Pippy had been racing around the courtyard, but she came to a halt at Gideon's feet and he bent down to scoop her up. 'Behave, little lady.'

'I'm sorry,' Sally said hastily. 'I only came across Pippy yesterday and she adopted me rather than the other way around. But she's a good dog really.'

'I can see that. She's young and she's intelligent. She just needs a firm hand.' Gideon passed Pippy to Sally. 'I'll look after Boney, but you'd better not bring your dog into the stables. She'll no doubt cause mayhem there.' He unharnessed Boney, leaving Sally to secure Pippy to the cart with a length of rope.

'Stay there and be a good girl,' Sally said firmly. 'I'll be back in a minute.' She shot a sideways glance at Gideon. 'I suppose you think I'm silly, talking to a stray dog like this.'

He laughed. 'No, you're quite right. She might not understand the words yet, but the tone of your voice will no doubt be a comfort to her. Follow me, Miss Suggs.'

When Sally broke the news to her father she could see that he was more upset than he would admit.

'Boney has done us well over the years,' he said gloomily. 'We old men should retire.'

'Don't say things like that, Pa. You're not old.'

Ted shook his head. 'I feel ancient sometimes, love. My whole body aches and I know I ain't the man I was. Me and Boney should be put to pasture together.'

'I won't allow you to think that way.'

'This is the end of our business, Sal. We can't carry on without Boney.'

Sally thought of Major, the splendid Shire horse who was now eating his way through as much hay as poor old Boney might consume in several days. She would have to return Major to the college tomorrow, but what then? The truth hit her like a lightning bolt. 'No, Pa. We can't sell Flower.'

'I'm sorry, love. It's that or the workhouse for us. You know it's the last thing I would want . . .' Ted broke off, his eyes reddened and moist with unshed tears. 'Don't look at me like that, Sal. What else can we do?'

'I don't know. Anything, but that. I could get a job at Astley's like my mother. I can ride well.'

'You'd be up against real professionals, Sal. Your ma was a wonderful performer, but in the end the riding killed her.'

'The fall did that, Pa. She could have fallen downstairs and hurt herself just as badly.'

'Well, all that is in the past, sad as it is. I hope to join your mother one day soon, and then I'll be a happy man.'

'Don't talk like that.' Sally gazed at her father and saw him suddenly as an old man. This last shock seemed to have sapped the life from him, and he appeared to have shrunk like a wizened apple. 'Forget what I said. We'll get another heavy horse. Maybe I can sell something to raise the money.' She looked round the small room with its shabby sofa and worn armchair. The square table set beneath the window was propped up by a book under one broken leg, and the clock on the mantelshelf had stopped, yet again. Like almost everything else in the room it seemed old, tired and ready to go back to the scrap heap.

'You'll have to face it, love. Flower has to go to Tattersalls. They'll get a good price for her, and maybe Kelly would like to make an offer for the cart.'

Sally felt her whole world slipping away beneath her feet. She sat down beside her father and clutched his hand. 'I can do the round until you're better, Pa. We'll get another horse and I'll work twice as hard, you'll see.' She stroked Pippy, who had leaped upon her lap and was trying to lick her face.

'That dog will have to go, too.' Ted glowered at Pippy. 'We can't afford to feed her, and she's no use to man nor beast.'

'She's a good ratter,' Sally protested. 'She'll earn her keep, as will I.'

'That's enough.' Ted shook his hand free from her grasp. 'I knows you mean well, love. But the rag-and-bone business ain't for a young woman on her own, and I don't see meself going back on the rounds.'

'You'll get better, Pa. We'll get the doctor to look at you and maybe he can give you something to ease your aching bones.'

'Maybe.' Ted raised himself with difficulty. 'I'm going to me bed, love.'

'Good night, Pa.' Sally watched her father hobble towards the door which led to his tiny bedroom. Her own bed was beneath the eaves on the opposite side of the building to where her father slept, with the living room in between. In the summer she could look through the cracks where the roof tiles had slipped and see the stars. In winter she had to wear her coat in bed and wrap a shawl around her head. If it rained she slept beneath a tarpaulin, and no matter how many times they reported the leaking roof to the landlord, nothing had ever been done. She knew that she would sleep little that night, and instead of getting ready for bed, she went downstairs to the stable with Pippy at her heels. Flower greeted her with a soft whinny and Major turned his head to give her a blank stare.

'I can't do it, Flower,' Sally said softly. 'I won't let you go, no matter what happens.'

Next morning Sally awakened early even though she had slept badly. She was up, washed and dressed before her father stirred. She took him a cup of tea, waking him with a gentle pressure on his shoulder. He grunted in acknowledgement and turned his face to the wall; a sure sign that he did not wish to be disturbed. Sally knew from experience that there was nothing she could do when her father was in one of his deep depressions. She sighed; it had been like this since her mother died, and she was afraid that the loss of Boney and the business would be too much for him to bear. Their future was in her hands now, but she was struggling to think of a way out of this dilemma. The rag-and-bone trade was a competitive and unforgiving occupation. There was no one to whom she could turn for help, and, to make matters worse, the rent was due.

She drank a rapidly cooling cup of tea before going downstairs to the stable. Every morning she had cleaned the stables and seen to the horses' needs, but today everything seemed different. Boney had been part of her life for almost as long as she could remember and it was strange to see Major in Boney's stall. Flower was edgy and nervous, as if she sensed that there was something wrong. Sally took the buckets to the pump in the back yard and filled them with water, but when she carried them back to the stable she was startled to find Gideon Lawrence waiting for her.

'The door was unlocked,' he said apologetically. 'I did knock but no one answered, so I let myself in.'

'You've come for Major?' Sally eyed him hopefully. Perhaps he would allow her to borrow the horse for one more day. If she could earn enough to pay the rent it would give them more time to find a way out of their predicament.

'Yes. I'm sorry, Miss Suggs. If Major was mine I'd loan him to you for as long as you needed him, but he belongs to the college.'

'I understand. Of course you must take him. He's a fine animal.'

Gideon gave her a searching look. 'Will you be able to find a replacement for Boney?'

'There'll never be another horse like him. How is he?' Sally held her breath.

'He's doing well enough, but I've given him a thorough examination and I'm afraid it's his heart. He could live quite happily for a number of years, but his working life is over. I'm sorry, it must have been a bitter blow for your father.'

'He's taken it badly.' Sally watched nervously as

Gideon turned his attention to Flower. He examined her as if he were a potential purchaser.

'She is a beautiful animal. You could sell her for a considerable sum of money.'

'No!' Sally raised her voice and was instantly sorry. She held up her hand. 'I shouldn't have shouted, but that would really be a last resort.'

'I can see that you're fond of her,' Gideon said thoughtfully. 'I know it's none of my business, but are you in a financial position to replace Boney?'

Sally shook her head. 'The only asset we have is Flower, but I can't bear to part with her. She's my only link to my mother. I can't let her go.' She took a deep breath and turned away to hide the tears that filled her eyes. She lifted Major's harness from the wall rack. 'I'd better get your horse ready for you to take back to the college. We're truly grateful for your help, Mr Lawrence.'

'It was nothing. Anyone would have done the same. I wish I could do more.'

Sally busied herself tacking up Major, who bore it stoically. 'Is Boney fit enough to come home? I can't expect you to look after him at the college – I mean, we can't afford to pay for his keep.'

'He should be taken to the country where he can roam free. Can you arrange that?'

'No. I can't, but I'll think of something.'

'I have a suggestion, although you must feel free to turn it down.'

Sally shot him a sideways glance. 'You've already

done so much. I wouldn't dream of asking you to do anything else.'

'Wait until you hear my proposition,' Gideon said, smiling. 'I was born and raised in the country. I recently inherited my late father's farm near Highgate and I was planning to go there on Saturday. If you and your father agree, your old horse could live out his days there. I have plenty of good pasture.'

'I don't know what to say.' Sally gazed at him in surprise. 'It seems an imposition when we hardly know you.'

'I entered the veterinary profession because I care for animals; not in a sentimental way, but in a practical sense. If I can heal a sick creature or make their life better in some way, that's what I'll do, and,' he added with a twinkle in his eyes, 'I get paid for my labours.'

'That's the main problem,' Sally said hastily. 'We can't afford to pay.'

'And I wouldn't dream of charging a penny. Boney will be company for the pet donkey I had when I was growing up. He is even older than your horse, so they can share stories of their lives. You are welcome to come with me, and I think Flower could do with a long ride. What do you say?'

Chapter Three

It was bitterly cold, but at least it had stopped snowing and the long ride to Hill Farm had been just what Sally needed to dispel some of the worries that had kept her awake at night. The air in the countryside was so much fresher and cleaner than the soot-filled atmosphere in Paradise Row, and the sight of snow-covered fields and hedgerows was a blissful change after the grime and dirt of the King's Cross area. It had been years since Sally had last ventured outside the city, and Ma had been alive then. The worn and faded riding habit that Sally wore with pride had belonged to her mother, and the scent of her still lingered in the merino cloth. The draped skirt was a couple of inches too short, revealing the boys' breeches and shabby boots she wore out of necessity, but Sally was determined to enjoy the outing, and she was not going to allow such trifles to spoil her day.

'We're almost there.' Gideon's pleasant voice brought Sally back to the present with a start.

'How far is it now?'

'Follow me.' Gideon encouraged his mount to a trot and then a canter as he rode on ahead.

Sally accepted the challenge and she flicked the reins. 'Come on, Flower. We can beat him.' Flower needed no further encouragement and they caught up with Gideon, passing him and then slowing down as it would be dangerous for the horses to go any faster. As they crested the steep hill Sally could see a black and white timbered farmhouse nestling in the wooden area below. It was surrounded by a neatly kept yard lined with redbrick outbuildings. She reined in and Flower obeyed by slowing down to a more sedate trot, allowing Gideon to catch up with them.

'That's a fine little mare. She goes like the wind,' he said breathlessly.

'You can see why I don't want to sell her.'

'It's obvious that you two have a strong bond. Maybe there's another way.'

'Do you really think so?'

'I might have an idea, but I don't want to say anything just yet.'

'Now I'm intrigued,' Sally said, laughing. 'You can't expect to drop hints like that without an explanation.'

'I need to give it more thought. Anyway, I'm starving and I expect you are, too. With a bit of luck Mrs Wallace will have done some baking. She's the best cook in the county.'

'Mrs Wallace?' Sally eyed him curiously.

'She cooks and keeps house for me, and her husband manages the farm. They've been with my family for years.'

'It looks like a lovely house,' Sally said wistfully.

'It's not grand like Fleet Hall.' Gideon smiled ruefully. 'I'm sorry, of course you don't know the locality, but our land abuts the Fleet Hall estate. I'll take you there after I've had a word with Wallace.' He drew his horse to a halt outside the farmyard and dismounted to open the gate.

Sally was about to ask him what was so important about a neighbouring estate, but she was forestalled by the appearance of a youth, who came running from the house. Gideon handed him the reins. 'Good lad, Bert. Take care of the horses.'

Bert grinned and did as he was asked, waiting until Sally had dismounted before giving her a shy grin and holding out his hand to take Flower's reins.

'She's quite nervous of strangers,' Sally said anxiously, but as if to prove her wrong, Flower whinnied softly and rubbed her head against Bert's shoulder. 'She likes you,' Sally added in surprise.

'I've grown up with horses, miss. Don't worry about her. We'll soon be the best of friends.'

Sally glanced at Gideon, who gave her a reassuring smile. 'Bert's been looking after my horses since he was a nipper and he took over from his father, so he knows what he's doing. He's the ideal person to keep an eye on your old carthorse.'

'Are you sure you want to keep Boney here?' Sally fell into step beside him.

'Yes, I am. We have plenty of good pasture and you could visit him when you wished.'

'I don't know what to say. It's a kind offer, and I'd accept straight away, but I really should check with Pa.'

'I understand.' Gideon stopped outside the farmhouse door, which Bert had left ajar. He sniffed the air. 'That smells like jam tarts and gingerbread – my housekeeper always bakes my favourites on the days when they're expecting me to visit.' He thrust the door open. 'Mrs Wallace, I've brought someone to see you, and I've been singing your praises as the best cook in the county.'

Sally glanced over his shoulder and she was amused to see the tiny woman blushing furiously.

'Get on with you, Mr Lawrence. You don't have to soft-soap me to get what you want.' She gave Sally a searching look. 'We don't get many visitors here these days, miss.'

'Miss Suggs is here to ascertain if our pastureland is suitable for her aged horse,' Gideon said hastily.

'I'm pleased to meet you, Mrs Wallace.' Sally stepped forward, holding out her hand. 'Mr Lawrence has been boasting about your cooking, and I must say it smells delicious.'

Mrs Wallace's flushed cheeks deepened in colour, but she shook Sally's hand. 'Nice of you to say so, miss.

If you'd like to take the young lady to the parlour, I'll bring a tray of coffee and cakes.'

Gideon pulled out a chair. 'We could have it here and save you the bother. What do you say, Sally?'

'Yes, indeed. Please don't go to any trouble on my behalf.' Sally sank down on the seat, gazing round the large room in admiration. Bunches of dried herbs hung from the beamed ceiling, filling the air with their aromatic scent, and the enormous black-leaded range glowed with heat from a blazing fire. A kettle sang on the hob and various pans bubbled merrily, sending out gusts of savoury-smelling steam. The homely atmosphere wrapped itself around her and she felt instantly at ease. Everything, from the highly polished brass rail on the range, to the burnished copper cooking pots and the rows of pristine china on the dresser, showed the love and care that Mrs Wallace had put into making the old farmhouse into a home.

'It's beautiful,' Sally said with a sigh. 'What a lovely house you have, Mr Lawrence.'

'Gideon, please.' He passed her a cup filled with hot coffee.

'I mean it, Gideon. I've never seen anything like this. Our rooms above the stable would fit into one corner of this kitchen.'

Mrs Wallace puffed out her chest. 'I'm glad you approve, miss. Some people take it all for granted,' she added, looking pointedly at Gideon.

It was his turn to flush with embarrassment. 'I probably do, but I've been spoiled all my life.'

'Well, it's not for me to say, Mr Lawrence, but I'd have to agree in part. You were always such a sweet boy it was impossible not to give you what you wanted.'

Sally laughed. 'I'm glad my pa isn't here to tell you about my childhood. I'm afraid I wasn't a model daughter. All I wanted to do was to become a rider like my mother. I saw her perform at Astley's Amphitheatre and I was inspired. She was such a wonderful horsewoman and so beautiful.'

'She's no longer with you, dear?' Mrs Wallace asked gently.

'She was thrown from her horse during a rehearsal and she broke her back. She died a couple of years later.' The explanation of her mother's early demise had become a mantra, but the pain of bereavement was still as sharp.

'That's so sad, dear.' Mrs Wallace picked up a plate of gingerbread. 'Would you like to try my gingerbread?'

Sally took a slice. 'Thank you. I can't wait to try it. I'm not much of a cook myself.'

Mrs Wallace beamed at her. 'Well, dear, it's so nice to be appreciated. I doubt if Mr Lawrence has ever given a second thought to the comforts he enjoys at home.'

'You're wrong there,' Gideon said with a wry smile. 'Living at the college has made me appreciate my home more than ever, especially the wonderful meals you've created over the years, not to mention the cakes.' He selected a jam tart and bit into it.

'As I said, it's nice to be appreciated.' Mrs Wallace refilled his cup with coffee. 'Will you be staying tonight?'

'No, I have to get back to London, but I'll be down again on Monday. It's Christmas Day and it's also Miss Appleton's birthday celebration at Fleet Hall.'

'So I heard.' Mrs Wallace eyed Gideon expectantly. 'Mrs Hart, the Appleton's housekeeper, told me in strict confidence that they're expecting the announcement of Miss Cecily's engagement. Your name crops up quite often, sir.'

'I don't know where she got that idea,' Gideon said casually.

Mrs Wallace turned to Sally with a confidential smile. 'Miss Cecily is an heiress and she's beautiful. I'm sure gentlemen are queuing up to ask for her hand.'

Gideon drank the last of his coffee and rose to his feet. 'If you're ready, Sally, I'll take you to see the field where Boney will have the freedom to roam, and – before you ask – if the weather becomes too inclement in winter, he'll be given a warm, dry stable.'

'Thank you for the coffee and the delicious cake, Mrs Wallace.' Sally stood up, brushing the crumbs off her crumpled skirt. 'Yes, of course. I'd love to look round the farm.' She waited until they were outside in the yard. 'Are you sure you want the bother of looking after an aged horse? I mean if you're thinking of getting married, you might sell the farm and . . .'

Gideon gave her a straight look. 'Hill Farm is mine and will remain so whatever happens in the future. Your animal will be safe with me. I've seen too many horses worked until they dropped with sheer exhaustion, so I'm happy to give Boney a chance of a peaceful retirement.'

Sally did not question him further. She sensed that he did not want to talk about the beautiful Miss Appleton, and that intrigued her. She walked beside him, keeping up with his long strides as he showed her the outbuildings, including the milking parlour, the dairy and the various animal pens. There was a hay barn and a coach house adjacent to the stable block. Sally could see Bert at work grooming a shire horse, while another one waited in its stall, munching placidly on hay.

They crossed the yard and walked down a lane bordered with hedgerows glistening with snow. The fields were wearing a blanket of white, but brave little spikes of green grass showed through in patches beneath overhanging trees, and Sally could imagine how lovely it would be in summer.

'This is where Boney will live out his days.' Gideon stopped at the five-bar gate. He whistled and a donkey came slowly towards them, braying loudly. Gideon leaned over to stroke the animal's head. 'This is Dobson, my old friend. He spends the night in a warm stable in the winter, but he enjoys being out here on a day like this. I think he and Boney will be good companions.'

Sally stroked Dobson's velvety muzzle. 'He's lovely. I'm afraid if he was mine I'd have him sitting on a rug by the fire. I can see why you love him.'

'I was an only child and Dobson was my best friend. We used to roam the countryside together.'

'I feel the same about Flower,' Sally said slowly. 'I can't bear to think of someone else owning her.'

'Do you think your father will be able to work again?'

The nagging fear was always at the back of her mind, even though Pa would never admit to being beaten by age or physical disability. He might have continued for a year or two, but they would be lost without Boney, and there was little or no possibility of finding the means to purchase another carthorse. She shook her head. 'To be perfectly honest, I doubt very much if he'll ever be able to lift heavy objects or even to drive round the city streets for hours on end. The rag-and-bone trade is tough, and it's hard to make a living if you're young and fit – my pa is getting old and he suffers from what he calls "the miseries" in all his joints.'

'Then it's obviously time for a change.'

'I expect you're right,' Sally said reluctantly. 'But I will be truly grateful if you would look after Boney. I'm sure he'll be very happy here in this lovely place.'

Gideon stroked Dobson's muzzle. 'I'll see you

soon, old chap, and I'll bring your new friend to share the field with you.'

Dobson snorted and pawed the ground.

'I believe he likes the idea.' Sally patted the donkey's neck. 'But I really ought to set off for home. I know the way, so you don't have to accompany me.'

'If you don't mind staying a while longer, I'd like to take you to Fleet Hall.'

She shot him a curious glance. 'Why?'

Gideon proffered his arm. 'I told you I had an idea, but I'd like to speak to Cecily before I say anything more.'

'I don't understand.'

'It's a short ride to Fleet Hall. Would you care to accompany me?'

'I don't know what you have in mind, but I'd like to meet this lady.'

'You'll love Cecily – everyone does.'

In her imagination Sally had pictured Fleet Hall as a huge Palladian mansion situated in the middle of a large deer park, but the reality was far more striking and surprising. Rising from the ground like some Gothic cathedral, decked with a coronet of snow, Fleet Hall looked so new that it might have been constructed yesterday. With its ornate façade, arched doorway and crenellated towers, it seemed as if a fairy-tale castle had been transported from the pages of a storybook to sit amongst formal lawns and a parterre garden.

Sally was momentarily speechless, which seemed to amuse Gideon. He reined in his horse to a walk. 'Striking, isn't it?'

'I've never seen anything like it,' she said truthfully.

'Sir Gregory Appleton's father bought the original mansion fifty years ago with the fortune his family made in the potteries. He spared no expense in having the place rebuilt to his satisfaction, and he furnished it with art treasures from all over Europe. It's not to everyone's taste, but it is very grand.'

'It's very imposing,' Sally said carefully. 'So this is where Miss Appleton lives?'

'Cecily is charming and beautiful and very accomplished.'

Sally eyed him warily. 'Why have you brought me here? I don't think I'm the sort of person that your friend would want to associate with.'

A look of genuine surprise crossed Gideon's handsome features. 'Cecily isn't like that, Sally. Wait until you meet her.' With a gentle nudge from his heels he urged his horse to a trot. 'Let's hope she's at home.'

Sally was desperate to question him further, but there was little she could do other than to follow his lead.

As they dismounted at the foot of the wide stone steps a stable boy appeared, seemingly from nowhere, to take their horses to the stables, and before Gideon had a chance to knock on the heavily embossed and studded oak door, it opened as if by magic. Sally stared in awe at the majestic butler, whose starched white shirtfront seemed to reflect the pale sunlight, and the high points of his collar threatened to pierce his plump cheeks.

'Good morning, Stafford. Is Miss Cecily at home?'

'Good morning, sir. Please come in and I'll announce your arrival.' Stafford looked down his long nose at Sally. 'Is the young lady with you, Mr Lawrence?'

'She is indeed.' Seemingly unperturbed by the butler's obvious reluctance to admit Sally, Gideon ushered her over the threshold. 'We'll wait here.'

Stafford closed the door and walked away at a measured pace, as if to underline his own importance. He returned minutes later. 'Come this way, please.'

'Is he always like this?' Sally asked in a whisper as they followed him across the highly polished floor. They walked past console tables where gilded cherubs supported ormolu-encrusted marble tops, on which were placed silver urns filled with hothouse flowers. Artistically draped marble statues were reflected in the many wall mirrors, and light flooded in from the tall mullioned windows. Most striking of all was an enormous, lavishly decorated Christmas tree. Sally felt as though she had stepped into a world so different from her own that it hardly seemed real, but catching sight of her own reflection she was shocked to see how shabby she looked. No wonder Stafford had thought twice before admitting her to such a grand establishment. She was tempted to turn and run, but that would be cowardly and she had to admit that she was curious.

Gideon ushered her into a large room that she would hardly describe as a parlour. The hand-painted wallpaper depicting colourful tropical birds and exotic foliage was a work of art in itself. The heavy mahogany furniture was upholstered in wine-red velvet, and matching curtains were held back by tasselled silk ropes, to reveal a splendid view of the parterre garden and the silver shimmer of a lake in the distance. As if all this magnificence was not enough, the young woman who rose from a chair by the fire was everything that Gideon had said and more. Cecily Appleton was almost too beautiful to be real. She was tall and slender and a welcoming smile lit her large blue eyes. Her golden curls were artlessly piled in a coronet on top of a well-shaped head and ringlets caressed her rosy cheeks. She seemed to glide as she moved towards Gideon with both hands outstretched.

'Gideon, this is a lovely surprise. I wasn't expecting to see you before the ball.'

He raised her hands to his lips. 'You look beautiful, as ever, Cessy.'

'Now I know you want something. You aren't usually so gallant.' Cecily glanced over his shoulder. 'Aren't you going to introduce me to your companion?'

'I'm sorry,' Gideon said hastily as he released her hands. 'Sally, I'd like you to meet my very good friend, Cecily Appleton.'

'Come now, Gideon. You and I are more than just friends.' Cecily turned to Sally, holding out her hand. 'I'm delighted to meet you, Miss . . .'

'Suggs.' Sally went to grasp Cecily's hand but it was withdrawn a little too quickly. 'But everyone calls me Sally.'

Cecily turned to face Gideon. 'So what brings you here? I thought your position at the college kept you busy all week.'

'It does normally, but Sally and I met by chance.'

'Twice, in fact,' Sally said, chuckling.

Gideon acknowledged her remark with a smile. 'The first time we quite literally bumped into each other during a snowstorm, but the second time it was an emergency concerning Sally's aged horse, which is why I took her to Hill Farm today.'

'How intriguing.' Cecily shot a sideways glance at Sally. 'I want to hear the whole story, however, where are my manners? Do take a seat. You must be tired after a long ride from London, and in such inclement weather, too.'

Sally perched on the edge of the nearest chair. She had never thought much about her own looks, and she had been quite happy to wear clothes that were practical for her daily life, but suddenly she felt drab and awkward. She tucked her feet under the chair in an attempt to hide her down-at-heel boots, and she folded her hands in the hope that the gorgeous Cecily Appleton would not notice that they were stained with black lead, and roughened by hard work. She found herself wishing that she had refused Gideon's invitation to visit Fleet Hall.

'It's a story that will appeal to you, Cessy,' Gideon said, smiling. 'You love horses and you are a good judge of quality.'

'Are you telling me that you've found a suitable mount for me, Gideon?' Cecily's eyes shone and she clapped her hands.

'Not exactly.' Gideon shot a worried glance in Sally's direction. 'Well, maybe. It all depends on the owner.'

'I have a fancy for an Andalusian, in particular a dapple grey.'

Gideon met Sally's anxious gaze with a sympathetic smile. 'Would you consider selling Flower to Miss Appleton?'

Cecily looked at Sally with renewed interest. 'You own a dapple grey?'

'Yes, I do.' Sally hesitated, clenching her fists so that her nails dug into her palms. The idea of selling Flower was agonising, and she had been putting off the decision, even though she knew in her heart it was inevitable. She had no doubt the stables here were far more luxurious than the tiny stall in Paradise Row, and Cecily Appleton seemed to be a nice enough person, but to part with Flower would be like cutting off her own hand.

'I'm only interested in thoroughbreds.' Cecily turned to Gideon, lowering her voice. 'It isn't stolen, is it?'

'I heard that.' Sally jumped to her feet. 'I've had Flower since she was a foal.'

Gideon frowned. 'Of course the animal belongs to Sally. You know better than to ask a question like that, Cessy.'

She blushed rosily. 'I'm sorry. I didn't mean to insult you, Miss Suggs. I have to be careful – there are so many rogues when it comes to buying and selling horses.'

'I don't want to sell her.' Sally's voice broke on a sob. 'But I can't keep her.'

Cecily was at her side in an instant and she put her arm around Sally's shoulders. 'You poor thing. How sad. Sit down and tell me how you came to be in such a pickle.' She pressed Sally back on her seat.

'That's putting it mildly,' Gideon said earnestly. 'Sally has had such incredible bad luck, Cessy. Her father can't work because he's infirm, and his horse is too old to carry on the business, even if Sally was able to continue on her own.'

'I could do it.' Sally met his gaze with a defiant stare. 'If Boney was a younger animal we could have kept up the round together.'

'What sort of business is it?' Cecily looked from one to the other.

'The rag-and-bone business, Miss Appleton.'

'I don't understand? I've never heard of such a thing.'

'We collect material and old clothes, scrap iron and bones,' Sally said patiently. 'Then we sell them to our contacts in the trade.'

'Trade!' Cecily's blue eyes widened as if Sally had just said a rude word. 'You poor girl.'

'We've done well enough until recently.' Sally was on the defensive. It was obvious that Miss Appleton knew nothing of the real world.

'It's a respectable business,' Gideon said firmly. 'Items that might have ended up on a rubbish heap are put to good use.'

'I see.' Cecily frowned thoughtfully. 'So how will you and your father survive without your horse? Forgive me for being so blunt, Sally, but I have no experience in such matters.'

'I don't know, and that's the honest truth.'

Cecily put her head on one side. 'Am I right in thinking that your horse is your only asset?'

'I won't sell her. I'd rather go to the workhouse.'

'I doubt if they have stables for residents' horses. I'm sorry for you, Sally, but I think you need to be practical.' Cecily rose gracefully to her feet and reached for the bell pull. 'I'd like to see your thoroughbred mare.'

'Is there any point, Cessy?' Gideon eyed her curiously. 'Sally has just said she won't sell her horse. In fact I was thinking along the lines of asking you to keep the animal here on a temporary basis. Your stables are well run and much more suitable than anything I could offer at Hill Farm, and you would have the pleasure of exercising a thoroughbred mare like Flower, but Sally would still own her.'

Cecily smiled sweetly. 'Why would I, or my father, agree to such a proposition, if the horse was simply eating its head off in our stables without earning its keep?'

'Come now, Cessy. You know that Sir Gregory will do anything you ask.'

'Very true, but why would I bother if there was no benefit to me?' Cecily turned to give Sally a calculating glance. 'If I like the look of your animal, I might just be persuaded to do what Gideon suggests with certain provisos.'

'I'm not sure I understand,' Sally said cautiously.

Cecily was prevented from answering by the appearance of a parlour maid.

'You rang, Miss Cecily?'

'I need my fur-lined mantle and the matching hat and gloves, Bertha. Fetch them for me, please.'

'Yes, miss.' Bertha bobbed a curtsey and hurried from the room.

'What are you up to, Cessy?' Gideon eyed her warily. 'Sally has made it clear that she has no intention of selling Flower.'

'I'll tell you when I've had a chance to look at the horse.'

'I'm sorry, Sally,' Gideon said apologetically. 'I should have spoken to you about this before I brought you here.'

Cecily gave him a sunny smile. 'Of course you should have, Gideon. But you invariably act first and think later.' She slipped her arm around Sally's waist. 'It's always left to us women to sort matters out.'

Sally moved away. She had a feeling that both she

and Gideon were being manipulated, although she could not say how it was being done. She had a suspicion that the lovely Cecily Appleton was an expert in getting her own way, but she was a guest in this palatial home and in no position to argue. One thing she did know for certain was that Flower belonged to her and her alone. Nothing and no one would separate them.

'Perhaps we should leave things as they are?' Gideon said worriedly.

'No, indeed. I'm looking forward to seeing Sally's horse and I fancy a walk to the stables. Don't be such a spoilsport, Gideon.'

'Flower isn't for sale,' Sally reiterated in desperation.

Cecily tossed her head. 'Maybe not, we'll see.'

Chapter Four

Cecily and Gideon walked arm in arm with Sally following at a discreet two paces behind them. It was only a short distance to the stables, and the outdoor servants had cleared the snow from the path. Sally tried hard not to stride along in her second-hand boots, but she felt very self-conscious in her shabby riding habit and she could not help envying Cecily's elegant outfit. She found herself wondering if people like the Appletons ever threw out unwanted items of clothing for the local rag-and-bone man; if so, she would be first in the queue.

The sight of Miss Appleton walking towards the stables seemed to cause a minor sensation amongst the stable boys, and the head groom came flying out of the tack room, struggling into his jacket as he ran.

Cecily seemed oblivious to the furore she was causing. 'Good morning, Jackson. I've come to see Miss Suggs's horse.'

'Do you intend to ride her, Miss Cecily?'

'I might, if I like the look of her. Have her saddled up and I'll make up my mind when I see how she behaves.' Cecily leaned on Gideon's arm, chattering eagerly about the coming ball while she waited for the horse to be brought from the stable, but Sally was filled with misgivings. The mere thought of leaving Flower here, even in such luxurious surroundings, was agonising.

'What do you think, Cessy?' Gideon looked on, smiling appreciatively as one of the young stable boys led Flower into the cobbled yard, which had been swept clear of snow.

'She's a very pretty mare,' Cecily conceded. She left Gideon's side and circled the animal, eyeing her critically. 'What's your opinion of the animal, Jackson? You're the expert when it comes to horseflesh.'

Jackson nodded. 'She's a true thoroughbred, Miss Cecily. I've had a look at her and she's in good shape.'

'I'll have to try her out,' Cecily said thoughtfully. 'I'd have to change into my riding habit, of course, and that saddle is no good to me.'

'It was good enough for my mother when she performed at Astley's,' Sally said angrily.

'I am not a circus performer, Miss Suggs. Ladies ride side-saddle.'

'What was your proposition, Cessy?' Gideon said hastily.

'I'm not prepared to say until I've ridden the animal, although I was thinking along the lines of a semi-permanent loan, as suggested earlier.'

'What does that mean exactly?' Sally asked anxiously.

'Your horse would be stabled here as if she were mine. The estate would bear the cost of taking care of your horse, and you would be allowed to visit and ride her whenever you were able.'

'I don't agree.' Sally shook her head. 'That means I would be giving Flower to you for nothing.'

Cecily shrugged. 'I thought Gideon said you were desperate.'

'Perhaps we ought to return to the house and talk it over,' Gideon said hastily. 'This is a big decision for Sally.' He turned to her with an apologetic smile. 'I know how difficult this must be for you.'

Sally snatched the reins from the stable boy. 'No, you don't. How could you know what it's like to be in my position? I'll find a way out of this without selling Flower or giving her away. Thank you for trying to help, but I'm leaving now.' She led Flower to the nearest mounting block and rode off before anyone had the chance to stop her. Sally was vaguely aware that Gideon was calling after her, but her one thought was to get away from Fleet Hall and the wealthy Miss Appleton. Cecily might be everything that Gideon had said, but he was welcome to her and her money. There must be another way out of their predicament.

It was late afternoon by the time Sally reached Paradise Row, and both she and Flower were close to exhaustion. Having unsaddled Flower, and given her a quick rub down, Sally went upstairs to let her father know that she had returned. She was greeted hysterically by Pippy, and it took her several minutes of fussing over the little dog to calm her down.

'I thought you was going to spend the day at the farm.' Ted's dark eyes twinkled mischievously. 'What happened? Did the honourable veterinarian prove to be not such a good fellow, after all?'

'Nothing of the sort, Pa. I didn't want to leave you on your own for too long, so I came home.' Sally placed the kettle on the hob. 'You must be hungry.'

'Well now, here's the thing. I was sitting up here, minding my own business at midday, when I heard someone calling my name. "Who's there?" I says. "It's me, Finn Kelly." So I says, "Come on up, Kelly," and he did.'

'What did he want?'

'Would you believe it? He wanted to know if I was recovered from my aches and pains.'

'That's not like Kelly,' Sally said thoughtfully. 'He's after something, although I can't think what, considering the fact that we're broke.'

'He asked me about poor old Boney, and I told

him.' Ted sighed heavily. 'Anyway, Kelly was moved enough to treat us to ham rolls and coffee from the stall next to the station.'

'Boney will be better off than both of us,' Sally said with a wry smile. 'I've seen the pasture where he'll spend his retirement with a donkey called Dobson. That is if Gideon is still willing to take him. I'm afraid I might have spoiled his chances there, Pa.'

'Sit down and tell me about it, love. I can't believe that you would have done anything wrong.'

Sally made the tea and pulled up a chair to sit close to the fire. She was uncomfortably aware that this was the last of the coal they had stored in the back yard, and if they wanted a fire tomorrow she would have to chop up anything that might burn for long enough to heat a kettle of water. It would be a lean Christmas and the rent collector was due at the end of the month. She had very little time in which to find the means to save them from eviction.

Later that evening, after she had settled Flower for the night, Sally was about to lock up when the outside door opened and Gideon walked into the stable.

'Why did you run off like that, Sally? We were only trying to help.'

'Flower is my horse,' Sally said stubbornly. 'I decide if I want to sell her and I'll choose the next owner. I certainly don't intend to give her away.'

'I'm certain that Cecily would see that Flower was

well cared for. You couldn't find a better home than the stables at Fleet Hall.'

'I'm sorry if I embarrassed you, but Flower is a special animal. Miss Appleton would take her out for a genteel trot if the mood took her, but otherwise Flower might be stuck in her stall for days on end. It's easy for her to say that I could visit when I pleased, but it's a long walk to Highgate.'

Gideon looked round the dilapidated stable and shook his head. 'Do you really think this is better than the conditions in which she might be living at Fleet Hall? I know it's none of my business, but as a veterinary surgeon it's the welfare of the animal that must come first. I feel I have a right to speak my mind.'

Sally looked him in the eye. 'You hardly know me. I'm truly grateful that you've offered to look after Boney, but if you feel in the circumstances you can't, I'll understand.'

'Of course my offer still stands. I'm pleased to be able to grant an old working horse a happy life in the country, but I don't know where you get the idea that you've offended me.'

'Miss Appleton is your future wife. I threw her offer to take Flower back in her face, so I would expect you to be annoyed.'

'I suppose that Jane Wallace gave you that impression, but Cecily and I are good friends. We've known each other since we were children. There is no such understanding between us.'

Sally was tempted to argue, but she could see that he was sincere and she held her tongue. 'Maybe I was mistaken, but Flower is not a rich lady's toy. Anyway, I'm sure that Miss Appleton has withdrawn the offer now, so please can we say no more on the subject. I'm very grateful for your attempts to help, but we will manage.'

Gideon smiled, shaking his head. 'I've never met two more stubborn women in my life. You might think that you and Cecily have nothing in common, but I can assure you that you're wrong. She is unlikely to give in once she's made up her mind, and I can see that you are similar. It's going to be interesting to see who wins.'

It was impossible to resist his humorous look and Sally relaxed just a little. 'This isn't a war. Flower is mine and that's an end to it.'

'So you may think. I'll say goodnight, but I have a feeling that we will meet again before very long.' Gideon let himself out into the street, closing the door behind him.

Sally fondled Flower's neck. 'I know he meant well, but I'm not so sure about Miss Cecily.'

Sally finished work in the stable and went upstairs to her room. They might not have a work horse but they still had the cart. She had toyed with the idea of pulling it through the streets herself, but she had abandoned the project as being unworkable. She sat on the edge of her truckle bed and counted out their meagre savings that she kept in a pouch beneath her mattress. There was only enough to keep them in food for two days, three at the most, and even then they would be living on next to nothing. Perhaps she could sell the cart as it was, although it had seen many years of hard labour. Sally settled down for the night. Maybe tomorrow she would find a solution to their problems.

Sally was in the yard, examining the cart with a view to putting it up for sale, when Kelly sauntered out of the back door.

'Ted told me that you were out here,' Kelly said affably.

Pippy bounced up to him, barking with obvious pleasure, and Kelly bent down to ruffle her fur.

'Pa said you bought him food yesterday. Thank you for that.'

'We all fall on hard times every now and then, mavourneen.' He strolled over to examine the cart. 'Would it be true that you're thinking of selling this old heap of splinters and woodworm?'

'Maybe,' Sally said warily. 'Why? Are you interested?'

'What? In that old pile of junk?' Kelly examined it from all sides. 'I've got a better cart than this.'

'Then why are you here? You never do anything for nothing.'

'That's not fair, mavourneen. Didn't I come round yesterday to offer my condolences about poor Boney?'

'How did you know about that?'

'Word gets round,' Kelly said mysteriously. 'But it was obvious that the old fellow wouldn't make it much longer. Your pa told me you'd gone to the country with the veterinary surgeon. What price did he extract from you for putting Boney out to pasture?'

'You have a devious mind, Kelly. Some people do nice things simply because they are decent and want to do the right thing.'

'Don't trust them, that's what I say. I'm a bad fellow, but you can rely on me to keep my word.'

'What do you want, Kelly? I'm getting tired of asking, and don't give me any of your blarney.'

'Well, now you come to mention it, I could offer you a few shillings for the cart, but I'd be doing meself down. It's only fit for the bonfire.'

Sally agreed with him in private, but she was not going to give in easily. 'A coat of paint and a new wheel or two, and it'll be as good as new.'

'So you're giving up, are you?'

'I'm not doing this from choice, Kelly.'

He leaned against the cart, stroking Pippy's small head as she vied for his attention. 'No, I gathered that from Ted. He feels bad because he can't provide for you any longer.' Kelly's serious expression melted into a wide grin. 'I told him he should marry you off to a bloke who could look after both of you.'

Sally knew Kelly well enough not to take him seriously. 'Are you offering?'

'Not me, mavourneen. I'm not the marrying kind.'

'Well, that's good because I wouldn't want to put

my life in the hands of a scallywag like you,' Sally said, smiling. 'But we do need money for the rent quite urgently, Kelly. Are you sure you don't want the cart?'

He shook his head. 'I'd buy it off you if only to help out, but I made a bad investment at the races a couple of days ago.'

'It's all right – I thought I'd ask. I'll handle it myself, Kelly.'

'I could lend you ten bob,' he said grudgingly. 'But that's all I've got.'

'Thank you again, but I couldn't take it from you. We'll manage somehow.' She could see that he did not believe her, but she did not want to be beholden to Kelly and she managed a smile. 'I'm considering an offer I had yesterday. A wealthy woman who lives in Highgate is interested in purchasing Flower. It's not something I want to do, but she would be safe and I could visit her often.' This was a lie, of course, but it made the arrangement sound more believable, or so she hoped.

'So why haven't you accepted her offer?'

Sally turned away. Kelly had the uncanny knack of knowing when she was lying. 'I wanted time to think about it.'

'You mean you don't trust her to look after your precious horse.'

'Not exactly – well, maybe. But Flower is mine and always has been. We belong together.'

'Have you thought about working for Astley's?'

She stared at him in surprise. 'I have, but I'm not a performer and neither is Flower.'

'You could learn and so could she.'

'Ma was a brilliant horsewoman. I'm a good rider, but that's all.'

Kelly shrugged. 'It was just a thought, mavourneen. I don't like to see my friends lose everything.'

'We aren't beaten yet,' Sally said firmly. 'I'll find a way.'

'Sure you will.' Kelly glanced round at the neat piles of scrap metal and other items that Sally and her father were preparing to sell. 'I'll take this stuff off your hands and I'll split the profits when I've sold it on. I can't say fairer than that.'

Sally thought quickly. She could not shift the items herself and the money would help to keep them until she had worked out a solution to what had seemed an unsolvable problem. She proffered her hand. 'It's a deal, Kelly.'

'And in the meantime I want you to accept the loan,' Kelly added firmly. 'I suggest we go to the Nag's Head and I'll treat you and your pa to a chicken dinner. We can settle things over a glass of hot rum punch.'

The loan from Kelly would cover the rent, but they would have to live on pea soup bought from a street vendor, and stale rolls that the baker sold off at closing time in the evening. It was only when Sally put the last of the fresh straw and sawdust down in the stable that she realised that matters had come to a head. It was one thing for herself and her father to cut their food and fuel down to a minimum, but when it came to an empty manger, it was another matter. Sally had not seen Gideon since the night he had called in after her somewhat undignified flight from Fleet Hall, but he arrived early on Christmas Eve, riding his own horse, with Boney on a leading rein.

Sally opened the stable door in answer to his knock, although she had seen him approaching from the upstairs parlour window. 'Have you brought Boney back to us?'

'Is that what you want?' Gideon was not smiling.

'No. I mean I want what's best for him.'

'Then you agree that I should take him to Hill Farm?'

'Yes, please. I'm very grateful, and, once again, I'm sorry if I offended Miss Appleton by leaving so abruptly.'

A slow smile lit Gideon's eyes. 'I'm sure that Cessy has forgotten the incident, but she was sincere in her wish to purchase Flower, and you both seem to have abandoned the idea of sharing her. Have you given any more thought to selling Flower?'

After a sleepless night, Sally had come to the only conclusion possible. She nodded. 'If she still wants her I'll consider it, but I must see where she's to be stabled and I want to speak to the head groom. Flower has very particular needs.'

'Cessy is very keen to have her, and if she makes up her mind to have something, money will be no object,' Gideon said, smiling. 'Today, as you might have gathered, is her birthday and there will be a grand ball tonight. Why don't you come with me now? Ride Flower to Fleet Hall and then you can have a word with Jackson and a tour of the stables. I can assure you they are very modern and the horses have every comfort.'

'I don't know.' Sally glanced over her shoulder at Flower, who was watching her with trusting eyes. 'I'm not sure I can do this.'

'Perhaps you could leave Flower in Jackson's care overnight, then you can judge for yourself whether or not she'll settle into her new home. I'm sure Mrs Wallace will make up a bed for you at the farm. She'd be more than happy to have your company.'

Sally knew that if she hesitated she would never be able to part with Flower, and Gideon's suggestion was not one to be dismissed lightly. 'All right. I'll come with you, but first I must make sure that Pa knows what to do for his supper. Give me five minutes and I'll be with you.'

Sally raced upstairs and found her father seated in his old chair by the empty grate. They had run out of coal and kindling and it was bitterly cold, but she did not dare break into the rent money.

'Where's the fire?' Ted gave her a wry smile. 'Joking aside, we could do with some coal, Sally love.'

'I know, Pa. I'm sorry but we've run out and there

isn't any money to buy more. That's why I'm going to do what's necessary. I don't want to leave you on Christmas Eve, but this might be my one chance to help us out of this mess.'

Ted was suddenly alert. 'What d'you mean? You're not going to sell Flower, are you?'

'Mr Lawrence is downstairs, Pa. He's taking Boney to his farm in Highgate and he suggested that I take Flower to Fleet Hall and leave her for the night to see if she'll settle.'

Ted dashed his hand across his eyes. 'What have we come to that you have to sell your horse in order to keep an old wreck like me.'

'Don't talk that way, Pa. I love you and I'll do anything to make your life more comfortable. I'll only sell Flower if I'm certain that she'll have a good home. With the money I get for her I could buy a horse to take Boney's place. That means we could stay here and I could take over your round.'

'It's not a job for a girl like you, Sally. It was different when we did it together, but I'll never be fit enough to take over again.'

'With the money I might get for Flower we could afford to pay for a doctor. We'll have you back on your feet in no time.'

'Don't do it, Sal. I know how much you love that animal.'

'I love you more, Pa. But I'll only leave Flower if I'm quite certain she'll be well treated and loved as I love her.' Sally took the crust of a loaf of bread from the cupboard and the last slice of cheese, which she placed on a plate at her father's side. 'There's your midday meal, Pa. I'll pop in to Mrs Maggs's shop next door. She'll bring you a cup of tea and a bite to eat for supper. She's bound to be on her own, so she'll be glad of the company.'

'She never stops talking.' Ted sighed. 'But she does bake good pies. I just munch away and shut me ears to her prattle.'

'You'll be fine, Pa. Mr Lawrence said I can stay at the farm tonight, and his housekeeper will keep an eye on me. I'll be home as soon as I can in the morning. Be good, Pa. Don't flirt with Mrs Maggs. I don't fancy her for a stepmother.'

Ted shuddered visibly. 'She's got a wart on her chin with hairs growing out of it. A fellow would have to be desperate to marry that one.'

'Or very greedy for her steak and oyster pies,' Sally added, laughing. 'I have to go now. Mr Lawrence is waiting outside.' She leaned over and dropped a kiss on her father's bald head. 'I'll see you tomorrow. I'll be home first thing, and we'll spend a nice quiet day together.'

Mrs Wallace seemed genuinely pleased to see Sally, and having plied her with tea and biscuits, she showed her to a room at the back of the farmhouse, overlooking an orchard.

'You'll be comfortable here,' Mrs Wallace said cheerily. 'Will you be staying long?'

'Just for tonight. Although I think I could live here quite happily. It's such a lovely place and so different from Paradise Row.'

'I wouldn't know about that, dear. I was born and bred in a cottage not far from here. My father was the gamekeeper on the Appletons' estate, so I grew up in the country.'

'You're very fortunate,' Sally said with feeling.

'I think so, and I have the best employer in the whole world. Unfortunately Arthur and I were never blessed with children, and I think of Mr Lawrence as my own son, although I wouldn't dream of telling him so.'

'He's been very generous in taking on Boney. I doubt if many people would do as much for a complete stranger.'

'A pretty face works wonders, my dear,' Mrs Wallace said, chuckling. 'But Mr Lawrence does have a kind heart, especially when it comes to animals. As a small boy he would bring home all manner of creatures that were sick or injured in some way. His poor mother never knew what sort of animal she would find crawling round the floor in her best parlour.' She cocked her head at the sound of Gideon's voice. 'I think he wants you, miss.'

Sally caught sight of her dishevelled state in the mirror on the dressing table. 'I was supposed to be getting ready to go to the Hall. Do I look all right?'

Mrs Wallace eyed her critically. 'Your hair is in

a bit of a tangle, and that outfit is not at all flattering, but Miss Appleton is interested in your horse, not you.'

'Yes, you're right.' Sally tucked stray strands of hair under her peaked cap. 'Thank you, Mrs Wallace. I'll see you later.' She hurried from the bedchamber and descended the stairs in a rush.

Gideon was waiting for her in the entrance hall. 'I was half expecting you to slide down the banister,' he said, laughing. 'We'd better go now or Cessy will be too engrossed in her preparations for the ball to take any interest.'

'Maybe this wasn't such a good idea after all,' Sally said nervously.

'You've come this far, but if you don't approve of the stables or you change your mind about selling Flower, we'll all understand.'

Sally had a sudden picture of her father huddled around an empty grate, at the mercy of Mrs Maggs with the hairy wart on her chin, and she knew that their future depended upon her and her alone. 'I've made my decision and I'll stick to it, but only if Flower settles down quickly.'

'A brave decision.' Gideon's smile was sympathetic. 'I know how hard this must be for you, so let's not waste any more time. The sooner we get Flower to her new home, the better.'

They left the house and were halfway across the yard when a tall, thin man emerged from the stable. He tipped his cap. 'Good morning, Mr Lawrence.'

'Good morning, Wallace. Is everything all right?'

'Yes, sir. I was just taking a look at the little mare. Bert was raving about her the other day, so I thought I'd see for myself.'

'Flower belongs to Miss Suggs.' Gideon turned to Sally. 'This is Arthur Wallace, my right-hand man. I wouldn't have been able to keep the farm going without him.'

'It's a pleasure to meet you, Mr Wallace.' Sally could see that he was shocked by her appearance and had probably made the mistake of thinking she was a boy. She smiled and shook his hand.

'Pleased to meet you, too, miss.' Arthur's weather-beaten skin darkened with a suspicion of a blush. 'It's a privilege to work here. Mr Lawrence senior took me on as a lad more than forty years ago, and I wouldn't want to live and work anywhere else.'

'It's a lovely setting,' Sally said earnestly.

'We'd better not keep you, Wallace.' Gideon beckoned to young Bert who was holding the two horses in readiness. 'We need to leave now, but Miss Suggs will be staying here for the night. I've been invited to dinner at the hall, so I hope you and Jane will keep her entertained.'

'It'll be our pleasure, sir.' Wallace tipped his cap to Sally before striding off towards the fields.

'He's a good man,' Gideon said confidentially. 'I would have had to sell up when my father died if it hadn't been for him and Jane.' He swung Sally onto the saddle and taking the reins from Bert he mounted his own horse. 'Walk on.'

'How much land have you got here?' Sally asked as they set off towards Fleet Hall.

'About a hundred acres. It's prime land and Sir Gregory is very keen to get his hands on it. His estate is the largest in the county, or it would be if he could incorporate Hill Farm. I think that's the only reason he tolerates my friendship with Cessy.'

'Why would that be?'

'If Cessy and I were to marry, our estates would merge. It's been done that way by ambitious landowners for centuries.'

'It sounds very mercenary.'

'I hadn't given it much thought.' Gideon encouraged his horse to a brisk trot, leaving Sally no alternative but to follow suit.

They arrived at Fleet Hall to find a flurry of activity. Servants were rushing around, stringing paper lanterns amongst the trees and placing flares at intervals along the drive. A huge Christmas tree had been transplanted to stand in the middle of the snowy lawn, and coloured glass balls glinted in the pale winter sunlight. Sally could imagine how it would look when the candles attached to the branches were lit, and the whole scene would have a touch of magic. She found herself wishing that she could be a guest at Cecily's birthday ball. 'It's beautiful,' she breathed. 'I've never seen anything like it in my whole life.'

'It's Sir Gregory demonstrating his affluence to the rest of the world.' Gideon shook his head. 'I'm sure he could do something better with his money.'

'But it's for his daughter's birthday.'

'Yes, of course, and Cessy deserves the best.' Gideon controlled his frightened mount as a smart phaeton bowled past, coming to a sudden halt just yards away.

'Who is that?' Sally struggled to calm Flower as the horse reared in fright.

'He's Cessy's father, and he's spotted us.'

Sir Gregory leaped down from the vehicle, flinging the reins to a groom. 'Lawrence, I thought it was you.'

A boy rushed up and swept away the snow as his master strode across the gravel carriage sweep, but Sir Gregory waved him away with an impatient flick of his gloved fingers.

'Save your efforts for the ladies, boy.' Sir Gregory came to a halt beside Flower, eyeing her up and down with an appreciative nod. 'That's a fine piece of horseflesh the young boy is riding. Let me see how she moves.'

'I'm not a boy,' Sally said crossly. 'And this is my horse, sir.'

'What the devil is a girl doing dressed like a ragamuffin?' Sir Gregory glared at Sally as if her outfit was an affront in itself. 'I don't believe you own such a thoroughbred. Is the animal stolen?'

'No, indeed. Flower is my horse, sir.'

Sir Gregory turned to Gideon. 'Is this the animal my daughter has been pestering me to purchase for her?'

'Yes, sir. But Miss Suggs is not certain that she wants to sell.'

'Nonsense. Everyone has a price. Walk on, girl. Show me what the little lady can do, but I warn you – I'm an excellent judge of horseflesh. You won't get a penny piece from me unless I approve.'

Chapter Five

Sally was tempted to turn Flower's head and ride off in the direction of home, but above all she wanted to wipe the smirk off Sir Gregory's face, and she put Flower through her paces. A capriole was followed by a showy pirouette and a series of dressage movements, ending in a beautifully executed piaffe.

'Impressive!' Sir Gregory said grudgingly. 'Are you a circus rider, girl?'

'No, sir. I'm a rag-and-bone man's daughter.' Sally could not resist the temptation to put the pompous man in his place. His smart attire did not disguise his portly figure, and the starched white collar and cravat did not flatter his florid complexion. At this moment he looked as though he might have an apoplectic fit, and he reminded her forcibly of Rags Roper, whose ramshackle warehouse at the back of the Imperial Gasworks was somewhere she did her best to avoid. Kelly had his uses, and one of them was accompanying her when she was forced to haggle for the best price for her goods with Rags, with whom no woman under ninety was safe.

'I suppose you think that's funny, boy!'

'It's the truth.' Sally took off her cap and shook out her long dark hair. 'And I am a girl, as you see.'

Sir Gregory was silent for a few seconds. 'I've never seen a woman ride like that.'

'Neither have I.' Gideon leaned over to stroke Flower's neck. 'This little mare is amazing, and you are an excellent horsewoman, Sally. I can see now why you want to keep Flower.'

'Well, now, I haven't made my offer yet,' Sir Gregory said hastily. 'Of course, all that fancy business isn't much use to my daughter. Cecily rides like a lady, but I do like that piece of horseflesh. She would be good breeding stock.'

Sally exchanged worried glances with Gideon. 'I haven't said I'd let her go yet. I want to see where she'll be stabled, and I'd like to find out who will look after her.'

'I'm the one with the bargaining power,' Sir Gregory said testily. 'I decide the terms, not you, miss.'

'Then you'd better find another mount for your daughter, Sir Gregory. Flower means everything to me.'

'But you could purchase another work horse,' Gideon said softly. 'Think about it, Sally. You have your father to support until he is fit enough to work, if ever.'

Sally nodded reluctantly. 'You're right, of course, but Flower's welfare is important too.'

'Make up your mind, miss.' Sir Gregory put one foot on the bottom step. 'I haven't got all day, and my patience is running out.'

'Papa. You're home, and in good time.' Cecily emerged from the house and ran down the steps, her velvet cloak wrapped tightly around her. She threw her arms around her father. 'I thought you must have been delayed in town.'

Sir Gregory's pinched features softened into a fond smile. 'Nothing would keep me away at such an important time, sweetheart.'

'And you're here, too, Gideon.' Cecily shielded her eyes from the brilliance of the sunlight reflecting on the fallen snow. 'And Miss Suggs has brought the horse. What do you think, Papa? Will you buy it for me?'

'Of course, darling. If that's what you want. Although you should have a ride first. The animal is highly strung and you might not be able to control it.'

'I'm an excellent horsewoman, aren't I, Gideon?' Cecily turned to him with an appealing smile.

'Yes, you are, Cessy. But your father is right. Flower might not suit you.'

'Then I'll go and change into my riding habit. I'll prove you both wrong.' Cecily turned on her heel, picked up her skirts and hurried back to the house.

Sir Gregory smiled and shook his head. 'My little pet can be wilful, but that only adds to her charm. Come indoors and share a glass of Madeira with me, Gideon.' He eyed Sally, frowning. 'Take the animal to my head groom, Jackson, and tell him to put a side-saddle on her. He'll show you round, but I can assure you that the stables here at Fleet Hall are the finest you will find anywhere in the country.' He made his way up the steps, pausing in the doorway to beckon to Gideon.

'Are you sure you're all right with this, Sally,' Gideon asked in a low voice. 'If you find it all too much, I'll understand.'

'I have very little choice, but I want to be sure that Cecily can manage Flower properly.'

'Hurry up, Lawrence.' Sir Gregory disappeared into the entrance hall. 'Stafford, we'll have a bottle of Madeira in the study, chop-chop.'

The stable block was almost more impressive than the mansion itself. Sally had been too anxious to take much notice of her surroundings on her first visit. She knew very little about architecture, but it was obvious even to the uninitiated, that the elegant buildings had been erected in the previous century. For some unknown reason they had escaped demolition when Sir Gregory's father decided that the neo-classical style of building was old-fashioned and outdated. The two-storey block had been constructed around a large cobbled yard and the stabling, accommodation and coach house were reached through an impressive archway. Sally drew Flower to a halt and dismounted. A stable boy rushed up to her but she held on to Flower's reins. 'I need to speak to Mr Jackson,' she said firmly.

'He's busy, miss. Got his hands full today with all the goings-on.'

'Sir Gregory told me to ask for Mr Jackson.'

The boy gazed at her with big brown eyes and backed away. 'Yes, miss.' He ran off and minutes later Jackson emerged from a doorway on the far side of the yard. His unhurried gait suggested a man who was used to command.

'What can I do for you, miss?'

'Sir Gregory wants my horse saddled up for Miss Appleton to ride.'

'Very well, miss.' Jackson signalled to the stable boy, who was waiting a few yards away. 'Fetch Miss Cecily's side-saddle.'

'Yes, guv.' The boy raced off into what Sally assumed must be the tack room. The scent of leather, dubbin, horseflesh, hay and dung was so familiar that Sally immediately thought of their cramped quarters above the stable in Paradise Row. The animals here lived in total luxury compared to the narrow stall inhabited by Flower.

'Do I take it that Miss Cecily wants to keep this animal?' Jackson asked curtly.

'Yes, she does.'

Jackson walked slowly round Flower, running his hand over her body with an expert touch. 'She's a nice Andalusian mare, but no good for hunting.'

'Does Miss Cecily ride to hounds?'

'Occasionally, but I'd say that this is a horse trained in classic dressage. Am I right?'

'My mother was a performer at Astley's. She bred Flower from her own mare and she trained her.'

'Well, she's docile enough. Miss Cecily is a good rider, and she prefers a quiet animal.'

'Flower is very well behaved. She has an excellent temperament, but I haven't decided whether I'm going to part with her.'

Jackson gave her a calculating look. 'If Miss Cecily really wants her you could name your price.'

'My main concern is that Flower would be well cared for.' Sally was impressed by the immaculately kept yard, but she did not want to give too much away. She could imagine Jackson repeating their entire conversation to his master, putting his own interpretation on her words.

'You won't find a better run stable anywhere in the country,' Jackson said, echoing Sir Gregory's words. 'I suggest you take a look round now. Your horse will be saddled up and waiting when you've done.'

'Thank you, I will.' Sally had no reason to doubt Jackson, but she was curious and she wanted to see how the wealthy took care of their horses. She explored the stables, avoiding the tack room where the grooms and stable boys were eating their midday meal, and she could not help but be impressed. A large bunch of mistletoe pinned to the lintel made her smile. In this entirely male domain, they would have difficulty finding any pretty young females to kiss. She dragged her thoughts back to the business in hand, and she had to admit that everywhere was spotlessly clean; the horses were healthy and well-groomed. She walked back to where Jackson waited with Flower, who was saddled up and ready to go. Sally could see that her horse was prepared to give the performance of her life, and she felt her heart swell with pride.

'Do you ride side-saddle, miss?' Jackson asked curiously.

'Yes, and I can ride bareback, too. Ma taught me well.'

'You said that your mother performed at Astley's Amphitheatre. It seems to me, although it's none of my business, that you could do well there yourself.'

'What makes you say that?'

'I saw you putting your horse through her paces when you were here previously. Very impressive, miss.'

'Thank you, but you should have seen my mother when she performed. She was brilliant and I fear I'll never live up to the standard she set. Anyway, I'd best take Flower back to the house. I'm sure Miss Cecily must be ready by now.'

Jackson gave her a wry smile. 'I wouldn't bet on it, miss.'

Sally led Flower over to the mounting block. She was surprised to find the side-saddle more comfortable than she had anticipated, and she felt quite secure.

'Miss Cecily should be ready by now,' Jackson said with an encouraging nod.

'Yes, thank you. I'd almost forgotten Miss Cecily. Walk on, Flower. Let's get this over and done with.'

Cecily was waiting at the foot of the steps and she did not look pleased. 'What kept you? I've been waiting a full five minutes, haven't I, Stafford?'

'I believe so, Miss Cecily.'

'And I didn't give you permission to use my saddle,' Cecily continued crossly.

Sally dismounted. 'You would've waited longer had I walked back from the stables. Do you want a leg-up?'

'Don't be vulgar,' Cecily said, sniffing disdainfully. 'Stafford, you may lift me onto the saddle as there is no mounting block to hand.'

Stafford muttered something unintelligible, and stepped forward to hoist her onto the saddle. It was not very dignified and Sally had to turn her head away as she struggled to control a chuckle. Cecily, however, seemed determined to prove herself as an excellent horsewoman and she used her crop to encourage Flower from a walk to a trot. Sally was tempted to shout at Cecily, but she managed to stop herself. This was going to be far more difficult than she had imagined. However, Cecily seemed satisfied with her own performance, but suddenly she reined in too hard for Flower's soft mouth, causing the animal to rear on her hind legs in alarm.

'That's not the way,' Sally said angrily. 'Flower has a very sensitive mouth. She needs just a little tightening on the reins, or a command and she'll do what you wish.'

'Lift me down Stafford.' Cecily held out her arms like a small child and Stafford stepped forward to oblige. He set her gently on the ground and stood back. 'You may go now,' Cecily said sharply. She turned back to Sally, frowning. 'I will take the animal for a trial period, as we agreed, but she needs schooling to suit my needs.'

'I'm sorry,' Sally said carefully. 'Do you mean that you want to retrain my horse?'

'Well, yes.' Cecily tossed her head. 'I'm not a circus rider, nor a rag-and-bone man's daughter. I like the look of her, she's a pretty little mare, but she will have to learn to do as I bid her.'

'I didn't agree to your proposition, and now I know why. Nothing in the world would persuade me to leave Flower in your care. You don't know how to handle a horse.' Sally unbuckled the saddle and dropped it at Cecily's feet. 'You can have your property back – I don't want to be accused of stealing.' She swung herself onto Flower's back and rode off in the direction of the stables.

If Jackson was surprised to see her riding bareback

into the yard he kept his thoughts to himself, and he sent the boy to fetch Sally's saddle.

'You might want to send one of your lads to fetch the one belonging to Miss Cecily,' Sally said awkwardly. 'I'm afraid I lost my temper when she handled Flower badly, and I dropped the saddle on the ground at her feet. She's not having my horse, and that's that.'

A muscle twitched at the corner of Jackson's mouth. 'I'd have given a week's pay to see her face,' he said solemnly. 'It's probably the first time that anyone has refused her anything.' He held out his hand to the stable boy who had come running up to them, puffing beneath the weight of saddle. 'Give it here, boy. You'll allow me to do this for you, miss. It's my pleasure.'

Sally's one thought was to get as far away from Fleet Hall as possible. She knew she ought to have returned to the farm, but that would have entailed explanations to Mr and Mrs Wallace, not to mention Gideon. It felt as though she was throwing his kindness back in his face, but she did not want to enter into an argument about the rights and wrongs of her decision to keep Flower. She knew that it defied common sense, and that she might regret it bitterly when she returned to the reality of life in Paradise Row, but she could not bring herself to leave her precious horse in the care of an over-indulged young woman like Cecily Appleton.

* * *

It was a long and difficult ride home. The snow had turned to slush and then it started to freeze, but Flower was sure-footed and Sally trusted her even in such adverse circumstances. It was pitch dark by the time Sally reached home, but a glimmer of candlelight in the window above the stables was all the welcome she needed. Christmas in Paradise Row might not be as glamorous as a birthday ball in Highgate, but it was home and she was glad to be there at last. As she let herself into the stable, she was surprised to see an occupant in Boney's old stall, which she recognised as Kelly's horse. She made Flower comfortable while she went upstairs, following the sound of male voices and Pippy's excited barking. The moment Sally opened the door she was met by an ecstatic little dog, who leaped into her arms and proceeded to lick her face.

'Sally, love. I didn't expect to see you tonight.' Ted half raised himself from his chair, sinking back with a grimace of pain. 'Look who came to keep me company on Christmas Eve.'

'That was kind of you, Kelly,' Sally said warily. She set Pippy on the floor and bent down to stroke her until she quietened down.

'I can be a decent fellow when it suits me,' Kelly countered, chuckling. 'Ted and I have been talking about old times when trade was good.'

'Kelly bought me a pie from Mrs Maggs. He saved me the trouble of having to listen to her prattling on about how hard it is for a poor widow woman to make a living.'

'And you've enjoyed a pitcher of ale from the jug and bottle, I see.' Sally tried to maintain a frown, but she could not help smiling at the guilty expressions on their faces.

'So how did your trip to the country go?' Kelly asked casually.

'I couldn't bring myself to leave Flower there.' Sally sank down on the worn seat of an armchair that had, like everything else in their accommodation, seen better days. Pippy took this as an invitation to jump onto her lap. 'Miss Appleton is a spoiled young woman who knows nothing about horses. I couldn't entrust Flower to someone who only wants her so that she can show off.' Sally turned to her father. 'I'm so sorry, Pa. I just couldn't abandon Flower, even though the stables are quite palatial and there were plenty of people to look after her.'

'How much did they offer for her, love?' Ted asked wearily.

'I didn't stop to find out, Pa. Miss Appleton would have ruined Flower's mouth, and broken her spirit.'

'Best find another buyer then,' Kelly said casually.

Ted heaved a sigh. 'What did your friend Mr Lawrence have to say about it, Sal?'

'I left without telling him.' Sally slid Pippy to the floor as she rose to her feet. She walked over to the small window, staring down at the wet cobblestones, noting that it had begun to snow again. 'I know it was wrong, and I should have stayed to explain, but I just wanted to get away as quickly as possible. I hope he doesn't turn Boney out because of me.'

'Why would he do that?' Ted's voice shook with emotion. 'Poor old Boney has earned a happy retirement.'

'Gideon Lawrence is virtually engaged to Miss Cecily, so he might take exception to the way I behaved.'

'Good luck to him. That's what I say.' Kelly rose to his feet. 'It sounds as if he'll be taking on a handful if he weds her. Anyway, I should be going. It's getting late and I'm sure you want to get some sleep, Ted.'

'I'm very grateful for the supper and your company, Kelly. You'll come again soon, won't you?'

'I will, unless Sally objects to entertaining a rogue like me.'

Sally shook her head. 'Why do you always put me in the wrong, Kelly? You know you're welcome to come and keep Pa company whenever you feel like it.' She followed Kelly downstairs to the stable. 'I have to give Flower a good rub down before I settle her for the night.'

Kelly led his horse from the stall. 'What will you do for money now?'

'I don't know and that's the truth, but I'll think of something and I will pay back the half sovereign you loaned me.'

'I'm not worried about that, girl. What does concern me is how you and your father are going to manage?'

'Why would that worry you? It means that we're not competing for business. I thought that would make you happy.'

He shook his head. 'I play fair when it comes to my friends. As I said before, your pa was good to me when I first started out, and now he's the one who needs help.'

'I'll find work,' Sally said with more conviction than she was feeling. 'Josie is always saying that the Grindles have difficulty in finding reliable servants. Maybe I could work for them.'

'I know that family. Old Grindle is a miser, and the rubbish they throw out is only fit for the nearest dust heap.'

'I'll bear that in mind,' Sally said, laughing.

'Be careful, that's all.' Kelly was serious for once. 'There are plenty of people out there who will take advantage of your present situation. You and I haven't always seen eye to eye, but you can call on me any time you need help.'

'Thank you, Kelly, and Merry Christmas.' She was about to enter Flower's stall when a feeling of dizziness almost overcame her and she reached out to clutch the wooden partition.

'Are you all right, Sally?'

She heard Kelly's voice coming from far away and she nodded. 'Yes. I'm fine.'

'When did you last have something to eat?'

'I don't know,' she said faintly. 'I can't remember.'

Kelly pulled up a stool and pressed her gently

onto the seat. 'I thought as much. Sit there until I come back. Mrs Maggs will have closed her shop, but Jarvis will still be open for business if I hurry. That man works late, even on Christmas Eve.' He left without giving her a chance to argue and Sally leaned back against the bare brick wall, closing her eyes until the world stopped spinning around her. It was only then that she realised she had eaten nothing since the refreshments that Mrs Wallace had provided, and that was hours ago.

She was more than ready to accept the food that Kelly purchased for her, despite the fact that the pie contained more gristle than meat and the bread rolls might have been freshly baked that morning, but they were now dry and stale. Kelly leaned against the wooden stall, watching her closely.

'You need to take better care of yourself, girl.'

Sally swallowed the last of the pastry. 'I know. I was so eager to get home that I forgot about eating. Thank you for the food, Kelly. How much do I owe you?'

He laughed. 'Don't worry about that. Old Jarvis likes to sell off the day's leftovers at knock-down price, otherwise the rats have a free meal during the night.'

'Maybe, but I will pay you back somehow, Kelly.'

'Have it your own way – I know you will, whatever I say. By the way, since you won't be able to do Ted's round, I'm taking it over. I've told him as much, and he doesn't mind.'

'It doesn't look as though we've much choice. I never thought I'd say this, but I suppose it's better you have Pa's round than one of the other totters.'

'I knew you'd come to my way of thinking in the end.' Kelly tipped his hat. 'I'll say goodnight, but when your friend the veterinary surgeon puts in an appearance, which I'm sure he will – make sure you stick to your guns. Don't let him or anyone talk you into giving up Flower, unless it's what you decide is right for her and for you. Merry Christmas, Sally.' He led his horse out into the street, closing the door behind him.

Now that he was no longer there, with his larger-than-life presence filling the room, Sally began to wonder if she had been selfish in her refusal to let Flower go, but she had only to look into her horse's intelligent eyes to confirm that her decision had been the right one. However, that did not solve her present predicament. If they wanted to eat she would have to pawn the only material thing she had that belonged to her mother, which was the narrow band of gold that Ted had slipped on Ma's finger twenty-two years ago. Sally had pawned it once before and she had been loath to let it go, even for a short while, but this time it might be gone for good. She was about to take it from its hiding place in a small box concealed behind a loose brick, when Kelly barged in without bothering to knock.

'Kelly!' Sally stared at him in surprise. 'Have you forgotten something?'

'I'll come straight to the point. I've had second thoughts about the old heap of wood in your yard. I might have some use for it after all.'

'Are you referring to Pa's cart?'

'The very same. I'm thinking of training up someone to help me on my rounds, and as I'm taking over your Pa's route, I'll need another cart. I'll give you a guinea for it, and you can forget the ten shillings you owe me.'

'But you told me that the cart was worthless.'

Kelly tilted his top hat at a rakish angle and grinned. 'That's business, mavourneen. Anyway, my better self has come forward, as it's Christmas. So what about it?'

'You really are a rogue, aren't you?' Sally said with a reluctant smile.

'Guilty, as charged. But I have a conscience when it comes to dealing with friends.'

'Are you serious, Kelly? Or is this one of your jokes.'

Kelly rolled his eyes, holding his hand to his heart. 'Do I look as if I'm joking? Of course I meant it.'

'I don't know whether to hug you or to slap you for being such a torment.'

'A hug would be nice, mavourneen.' Kelly blew her a kiss as he stepped outside into the street.

Sally locked the door after him, not knowing whether to laugh or cry.

* * *

Next morning, refreshed after a surprisingly good night's sleep, Sally was up early. It was not yet light and she decided to take Flower for a ride in Regent's Park. It was Christmas Day and the streets were deserted of traffic, apart from the odd hansom cab, and they had Rotten Row all to themselves. The ground was too hard and icy for a gallop, nevertheless it was a brisk ride and Sally was certain that Flower enjoyed it as much as she did. This was the time of day she loved when the city still slumbered, and the world seemed to be starting anew. Thanks to Kelly's unusual generosity, they would have enough food to eat and a week's supply of coal, kindling and candles. There was money to pay the rent, although Sally knew that she would have to find work soon, or they would be in the same predicament as before.

As she rode slowly home through the park and the gaslit cobbled streets, she could not help wondering whether Gideon had proposed to Cecily at the ball. Sally had glimpsed a world far removed from the way people lived in Paradise Row, and although she did not envy them their riches, the brief experience had left her feeling oddly unsettled. She told herself that she did not care what happened to Gideon, and if he married for money that was none of her business, but even so she had an uneasy feeling in the pit of her stomach. She had always been told that wealth did not necessarily bring happiness, and now she had seen it first-hand. She leaned forward to pat Flower's sleek neck.

'You and I are still together, Flower, and that's the way it's going to stay. We're happy as we are, living in Paradise Row.'

The sound of church bells ringing out joyously reminded Sally that it was Christmas morning, but there was little sign of festivity in Paradise Row. When she reined in Flower outside the stable she was surprised to see a shadowy shape wrapped in a voluminous cloak, hovering in the doorway.

Chapter Six

'Mrs Maggs? Is that you?'

'I've been knocking on the door for the past ten minutes,' Mrs Maggs said peevishly. 'I was beginning to think you'd gone away.'

Sally dismounted and unlocked the door. 'Is anything wrong?'

'I thought I'd bring you and your pa a little gift. In accordance with the spirit of the season, you understand.' From beneath the cloak Mrs Maggs produced a loaf of bread, still warm from the oven, and a saucepan. An appetising aroma wafted into the frosty air as she lifted the lid. 'Frumenty,' she said triumphantly. 'My own special recipe with the addition of a tot of rum, plump raisins and egg yolks. This will set you and your dear pa up for the day.'

'That's incredibly kind of you, ma'am.' Sally ushered Mrs Maggs into the stable before leading

Flower to her stall. 'Will you share it with us?' she added, hoping that her father would put a brave face on having to take breakfast with Mrs Maggs and her hairy wart.

Mrs Maggs beamed from ear to ear. 'Well, that's uncommon kind of you, Miss Sally. But I have to get back to the shop. You'd be surprised how many people need my services. I do good business by opening up on Christmas Day.'

'Perhaps you'd like to have supper with us this evening.' Sally knew her father would object, but it was obvious that the poor woman was very lonely.

'Oh, my! Well, I'd like nothing better, but you must allow me to bring something to the feast. I have a York ham, cooked to perfection. I'll bring what's left after I've served my regulars, and that together with a glass or two of rum punch will go down very nicely.'

'I'll look forward to it,' Sally said, steering her towards the door. 'Now I mustn't keep you from your shop, but we'll see you at six o'clock this evening.'

'I'll be there.' Mrs Maggs stepped outside. 'Merry Christmas, my dear.'

'Compliments of the season to you, Mrs Maggs.' Sally put the pan on the bottom stair tread and went to close the door. Quite what her father would say was another matter, but Mrs Maggs was a kind-hearted soul and the frumenty smelled delicious.

Having settled Flower with a fresh supply of hay,

Sally took the saucepan upstairs to set it on the trivet by the fire where it would keep warm until her father rose from his bed. She was in the process of making a pot of tea when she heard someone banging on the stable door, and she hurried to answer the urgent summons.

'It's you again, Kelly,' Sally said crossly. 'I thought there must be a fire at least.'

He tipped his hat. 'I've come for the cart, but I've also brought a little seasonal cheer for Ted.' He put his hand in the pocket of his greatcoat and took out a bottle of brandy, and from behind his back he produced a fruit cake decorated with glacé fruit and nuts. 'Brandy for Ted and the cake is for you. I'd like to think of you having a nice festive meal, even though I'll be taking supper alone.'

Sally resisted the urge to laugh. Kelly was the most unsubtle person she had ever met. 'Are you angling for an invitation to share a meal with us this evening?'

'Me? No! Would I be so crass as to invite myself to dinner with old friends, even if I have done them a great favour by taking a worm-eaten cart off their hands?'

'Stop! You'll have me in tears in a moment. You are most welcome to share our supper tonight. Come at six o'clock and we'll eat together.'

Kelly's face split in a wide grin. 'Thank you, mavourneen. I knew I could rely on your kindness. Now, I've got my old nag outside. I'll take him round to the back to collect the cart, if you'll be kind enough to unlock the gate.'

'I'll do that with pleasure.' Sally was tempted to tell him that she had already invited Mrs Maggs to dine with them, but she decided to let him find out for himself. At least his presence meant that Pa would have someone other than the over-eager Mrs Maggs to entertain.

Later, after Kelly had harnessed his horse to the cart and taken the last of the unwanted items that Ted had collected, Sally closed the gates and locked them. It was the end of the rag-and-bone trade for the Suggs family and she felt sad for her father, and for herself. The last links with her mother were rapidly disappearing and sometimes she had difficulty in picturing Ma's lovely face. It felt as if a mist was gradually blotting out the past, and as yet the future was unknown. Sally put such thoughts behind her and hurried upstairs to wake her father. She would share the breakfast treat with him, after which she would break the news that she had invited Mrs Maggs to supper.

Ted was dismayed at first, but the knowledge that Kelly would also be joining them cheered him up to the extent that he was gracious about Mrs Maggs and her hairy wart.

'The poor woman will never find another husband.' Ted scraped the last of the frumenty from his bowl. 'But I'll say this for her, she's a fine cook. Maybe someone with failing eyesight would take her on.'

'Don't be cruel, Pa,' Sally said, trying not to laugh. 'She can't help her looks and she is very generous.'

'Is there any more of that frumenty left, Sal? I haven't tasted anything like that for many a year. Your dear mother wasn't a good cook, although, to be fair, we haven't much in the way of cooking facilities, so I couldn't expect either of you to learn. You say Mrs Maggs is bringing a York ham for supper?'

'Yes, Pa. That's right.'

'In that case I'll do my best to be civil. Where's my best cravat, love? It is Christmas after all.'

That evening Sally changed into the only dress she owned. It was plain linsey-woolsey in a delicate shade of blue with a high neck and a full skirt that accentuated her tiny waist. Her dark hair was confined in a chignon at the back of her neck, but strands escaped and curled wildly about her forehead. She had long ago given up all attempts to tame her rebellious locks into the fashionable smooth hairstyles adopted by Queen Victoria and her ladies. Vanity, she hoped, was not her besetting sin, but sometimes it was nice to dress like a woman instead of looking like a stable boy. She knew by the appreciative expression on Kelly's face that the change in her appearance was a success, and Mrs Maggs remarked on the difference that clothes could make.

'Fine feathers make fine birds,' she said tipsily, after the second glass of a potent rum punch concocted by Kelly.

Sally suspected that he had been overgenerous with the spirit and mean with the water, but the spices and sugar made it very palatable. She had never seen her father so relaxed and he made an effort to be civil to Mrs Maggs, who had lived up to her promise. Not only had she brought what was left of the York ham, but out of her capacious basket she produced a large pork pie and a bottle of port. The meal went down well and afterwards, when they could eat no more, they sat round the fire and Kelly amused them with tales of his exploits. Sally joined in the laughter, even though she did not believe a word he said. Then, having drunk a glass or two of port, Mrs Maggs fell asleep in the armchair by the fire, snoring gently, with her double chins resting on her generous bosom. Ted brought out a pack of playing cards and Kelly lit a cigar for himself. He handed another to his host and they sat opposite each other at the table, glasses of punch at hand while they played. Pippy had eaten her fill of scraps from the table and she curled up on the hearth. Sally took the opportunity to go down to the stable to make sure that Flower was comfortable. She took a curry comb from the shelf and began to groom Flower, talking to her as if she were a human.

'You would have had the best of everything at Fleet Hall. Was I wrong to keep you here?'

Flower turned her head, gazing mutely at Sally with soft brown eyes.

'You can't answer that, of course. But I wonder

if Gideon did propose to Miss Cecily. She's beautiful, and she's very rich. He would own that huge house one day, and all the land around it. Who in their right mind would miss such an opportunity to better themselves? But perhaps he doesn't love her. What do you think Flower?'

'You won't get a sensible answer from her, Sally. She can't speak.' Kelly's amused voice broke into Sally's reverie and she dropped the curry comb.

'You made me jump.' She turned her head and saw that he was supporting a very tipsy Mrs Maggs.

'Open the door for us, mavourneen,' Kelly said, chuckling. 'The lady is a bit tired, so I'm seeing her safely home. Maybe you could come with us. I think she might need putting to bed, and I don't think she'd approve of having me in her room.'

'Of course I will.' Sally retrieved the curry comb and placed it back on the shelf. 'I'll finish it off later, Flower,' she told the horse apologetically.

Together they managed to get Mrs Maggs to her shop next door, and it took both of them to manoeuvre her up the narrow staircase to her room.

'I'll leave you to it,' Kelly said from the doorway. 'I'm going back to finish my game with Ted.'

'Thank you, Kelly.'

'Thanks for what?'

'Thank you for everything. It's been a long time since I last saw Pa so happy. You're good for him.'

'That means I must be good for you, too.'

She tugged at the strings of Mrs Maggs's corset.

'Go away. This isn't the sight for a gentleman. But I did mean it, Kelly. You've made our Christmas a happy one, and I was afraid it would be miserable.'

'Always glad to oblige.' Kelly backed out onto the narrow landing and Sally heard his booted feet clattering on the wooden stair treads. She sighed. It had been a pleasant evening, but what would happen in the future was still anyone's guess. She had never felt so unsettled in her life.

Mrs Maggs stirred and opened one eye as Sally covered her with a quilt. 'Is there any more port, dear?'

'I think you've had quite enough, Mrs Maggs.' Sally laid the large corsets on a chair beside the bed. 'Thank you for the ham and the pie.'

'My pleasure.' Mrs Maggs rolled onto her side and began snoring loudly.

Sally took the opportunity to leave the shop and returned home. The parlour was thick with cigar smoke and the fire blazed up the chimney. It was a profligate waste of expensive coal, but she could not begrudge her father his comfort, or the companionship of a former business rival. She was happy to see Pa enjoying himself, and with Pippy at her heels, Sally went to her room, leaving them to finish their game.

Next morning the smell of stale cigar smoke and alcohol fumes lingered in the parlour as Sally cleared away the debris. She wondered whether Mrs Maggs was up and about, or whether she would be suffering from the after-effects of imbibing too much punch and port. Sally took a bucket of ashes downstairs to the back yard, which was covered by a fresh fall of snow, shining pure and pristine in the light of early dawn. It seemed impossible to think that just a few short days ago the yard had been piled high with the unsold remainder of their collection, but Kelly had cleared everything away including the last scraps of iron. However, knowing him as she did, Sally suspected that he would manage to make money from each piece, down to the last rusty nail. She trod carefully on the frozen surface, taking care not to slip and spill the contents of the pail as she opened the gate. She walked to the ash-pit at the end of the back alley where she emptied the contents, to be collected later by the city dustmen. It was still very early but it was a working day and Paradise Row was already buzzing with life. The better-off householders in the nearby streets and squares would still be sleeping off the excesses of their Christmas celebrations, while their servants lit fires, emptied night-soil and began preparations for breakfast. The workers who lived in the poorer area were already hurrying to their places of employment, to begin another long day. Trains were leaving the station accompanied by shrieks of steam whistles, and in the goods yard the sound of engines shunting, and the rattle and bumps of the buffer and chain couplings vied with the blaring of factory hooters summoning people to work.

Sally had a sudden longing for the peace and quiet of the countryside. Hill Farm had seemed like heaven on earth, but she doubted if she would ever see it again. She would not blame Gideon if he refused to see her after the way she had left so abruptly, not once, but twice. She wrapped her shawl more tightly around herself and hurried as fast as the slippery conditions would allow, making her way back to the stable. What had happened was in the past, and there was little she could do about it now. Life had to go on and she must concentrate on finding work, or else face the prospect of eviction if she could not raise the next month's rent. Number seventeen Paradise Row might not be much compared to Hill Farm or the magnificent Fleet Hall, but it was the only home she had ever known, and losing it would be heart-breaking.

Sally went about her usual morning tasks of filling the empty bucket with coal and another with water from the pump. She made sure that Flower was comfortable before she went upstairs to light the fire and put the kettle on the trivet. She had just got a reasonable blaze going when her father staggered into the room.

He clutched his hand to his head. 'I shouldn't have had that second glass of brandy last night. It's all Kelly's fault. He encouraged me to drink.'

'You didn't need much encouragement, as I remember it, Pa.' Sally replaced the bellows on their hook by the fire and rose to her feet. 'You'll feel better when you've had a nice hot cup of tea and some toast.'

Ted sank down on his favourite chair. 'What? No frumenty?'

'We ate it all yesterday. I'm afraid you'll have to make do with toast. That's if you don't mind using the toasting fork yourself.'

'My head aches and my throat is dry. I don't fancy toast, Sal.'

'I'll get you some seltzer when I go out, Pa.'

Ted eyed her warily. 'Kelly is a good man.'

'Yes, I suppose he is.'

'There's no suppose about it, love. You could do worse.'

Sally stared at him in amazement. 'What are you saying, Pa?'

'He's doing well, and he's in the trade. You'd be well looked after.'

'Pa! Finn Kelly is a rogue. You've always said so.'

'A man can change his opinion.' Ted stared moodily into the fire. 'Like I said, you could do worse. Don't turn your back on an old friend.'

'You'll feel better after a cup of tea. I'm going to Mrs Maggs's shop for some milk. Maybe she's got some seltzer. She stocks all sort of things.'

'Think about what I said. We could live here for ever if you was to marry Kelly. He could use our yard, and stable one of his horses here.'

'Is this your idea, Pa? Or did Kelly say anything about me?'

'He didn't have to, love. I can always tell when a man fancies a woman.'

'You're imagining things, Pa.' Sally picked up the empty milk jug from the table and reached for her shawl. 'I'll be back in two ticks.'

She did not wait for him to argue.

In the stable Flower was pawing the ground as if asking to be taken out for a long ride, but Sally let herself out into the street and went next door to Mrs Maggs's shop. To her surprise the lady herself was busy serving as if nothing had happened. The tipsy woman from last evening had been transformed into the businesswoman. She had changed into a clean frock, with a spanking white pinafore and mobcap.

'Good morning, Mrs Maggs,' Sally said when it was her turn to be served.

Mrs Maggs pulled a face as the previous customer slammed out of the shop. 'It says clearly "No credit", but some people either can't read or they think they can bamboozle me into giving them stuff on tick.'

Sally handed her the jug. 'Would you be kind enough to fill this, please, and have you any seltzer powders? I'm afraid Pa is feeling a little worse for wear this morning.'

'Poor dear. I don't hold with strong drink, but it was the festive season, and he could be forgiven for overindulging.' She dipped the jug in a large milk churn, shook off the excess and handed it back to Sally. 'As it happens I do keep seltzers in, as the drunkards round here often ask for them, if they don't want to bother the apothecary or it's too far for them to stagger.'

Sally accepted the powders wrapped in slips of paper and paid for her purchases while Mrs Maggs went on and on about the good time she had had the previous evening. It was a relief when another customer breezed into the shop, followed by some young boys, who sidled round, peering into the open boxes of broken biscuits and fingering the goods. Mrs Maggs was round the counter in a flash.

'Get out of here you young scallywags. You don't get nothing unless you've got the money.'

The boys fled, but stopped outside, staring longingly at the food displayed in the window. Sally had also made her escape, but she hesitated, eyeing the boys who were skinny, dirty and barefooted, even though there was still slushy snow on the pavement. She opened her purse and took out some coppers. 'Here, boys. Go to the pie man and buy something to eat. Mind you spend it on food, though.'

The eldest of the three snatched the money. 'Ta, miss. We ain't eaten since the day afore yesterday.'

'Where are you parents?' It was a silly question – Sally knew the answer without waiting to hear the excuses the boys made. She had seen it all before. 'Come with me, boys. I want to make sure you buy food for yourselves. I don't want you giving the money to your good-for-nothing dad to spend on drink or tobacco.'

There was a stall on the corner, close to the station, and Sally knew the stallholder. 'Good morning, Ned.'

He tipped his cap. 'Morning, Sally. What have we here?' He eyed the boys suspiciously.

'Give them what they want to eat and some tea with lots of sugar, please.'

The eldest boy eyed her warily. 'Why would you treat the likes of us?'

'Don't ask questions, Jim.' His younger brother grabbed a ham roll that Ned offered him, and he passed it to the youngest boy. 'Eat it slowly now, Benny. Don't gobble.'

'Ta, Eddie.' The smallest boy took a bite and was about to hand it back to his brother when Sally stopped him.

'That's yours Benny. You may have one each,' Sally said hastily.

'You shouldn't encourage them. You'll have a whole pack of guttersnipes on your heels if word gets round.' Reluctantly, Ned handed two more rolls to the eldest boy. 'I know your sort, Jim Cotton. Your dad is a wrong 'un.'

Jim snatched the food, and passed one roll to his younger brother before taking a bite from his own. 'I won't argue with that, but it ain't our fault,' he said, swallowing a mouthful of bread and ham. 'Ta, miss. We won't tell no one what you just done.'

Sally gazed at Benny's small feet, which, despite the layer of ingrained grime, were rapidly turning blue. 'Why aren't you wearing shoes?'

'Shoes cost money what we don't have, miss.' Jim faced her with a defiant scowl. 'I can take care of me brothers, miss. We ain't going to the workhouse.'

'Good heavens! I never even thought of the workhouse, Jim.' Sally leaned across the barrow, lowering her voice. 'Is that likely, Ned?'

'Their ma ran off with another man a year ago, and their dad spends any money he earns on the railway in the pub. There's not much hope for such as them.'

'I ain't deaf,' Jim said angrily. 'Give us the tea, mate, and we'll be off.'

'Can you spare some milk for the little one?' Sally took some coins from her purse. 'I can pay extra.'

Ned poured tea into two mugs, adding a generous amount of sugar, and filled another with milk for Benny. He shook his head, tut-tutting, making his disapproval clear.

Sally waited while the boys finished their food and drink. Her own problems seemed minor when she thought about their sad predicament. She still had most of the money that Kelly had given her for the cart, but her heart was touched by the boys' plight. She came to a sudden decision.

'Come with me, boys. I'm taking you to the second-hand shop round the corner. I can't stand to see you barefoot and shivering in this weather.'

'You might as well throw your money down the drain,' Ned said grimly. 'Ten to one, they'll sell them before the day's out.'

'That's a chance I'll have to take.' Sally grabbed Benny by the hand. 'You're not going barefoot one minute longer than necessary.' She walked off, towing a protesting Benny, safe in the knowledge that his older brothers would follow. Sally was used to handling horses, and she reasoned that small boys needed to be treated much the same – love, kindness and a firm hand were what was needed.

Chapter Seven

Baines was not pleased when he came to collect the rent at the beginning of January. Out of sheer necessity, Sally had kept back enough money to buy food, coal and kindling for the next couple of days, not to mention a bale of hay and fresh straw for the stable – all of which left them in arrears. There might have been enough had she not spent so much outfitting the Cotton boys in the second-hand shop. She had bought extra food so that they had at least one decent meal a day, and they had taken to turning up late in the evening, sometimes black and blue from beatings their father had handed out. It was on these occasions that Sally let them sleep in Boney's old stall, having made up a bed of straw covered in a horse blanket. Pippy had seemingly adopted Benny, and she curled up with him, licking the salty tears from his cheeks. Sally hated sending the boys back to their father next day, but the law was on his side and the children belonged to him.

'This isn't good enough, Miss Suggs,' Baines said angrily, having counted the coins she gave him. 'You and your father will have to find other accommodation if you can't keep up regular payments.'

Sally squared her shoulders. She knew that he was right, but she was not going to plead their case. 'You'll get the money in full as soon as I have it, Mr Baines.'

He glanced over her shoulder at Boney's empty stall. 'You pa is out on his rounds, is he?'

'We'll make up the difference when you call again,' Sally said firmly. 'Good day to you, sir.'

He did not look convinced. 'Word is that your horse ain't up to the job any more and your pa is all but crippled by the rheumatics. That's what they're saying on the street.'

'Gossips always get things wrong. We're doing well enough.' Sally closed the door before he had a chance to argue. Baines was no fool and there were plenty of people willing to spread spiteful rumours. But there was no getting away from it – things were desperate and she needed to find a way to earn money.

'Who was that at the door, Sal?'

Her father's voice was querulous and Sally knew that he had suffered a sleepless night. She had heard him groaning from her tiny room beneath the eaves, but there was nothing she could do to ease his pain.

'It was Mr Baines, Pa.' Sally called from the foot of the stairs. 'He came to collect the rent.'

'Did you have enough?'

'Yes, Pa. You don't need to worry. I'm just going out on an errand, but I'll be back soon.' She did not wait for his answer and, snatching her shawl from a peg behind the door, she let herself out into the cold and wet. It was no use sitting at home worrying and she headed for the Grindle house.

Situated in the respectable terraces of Percy Street, the Grindles' establishment was a more humble establishment than some of the imposing buildings that graced the area, with their white-columned porticos, wrought-iron balconies and ornate brass door furniture. Even so, it was still a substantial four-storey dwelling with steps leading up to the front door, and the servants' entrance in the area below street level. Sally opened the gate and made her way carefully down the narrow stone steps. She knocked and after a minute or so the door was opened by none other than Josie, whose face lit up with a wide smile.

'What brings you here, Sal? Got tired of doing the rounds on the old cart, have you?'

'I need to find work quickly, Josie. D'you think Mrs Grindle would take me on?'

'You'd best come in.' Josie stood aside and Sally stepped into the narrow hallway.

'I don't mind what I do,' Sally said in a low voice.

'Who's that at the door, Josie, you lazy slut? If it's your gentleman friend, you can tell him to sling his hook.' A red-faced woman, enveloped in a grubby white pinafore, stepped out of the kitchen. Her sleeves were rolled up to expose muscular forearms coated with flour. 'Who's she?'

'She's the cat's mother,' Josie said with a cheeky grin, which was wiped away by a clout round the head from Cook.

'You'll go too far one of these days, Josie Bates.' Cook turned to Sally with an angry frown. 'Well? Who are you and what d'you want?'

'My name is Sally Suggs and I'm looking for work.'

Cook looked her up and down, curling her lip. 'You don't look like a skivvy to me. You ain't a friend of this one here, are you? Because if you are, you ain't no use to me.'

'I ain't never seen her before in me life.' Clutching her sore ear, Josie winked at Sally.

'I'm a good worker,' Sally said hastily. 'I can scrub floors or do the laundry.'

Cook leaned forward, peering at Sally with narrowed eyes. 'Are you sure you ain't a friend of this little trollop?'

'Who are you calling a trollop?' Josie demanded angrily. 'Just because I got a fellow and you ain't, don't give you the right to call me names – you old bat!'

'One more word from you and I'll wash your mouth out with lye soap.' Cook clenched her fists and her cheeks reddened. 'Get out of my sight before I change my mind.'

Josie tossed her head and stalked off, leaving Sally alone with the angry woman. 'All right,' Cook said reluctantly. 'I'll give you a trial. As it happens the scrub woman didn't turn up this morning and the kitchen floor is a pool of grease, but before that you can empty the chamber pots ready for the night-soil collector. Which, I might add, should have been done an hour since, but Miss Hoity-Toity thinks she's above such work.'

'I'll do it.' Sally could see that Cook was working herself up into a fine old temper and Josie would suffer for it. 'I'm used to mucking out stables, so I don't mind at all.'

'Stables?' Cook stared at her, frowning. 'Don't mention it to Mr Harvey or he'll have you working in the mews where he keeps his old nag.'

Sally nodded, although she had no idea who Mr Harvey was. 'Have I got the job, Mrs er . . .'

'Mrs Flitch is the name, but you can call me Cook. I'll give you a trial and we'll see how you get on. You'll find the chamber pots on the first landing and you empty them in the back yard privy.'

'Yes, Cook.' Sally took off her shawl and was about to hang it on the hallstand when a meaningful scowl on Mrs Flitch's face warned her that this was unacceptable behaviour.

'Leave it in the kitchen. Josie will show you where to find a pinafore and cap.'

'Yes, Cook.' Sally followed Mrs Flitch into the large, steamy kitchen where Josie was adding coal to the fire in the range.

'Stop that, Josie. Take Suggs to the linen cupboard and fit her out with her uniform. Show her where things are and then you can fetch more coal from the cellar.

'Yes, Cook.' Josie sounded demure, but Sally recognised the mischievous glint in her friend's eyes and she could see now why Josie had been sacked from almost every job she had ever had.

Josie led her down a long, narrow passage to the linen cupboard and, after a lot of giggling and trying on aprons and caps that were either too large or too small, Sally was kitted out with the appropriate uniform of a domestic.

'There you are, you look ridiculously pretty, even in that hideous outfit,' Josie said enviously. 'Life isn't fair. I look a sight in my cap and pinny. You'd best watch out for Mr Harvey, that's all I can say. Very free with his hands, he is.'

'Who is Mr Harvey? Mrs Flitch mentioned him.'

'He's the Grindles' son and heir. Mr Harvey must be forty if he's a day, but he's never left home and his mother dotes on him, so does old man Grindle, who's also best avoided. The only reason I haven't yet had the sack is because both of them fancy me, and I occasionally allow them to take a few liberties.'

'You don't!'

'A bit of a cuddle or a pinched bum is better than

begging for food on the street, as you'll find out if you have to earn your living as a skivvy.'

'I'm not sure I like the sound of that.'

'Well, give it a try. A shilling a day is all you'll get, but it's better than nothing. Go upstairs and follow your nose – you'll find the disgusting pots waiting to be taken to the privy, and don't forget to scrub them out. Mrs Grindle is very fussy about the state of her china.'

'All right. Thank you, Josie. I'd better get this over and done with, or I'll get the sack before I've done a day's work.'

'Good luck, and remember what I said.' Josie was about to leave but she hesitated. 'And if you should bump into Mr Harvey, don't mention horses or he'll have you round at the mews cleaning out the stable. He's thinks he's got the next winner of the Derby.'

'I won't speak unless I'm spoken to. Don't worry about me, Josie.'

Sally worked hard. She was given the dirtiest jobs in the house, which, after sorting out the chamber pots, included scrubbing the floors of the scullery, kitchen and the flagstone passages below stairs. Above stairs, the wooden floors had to be swept and polished and Sally spent most of the day on her hands and knees. Mrs Flitch appeared to be both cook and housekeeper to the Grindles and she was not easy to please. Her standards were set very high and she inspected every task that Sally undertook, running her finger over the surface of furniture that she had told Sally to dust, and even going as far as holding the chamber pots up to the light to make sure they were absolutely spotless. At the end of the day Sally was exhausted and wondering why she had complained about the rag-and-bone trade being hard work. Her heart went out to all the skivvies who slaved away for so little money in order to keep the homes of the wealthy clean. The only bonus was that Cook was generous when it came to feeding the staff. They ate in the back room at a long trestle table laid with a white cloth, and the food might be plain but there was plenty of it. Sally secreted a couple of bread rolls in her pocket to take home to her father, but Cook spotted her and she ordered Sally to put them back on the plate. As a punishment she was forced to sit and watch while the rest of the servants ate treacle pudding.

'I'll let you off this time,' Cook said sharply. 'But if I catch you stealing anything in future you'll be out on your pretty little ear.'

'Yes, Cook. I'm sorry.' Sally tried to ignore the sniggers from the parlour maid and the young girl who slaved away in the scullery. Josie rolled her eyes and turned away.

At the end of the day, Cook dropped some coins into Sally's hand. 'Here's your wages.'

Sally accepted the money but it was twopence short of a shilling. 'I was promised a shilling a day, Cook.'

'Yes, but you didn't do a full day.' Mrs Flitch turned away, glancing at Sally over her shoulder. 'Although you did quite well. Come at half past six tomorrow morning and you'll earn a shilling, providing I'm still satisfied.'

Josie was hovering in the distance, pulling faces behind Cook's back. Sally tried to ignore her. 'Thank you, Mrs Flitch.' She left the house and had reached the top of the area steps when a hansom cab drew up outside and a short, stocky man wearing a frock coat and top hat alighted and paid the cabby. He looked her up and down, his pale grey eyes the colour of a winter sky.

'Who are you?' His voice was oddly high-pitched.

'I'm Sally Suggs. I work here, sir.'

'I haven't seen you before. Are you sure you're not a tinker?'

'Certainly not. I've just started here.'

'You won't last,' he said gloomily. 'They never do.'

Sally could only guess that this strange man must be Harvey Grindle, and she hung back respectfully while he mounted the steps and hammered on the front door. Her assumption was proved correct when it was opened by Josie.

'Your ma has been asking for you, Mr Harvey. She's in a bit of a state so I wouldn't keep her waiting if I was you.'

'When I want your advice I'll ask for it, you saucy minx.' He pinched Josie's cheek and guffawed with laughter.

Sally took the opportunity to slip away unnoticed. It was becoming obvious that Josie was up to her old tricks again, and although Sally had not met Mrs Grindle, she doubted if Josie's employer would take kindly to her maidservant encouraging a dalliance with her son. But that was Josie's business, and the sixpenny bit and four pennies rattled comfortingly in her pocket as she set off for Paradise Row. On the way home she purchased hot baked potatoes from a street vendor and two ham rolls. They would eat well tonight, and tomorrow she would earn a whole shilling. She did not relish the thought of returning to Percy Street, but Flower was safe for the time being and Pa would go to bed with a full stomach this evening. When he was settled after supper with a cup of tea and his favourite pipe, she would exercise Flower in Regent's Park. Late in the evening was not a fashionable hour in Rotten Row, and more than likely she would have the lane to herself. It was something she had been looking forward to all day. But when she reached home she was surprised to find another horse in the stable. She could hear the sound of male voices come from the parlour upstairs.

Clutching the parcel of food wrapped in newspaper, Sally entered the room with a feeling of trepidation. She had recognised his horse even before she heard the sound of Gideon's voice. She was wary about seeing him again after their last encounter, but Pippy had given away her presence by barking and jumping joyously up and down.

Gideon rose to his feet as she entered the room. 'I came to apologise, Sally.'

'I was the one who left in such a hurry. I'm the one who should say I'm sorry.'

'You've both admitted you were wrong, so let's forget it, shall we?' Ted raised a glass of ale to his lips. 'Gideon was kind enough to bring some beer and we've been having a good chat.'

'I'm still not selling Flower,' Sally said firmly.

'I wasn't going to ask it of you.' Gideon resumed his seat. 'What happened at Fleet Hall was my fault. I should have stayed to make sure that you weren't overwhelmed by everything. Cecily can be very determined when she sets her mind on something, and her father is even more stubborn. He thinks that money can buy anything, but he's mistaken.'

'What I don't understand is why they want Sally's horse in the first place.' Ted sipped his drink, frowning. 'There must be plenty of choice if money is no object.' He sniffed the air. 'Can I smell baked potato? I'm starving, Sal. I haven't eaten all day.'

Sally shot an anxious glance in Gideon's direction. 'I'm afraid there isn't enough for three, although I could split my ham roll in half. I had a good meal at midday.'

'Thank you, but I wouldn't hear of it,' Gideon said, smiling. 'My landlady provides an evening meal. She's not the best cook in the world, but she'd be very offended if I ate out.'

'So where've you been, Sal?' Ted demanded. 'You

said goodbye and disappeared. I was beginning to worry.'

'I have a job in Percy Street. I'm working for Mrs Grindle.'

'No relation to Harvey Grindle, I hope,' Gideon said grimly.

'Why?' Sally rounded on him. 'What do you know about Harvey Grindle?'

'The man is a menace. He's set up a stable where he's attempting to train race horses, and he doesn't know what he's doing. We've had several of his nags in for treatment of entirely avoidable injuries.'

'I'm only there to scrub floors,' Sally said hastily.

'You're worth better than that.' Ted accepted the plate of food that she handed him. 'I don't want you doing that sort of thing, Sal.'

Gideon glanced at Sally's reddened hands. 'Are matters that serious?'

'We'll manage,' Sally said firmly. 'Working for the Grindles is only temporary. I'm sure I'll find something better soon.'

'Of course you will, Sal. You're a clever girl.' Ted spooned hot potato dripping with butter into his mouth. 'Ta for the beer, Gideon. You can call again any time. I've enjoyed our chat.'

'I'll come again, if it's all right with you, Ted. Your stories about the old days are fascinating.' Gideon leaned over to pat Ted on the shoulder. 'I'd better go now or my dinner will be spoiled. My landlady only knows how to cook one thing.'

This made Sally laugh. 'That's one more than I can cook. I've never had the chance to use a range and I wouldn't know where to begin.'

'You have other talents. You showed everyone how you handle a spirited horse like Flower. Not many people can do that with such skill.' Gideon hesitated in the doorway. 'Perhaps you'd like to come to Hill Farm sometime soon, Sally? Boney is doing really well, but I'm sure he misses you. If I bring the trap we could take your father to see him.'

'That would be wonderful,' Sally said, smiling. 'Pa would love that. But wouldn't Miss Appleton mind?'

'We aren't engaged, if that's what you're hinting at, Sally.'

'I thought it was to be announced at the ball. Mrs Wallace seemed to think so.'

'Jane Wallace is a romantic, and she wants to see me married with half a dozen children. However, that will happen when and with whom I choose.'

'There, Sal. You've been told.' Ted wagged at finger at her. 'Never assume anything, my duck.'

Gideon smiled and nodded. 'Anyway, forget all that, Sally. Mrs Wallace would like to see you again. You made a hit with her, and she was very disappointed that you didn't stay the night.'

'I know, and I still feel guilty about that. Of course I'd love to see her so that I could explain. I'm sure she'll understand.'

'How about Sunday? I'll bring the trap. We'll make a day of it and hope that it's fine.'

'I'll look forward to it,' Sally said with feeling. 'And if Mrs Grindle won't give me the whole day off, I'll tell her I'm taking it anyway.'

Next morning Sally was up before five and she rode Flower to Regent's Park, eagerly anticipating an early morning gallop along Rotten Row. At this hour it was usually deserted, but quite suddenly, coming out from seemingly nowhere, a pair of horses ridden at breakneck speed passed so close that Flower reared in fright, almost unseating Sally. She managed to regain control.

'What do you think you're doing?' Sally demanded when she caught up with the two boy riders, both of whom looked very sheepish. 'This isn't a racecourse.'

'We come here every morning at this time.' The elder of the two boys wheeled his mount round as if to ride away.

'Who owns these horses?' Sally demanded. 'Look at the state of them. They're not fit enough to be treated this way.'

'Tell that to the boss.' The boy nodded in the direction of a phaeton bowling along the carriage drive. It was an old vehicle, painted a garish yellow with red spokes to the wheels. The man holding the reins jerked the horse to a halt.

Sally turned in the saddle to take a look at the owner of the unfortunate animals, and she recognised Harvey Grindle.

'Are these your horses?' Sally demanded angrily.

'They are indeed. Not that it's any of your business, young man.' Harvey turned to the two riders. 'Is this person bothering you?'

Sally was torn between the desire to stand up for the poor animals and the need to remain anonymous as far as Mr Grindle was concerned. She might work for his family, but she did not want to bring attention to herself. In the dim light of approaching dawn he had assumed that she was male, and it suited her to leave him in ignorance.

When neither of the boys offered an answer, Harvey shrugged his shoulders. 'I suggest you move on, fellow,' he said, addressing himself to Sally. 'You're in the way of the professionals. You've been warned so leave now before I take a horsewhip to you.'

'You ought to be reported for cruelty to animals,' Sally said as a parting shot. She wheeled Flower's head round and galloped off in the direction of home. Gideon had been right – Harvey Grindle knew nothing about horses and something should be done to put a stop to his antics.

The clock in the church tower struck six as Sally was dismounting outside the stables and she realised that she had only half an hour to get ready for work, but first she had to make sure that Flower was unsaddled, fed and watered. Sally's own needs always came second to those of her horse and her father. She filled the kettle and placed it on the trivet in front of the fire, which she had already banked up with enough coal to keep it going for several hours. She put the teapot, tea caddy and milk jug on the table close to Pa's chair, together with slices of bread, and a small pat of butter. It was a frugal breakfast but Sally had not eaten and she left for work trying to ignore the pangs of hunger that cramped her stomach. She could only hope that Cook was as generous with breakfast as she had been with the midday meal yesterday.

'You're five minutes late.' Mrs Flitch greeted Sally with arms akimbo, and her mobcap tilted over one eye. 'You can miss breakfast when the others eat. Maybe that will teach you to be on time.'

'Yes, Mrs Flitch.' Sally knew that it would be useless to make excuses. 'Where shall I start this morning?'

'Lord above! Do I have to tell you everything, you stupid girl? Do what you did yesterday. When you've finished you can come to me for further instructions. Now get about your work.' Cook went to the door and opened it. 'Josie Bates. Where are you?' She waited for a few seconds, shaking her head and tut-tutting. 'Damned slut. I haven't seen her this morning. If she doesn't turn up in the next ten minutes, you'll have to do her work, Suggs.'

Sally stared at her in dismay. 'She's probably been held up, Mrs Flitch.'

'Held up! Bah! She'll be in someone's bed, too lazy to get up for work, if I know that girl. She's been warned enough times.'

'I'm sure she'll be here directly.'

'Never mind your fancy words. She's late and that's that.' Mrs Flitch pointed to a skinny little kitchen maid. 'Show Suggs where to get the coal and kindling. You'll have to light the fires in the family bedrooms, as well as the breakfast parlour, Suggs.'

'Yes, Mrs Flitch.' Sally followed the girl down the cellar steps to the coal hole where it was dark, damp and dirty.

Snivelling pathetically, Biddy started shovelling coal into a large pail. 'I can't carry it when it's full,' she whined. 'But she'll box me ears if I spill any on the floor.'

'You've done your bit. I'll do the rest. Just show me where the kindling is kept and you can go back to the kitchen.' Sally took the shovel from the child's limp hand.

'Kindling's in the back yard under a heavy cover. I can't lift that either. You'll find old newspapers and matches in the boot room.'

'Never mind, Biddy. Go back to whatever you were doing, and if Mrs Flitch asks you, tell her that you showed me all I needed to see. I can manage on my own.'

Biddy wiped a filthy hand across her eyes, smearing her cheeks with coal dust. 'Ta ever so, miss.'

'It's Sally. You'd best wash your hands and face under the pump in the yard before you return to the kitchen.'

'Yes, miss. I mean, Sally.' Biddy scuttled up the stairs, taking two at a time.

Sally finished loading the pail with lumps of shiny black coal. Armed with kindling, newspaper and matches, Sally hefted the heavy bucket upstairs. She had a vague idea which rooms needed to have fires lit, and she decided to start with the master's bedchamber. From outside the door she could hear loud snores and she judged it safe to enter. A beam from the streetlight outside filtered through a gap between the heavy damask curtains, enabling Sally to make her way to the fireplace without mishap. She set about her task quickly and efficiently. After years of lighting fires in the temperamental grate at home, she was expert in coaxing the stubbornest of kindling to burst into flames. Mr Grindle senior was beginning to stir and that spurred Sally on to finish quickly. She left the room as quietly as she had entered and made her way to Mrs Grindle's bedchamber, where she managed to light the fire without waking the sleeping woman.

'Where are you when I need you, Josie?' Sally murmured as she hesitated outside Harvey Grindle's room. She could only hope that he had not returned from his jaunt in Regent's Park as she knocked gently on the door. Encouraged by the silence that ensued, Sally let herself into the room, and for the second time that morning she came face to face with Harvey himself, only this time he was in a state of undress.

Chapter Eight

'Who the hell are you?' Harvey demanded angrily. 'Where's Josie?'

Sally stared at him dumbstruck. What could she say to a man who was stripped to his unmentionables and clearly not amused?

'Heavens above, Suggs. I told you the wrong room.' Josie appeared as if from nowhere. She pushed past Sally. 'You'll have to forgive her, Harvey, love. She's new.' Josie shooed Sally out of the room. 'Leave him to me,' she said in a whisper. 'I can handle Harvey.' She winked and closed the door.

Sally retreated hastily. Josie was playing a dangerous game, one that would most probably end badly, but that was how Josie lived her life. She had been sacked from every job she had taken on, and always for the same reason. Josie simply could not say no. A man only had to smile at her in the right way and Josie was ready to risk everything. Sally hurried downstairs to light the fire in the breakfast parlour. It was quite obvious that Josie was not going to be much help, so Sally finished off the chores that her friend should have done, before taking on the onerous task of emptying and washing out the chamber pots. Her patience was tested to its limits, however, when Josie sauntered downstairs to join the other servants and she was allowed to eat with them, while Sally was excluded. Hungry and frustrated, Sally went about her work on an empty stomach.

She was in the drawing room, having lit the fire and refilled the coal scuttle, when Josie popped her head round the door. She slipped into the room, placing her work box on the floor. She reached into her pocket and produced a bread roll with the air of a conjuror pulling a rabbit out of a hat.

'I thought you'd be hungry since the old bat refused to let you eat with us. This is all I could smuggle out.' She handed it to Sally. 'It's not much but it's better than nothing.'

Sally took a large bite. 'This is so good. You put some bacon in it. Thank you, Josie.'

'You'd do the same for me.' Josie shrugged and retrieved her box of polish and dusters. 'Anyway, I'd better get on.'

'Wait a minute.' Sally reached out to grasp Josie's hand. 'What did Mr Harvey say about me?

'Just the usual questions about a new servant,

particularly a pretty one. If I had your looks I'd be mistress of a big house by now.'

'You're playing a dangerous game, Josie. You know what will happen if his mother finds out.'

Josie shrugged. 'Harvey's pa will stand up for me. He might be old, but he's not averse to a bit of slap and tickle – the dirty dog.'

'You're the end, Josie Bates. What will I do with you?'

'Not a thing, my duck. I get along in my own way,' Josie's smile faded. 'But take my advice and keep away from Mr Harvey. He's not as stupid as he looks, and he told me about you and the horses on Rotten Row.'

'He knew it was me?'

'No. Lucky for you he didn't recognise you. In fact he thought you were a boy, but I know you have a habit of riding out early. Don't cross him when it comes to his old nags. He's obsessed with the idea of winning the Derby. In fact, he's promised to take me with him this year, if I'm still here, that is.'

'He's not fit to own horses, let alone to train them,' Sally said hotly. 'He should be reported for animal cruelty. The pair I saw looked underfed.'

'Please don't say anything. He's happy when he thinks he's the owner of a future winner. Leave him be, Sally, there's a good girl.'

'I can't promise something like that. If I find out he's ill-treating those animals, I'll have to report him to the RSPCA.'

'They are just animals, Sal. If you want to put food on the table and pay the rent, you'd better keep your mouth shut. I'm saying that as a friend, you understand.'

'Yes, I know that,' Sally said, smiling. 'I'll do my best to keep out of his way, so don't worry.'

'That's enough chit-chat for now. I'd better get on with the dusting, or I'll be the one who's in trouble.' Josie snatched up a duster and whisked around the room, flicking the furniture so that the dust flew up, only to settle again when she moved on. Sally chuckled as she left the room, heading for the scullery. Josie must be the worst chambermaid ever, but she relied on her innate charm and wit to keep her going. Sally went on to her next task, which was to sweep the front steps and polish the brass door knocker.

It was one of those rare winter days when the sun shone from an azure sky, and, despite a bitter east wind, it was good to be outside, even for a short while. Sally realised that she actually missed going out on the rounds with her father. At least there had been freedom of a sort, and each day had been different. Even after a short time in the Grindles' employment, she realised that her job was going to be boring and repetitive, as well as gruelling. She swept the steps, and having done that she propped the broom against the railings while she polished the brass lion's head door knocker.

There was a steady flow of horse-drawn traffic

and hand-carts at that time in the morning. Butchers, bakers and grocers arrived at the more affluent houses delivering their goods to basement kitchens, while hansom cabs dropped off well-dressed visitors whose right it was to use the front door. Sally paid no attention when a vehicle drew up alongside the kerb, but she did turn her head at the sound of Kelly's voice calling her name.

She held her finger to her lips. 'Don't make such a noise. I'm not allowed to have gentlemen callers.'

'Then it's as well that I'm no gentleman.' Kelly's disarming smile faded. 'This is strictly business, mavourneen. As you can see I'm working.'

'So am I, Kelly. Now drive on.'

'I'll ring my bell and shout, if you don't come down and talk to me.'

'Don't you dare.' Sally hurried down the steps. 'What do you want?'

'I don't like to see you skivvying for anyone, let alone the Grindles.'

'Keep your voice down.' Sally glanced anxiously over her shoulder to see if anyone had heard him. 'I can't afford to lose this job.'

Kelly leaned towards her. 'That's why I'm here. I'm offering you work.'

'What sort of work?'

'Don't look so suspicious, mavourneen. You know that I need someone to take your pa's old cart on his old round. You've done it before and you know the routes better than anyone.'

'Are you serious? If it's a joke, it's not funny.'

'I was never more serious. I don't like to see your pa fretting about you working all hours for a pittance. With my help you could earn enough to keep you both fed and a roof over your heads.'

'There's only one flaw in your proposition, Kelly. I can do most things, but there are some things I can't do on my own because I lack the strength.'

'I've thought of that, and I know you've been looking after the Cotton nippers. Jim is a strong boy, for his age. You can take him with you.'

'He's only nine, Kelly.'

'Nearly ten, so he told me this morning. I came across the three of them wandering round my scrap yard, looking for anything they could sell in order to buy food. It seems that they slept there last night under a tarpaulin because their dad was even more out of control than usual.'

'That's terrible.'

'I agree, and I gave Jim some money to buy them a meal, but if you employ the child he could take care of his brothers. He's eager to work.'

'Yes, but who would take care of the two younger ones?'

'They could go to the ragged school. Maybe with a basic education they could aspire to something better.'

Sally eyed him curiously. 'I never took you for a fatherly type of person, Kelly.'

'I'm full of surprises, and I know what it was like

during the potato famine. I was young then but I remember the grim sights I saw, and the suffering. My family were lucky enough to have the means to get away from Ireland and start again. Anyway, that's not what we were talking about. Would you like to work with me, Sally?'

'I don't know.' Sally met his intense gaze with a frown. 'I'd have to talk it over with my pa.'

'But you will think about it?'

She smiled. 'Yes, Kelly. I promise that I'll give you an answer quickly. Now, please go before I get the sack.'

'Then you'd have to accept my offer.' Kelly flicked the whip above his horse's head. 'Walk on.'

Sally went back to polishing the door knocker, but as she raised her duster the door opened and she found herself face to face with Harvey Grindle.

'Get out of my way, girl,' he said crossly

'I'm sorry, sir.' Sally stepped aside, bowing her head to avoid meeting his angry gaze.

Harvey was about to walk past her, but he stopped suddenly. 'I know that voice.'

Sally edged towards the door, but he sidestepped her, blocking the entrance to the house. 'Look at me.'

Reluctantly she raised her head and looked him in the eye. 'I have work to do, sir.'

'I knew it. You are the insolent person I met in the park, only then you were dressed as a boy, but you were riding a decent piece of horseflesh, if I remember correctly.'

'I didn't mean to speak out of turn, sir.' Sally put one foot over the threshold.

'Where did you get that animal? Where would a skivvy like you find the means to purchase a horse like that?'

'Is this young person bothering you, Mr Grindle?'

The sound of Mrs Flitch's irate voice coming from the bottom of the area steps made both Sally and Harvey turn their heads.

'Where did you find this girl, Mrs Flitch?' Harvey leaned over the gate.

'I've just discovered that she's a friend of Josie's, and I've a good mind to sack the pair of them, sir.'

Harvey shot a sideways glance at Sally. 'So, you're her friend, are you?'

'I am, sir.'

'There's no need to be hasty, Mrs Flitch,' Harvey said cheerily. 'This girl has done a good job so far.'

'If you say so, sir.' Mrs Flitch retreated into the kitchen, slamming the door behind her.

'You'd better keep on her right side, girl. My mother will take Mrs Flitch's word against yours whatever the circumstances.'

'Thank you, sir.'

'What's your name?'

'Sally Suggs.'

'Well, Sally, you and I will be good friends, providing you don't anger me, and I'd like to take a closer look at your horse. If, in fact, it is your property.'

Sally thought quickly. She could imagine a variety

of complications if she admitted that Flower belonged to her. 'I'm just looking after the mare, sir. She belongs to someone else.'

'And who might that be?'

'A veterinary gentleman, sir.'

'I'd like to meet this person. I have a mind to purchase another horse.'

'I don't think he has a mind to sell, sir.'

'It's not up to you to speak for him, Sally Suggs. Arrange a meeting with this gentleman at his convenience. Tell him money is no object.'

'Yes, sir. May I get on with my work now?'

Harvey dismissed her with a wave of his gloved hand, and Sally retreated into the house. She took the back stairs and was putting the cleaning materials away in the broom cupboard when Josie rushed up to her.

'What did he say to you? I heard Ma Flitch shouting and I looked out of the upstairs window. What was Harvey saying to you?'

'Don't worry, Josie. Harvey isn't interested in me – he wants to buy Flower.'

'Is that all? The way he was leaning over you I thought he was up to something.'

'I'd rather work as a crossing sweeper than have that man pawing me. I don't know how you stand it, Josie.'

'Needs must, love. I might as well be an orphan for all the good my parents did me. I never knew who my pa was, and Ma is never sober, so I take every chance I get to have a bit of fun, especially if there's money in it.'

Sally gave her a quick hug. 'I'm sorry, I spoke out of turn.'

'I'm all right, Sal. I've learned to get by and I don't take no notice of what people say, except you, of course.' Josie slapped her on the back. 'Let's forget it, shall we?'

Sally nodded, too choked with emotion to speak. Josie rarely said anything about her past, and now Sally understood why her friend was so reticent when it came to speaking about her family. She took a deep breath. 'What do I do now, Josie? Should I ask Mrs Flitch?'

'That's the best idea. If I tell you it's bound to be wrong. Keep on the right side of old Fanny Flitch and you won't go far wrong.'

Sally spent the rest of the day making an effort to please the irascible Mrs Flitch, but she narrowly avoided a complete disaster while polishing the floorboards in the entrance hall. Mrs Grindle, Sally discovered to her cost, was a large woman who still favoured the wide crinoline cage, even though it was no longer the height of fashion. That piece of information was passed on by Josie, who studied ladies' journals even though she could never afford to dress in such style. It was late afternoon when Mrs Grindle appeared, moving like a ship in full sail, head held high, advancing on Sally without looking where she was going. She trod on a cake of beeswax and skidded uncontrollably, arms flailing in an attempt to steady herself. She crashed to the floor and lay on her back like an upturned beetle, legs kicking frantically as she attempted to right herself. Her screams brought Josie running to her aid, and Mr Grindle emerged from his study, blinking like a sleepy owl. Sally tossed aside her polishing rags and jumped to her feet. Together with Josie she managed to heave Mrs Grindle to a standing position.

Red-faced and sweating profusely, Mrs Grindle pointed a shaking finger at Sally. 'You stupid girl. What are you doing, polishing the floor at this time of the day? Haven't you a grain of sense? I might have broken my neck.'

Mr Grindle, who was almost as obese as his wife, waddled up to them, his face contorted in a scowl. 'What's going on? Can't a fellow have peace and quiet in his own house?'

'Percival, I want you to speak severely to Mrs Flitch. I don't know this girl, but she is obviously not the quality of servant we require.'

Sally bobbed a curtsey. 'If you please, sir, it was an accident.'

Percival Grindle glared at her, puffing out his flushed cheeks. 'Who gave you permission to speak?'

Sally hung her head. 'I'm sorry, sir, but it wasn't my fault. If Mrs Grindle had been looking where she was going it wouldn't have happened.'

A sharp intake of breath from Josie made Sally realise she had gone too far, and she raised her head to meet her employer's angry gaze. But to her astonishment, Mr Grindle's stern features melted into a smile and he threw back his head and laughed.

'Percival! Are you going to allow a menial to speak to your wife in that manner?' Mrs Grindle's large bosom rose and fell with alarming rapidity.

Sally was afraid that the tiny buttons down the front of Mrs Grindle's gown were going to fly off in all directions as the material stretched to its limits.

'Oh, come now, Adelaide, no harm done.' Mr Grindle walked up to Sally, gazing at her critically. 'You're a pretty little thing. If you were dressed well and cleaned up, you could even pass for a lady.'

'That's enough, Percival,' Mrs Grindle said angrily. 'Leave the little trollop alone.' She turned on Josie. 'And you can get on with your work, too. I've got your measure, miss. Don't think you can fool Adelaide Grindle. Your days here are numbered as well as hers.' She turned her back on them and stalked off in the direction of the dining room. 'I'm going to count the silver,' she called over her shoulder.

Mr Grindle rolled his eyes and retreated to his study, leaving Sally and Josie to clear up the mess of crushed beeswax.

'What did she mean by counting the silver?' Sally asked in a whisper.

'One of the servants stole some cutlery – the old girl's never forgotten it. She thinks we're all out to pinch things from the house, but I know it's silver plate.'

'How do you know that, Josie?'

Josie grinned. 'Because I tried to sell a couple of spoons to Rags Roper, and he told me it was only silver plate.'

'Did she find out what you'd done?'

'No, I put them back so they were never missed. I learned my lesson – always check the hallmark before you pinch anything.'

Sally threw back her head and laughed. 'You really are a terrible person, Josie.'

That evening, after a supper of pea soup from Sid's stall, hard-boiled eggs and watercress, Sally was settling Flower down for the night when there was a knock on the stable door. She opened it, expecting to see Kelly, but to her dismay it was Harvey Grindle. He tipped his top hat, his fleshy lips twisted in an ingratiating smile. Pippy had been curled up on a pile of straw, but she leaped to her feet and snarled at Harvey.

'Good evening, Miss Suggs.'

'How did you know where I live?' Sally asked angrily.

'A little bird told me,' Harvey said, chuckling. 'It's surprising what you can get for half a crown.'

Sally eyed him suspiciously. It was obvious that he had bribed Josie to give him her address, but she decided to ignore the insinuation. 'Is there anything wrong, sir?'

'Not at all. I've come to take a look at that little

mare of yours. Fine piece of horseflesh, if I remember correctly. Frisky little thing, just like you.' He pinched Sally's cheek.

She recoiled at his touch. 'It's not convenient at the moment.'

Harvey pushed past her. His heavy overcoat, complete with a fur collar, served to emphasise his bulk, and Sally could not have stopped him had she tried. As it was she stood aside, watching helplessly while he strode over to Flower's stall.

'Don't touch her,' Sally warned. 'She's nervous around strangers.'

'I'd soon knock that out of her,' Harvey said grimly. 'I know how to handle skittish females, whether they're horses or women. How much do you want for her?' He kicked out at Pippy, who was nipping at his ankles.

'As I told you this morning, she doesn't belong to me.' Sally snatched the dog up in her arms. 'Quiet, Pippy.'

'Yes, I seem to remember you mentioned a veterinary gentleman, but I can recognise a lie when I hear one. I'm not a fool, Suggs. A man of means wouldn't keep a thoroughbred animal like this in conditions like these.'

'Flower is not for sale, sir. Now I'm asking you politely to leave.'

'If you want to keep your position in my household, you'd better adopt a more reasonable attitude.'

'Are you threatening me, sir?' Sally held Pippy

tighter as the small dog bared her teeth at Harvey, growling deep in her throat.

'I'm simply telling you that I want to purchase this animal. It's up to you how you choose to comply with my wishes. If she does belong to someone else, I expect you to mediate, but I'm a generous fellow and money is no object if it's something I truly desire.' Harvey moved closer to Sally and his breath was laced with garlic, wine and cigar smoke, but at that moment, the door opened and Kelly walked in. He came to a halt, staring at Harvey.

'Is this fellow bothering you, Sally?'

'Mr Grindle is just going,' she said, putting Pippy down on the floor.

'Do I know you, sir?' Harvey fisted his hands at his sides. 'You're interrupting a private conversation.'

'I've said all I'm going to say, Mr Grindle.' Sally moved instinctively to stand beside Kelly. 'Flower is not for sale.'

'There you have it, Grindle,' Kelly said casually. 'Now will you leave quietly, or do I have to eject you forcibly?'

Harvey posed in a boxing stance with his fists raised, and began to dance about on his toes. Sally had a sudden vision of a walrus attempting a waltz, and, despite the seriousness of the situation, she had to stifle a giggle.

'You, cully, are ridiculous.' Kelly caught Harvey off balance and twisted him round so that he was facing the door. Grabbing him by the collar, Kelly marched Harvey out into the street. Sally heard the sounds of a scuffle then a thud and a torrent of abuse from Harvey. Kelly entered the stable wiping his hands together. 'I don't think he'll be bothering you again, mavourneen.'

Pippy bounced up and down, barking in delight as if approving of Kelly's handling of the situation, and Sally picked her up in case she tried to rush outside.

'Thank you, Kelly, but you've just lost me my job at the Grindles' establishment. Now I'm out of work.'

'What did he want, anyway? If he came here to proposition you I'll give him a good thrashing.'

'Stop it, Kelly. There's no need for violence. Harvey wanted to buy Flower, and of course I said no. I saw the way his horses are treated and I wouldn't put a rat in his care.'

'He looked as if he was getting very familiar when I walked in.'

'That's the way he treats servant girls. Josie is his current favourite but he has a roving eye, and I would probably have been his next target. It just happens that he wanted Flower more than he wanted me – thank goodness.'

'Sally, love. What's going on down there?' Ted poked his head over the banister rail, peering down at them. 'Is that you, Kelly?'

'Sally had an unwelcome visitor, Ted.' Kelly slipped his arm around Sally's shoulders. 'But she's fine. I sent the chap packing.'

Sally slipped free from his grasp. 'Yes, and now I'll have to look for another job.'

'Then you're free to take up my offer, mavourneen. Together we'll build a rag-and-bone empire such as the world has never seen.'

'What are you saying, Kelly?' Ted asked peevishly. 'I can't hear you. Come upstairs and tell me what's going on.'

Sally put Pippy down and laid her hand on Kelly's arm as he was about to mount the stairs. 'Don't tell him you've offered me work. I want to think it over.'

Kelly gave her an appraising look. 'It's a good offer. Don't turn it down out of hand.'

'I won't,' Sally said earnestly. 'I have to do what is best for me and for my pa.'

'Of course you do.' Kelly patted her hand and continued up the narrow wooden staircase with Pippy close on his heels.

Sally heard her father greet Kelly with obvious pleasure and she sighed. Life was filled with difficult choices and she had a very important decision to make. Kelly's offer was a generous one in the circumstances, but she had enough experience of the rag-and-bone trade to know that it was a hard life, requiring physical strength and stamina. She could not rely on a young boy to help her manage some of the heavy objects that they would inevitably collect, and Jim was undernourished and puny for his age.

Flower whickered softly in her stall, an invitation to fondle her that Sally could not resist. She stroked

Flower's head, leaning against her. 'I have to do what's best for all of us. You do understand that, don't you, girl?' Sally shivered as an icy draught whistled through the cracked windowpanes, and she gazed round, seeing the dilapidated building as if for the first time. Maybe Harvey had been right when he said that the stable was in too poor a state of repair to house a horse like Flower.

Sally busied herself in the stable until Kelly had left and then, having locked up and made everything secure for the night, she helped her father to his bed, settling him down with a cup of cocoa.

'Kelly is a good man.' Ted leaned against the bare brick wall, sipping his hot drink. 'He'd look after you when I've gone, Sal.'

She tucked him in. 'Don't talk like that, Pa. You'll be better when spring comes. You're always more mobile in the warm weather.'

'You're not taking me seriously, my duck. Kelly is fond of you, I've no doubts about that.'

'Get some sleep, Pa. We'll talk about it tomorrow. I'm too tired to think straight at the moment.'

'Of course, love. I should be more thoughtful.'

Sally leaned over to kiss him on the brow. 'Goodnight, Pa. I'll have gone to work before you get up, but I'll leave your breakfast out for you.'

'You're a good girl, Sal. I couldn't have a better daughter.'

Sally bit back tears as she left his room and made her way to the place beneath the eaves where she slept. Tomorrow she must make the big decision that would change the course of their lives, but what was it to be? She undressed and slipped her night-gown over her head. The old, flock-filled mattress was worn to the shape of her body and she could feel the wooden boards of the truckle bed digging into her spine as she lay down. Perhaps the time had come to say goodbye to Paradise Row, but where would they go from here?

Chapter Nine

Sally awakened next morning with her mind made up. She went about her normal routine of collecting water, lighting the parlour fire and setting out her father's breakfast of bread and a sliver of cheese. She filled the kettle and set it on the trivet in front of the fire, and when she was satisfied that everything was in order, she went downstairs to the stable to tack up Flower. It was much later than normal and the sky in the east had a pearly pink glow as she set off for the Veterinary College. It had come to her in the early hours of the morning that the most sensible course would be to put the case to Gideon. He, like herself, had Flower's best interests at heart and she valued his opinion. Whatever happened, she knew that in fairness to all concerned she must part with her beloved horse.

Sally rode slowly, putting off the evil moment

as long as possible, but eventually she arrived at the college, dismounted and went in search of the doorkeeper.

Gideon had not yet arrived when Sally made enquiries, and she waited in the courtyard, walking Flower up and down in an attempt to keep them both warm. She had to wait at least half an hour and, despite the earlier promise of a fine day, sleety rain had begun to fall from the lowering clouds. Then, just as she was thinking that Gideon had taken the day off, he came rushing into the courtyard, losing his hat in a gust of wind. He retrieved it and was wiping it dry when he spotted Sally and Flower. He crossed the yard in long strides.

'Sally, this is a pleasant surprise.'

'I couldn't wait until Sunday, Gideon. I wanted to ask you for a big favour.'

Gideon stroked Flower's neck. 'Let's get this lady into the stable, one of the boys will look after her. I've got half an hour before my first lecture, so we can have a quiet chat in my office.'

Sally nodded wordlessly. She followed him to the stables where he placed Flower in the hands of the senior groom. 'Treat her like one of your own, Armstrong. She's a valuable animal.'

Armstrong nodded and led Flower away.

'Thank you,' Sally said with feeling. 'You're very kind considering the way I've behaved in the past.'

'That's all behind us and you mustn't blame yourself. Come with me, Sally. My office should be considerably warmer than out here.' Gideon strode off and Sally followed him into the building. He led her up a flight of stone stairs to an office on the first floor. The walls were lined with bookshelves and a large desk was partially buried beneath piles of documents, leaflets and textbooks. A fire burned in the grate and someone had thoughtfully placed a kettle on the hob.

'I have the staff well-trained,' Gideon said, chuckling. 'I don't always have time for breakfast at my digs, so if you'll take a seat, I'll make us both a cup of tea.'

Sally perched on the edge of an upright wooden chair. 'Thank you.'

'What brought you here today, Sally? What couldn't wait until Sunday?'

She clasped her hands, knotting her fingers together. 'Pa is quite infirm now. I doubt if he could work even if Boney was still young and healthy.'

Gideon took a caddy from a cupboard and, having warmed the pot, he added three teaspoons of tea before filling it with boiling water. 'The rag-and-bone trade must be very hard even for a much younger man.'

'Yes, it is, and now it falls to me to be the breadwinner.' Sally eyed him warily. 'Finn Kelly has offered me the chance to work with him. He bought Pa's cart and he wants me to do the old round.'

'I thought you were working for the Grindles, although I'm sure you could do better. Harvey Grindle is a menace.'

'I'll almost certainly have lost my job, but you're right about Harvey Grindle. He's a horrible person, but unfortunately he saw me riding Flower in Rotten Row. He was impressed by her, even after such a brief acquaintance, and now he wants to buy her from me.'

'And you very sensibly refused.'

'Of course I did, but he persisted, so I told him that Flower isn't mine. I said she belongs to a veterinary gentleman. I didn't mention your name.'

'Would that it were true,' Gideon said, smiling. 'I would be proud to own such a beauty.' His smile faded. 'But I suppose he didn't take no for an answer or you wouldn't be here today?'

'I don't think he believed me. He came to my home last evening and he threatened to have me sacked if I didn't let him have Flower. If Kelly hadn't arrived at that moment it might have turned nasty, although I'd have stood my ground. I'm not the sort of woman who faints or has hysterics when things go wrong.'

'I believe you, but it's probably just as well that Kelly turned up.' Gideon sipped his tea, frowning. 'If Grindle comes to see me about Flower, I'll have an excuse to visit his stable. It would give me great pleasure to report him to the authorities.'

'From the little I saw, the animals he owns are underfed and overworked. He should be banned from keeping horses, let alone attempting to train them.'

'What will you do now?'

'I'm sure he's told his horrible mother that I did something very wrong. I have a suspicion that he gets rid of servants who won't do as he wishes by accusing them of stealing the silver.'

'A novel way to cover up his indiscretions. I dislike him even more now.' Gideon's smile faded. 'But what about you, Sally?'

'I'm seriously thinking about taking up Kelly's offer. It's not as if I have much choice now, thanks to Harvey Grindle.'

'So how can I help?'

'Pa and I might be able to manage on what I could earn working with Kelly, but Flower deserves better. Besides which, I think we will have to find somewhere cheaper to live. A small cottage would be best for Pa, and almost certainly it would be easier to keep warm. Perhaps a fresh start would be good for both of us.'

'I think you're right,' Gideon said thoughtfully.

'Which brings me to the point of my visit this morning. I wouldn't be able to afford to pay very much, but would you be prepared to keep Flower at Hill Farm for me? Just until I can save enough to bring her back to London?'

'Are you sure you don't want to sell her to Cessy? Sir Gregory would pay well.'

'That would be so final. This way, if you agree, it would give me time to earn enough to make other arrangements.'

'Perhaps you ought to come to the farm on

Saturday, and take a closer look at the stables before you decide. I'd be happy to have Flower there, but I want you to be sure.'

'Thank you, Gideon.' Sally rose to her feet. 'If I have to part with Flower, at least I know that she'll be safe and well treated at Hill Farm, and I'll be sure of seeing her every once in a while.'

'You know you're always welcome.'

'Thank you, but I'd better go now and face Mrs Grindle. Although I'm quite certain she'll sack me on the spot.'

'Might I suggest that you leave Flower here now? You wouldn't want to take her to the Grindles' establishment, would you?'

'No. That would be a fatal mistake.'

Gideon followed her to the door and was about to open it when he paused. 'If you're free for the rest of the week you might like to help me in some of my classes.'

Sally stared at him in amazement. 'How would I do that?'

'Well, you could put Flower through some of her paces so that my students could see how such actions might cause injury to a horse, if not executed properly. You could talk to them after the demonstration and share the knowledge that your mother passed down to you.'

'It's very tempting,' Sally said cautiously.

'You would be paid, although it wouldn't be as much as you deserve.'

'I'll do it.' Sally proffered her hand. 'I'd do it for nothing if I didn't need to buy food and pay the rent.'

Gideon shook her hand. 'I heard that you'd been helping out the Cotton children, too.'

'How did you know about that?'

'I often stop by Sid's stall for a coffee or a ham roll. That man knows everything that goes on in this part of London, and I'm familiar with Fred Cotton – he used to work here in the stable until he was found asleep in one of the stalls, dead drunk. He had to go because he was a danger to himself and the animals.'

'They're good boys. They deserve better.'

'I fear that Fred will drink himself to death and they'll end up in the workhouse.'

'I hope not, for their sakes,' Sally said with a shudder. 'I'd do more for them if I could. Sometimes they sleep in Boney's old stall if they have nowhere else to go. It's so sad.'

'I'm afraid there are many others like them, living rough on the streets of London, and elsewhere.'

'I'll do my best to keep an eye on the Cotton boys, but I have to go now.'

Gideon opened the door. 'Tomorrow is Thursday, so you could start in the morning, if that's convenient.'

'Thank you, Gideon. I will take you up on your offer.' Sally hurried from the building and set off for Percy Street. It was a relief to know that Flower would be safe at Hill Farm – now all she had to do was to find alternative accommodation for herself and her father.

She arrived at the Grindles' house three hours late for work, breathless and damp from getting caught in a heavy shower. Josie opened the door in answer to Sally's knock.

'You're in trouble,' she said gleefully. 'There's been such goings-on this morning. Mr Harvey discovered that there were two silver serving spoons missing, or so he said, and we all know they're only plate. Anyway, Mrs Grindle is fuming and the master isn't too happy neither because his breakfast got burned while Mrs Flitch and the rest of us were running round searching for the dratted spoons.'

'I bet they're in Harvey's room,' Sally said grimly. 'He came to see me last evening and he threatened to have me dismissed if I wouldn't sell him Flower.'

'He's a bad man.' Josie pulled a face. 'That's why we get on so well.' She glanced over her shoulder. 'You'd best go, Sal. I can hear Ma Flitch coming. I'd know the slap of her flat feet on the flagstones anywhere.'

Sally stepped over the threshold. 'I'm going nowhere until I've proved my innocence. I'm not leaving here until I have a formal apology from Mr Harvey himself.'

'Are you sure about this?' Josie asked nervously.

Mrs Flitch came storming up to them before Sally had a chance to reply. 'You've got a nerve, miss. I don't know how you can show your face here after what you've done.'

Sally brushed past Josie. 'I haven't stolen your mistress's silver plate, Mrs Flitch. But I have a very good idea where you might find it.'

Mrs Flitch grabbed Sally by the arm, closing her fingers spitefully round the soft flesh and pinching hard. 'You'll tell that to Mrs Grindle. She's about to send for a constable.'

'Gladly,' Sally said angrily. 'I've had enough of this sort of treatment. Mrs Grindle needs to hear a few home truths.'

'Oh, the cheek of the girl. We'll see you grin on the other side of your face when the mistress has finished with you.'

Sally wrenched her arm free. 'I want to see her. You don't have to hold on to me. Where is your mistress?'

'You'll get your comeuppance, you insolent creature. You'll find her in the breakfast parlour. She'll sort you out for once and all.' Mrs Flitch stormed off in the direction of the back stairs.

Mrs Grindle had just finished her meal when Sally and Josie entered the breakfast parlour.

'So, you've come back, have you?' Mrs Grindle mopped her lips on a table napkin. 'You've saved the constable the trouble of going to look for you, Suggs.'

'I haven't taken anything from your house, Mrs Grindle,' Sally said coldly. 'You need to look closer to home for the culprit.'

'What d'you mean by that?'

'Your son came to my home last evening, Mrs Grindle. He threatened to have me sacked if I refused to sell him my horse. I suggest you look in his room for the missing items.'

Mrs Grindle rose majestically to her feet, but was overcome by a sudden belch, which shook her whole frame. She covered her mouth with her hand, her cheeks flushed to a dark red. 'You've done this to me, you lying trollop. You've upset my delicate digestion and turned my household upside down. How dare you suggest that my silver will be found in Harvey's room?'

'There's only one way to find out.' Sally forced herself to sound calm, although inwardly she was trembling. 'Lead on Josie, you know the way better than I do.'

Josie shot her a sideways glance. 'Here, steady on, girl. You'll have Mrs Grindle imagining all sorts.'

Mrs Grindle tossed her head. 'You stupid girl, d'you think I don't know what goes on in my house? I only allow you to stay because my son seems to enjoy your company, but the minute he tires of you – out you go.'

'Ta for that,' Josie said cheekily. 'If I'd known you was running a kip-shop I'd never have taken the job in the first place.' She flounced out of the room with Mrs Grindle waddling after her. Sally followed on.

'You're sacked, Josie Bates,' Mrs Grindle said

breathlessly. 'If you search my son's room I'll get the constable to arrest you.'

But Josie was too far ahead for Mrs Grindle's threats to make any difference and Sally hurried after her. She could hear the policeman's heavy tread on the stairs behind them but she had no intention of stopping now. Harvey was still in bed, but he snapped into a sitting position with his nightcap askew.

'What's going on?' he demanded angrily. 'What's he doing in my room?' He pulled the coverlet up to his chin at the sight of the constable.

'He's here at my request, Harvey,' Mrs Grindle said breathlessly. She leaned against the wall, clutching her hands to her heaving bosom. 'I feel faint. Someone bring me a chair.' She gazed round the room but Josie was rushing round like a whirlwind, opening drawers and pulling out garments and Sally had gone down on her hands and knees to peer under the bed.

'I bet he's hidden them in the chamber pot,' Josie said, giggling.

'Get them out of here, Mama.' Harvey's voice rose to a screech. 'I'll sue everyone.'

The young constable cleared his throat nervously. 'Shall I arrest the young women, missis?'

'Yes, take them away,' Mrs Grindle cried, fanning herself with her hand. 'I think I'm going to have an apoplectic fit.'

'Shut up, Mama,' Harvey said crossly. 'You're perfectly all right. Get them out of my room.'

A cry of triumph from Josie brought the constable to a sudden halt as he was about to make a grab for her. 'I've found them all.' She straightened up clutching a linen bag, which she emptied onto the rug with a clatter of metal on metal. 'They're all there, including the ones that poor little Mabel was accused of stealing.'

'My silver!' Mrs Grindle rolled her eyes as if she were about to swoon, but when no one took any notice of her she made a quick recovery. 'Who would have hidden my spoons in your room, Harvey?'

'Isn't it obvious?' Sally went to help Josie retrieve the silver plate. 'It looks as if all your missing cutlery is here, ma'am.'

'Yes, you old bitch, even you can see that this is your precious son's way of getting rid of maids who won't do as he wants.' Josie moved closer to the bed, waving a serving spoon in Harvey's face. 'Was I going to be next? What were you going to say I'd pinched?'

'It doesn't matter – you're sacked. Get out of my house now, both of you.' Mrs Grindle straightened up. 'Constable, make sure these creatures leave immediately.'

'We're going, Constable,' Sally said firmly. She made a grab for Josie, who looked as if she was about to do Harvey a mischief with one of the serving spoons. 'Come on, love. He's not worth it.'

Josie tossed the spoon at Mrs Grindle's feet. 'There, keep your silver plate. It's not worth tuppence, anyway.'

It was only when they were outside on the pavement that Sally realised they had left without collecting their pay. She shot a wary glance at Josie. 'How will you manage without your wages?'

Josie grinned and took a leather pouch from her pocket. 'How much do they owe you, Sal? I found this in Harvey's room. I knew the old bitch wouldn't pay either of us, so I helped myself.'

'Josie, the constable is still in there,' Sally said, aghast. 'We really will be accused of stealing.'

'Harvey must have been at the gaming tables again. His mother doesn't know about his nightly visits to the gentlemen's club in Shepherd Market. He won't dare tell her that he's lost his winnings, and they owe us our wages. Let's get away from here.'

'You'd best come home with me, Josie. You can't wander round the streets with only a thin shawl to keep you warm.'

'There should be enough in here to replace the duds I left behind. They was all in rags anyway. I'll dress meself up nice and meet Ned when he finishes his shift. He says he's going to leave his miserable harpy of a wife and we'll go away together and start afresh.'

Sally glanced at the dark clouds that were threatening more rain. 'We'll go home and you can tell me all about it.'

Josie shook her head. 'Like I said, I'm going to get something nice to wear with old Harvey's money. I reckon I've earned it. Then I'm going to meet Ned as usual, only this time I'm telling him what we're going to do.' Josie took some coins from the pouch before handing it to Sally. 'You look after the rest. I'll come round to your place and collect my share when I know exactly what me and Ned are going to do.' Josie hurried off without giving Sally a chance to argue.

Huge drops of rain began to fall and Sally tucked the pouch into her pocket. She headed for home, but she came to a halt by the railway arches where she spotted the youngest of the Cotton brothers begging for money. Benny appeared to be on his own, there being no sign of either Jim or Eddie. Sally hesitated; she had enough problems of her own without taking on those of the Cotton boys, but when she saw Rags Roper approaching the five-year-old, she remembered hearing stories about the man's reputation when it came to young children. It was common knowledge that Rags trained boys and girls to pick pockets, and it was rumoured that he used some of the most agile children to clamber through narrow openings to steal household silver or trinkets.

Rags moved closer to Benny and leaned over him, but Sally managed to forestall him. She swept Benny up in her arms and was alarmed to discover how light he was.

'Put me down, missis,' Benny cried, kicking and struggling.

'Now, now, dear. That's not the way to behave,'

Sally said firmly. 'I promised your pa that I would keep an eye on you today.'

'Put the nipper down, Sally,' Rags growled. 'He's nothing to you.'

'And he's nothing to you,' Sally said angrily. 'I know all about you and the children you use for your illegal dealings.'

'That's slanderous, missy. I could take you to court for saying things like that.'

'That's rich, coming from someone like you.' Sally placed Benny on the ground, keeping a tight hold of his hand. 'Leave the Cotton boys alone, Rags. They've suffered enough at the hands of their father, without you leading them into a life of crime.'

Rags's expression changed subtly. 'Come now, my dear. Those are harsh words indeed. I'm a respectable businessman.'

'Come along, Benny,' Sally said, dragging the unwilling boy away from the railway arches. 'I'm sure you'd like something to eat.'

Benny gazed up at her, his dirty face alight with expectation. 'Yes, miss. But what about Jim and Eddie?'

'Take me to them and we'll all go together.' Sally led him away without a backwards glance, although she could feel Rags's gaze boring into her back and she knew that she had made an implacable enemy. She was not certain whether it was the promise of food, or the fact that he wanted to be with his brothers, but Benny snatched his hand free and ran on ahead. With little alternative but to follow him, Sally found the two older boys scavenging for anything remotely edible in the rubbish put out for the dustmen. It took some persuading to convince Jim that she would not abandon them to the workhouse. But eventually they arrived back in Paradise Row and Sally took them into Mrs Maggs's shop, where they purchased pies, sticky buns and, as a special treat, she selected three oranges.

'What are those?' Jim demanded suspiciously.

'Ain't you never seen an orange?' Mrs Maggs pulled a face. 'You be careful, Sally. Kids like these will rob you blind if you give them a chance.'

'Oy, missis,' Jim protested. 'That's a lie. We ain't thieves.'

'Of course not,' Sally said hastily. 'They're just unfortunate, Mrs Maggs. I'll take the oranges as well as the rest. I'm sure the boys will enjoy the taste.'

'Well, I suppose I could let you have them cheap. I got the box in for the Christmas trade, but folks in Paradise Row can't afford such luxuries. I should have known better.'

'Thank you, Mrs Maggs. I'm sure the boys will be grateful for your generosity.'

'That's me, all right. Generous to a fault, as they say.' Mrs Maggs placed the oranges in a paper bag. 'I'm afraid I haven't been up to see your dear pa recently, Sally.'

'I'm sure he understands how busy you are, Mrs Maggs.'

'I've got a gentleman friend,' Mrs Maggs said coyly.

'Really? I mean, that's lovely. I'm happy for you.' Sally opened the door and ushered the boys into the street.

'It's Mr Jarvis,' Mrs Maggs said loudly. 'We have so much in common, us both being shopkeepers and all, and Frank enjoys a drop of tiddly every now and then.'

Sally smiled. 'That's very good news, Mrs Maggs.'

'You will tell your pa, won't you? I mean, you can let him down gently. I don't want to hurt his feelings by taking up with another gentleman.'

'I'm sure he'll understand, and wish you well, Mrs Maggs. Wait for me boys.' Sally hurried from the shop, keeping her head down so that Mrs Maggs could not see that she was chuckling.

'What's funny?' Jim demanded suspiciously.

'Just a private joke between me and my pa. Anyway, never mind silly grown-up things. The pies are still warm from the oven, so let's get you fed before they get cold.'

With the boys settled round the fire in the parlour, Sally told her father about her conversation with Mrs Maggs.

Ted grinned and slapped his knee. 'That's the best news I've had this week. Give us a pie, Sally. I can enjoy them now without worrying that Mrs Maggs will think it's a sign that I have tender feelings for her.'

'Mrs Maggs is kind-hearted, Pa. Although what she sees in Mr Jarvis is anyone's guess.' Sally placed a pie on a plate and passed it to her father. She was about to pour the tea when a thunderous noise downstairs made them all jump.

'Open up or I'll break the door down.' The angry voice echoed round the room, causing the two younger boys to huddle together and Benny started to cry.

Jim leaped to his feet, sending what was left of his pie falling to the floor, which Pippy gobbled up before anyone could stop her.

'It's Pa.' Jim grabbed Sally by the hand. 'Don't let him in. He'll kill me this time for sure.'

Chapter Ten

Sally patted Jim on the shoulder. 'He won't hurt you, I promise.'

'Pa drinks a lot.' Eddie wrapped his arms around his younger brother. 'He beats us when he's drunk.'

'That's not right.' Ted struggled to raise himself from his chair. 'I'll sort him out, Sal. You and the boys stay here.'

Sally snatched up Pippy, who was barking furiously. 'No, Pa. You'll come off worst if you try to reason with Fred Cotton. Maybe he'll calm down if I go and speak to him.'

Jim clutched her hand even tighter. 'No, don't go, miss. He'll knock you about like he did our mum.'

'Pippy will bite him if he tries to harm me,' Sally said with more confidence than she was feeling. 'Keep the boys here, Pa. I'll see if I can reason with

Fred Cotton.' She hurried from the parlour with Pippy tucked under her arm.

Downstairs the timbers on the old stable door were splintering beneath the weight of a man's heavy boot, and it seemed likely that Fred would break in at any moment – then suddenly all was quiet. Sally unbolted the door and opened it just far enough to peer outside. Kelly was standing over the prostrate form of a man she assumed must be the boys' father.

'Thank you, Kelly,' Sally opened the door and stepped outside. 'I thought he was going to smash his way in.'

Kelly rubbed his bruised knuckles. 'It was lucky I came along. I wanted to find out if you'd come to a decision about my offer.' He put his booted foot on Cotton's chest as the man attempted to rise. 'You can stay there until you calm down, mate.'

'Get off me.' Fred Cotton slithered away, glaring blearily at Kelly. 'I'll get you for this.'

'Crawl back into the gutter, you old soak. I'm not afraid of you.' Kelly turned his back on Cotton, and he stroked Pippy's head as the little dog tried to lick his hand. 'At least she's got the right idea. She'd have a go at anyone who tried to harm you, Sally.'

'She would,' Sally nodded, but she kept an eye on Cotton, who had managed to get to his feet, but he teetered away, cursing volubly.

'Well, can I come upstairs after my heroic actions?' Kelly demanded, grinning.

'Yes, of course.' Sally stood aside and Kelly sauntered into the stable. 'Pa will be pleased to see you, but Fred Cotton is sure to come back when he sobers up.'

'Why was he trying to break in anyway?'

'I have the boys here. I was just giving them some food.'

'They aren't your responsibility, mavourneen.'

'What would you have done, Kelly? I found young Benny under the railway arches, begging. Then Rags Roper spotted him and I'm sure he was going to lure the poor little fellow away. He'd put him to work picking pockets and worse.'

Kelly shook his head. 'You don't want to get on the wrong side of him, Sally. He's a mean one, even when he's in a good temper. Cross him and you'll know all about it.'

Sally gave him a searching look. 'Don't tell me that you're afraid of Rags Roper.'

'I'm not when it comes to myself, but he's in with all the roughest gangs in this part of London. Steer clear of him, that's all I'm saying.'

'I will,' Sally said earnestly. 'Don't worry on that account. It was bad enough when I had to deal with him in the trade. Anyway, come upstairs and see Pa. You always manage to cheer him up.' She made a move towards the stairs, but Kelly sidestepped her.

'Wait a minute. You haven't told me what you think about us working together.'

'I'm still considering it seriously, Kelly.'

He frowned. 'Don't leave it too long, mavourneen.'

'I can't think about anything at the moment,' Sally said with a break in her voice. 'I've decided to look for somewhere smaller for us to live, and Flower is going to stay at Hill Farm until I can afford to look after her myself.'

'I'm sorry, I know how much she means to you.' Kelly laid his hand on Sally's shoulder, but she moved away.

'Pa will be waiting to speak to you, Kelly. Don't disappoint him.'

'What are you going to do with the boys? They'll get the living daylights knocked out of them if you send them home now.'

'I thought I'd make them up a bed in Boney's stall. They've slept here before.'

'They'll be safe enough for tonight, but Cotton will be back when he sobers up enough to remember where his nippers are. Next time he'll probably bring some of his cronies with him.'

'I'll have to find somewhere safer for them, but they're little kids, Kelly. They need someone to look after them.'

'They'll probably end up in the workhouse like so many others. You can't save them all, Sally.'

She shrugged. 'No, but I might be able to do something for the three boys upstairs. At least I'll try.'

* * *

Next morning Sally arrived bright and early at the Veterinary College, where she put Flower through her paces in front of enthusiastic students. She dismounted and held onto Flower's reins while Gideon went through the various movements, explaining how each one, if executed without due care to the animal's welfare, could cause irreparable damage. There followed a barrage of questions, involving both Gideon and Sally, which she was pleased to answer in full.

'Your mother taught you well,' Gideon said while they waited for the next group to assemble. 'You could teach me a few things about the finer points of schooling high-spirited thoroughbreds.'

'Maybe,' Sally said, smiling. 'But you have the knowledge and expertise to cure sick and ill-treated animals.'

'Nevertheless, this has been a very successful demonstration, and my students learned a great deal more than studying from textbooks on the subject.' Gideon turned his head as the door opened and they were joined by a group of more senior students. 'Are you ready to go through it all over again, Sally?'

She mounted Flower and settled herself on the saddle. 'This isn't work, Gideon. This is a pleasure.'

Gideon stepped forward to address the students. 'Gentleman you are about to witness an expert horsewoman in control of a remarkable thoroughbred animal. Miss Suggs will perform a routine such as you might be lucky enough to witness at Astley's

Amphitheatre. We will then go through each movement in turn, discussing how a badly trained rider could cause pain and injury to an intelligent and beautiful animal, and then I'd like you to suggest methods of treatment.' He turned to Sally with an encouraging smile. 'Miss Suggs – if you please.'

The morning passed so quickly that Sally was genuinely surprised when Gideon announced that it was time for a break at midday.

'We'll start again at two o'clock.' Gideon stroked Flower's neck. 'She deserves a rest after all that hard work.' He signalled to Armstrong. 'Take good care of her, please. She's been a star performer this morning.'

'Aye, sir. I was watching when I had a minute or two to spare.' Armstrong winked at Sally. 'I ain't easily impressed, miss. But you're good enough to join Pablo Fanque's circus. I seen him once performing at Astley's – he was amazing.'

'We'll start again at two o'clock, Armstrong,' Gideon said firmly.

'Yes, sir. I'll have Flower ready for Miss Suggs.' Armstrong tipped his cap to Sally and led Flower away.

Gideon waited until the groom was out of earshot. 'Can I tempt you to a cup of coffee and a ham roll for luncheon, Sally? I'm going to Ned's stall.'

She was hungry, but she was also worried about the children. 'Thank you, but I must go home and check on the boys. They slept in Boney's stall last night.'

'Why was that? Is Fred up to his old tricks again?'

'I'm afraid so. I was just giving them some supper when he turned up and he tried to break the door down. I hate to think what might have happened if Kelly hadn't come along at that moment.'

'You're seeing a lot of Finn Kelly lately.'

Sally shot him a curious glance. 'He comes to see my father.'

'Yes, of course.'

He did not sound convinced and Sally experienced a sharp twinge of resentment. Her relationship with Kelly was her own business. 'I really must go home, Gideon.'

'Would you like me to come with you? I mean, if Fred Cotton should be there I know how to handle him. Heaven knows I had enough practice when he worked here. The man was a liability.'

'Thank you,' Sally said reluctantly. 'But I think it would be better if I went on my own. If Fred should turn up, and if he's sober, I might be able to reason with him.'

'You might, but I doubt that he'll be sober. Just be careful, that's all I ask. After all, I can't afford to lose such an excellent exponent in the art of dressage.'

'I'll be back by two o'clock,' Sally said firmly. 'Don't worry about me, Gideon. I can take care of myself.' She walked off quickly without giving him a chance to argue.

When she arrived home she found the stable empty, but she could hear the babble of youthful voices in the parlour and she hurried upstairs. The sight that met her eyes made her come to a sudden halt. Her father was seated in his usual chair by the fire but he had Benny on his knee and Eddie sitting at his feet with Pippy on his lap. Josie was curled up on the sofa, and she and the boys were enjoying what sounded like a fairy story. It was only when she listened carefully that Sally realised Pa was telling them about his misspent youth as a mudlark, and sometime pickpocket.

Ted looked up and grinned when he spotted his daughter standing in the doorway. 'Just keeping the nippers amused, Sal.'

'Go on Ted,' Josie said eagerly. 'Finish the story.'

'Maybe later.' Ted set Benny down on the floor next to Eddie. 'Sal's here, boys. She'll get us something to eat. I'm blooming starving. I don't know about you.'

'Yes, Uncle Ted.' Benny turned to look up at Sally. 'I'm hungry, too.'

'And me,' Eddie added, jumping to his feet. 'Shall I go out and pinch something from Ned's barrow? I like hard-boiled eggs, meself.'

'Me, too.' Benny eyed Sally expectantly.

She shook her head. 'Stealing things is wrong. As a matter of fact, I stopped off at Ned's stall, hoping you were still here.' She took eggs from her pockets and set them on the table together with a loaf of bread and half a pound of butter wrapped in a cabbage leaf, which she had purchased from Mrs

Maggs's shop. It was only then she realised that someone was missing. 'Where's Jim?'

'He went out with Kelly.' Ted caught Benny by the collar of his tattered shirt, holding him away from the food. 'You'd best feed these two first, Sal. They've been good all morning, but they haven't had anything to eat.'

'I'm broke,' Josie said hastily. 'I spent all my money on new duds last evening, and a fat lot of good that did me.'

Sally moved swiftly to the dresser and opened the drawer. She handed a knife to Josie. 'Never mind that now. You can tell me all about it later. Slice the loaf and I'll butter the bread.' She took plates from the rack and set them on the table. 'Just wait a bit longer, boys, and then you can eat as much as you like.'

'Steady on, Sal.' Ted held up his hand. 'Don't spoil them or they'll want to stay with us for ever.'

'Yes, please,' Eddie said fervently. 'Don't send us back to our dad.'

'We'll see.' Sally peeled an egg and put it on a plate with a slice of bread and butter. 'Here you are, Benny. Eat it slowly.' She turned to Eddie, who was eyeing her hopefully. 'I'm just doing yours now.'

'You're a proper little mother,' Ted said, chuckling. 'You're just like your dear ma, Sally. She took care of everyone.'

'I only wish I was more like Ma, but thank you for saying so.' Sally passed Eddie a plate of food.

She turned back to her father. 'Why did Jim go with Kelly?'

'Kelly offered to pay him. He said you were thinking about taking up his offer of using our old cart. You never told me that, Sal? You don't usually keep secrets from me.'

Josie handed him his food. 'Here you are, old fellow. Don't you ever stop nattering? Leave poor Sally alone to enjoy her meal.'

Sally held her breath, waiting for her father to snap back angrily at Josie, but he merely grinned. 'Cheeky madam.'

Josie winked at Sally. 'Don't worry. Your pa and I have an understanding. I say what I think and he does the same. We've had a good long chat this morning, haven't we, old man?'

Sally helped herself to a slice of bread and scraped it with butter. Even with the pay from the college, she would have to be careful with money. She went to sit beside Josie. 'Why are you here? What happened with your Ned?'

'He ain't mine now, so he said. He's going to stay with his harpy of a wife. It's over, Sal.' Josie's eyes filled with tears. 'I thought it was real. But he's just the same as the rest of 'em.'

'What's the matter with the lady?' Benny stared up at Josie.

'She has something in her eye. Don't worry,' Sally said hastily. 'Eat your bread and butter and if you're good boys I'll see if Mrs Maggs has some toffee.'

Benny seemed satisfied with this answer and Eddie was more interested in eating than Josie's problems. Sally ate her food in silence, giving Josie time to regain control of her emotions.

Ted ate slowly, savouring every mouthful. 'What about a cup of tea, Sally?' he asked plaintively. 'Aren't we having any today?'

'I'll go downstairs and fetch water.' Sally rose to her feet. 'Do you want to come with me, Josie? You could carry the coal.' She picked up the scuttle and thrust it into Josie's hands.

As soon as they reached the back yard, Sally turned to Josie with a questioning look. 'What's the matter? It's not just Ned, is it? You've had more disasters with gentleman friends than I can count on both hands.'

'That's not fair,' Josie said tearfully. 'Well, it's true, but this time it's different.'

'I'm sorry. Did you really love him?'

Josie shrugged. 'I dunno, but I'm in the family way. I can't believe it. After all this time and now I've fallen with Ned's kid, which he doesn't want.'

Sally's hand flew to cover her lips. 'Oh, I'm so sorry. Truly I am. Did he say that?'

'Yes, he did. He said we was just having a bit of fun and it's all my fault. Anyway, he said it might be anybody's baby so he isn't responsible – and he just walked away.'

'Are you sure it's his?'

'Yes. Well, reasonably sure. Anyway, what does it

matter? I'll have to go to Mother Norris. She'll sort it out.'

'You can't, Josie. Girls have died after she's "helped" them.'

'What else can I do? I got no one to support me and the nipper. There'll be a time when I can't work for a while. It's the workhouse or Mother Norris and I'll take me chances.'

'No. I won't let you risk your life, Josie.'

Josie leaned against the coal shed, glaring at Sally. 'You tell me what I can do then. Can you magic this away?'

Sally thought for a moment. 'I suppose it couldn't be Harvey's, could it, Josie?'

'No. I never let it go that far.'

'It's just as well, but that isn't much help. At least he would have helped you out with money.'

'Harvey wouldn't give me a penny, even if the kid was his. No, it's Ned's and he doesn't want anything to do with me now.' Josie's eyes brimmed with tears. 'I haven't any other choice. I can't keep it.'

'Maybe you should tell you mother, Josie. She might surprise you.'

'It would be a surprise if she recognised me. It's years since I left home, if you could call where we lived by that name. The sewer rats were housed in better conditions, and all Ma was interested in was having a good time and where the next drink was coming from. I had so many "uncles" when I was a nipper that I couldn't remember their names.' Josie shook her head. 'There's no use going along that road. It ends in disaster.'

'You could go through with it, Josie. I'll do all I can to help you.'

'You're a good friend, Sal. But before I do anything I need to find work, and it's no use asking Mrs Grindle for a reference. I've got to find somewhere to doss down, and the money I took from Harvey isn't going to last long.'

'You can stay here for tonight at least. I'm afraid you'll have to sleep on the sofa, but at least you'll be safe and warm.'

Josie flung her arms around Sally, giving her a hug. 'You're the best friend anyone could wish for, Sal.'

'You might not say that after a night on the sofa,' Sally said, disengaging herself with a wry smile. 'The springs stick up in awkward places and the horsehair pokes through the worn material, but you can lie on a blanket and wrap it round you. It's better than sleeping in a shop doorway.'

'Ta, Sally. I don't know what I'd do without you.' Tears welled in Josie's eyes and she wiped her face on her sleeve.

Sally handed her the bucket. 'Don't cry, love. We'll sort this out somehow. Fill this and take it upstairs and I'll fetch the coal.'

Josie filled the bucket with water and took it indoors, leaving Sally to shovel coal into the scuttle. She had just finished when a cheery voice called out to her from the other side of the gate.

'Let the boy in, Sal. He's done a man's job today.'

Sally hurried across the yard to open the gate. Jim was filthy and pale with fatigue, but his brown eyes shone with pride.

'I done well, miss. The boss said so.'

'Good for you, Jim.' Sally held the gate open. 'Are you coming in, Kelly?'

He shook his head. 'Not now, mavourneen. I have business to discuss in the Skinners Arms, but the lad did well. He'll be a great help to you when you work for me.' Kelly drove off before Sally had a chance to argue.

She closed the gate with unnecessary force. Kelly was impossible and he assumed too much. She retrieved the coal scuttle and followed Jim into the stable, shutting the door and locking it, just in case Fred Cotton tried to get in through the back yard.

'I did work hard, miss,' Jim said eagerly. 'The boss gave me sixpence for what I done.'

'That was generous of him, but don't expect that every day, Jim.'

'It's more than I ever earned begging.'

'You won't have to do that again, Jim.'

He gazed up at her with patent disbelief in his large eyes. 'Who says?'

'I say so. I don't quite know how I'm going to do it, but I'm going to look after you and your brothers, too.'

Jim shook his head. 'Dad won't like it, miss. He relies on us to bring in a few pennies to buy him ale.'

'That's going to end,' Sally said firmly. 'Do you want to go back to your father, Jim?'

'No, miss.'

Sally grasped him by the shoulders. 'Then I promise you I will do my utmost to find a way to keep you boys safe. Do you trust me?'

'I do, miss.'

'Leave it to me, Jim. Now go upstairs and get your supper before the others eat the lot and I'll go to Mrs Maggs's shop for some toffee.'

Next day at the Veterinary College, Sally went through her routine automatically, and she answered the questions from the students, but her thoughts kept returning to the problems at home.

Gideon drew her aside during the short break between demonstrations. 'What's the matter, Sally? You seem distracted.'

Sally was tempted to lie and tell him that all was well, but meeting his sincere gaze, she was compelled to explain why her attention had wandered, albeit briefly.

He listened without making any comment until she finished speaking. 'You seem to have taken the troubles of the world on your shoulders.'

'Only a very small part of it,' she said, smiling. 'If I'm to help the boys and Josie, we will need to find somewhere much larger to live than I was planning.'

'Are you sure that's the right thing for you, Sally?

The Cotton children are their father's responsibility, not yours.'

'You didn't see them last evening, Gideon. They were so grateful for a very simple supper and they slept in Boney's old stall on a bed of straw. They looked like little angels when they were asleep.'

'But they're far from being cherubs. They've been raised like gypsies, going from one cheap lodging to another. They probably pick pockets for their father when he's desperate for a drink, and goodness knows what sort of things they've seen and heard.'

'All the more reason to give them a better life. Fred Cotton obviously doesn't want them, and if they carry on like this they'll end up in the workhouse, or even worse, in prison.'

'Very well, I won't try to dissuade you, but please think it over carefully before you commit yourself.'

Sally managed a smile. 'I will.'

'And tomorrow is Saturday. Are you and your father still able to come to Hill Farm?'

'Yes, of course. I'll be eternally grateful to you, Gideon.'

He patted her on the shoulder. 'What about the boys? Do you trust them to stay on their own?'

'Probably not, but Josie hasn't got a job at the moment, so she can spend the day with them. It will give her an idea what motherhood is like.'

'I was going to say that it might put her off forever, but from what you told me it's already too late.'

'I shouldn't have mentioned it, Gideon. It's just

that I'm worried about her and I blurted it out. You won't let on that you know, will you?'

He grinned and crossed his heart. 'Wild horses wouldn't drag it out of me, Sally.' He turned to the group of students who were watching them avidly. 'Good morning, gentlemen. Shall we begin?'

Sally put Flower through her paces, but all the while she was uncomfortably aware that they were going to Hill Farm tomorrow morning, and from there it was only about a mile to Fleet Hall. Despite his promise to keep Flower in his own stables, Sally had a nagging suspicion that Cecily Appleton would use all her considerable persuasive powers to convince him that she ought to be Flower's owner. Sally did her best to put her fears out of her mind, and it seemed that Flower sensed her mistress's anxiety. It was as if she knew that this would be their last performance, and every movement was executed perfectly. At the end of their first demonstration the students applauded enthusiastically, and Sally was suddenly aware of a stranger standing at the back of the crowd. She turned away to ask Gideon if he knew the man, but Gideon was speaking to one of the younger students, and when Sally looked again, the stranger had gone. When she managed to get Gideon's attention, he denied having seen anyone, and Sally began to think she had imagined the tall bewhiskered man, who had been wearing a dramatic opera cloak and top hat. It was only when she left the building, intending to make her way home to satisfy herself that the children were safe, that she almost bumped into the person she had seen in the college courtyard.

He doffed his hat and bowed. 'I've been waiting to see you, Miss Suggs.'

'How do you know my name?'

'I knew your mother, Sally, and I knew you when you were a small child.'

'I'm sorry, sir, but I don't remember you.'

He threw back his head and his laughter echoed off the buildings on the far side of the street. His brown moustache, streaked with white, curled at the tips, and when he closed his mouth his pointed beard seemed to snap shut, reminding Sally of a nutcracker she had once seen in a shop window. 'You were too small to take much notice of me, but you rode your mother's horse with the confidence and expertise of a professional equestrienne.'

'I still can't place you, sir. If you'll excuse me I have to go home.'

'I'll walk with you, Sally. I may call you, Sally, mayn't I?'

'Please, just go away,' Sally said wearily. 'I really don't know you, sir.'

'My name is Orrin Vasey.'

Sally quickened her pace. She had half hoped that Gideon might have followed her out of the building, but there was no sign of him. 'Please, leave me alone, Mr Vasey.'

'But you haven't heard what I have to offer you,

Miss Suggs. I've been making some enquiries and I think I might be of help to you.'

Sally came to a halt. 'What could you possible say that would interest me, sir?'

'I have a proposition to put to you, Miss Suggs. Are you prepared to listen?'

Chapter Eleven

'What is your proposition?' Sally demanded impatiently. 'I'm listening.'

'Is there a coffee house nearby? I'm parched and I am always more eloquent if I have a cup of good strong coffee in my hand.'

'I'm sorry, Mr Vasey, but I haven't got time to spare. I need to get home to check on my family before I return to the college for the afternoon session.'

'Excellent though the demonstration undoubtedly was, I think you're wasting your talents and those of the beautiful Andalusian mare. I've only seen the like of her once in my life and that was Gaia, your mother's horse. I'd say that your mare is her foal. Am I right?'

'Yes, you are as it happens. Did you really know my mother?'

'My dear, I taught her everything she knew about

performing in the circus ring and at Astley's. She was a brilliant horsewoman and you have inherited her talent.'

'Thank you. It's nice to speak to someone who knew her so well, but I'm afraid I won't have Flower for much longer.'

'What?' Vasey came to a sudden halt, and his moustache drooped, losing its curl.

'I have to think of her welfare as well as my father's and my own, Mr Vasey. Flower is going to a very good home in the stables of a good friend. In fact she will be housed better than we are.'

'No, my dear. You cannot part with her.'

'I felt like that at first, and it's not forever, but I have to be practical. My father is crippled by rheumatics and no longer able to continue in the rag-and-bone trade. We are at present living above the stables, but without work we can't afford the rent so we must move somewhere cheaper.' Sally shook her head. 'I don't know why I'm telling you all this. It has nothing to do with you.'

'But, my dear, it does. I cannot allow you to make this foolish mistake.'

'It really isn't your problem, Mr Vasey. If you'll kindly stand aside, I have to get home.' Sally was about to walk on, but he caught her by the arm.

'No, please listen to me. I've been looking for a talented equestrienne for years. You could command a good wage for appearing every night at Astley's and you could keep your horse. She would be doing what she was bred to do, and you would be following in your sainted mother's footsteps.'

Sally hesitated. It was clutching at straws, but she was desperate. 'How much would I be paid for such work?'

'I'd say a minimum of five pounds a week, maybe much more if you brought in the crowds. Someone young and pretty like you should be able to command a much higher wage.'

'Five pounds!' Sally gasped. It was a small fortune and they could live in comfort on less than half of that sum. 'But I would need to find a house large enough to accommodate my family. There are six of us,' she added, including Josie and the boys.

Vasey threw up his hands and his moustache sprang back into curl like a spring that had been stretched and suddenly released. 'That is not a problem, my dear. I know of a suitable abode in Horse and Groom Yard. It's not the most salubrious area, but that means the rent is reasonable.'

'Wait. You're going too fast.

'When are you supposed to be taking Flower to the countryside?'

'Tomorrow.'

'Then I suggest you think over what I've just said.' With a flourish, Vasey took a silver visiting card case from his pocket. 'This is where you'll find me, Sally, my dear.'

She studied the gilt-edged card. 'But this is a tavern.'

'Quite, it's where I live when I am in town,' Vasey said grandly. 'If I don't hear from you by tomorrow, I'll assume you have taken that beautiful little mare to the country.' He was about to walk off when Sally called him back.

'Wait. I'm thinking about your offer, but I would need to see this house before I agree to anything.'

'Of course, my dear. I can take you there this afternoon.'

'I have another session at the college.'

'I'll be waiting for you at the gate when the session ends. We'll take a cab.'

Sally did not tell her father about the house near Westminster Bridge, nor did she mention the possibility of working for Astley's. It would be foolish to raise his hopes and then dash them if she failed to gain employment at the celebrated establishment, and the house Vasey had found for them might not be suitable for their needs. She toyed with the idea of confiding in Gideon, but she came to the conclusion that it would be better to wait until she had decided which course to take. Even so she was nervous as she left the college at the end of the afternoon demonstration, and she half hoped that Vasey had changed his mind, but he was waiting for her in a hansom cab. She had little alternative but to climb up and take a seat.

'I've spoken to the manager,' Vasey said smugly. 'He also knew your mother and he's willing to give you and Flower a month's trial, so it only remains for you to take a look at the accommodation.'

Sally turned her head, giving him an appraising glance. 'What do you gain from this, Mr Vasey?'

'I take a small fee from Astley's for finding them new and exciting acts, and the house belongs to my uncle Mortimer Vasey, who is an old skinflint and he owns half of the properties in the Devil's Acre, as Mr Dickens described the area in *Household Words*. My uncle was not amused and he forbade me to subscribe to the weekly journal.'

'I see, but I haven't said I would accept the job or the house as yet.'

'Quite so, my dear Sally. Wait until you've seen the place before you make up your mind.'

Sally sat quietly for the rest of the cab ride. She knew that she would have to make a snap decision without the benefit of her father's advice or agreement. Then there was Kelly – she had not given him a definite answer, and yet he was already training young Jim to help her should she take over Pa's old round. Sally's head was beginning to ache by the time they reached their destination. Added to her worries, the area they were now travelling through lived up to the name of Devil's Acre. The narrow streets were poverty stricken, teeming with rats and half-buried in piles of filth. Many of the buildings were so ancient that they had to be propped up by hefty black beams, and the inhabitants were unwashed and ragged. Old women slumped in doorways, begging for money, and disreputable-looking men hung about, warming themselves over flaming braziers.

'This area makes Paradise Row seem quite respectable,' Sally said anxiously.

'But we are very close to the Houses of Parliament and Westminster Abbey. So just forget the poorer area and concentrate on the dwelling I am about to show you.'

They were nearing the river. Sally could smell the mixture of mud and the effluent that poured into the water from the underground rivers containing sewage. The various cargoes contained on the vessels tied up alongside the wharfs sent out their own particular aromas, some of them pleasant and mingling with other odours that were particularly nasty. Sally was not very familiar with living so close to the Thames, and the sounds were strange to her ears. There seemed to be a continuous background noise of cranes shrieking on rusty rails as they moved painfully like old men. The creaking stays of sailing barges mingled with the rumble of barrels being rolled over cobblestones, and all this noise was punctuated by the hoots of steam vessels. Adding to all this cacophony were the shouts of men on shore and those on board as they attempted to communicate with each other. Sally was tempted to cover her ears with her hands – Paradise Row was a haven of peace and tranquillity in comparison with this part of Westminster. By the time they reached Horse and Groom Yard she was ready to refuse Vasey's offer. To bring Pa and the children to this place was unthinkable, even for five pounds a week.

'Stop here, cabby,' Vasey said, tapping on the roof window. He leaned forward, pointing to a terrace of tall, narrow town houses that had obviously seen better days. 'The one in the middle is my uncle's house,' Vasey said proudly. 'Would you like to see inside, Sally?'

She looked round apprehensively. The houses loomed above her on three sides of the court, leaving them in a shadowy canyon beyond the reach of the pale winter sun.

'No, thank you, Mr Vasey.'

He turned to give her a startled look. 'No? But I thought this is what you wanted. The house is large enough for a family and Astley's is just over Westminster Bridge. There are stables there for your valuable horse, and she would have the best treatment.'

'I'm sorry, Mr Vasey, but I couldn't bring my family to this place. My pa needs rest and clean country air. I can hardly breathe here for the stink from the river and the overflowing drains. It's not healthy.'

'But, my dear girl, work is being done as we speak on the new sewage systems both north and south of the river. I believe the new pumping station at Crossness is the most amazing piece of engineering.'

'I believe you, sir, but this isn't the place for me or my family, and I couldn't leave Flower in Astley's stables, however good they might be.'

'Are you saying you don't want to take the opportunity that Astley's is offering you?'

'I'm afraid that is exactly what I'm saying.' Sally looked up at the sound of a woman's warning cry from one of the first-floor windows, which was followed by a loud splash on the cobblestones as the contents of a chamber pot hit the ground.

The cabby opened the window in the roof. 'Either you're getting out and paying my fare, or I'm driving off and you can pay the extra. I ain't staying here.'

'Drive on, my man,' Vasey said hastily. 'We'll return to the Veterinary College.' He shot a resentful glance in Sally's direction. 'Is that what you want?'

'Yes, it is. Flower will be waiting for me to take her home.' Sally leaned back in the seat, covering her nose with her hands. The cabby urged his horse to brisk walk and Sally uttered a sigh of relief as they headed back towards Millbank Street. She edged as far away from Vasey as was possible in the narrow confines of the cab, and they travelled on in silence. She shot him a sideways glance occasionally, but his profile was set in a stern expression, his mouth clamped into a straight line as he stared straight ahead.

When they reached the college Sally alighted quickly. 'Thank you for trying to help us, Mr Vasey. It is much appreciated, even if I cannot take you up on your offer.'

'You'll regret your decision one day, Miss Suggs.

Opportunities like that don't come along very often. Drive on, cabby. Fitzroy Street.'

Sally watched the cab drive off in the direction of the more exclusive neighbourhood, and yet he had said he lived in a tavern. She wondered why a man like Orrin Vasey had taken such an interest in her, or perhaps it was merely a ploy to get his hands on Flower. She was beginning to realise just how much her beloved horse was worth, and it was a frightening thought. She walked slowly into the courtyard and made her way to the stable where Flower whinnied with pleasure at the sight of her. There was no sign of Gideon and Sally was not in the mood to talk about her recent experience. One thing the trip to Devil's Acre had shown her was that there were worse places to live than Paradise Row. She thanked Armstrong for taking care of Flower, and she rode off slowly in the direction of home. Tomorrow was the day she must make the final decision that would change their lives forever.

But when Sally reached home she found Harvey Grindle sprawled on the sofa, chatting amicably with her father. There was no sign of Josie or the children and Pippy was also missing.

'What is he doing here?' Sally asked angrily. 'Why did you let this man in, Pa?'

'Really, love. That's no way to speak to a guest.' Ted turned to Harvey with an apologetic smile. 'You'll have to forgive my daughter, Harvey. She's upset about letting Flower go.'

'Of course, Ted. I understand perfectly,' Harvey said smoothly. 'Flower is something special.'

'Yes, she is,' Sally countered. 'And I'm not selling her to you.'

Harvey's smile froze and his eyes narrowed. 'I could report the theft of money from my room to the police. You and that trollop you befriended are to blame for that. Don't deny it.'

Sally held the door open. 'I'm asking you politely to leave.'

'Hear him out, Sal.' Ted gave her an anxious smile. 'He's got a plan.'

'Really? I suppose it concerns Flower.' Sally faced Harvey with a challenge in her eyes. 'Say what you have to say and then get out.'

Harvey leaned forward in his chair. 'I understand that you do not wish to sell your precious animal, but if you would allow me to keep her in my stable and train her for the racecourse, I will pay you . . .' he put his head on one side as if doing mental calculations. 'Well, it would be a sum large enough for you to remain here in your childhood home, and you could devote yourself to looking after your dear pa, instead of working as a skivvy.'

'Flower must be even more valuable than I thought,' Sally said slowly. 'That's the second proposition I've had today, Pa.'

'Really, Sal? What was the other one?'

'A man called Orrin Vasey offered me a job at Astley's and a house in Horse and Groom Yard.'

Harvey leaped to his feet. 'Don't have anything to do with Vasey. He's a criminal if ever I saw one. He's a horse thief and a cheat. You'll rue the day you became involved with a man like him.'

'Why do you say that?' Sally gave him a searching look. 'What proof have you got?'

'Orrin Vasey owns racehorses. He also deals in show horses of all kinds, taking payments from circus owners for finding animals suitable for training. Some of these establishments are less than respectable, but Vasey doesn't care about that. All he's interested in is money.'

'You didn't agree to let that man have Flower, did you, Sal?' Ted stared at her in alarm.

'No, Pa. He promised me work at Astley's, and he said he could let us rent a house in a place they call the Devil's Acre. He took me there, but I didn't bother to inspect the property. It was a disgusting place.'

'You shouldn't have gone with him, Sal,' Ted said anxiously. 'You ought to know better.'

'I wasn't in any danger, Pa. But it was a dreadful slum.'

'Even worse than Paradise Row?' Ted asked with a wry smile.

'Yes, Pa. Much worse.'

'That's typical of Vasey,' Harvey said, nodding.

'He said he knew my mother,' Sally said in a whisper. 'Was that a lie, too?'

'Of course it was.' Harvey preened himself, grinning widely. 'You might think I'm the villain of the piece, but I'm a saint compared to Vasey. Now I am prepared to make you a good offer for your horse.'

Ted struggled to his feet. 'That's enough, Grindle. My daughter doesn't want to sell her horse to you, or to this man Vasey. I want you to leave.'

'All right, I'm going, but I'm not giving up. I know people,' Harvey added, tapping the side of his nose with the tip of his forefinger. 'I could put the word out that you'd crossed me, Sally Suggs. You'll wish you'd been more cooperative then.' He left the room before either Sally or her father had a chance to question him.

'Why did you let him in, Pa?' Sally demanded as the door closed on Harvey.

'He seemed a decent enough fellow at first.' Ted scratched his head. 'I dunno, love. I'm getting a bit long in the tooth for all this. The only life I know is going on me rounds and relieving folk of their unwanted items. I can't be doing with this horse-racing business. It was bad enough when you dear mother was riding at Astley's.'

'Yes, Pa. I'm sorry that you've been bothered, but I don't think Harvey Grindle will call here again.'

'We'll manage without the help of men like him and that Vasey fellow.' Ted settled back in his chair. 'Put the kettle on, love. I could do with a cup of tea and a bit of peace and quiet before those nippers come home.'

'Where are Josie and the boys?'

'Young Jim is still out with Kelly, and I sent Josie with the two younger ones to fetch food for supper. We can't afford to keep feeding them, Sal. Those boys need a proper home, away from that wastrel they call their father.'

'Yes, Pa. I realise that and I'll think of something, I promise.'

'I'm fond of the little chaps, but they should be in school or out at work, and Josie needs to sort that fellow out who's led her astray.'

'I agree and I promise I'll have a chat with Jim and Josie this evening. There's so much to think about.'

A loud 'Halloo' from downstairs put a stop to any further conversation, and Sally opened the door. 'Is that you, Kelly?'

Kelly took the stairs two at a time. 'I hope you're ready to give me an answer mavourneen.'

'Why are you in so much of a hurry?'

'Because I have a cart idling away and a horse eating its head off in the stable.' Kelly put his head on one side, eyeing her speculatively. 'And I would like to have you as my business partner.'

'Really? A partner?' Sally put her head on one side. It was hard to know when Kelly was being serious. 'Do you mean equal partners?'

'Of course I do. Would I insult you by offering any less?'

'You could marry my girl and be done with it, Kelly.' Ted raised himself from his chair. 'I'm too long in the tooth to sit here and watch you two sidestepping each other. Heaven knows you've been paying my girl marked attention for months, if not years.'

'Pa!' Sally felt the blood rush to her cheeks. 'Don't say things like that.'

'What if he's telling the truth, mavourneen?' Kelly said softly. 'What would you say then?'

'I'd say this is neither the time nor the place to talk about such things, and anyway, it's nonsense, isn't it? You've had so many lady loves that I know of, so if I'm on your list I must be at the very bottom.'

'The ladies you mention were mere flirtations,' Kelly said casually. 'I think I can safely say that all of them enjoyed my attentions, and there were no broken hearts when we parted.'

Sally shook her head, smiling. 'If you say so. Sit down and talk to Pa. I'll fetch some water to make a pot of tea.' She left the room before her father could have his say. She knew that Pa was very fond of Kelly, but in her opinion the only person that Kelly really loved was himself. He was amusing, frustrating and often annoying, but he was not the sort of man with whom she could imagine sharing the rest of her life.

She could hear the sound of youthful voices and she hurried downstairs to meet Josie and the two younger boys, who had just returned with Pippy. Jim was outside, holding the reins of Kelly's horse while he minded the overloaded cart. Some of the local boys were hovering in a doorway on the other side of the street, just waiting their chance to snatch anything they could sell for a couple of coppers. All of them were older and bigger than Jim, who would not stand a chance if it came to a fight.

'I'll send Kelly down, Jim,' Sally said in a low voice. 'Keep an eye on those lads across the street. Use the whip if you have to.'

'I can look after meself.' Jim puffed out his chest, but his hand went out to clutch the handle of the horsewhip.

'I'll stay with him, Sal,' Josie said calmly. 'I can deal with those ragamuffins.'

'Are you all right?' Sally asked in a low voice.

'Never better,' Josie said chirpily. 'Don't worry about me, Sal.'

'You won't do anything silly, will you?'

'No, not me.' Josie tossed her head. 'Go and get Kelly, or I will, and I won't be as polite as you.'

Later that evening, the boys had been fed and had suffered the indignity of being washed in ice-cold water in the back yard. Eventually, after drinking mugs of hot cocoa, they settled down for the night on a palliasse stuffed with clean straw. Sally covered them with a large patchwork quilt and kissed the two younger boys goodnight. She patted Jim on the shoulder, knowing that any overt show of affection would only serve to embarrass him. She doused the lantern and went upstairs to join Josie, who was sitting by the embers of the fire, drinking tea.

'Your dad went to bed,' Josie said, stretching her

feet out to warm them on the hearth. 'He said he was tired.'

'I'm sure he was. He tires easily these days.' Sally filled a cup with tea and sat down on the chair closest to the fire. She lowered her voice, even though there was no one to overhear their conversation. 'Have you decided what to do about the baby?'

'I can't think about anything else.' Josie sipped her tea with a faraway expression in her green eyes. 'It will be the first thing that's really belonged to me. Ned made it clear that he didn't want anything to do with it or me, so he can stay with his wife for all I care.'

'But you do care, you know you do.'

'Yes,' Josie admitted reluctantly. 'But he's not going to know that, and I'm going to manage somehow. My mum raised me, although it was more by luck than anything else that I survived. Anyway, it'll be some time before it begins to show, so I'll find work somewhere. I think it must be due in July. That's a long way away.'

'Pa and I are going to Hill Farm tomorrow with Gideon, so perhaps you could stay here with the boys, if that's all right with you? You can practise being a mum to them.' Sally added, smiling. 'I hate the thought of them going back to their father, but the law is on his side, unfortunately.'

'There's not much we can do about it, Sal. We've got our own problems.'

'Yes, you're right. We've all got big decisions to

make, Josie. I don't know what to do for the best, I really don't.'

'Will you work with Kelly? He seems very keen to keep you by his side.' Josie set her cup down on the hearth. 'He's a decent enough chap. You could do worse.'

'I wouldn't be working with him,' Sally said hastily. 'It doesn't matter what Kelly says, I'd be in his employ. I'd be driving Pa's old cart with Jim to help me, but I'm not sure it would work out.'

'He seems very keen on you, Sal. You could do worse than marry him.'

'I'm not going to wed a man just to keep a roof over my head.'

'Most women don't have much choice,' Josie said gloomily. 'I reckon I'd say yes, if I met a man who offered me a wedding ring. I fancy being respectable for a change.'

'I'm sure you'll meet someone suitable one day. You deserve a happy life, Josie.'

Josie threw her head back and laughed. 'That's what I keep telling meself, but what about you? Are you really going to leave Flower at Hill Farm?'

'I don't think I have much choice,' Sally said sadly. 'She seems to be much more valuable than I ever imagined.'

'Why do you say that? I mean old Harvey doesn't know one end of a nag from the other.'

'Maybe not, but Orrin Vasey wants her and I know that Rags Roper would love to get his hands on

Flower, if only to sell her to the highest bidder. If I can't earn enough to pay the rent, Baines will send the bailiffs in to seize our property and they might take my horse, because she's the only thing of value we own. I have to act now, Josie, before it's too late.'

'I'll do anything I can to help, my duck.' Josie rose to her feet. 'But now I'm ready for bed. Me and that sofa are getting to be the best of friends.'

Sally raised herself reluctantly. It was warm by the fire and the cramped space where she slept each night was cold and draughty. 'Wouldn't it be nice to have a real house, with an upstairs and a downstairs, and a back yard with its own privy, instead of sharing with the neighbours?'

'And a kitchen range with a large oven. I'd like a garden where I can grow vegetables and flowers. You never see anything green or pretty growing in Paradise Row, not even a dandelion.'

Sally yawned and rose to her feet. 'That's what I'm looking forward to most when Pa and I go to the country with Gideon. It might be midwinter, but the grass is green and trees are beautiful, even if they've shed their leaves. I think I could live quite happily in the country.'

'Maybe Gideon will propose,' Josie said, chuckling. 'He might abandon the beautiful, wealthy heiress and choose you instead.'

It was Sally's turn to laugh. 'He'd have to be mad to choose me over Miss Cecily Appleton. That's never going to happen.'

'Says you,' Josie said, winking. 'I'll bet if you was dressed up in fine clothes, with your hair all coiffed and elegant, you'd be a match for any of them fine ladies.'

The sound of Pippy whining and scratching the woodwork made Sally open the door. 'What's the matter, you silly dog? Don't you want to sleep with Benny?' She sniffed the air, frowning. 'Can you smell smoke, Josie? I think something's burning . . .'

Chapter Twelve

'Fire!' Sally cried, as she opened the parlour door and smoke billowed into the room, filling it with a noxious, choking cloud. 'Get my father up, Josie. I'll see to Flower and the boys.' Covering her mouth with her apron, Sally made her way downstairs into the darkness of the stable. 'Boys, wake up.'

Pippy raced on ahead, barking excitedly, and Flower whinnied as she reared, striking out with her flailing hoofs. Sally grabbed the two youngest boys and practically threw them out onto the street, still wrapped in the quilt. Jim was already on his feet and he helped her to get Flower from the stall and outside to the relative safety of the street. Men were staggering sleepily from neighbouring buildings, shouting warnings to those whose property adjoined the stables.

'Send for the fire brigade.' The word was passed

on down the street. Everyone knew that fire could devastate an area like Paradise Row in minutes if the wind was in the wrong direction.

'Hold Flower.' Sally slipped a halter over Flower's head and passed the lead rope to Jim. 'Keep her safe, Jim. I'm going back to help Josie with my father.'

'Don't go in there, Sally,' Jim said urgently. 'I can see flames.'

But Sally ignored his warning and she dashed back into the stable and headed up the stairs. She could see almost nothing and once again she covered her mouth with her apron, but she was only halfway up the stairs when she came across Josie, who was having great difficulty in getting Ted to safety. Together they managed to get him out into the street, where he collapsed to the ground. Mrs Maggs emerged from her premises, wearing only her flannel nightgown, with a shawl thrown hastily around her shoulders. Her curl papers stuck out at angles beneath her mobcap and she clutched her hands together, tears spurting from her eyes.

'Oh, Lord!' she sobbed. 'My shop will go up next. What will a poor widow do then?' She leaned over Ted, stroking wisps of grey hair back from his forehead. 'You poor dear, are you hurt?'

'Leave me alone, woman,' Ted said crossly as he struggled to a sitting position. 'Never mind your dratted shop. We're going to lose everything.'

Sally stood and watched helplessly as the only home she had ever known went up in flames. It seemed like an eternity before the horse-drawn fire engine came thundering down the street to cheers from the crowd. It was too late to save the stable and the accommodation above it, but Mrs Maggs's shop was virtually untouched, and the end wall of the building on the other side was smoke-blackened, but otherwise unharmed. When the last flame was extinguished, the fire brigade packed up their equipment and drove off to attend another blaze a few streets away.

'You must come into my parlour,' Mrs Maggs said firmly. 'I'll put the kettle on and make a pot of tea.' She glanced at the boys and smiled. 'I daresay I can find some cakes for the little ones.'

'Ta, but we'll be fine.' Ted backed away, shaking his head.

'Don't be silly, Pa.' Sally took him by the arm and led him towards the shop door. 'You'll catch your death of cold out here, and so will the children.'

'But Sally, we must go back into the stables and see what we can salvage.'

'No, Pa. It's all gone. Can't you see?' Sally pointed to the gable ends, which were the only part of the roof left standing, and it was obvious that nothing could have survived the inferno. Two police constables had arrived and were waiting to speak to her. 'Go into the warm, Pa. I'll deal with this.'

'That woman has her eye on me, Sally. Tell her I'm a married man. Your mother will be home soon from Astley's. She'll put her straight.'

Sally put her arm around him. 'I think Frank Jarvis has taken your place in Mrs Maggs's affections.'

Ted sniffed. 'You can't trust women. Except my dear Emmie. She's a diamond.'

Sally turned away, biting her lip. It must be the shock of the fire that had affected her father's grip on reality.

'Come on, Ted.' Josie slipped his hand through the crook of her arm. 'I'm blooming freezing, and so are the nippers. Tea and cake never sounded so good.'

'Take them into the shop.' Sally forced herself to sound calm and in control. 'I'll have to find somewhere safe for Flower to spend the rest of the night. She can hardly climb the stairs to Mrs Maggs's parlour.'

'I'll come with you, miss,' Jim said eagerly.

'Don't you want to go with your brothers?' Sally stared at him, frowning. 'It's bitterly cold and you haven't got a jacket.'

He looked up at her with a faint grin. 'Neither have you, miss.'

'That's true. All right then, I think we'll take Flower to Mr Lawrence's lodging house. It's near the college and he's sure to have a key to the stables, but I have to speak to the constable first.' Sally walked over to where the older of the two policemen was examining the front door.

'I don't know how it started, Constable,' Sally said hastily. 'I doused the lantern when I went upstairs.'

'It looks like arson, miss. We found rags soaked in lamp oil round the back of the building, or what's left of it. Someone set fire to your place deliberately, I'd say.'

'Who would do such a wicked thing? Sally stared at him in disbelief. 'I have an elderly father and there were three children sleeping in the stable.'

'Well, miss, someone has it in for you or your dad, and no mistake. I'll write a report and give it to my superior, but I doubt if there's much to go on. Unless, of course, you could give me names.'

'Names?' Sally said dazedly. Somehow her brain seemed to have slowed right down and everything seemed unreal.

'People who might carry a grudge against you or your dad, miss.'

'I see.' Sally could think of several people who fitted that description, but she was unwilling to cast blame without proof. 'I'll think about it, Constable. Will that be all for now? I must find somewhere to stable my horse for tonight.'

'Yes, miss. We'll let you know if we uncover anything further.' The constable saluted and strolled off at a leisurely pace with his colleague following at his heels like a well-trained dog.

Sally forced herself to be positive. 'All right. Let's go before we freeze to the spot.'

'Now the fire's gone out it's perishing taters.' Jim stamped his feet as if to emphasise his point.

'Come on then. We'll walk together, unless you can ride bareback. All Flower's tack was lost in the fire.'

Jim shot her a sideways glance. 'Lucky you wasn't in your nightgown, miss. Not like old Ma Maggs – she didn't half look a sight.'

'She has a kind heart, Jim. You'll be old like her one day, so don't make fun of her.'

'Sorry, miss. Can I really ride Flower bareback?'

Sally nodded and helped him to mount. 'Hold on to her mane, we're only going slowly, so you won't fall off.'

'I never rode a horse before,' Jim said happily. 'I could get used to this.'

A terrified maidservant opened the door of Gideon's lodging house in answer to Sally's insistent rapping on the knocker. The girl clutched a candle in one hand and she held the door with the other, as if ready to slam it in their faces.

'Who's there?'

'I'm sorry to disturb you,' Sally said apologetically. 'I need to speak to Mr Lawrence urgently.'

'I daren't wake him, miss. I'd lose me job.'

'You won't, I promise. I really must speak to him.'

'All right, I'll try, but I ain't promising nothing. If Mrs Tompkins finds out what I've done she'll be furious.'

'Go quietly and she'll never know,' Sally said urgently.

The maid closed the door and Sally waited for what seemed liked hours, but could only have been a few minutes, before Gideon appeared. His hair was tousled and he wore a dressing robe, but his feet were bare. Sally felt herself blushing despite the stinging cold. Seeing a man in a state of undress was disturbing, and a little too intimate for comfort.

'I – I'm sorry,' she stammered. 'There was a fire – our home and the stables were razed to the ground. I didn't know where else to bring Flower.'

'Was anyone hurt? Are you all right?'

She nodded. 'Yes, I'm fine, but it's Flower I'm worried about. We've lost everything, but she needs to be stabled for what's left of the night.'

As if acting on cue, the clock in the church steeple nearby struck the midnight hour.

'You're shivering. Come in and get warm.' Gideon glanced over her shoulder. 'Is that young Jim?'

'Yes, the boys were sleeping in Boney's old stall when the fire broke out, but they and Pa and Josie are safe with Mrs Maggs. Luckily the fire didn't spread to her premises. I wondered if there was room in the college stables for Flower. Just for tonight.'

'Of course. Come inside while I get changed into something more respectable.' He left her in the entrance hall and took the stairs two at a time, returning minutes later fully dressed.

Gideon had keys to all the main doors of the college, and, having settled Flower in a nice warm stall, he insisted on escorting Sally and Jim back to Paradise Row.

The stark reality of the devastation was clear, even in the dim light of the street lamps, and the acrid smell of burning hung in a pall over the whole area.

'This is worse than I imagined,' Gideon said slowly. 'How did it start?'

'The police said someone had set fire to the building on purpose.'

'Who would do such a thing? Do you suspect anyone?'

'I don't know. I can't think straight at the moment.'

'Little wonder after the shock you've had.' Gideon slipped his arm around Sally's shoulders. 'I am so sorry.'

'I don't know what we'll do,' she said, sighing. 'We've lost everything.'

Jim tugged at her sleeve. 'Can we go inside? I'm tired and I'm cold.'

'Yes, of course. I'll follow you in a minute.' Sally moved away from the shelter of Gideon's arm. 'Thank you for taking Flower in. That's one thing off my mind.'

'What else would I do? But it's you I'm worried about, Sally.'

'Thank you, but I'll find somewhere temporary for us to stay.' Sally spoke with more conviction than she was feeling. They had no relatives in London, and there were some distant cousins in the country, but she had not seen them in years. She was about to follow Jim, who had been admitted into the shop by Mrs Maggs, when Gideon caught her by the hand.

'We can still go to Highgate this morning. After daybreak, of course,' he added with a wry smile. 'I'll borrow the college's old growler and we can fit everyone in.'

'Are you suggesting that I bring Josie and the boys as well as Pa?'

'Precisely. You can stay at the farm while you decide what to do next. There's plenty of room, and Mrs Wallace will be in her element with three children to fuss over.'

'We can't impose on you like that, Gideon.'

'Why not? Anyway, it will be my pleasure to be of assistance. I can't help feeling somewhat responsible for what's happened.'

Sally stared at him in astonishment. 'How could you possibly be to blame for an act of arson?'

'It all seems to stem from the knowledge that Flower is an extremely valuable animal, doesn't it? Since Cessy offered to buy your horse, you've had other people showing an interest, including Grindle.'

'And Orrin Vasey,' Sally added thoughtfully. 'But surely you don't think either of them had a hand in setting fire to my home?'

'Someone holds a grudge against you and your father. I'd suspect Fred Cotton, but he wouldn't want to harm his boys. He's a hopeless drunkard and good-for-nothing, but I don't think he's a murderer.'

'Murder?' Sally swayed on her feet. 'Do you think whoever it was intended to kill us?'

'It was probably done to frighten you into selling

Flower; that's the only reason I can think of for someone committing such a dastardly act. Anyway, you look dead on your feet, Sally. Go with Jim and I'll come round later. Get some rest, if you can.'

'Yes, thank you.' Sally entered the shop in a daze. She could hardly believe that someone would deliberately set fire to their home. She decided to keep the knowledge to herself, for the time being at least. She went upstairs to the parlour where her father was asleep in a chair by the fire, which had long ago burned down to ash, and Josie was sprawled in another chair, snoring gently. The two small boys were asleep on the hearth rug, curled up like puppies with Pippy, and Jim was seated at the table, stuffing cake into his mouth. There was no sign of Mrs Maggs, and Sally assumed that their hostess must have gone back to bed.

'You'd best try to get some sleep, Jim,' Sally said gently. 'Later this morning we're all going to Hill Farm in Highgate.'

'But I have to work. Kelly will be expecting me.'

The fire had put everything out of Sally's mind other than their immediate needs. She brushed her tangled hair back from her forehead with an impatient gesture. 'I'm sure Kelly will understand.'

'He'll be here to collect me at seven o'clock prompt. I like working for Kelly. He treats me like a grown-up.'

'The thing is,' Sally said patiently, 'we will have to stay at the farm until I can find accommodation here in London. It's the last thing I wanted to do, but I might have to sell Flower to a very rich lady, who will treat her well, and when I get the money we can start again.'

'Do you want us to go back to our dad?' Jim's bottom lip trembled. 'I know we're a nuisance. Dad is always telling us that.'

Sally reached out to clasp Jim's hand. 'You are not a nuisance, my dear. You are a good, hard-working boy that any man would be proud to call his son, and your brothers will grow up to be just like you. But that will only happen if you have a decent home and someone who cares about you.'

'Do you mean the workhouse, miss?'

'No, certainly not. And my name is Sally – I'd like you to call me that, as if I was your big sister.'

'Could you be our mother? We ain't got one of those.'

Tears welled in Sally's eyes, and she wrapped her arms around him in a hug. 'I can be anything you want, Jim. Now try to get some sleep, and when Kelly comes round I'll explain the situation. He's a very reasonable man, most of the time.'

Kelly arrived, as Jim had predicted, on the dot of seven o'clock. Sally had finally fallen asleep, leaning over Mrs Maggs's table with her head resting on her arms. She awakened at the sound of Kelly's voice shouting from the street below and she dragged herself to the window. She opened it and leaned out, blinking sleepily in the bright daylight.

'Wait a minute, Kelly. I'll be down.' She ran her fingers through her hair in an attempt to tame the tangles as she hurried downstairs to open the shop door.

'Why didn't you come to me for help?' Kelly demanded angrily. 'I had the shock of my life when I pulled up and saw your place razed to the ground.'

'It happened late last night, Kelly. I had to get Flower to safety as well as Pa, Josie and the boys.'

'You should have come to me. I'd have taken you all in.' Kelly looked her up and down, shaking his head. 'You look terrible.'

'Thank you. That makes me feel much better.'

'I'm sorry, Sal. It's an appalling thing to happen to anyone. Is Ted all right?'

'He was very confused last night. He thought that Ma was still alive and he was waiting for her to come home.' Sally's voice broke on a suppressed sob.

'He's an old man, mavourneen. It must have been a terrible shock. No wonder he was bewildered by it all.'

'He's asleep now, as are the others. I'm afraid you'll have to do without Jim for a while.'

'I'll manage, but you can't stay here with Ma Maggs. What do you plan to do?'

'I've decided to sell Flower to Cecily Appleton. The fact that we've lost our home and the stable leaves me no alternative. I have to be practical, Kelly. With the money I get for Flower I can find us somewhere cheap to rent until I can earn enough to keep us all. In the meantime Gideon has invited us to stay at his farmhouse.'

'I could find you somewhere to live, and my offer of a partnership still stands.'

'I'm too tired to make any decision at the moment, and I have Pa to consider, as well as the children.'

'Jim can stay with me. He's a hard worker and I'll take good care of him until you return.'

'You'd better ask him.' Sally glanced over her shoulder at the sound of footsteps. Rubbing his eyes, Jim gazed at the ruined stable.

'Crikey. What a mess. We was lucky to get out alive.'

Sally slipped her arm around his shoulders. 'Yes, we were, but we have to make the best of things. Mr Kelly has something to say to you, Jim.'

'Would you like to stay with me and help me on my rounds, Jim?' Kelly said, smiling. 'Or do you want to go to the farm with your brothers?'

Jim hesitated. 'I have to look after them.'

'If you want to go with Kelly, I promise you that I'll take good care of your brothers, Sally said gently. 'We'll be back as soon as we can, and we'll find somewhere nice for us all to live. But if you want to go back to your father, then that's what you must do.'

'No!' Jim backed away from her. 'Don't say that. I won't go near him.'

'And no one is going to make you,' Sally said calmly. 'If you want to stay with Kelly that's all right.'

'Yes, if you look after Ed and Benny, I'll go with Kelly.'

Kelly grinned. 'You have your answer, mavourneen. We men must stick together. Isn't that right, Jim?'

'Yes, sir.' Jim climbed up onto the cart and made himself comfortable on the driver's seat.

'He hasn't got any clothes other than what he's wearing now,' Sally said hastily. 'None of us have, if it comes to that. Everything went in the fire.'

'All the more reason for you to reconsider my offer, mavourneen. You may think I was jesting, but I was sincere.'

'Were you, Kelly? Have you ever meant anything you said when a woman was concerned?'

'You've cut me to the quick, Sally.' Kelly's smile faded as he glanced over her shoulder. 'That looks like your horse doctor.'

Sally turned to see Gideon on the driver's seat of an ancient Clarence, which was living up to its nickname of 'growler' as it rumbled over the cobblestones.

'Are you sure you want to go with Kelly?' Sally gave Jim a searching look. 'You can still change your mind.'

'I want to go with Kelly, miss,' Jim said firmly.

'The boy will be fine with me. Don't worry, mavourneen. We'll have you back in London before you know it.' Kelly climbed up onto the cart and flicked the whip above the horse's head. He drove off, acknowledging Gideon with a curt nod.

Gideon reined his horse in and leaped to the ground. 'It's terrible, but it could have been a lot worse, Sally. At least no one was hurt.'

She nodded. 'I know, but we've lost all our possessions. We've only the clothes we stand up in.'

'Let's get you and the family away from here. We'll stop at the college and collect Flower, if you feel up to riding her.'

'Yes, of course I do.'

'That's settle then. There's a warm welcome waiting for you at Hill Farm.'

Mrs Wallace fussed over the children and she welcomed Sally and her father with genuine pleasure. She seemed equally happy for Josie to stay in the sprawling farmhouse and Pippy bounded round the yard, making friends with the two sheepdogs. Mrs Wallace paid particular attention to Ted, who was still in a confused state and convinced that his dear Emily would come to join him soon. He was clearly suffering from shock as well as exhaustion, and Arthur Wallace helped him upstairs to a room at the back of the house.

'We lost everything in the fire,' Sally said apologetically when Mr Wallace announced that he had put her father to bed wearing one of his nightshirts. 'I'm sorry to be such a nuisance.'

'Nonsense.' Mrs Wallace spoke before her husband had a chance to respond. 'We're only too happy to help out, aren't we Arthur? Anyway, the two little ones are happy with their milk and cake, so if you young ladies would like to follow me, we'll go upstairs and you can choose your rooms.'

'Thank you, Mrs Wallace,' Sally said gratefully. 'You're very kind.'

'Yes, indeed,' Josie added.

'This old place was meant to be a home for a large family,' Mrs Wallace said as she led Sally and Josie upstairs. She came to a halt on the landing. 'Sometimes I imagine that I can hear nippers running around, laughing and teasing each other, but it's just my fancy. I lost my baby boy when he was a few months old, God bless his innocent little soul.'

'I'm so sorry, Mrs Wallace,' Sally said softly. 'How awful for you.'

'That's sad.' Josie sniffed and dashed her hand across her eyes.

Mrs Wallace gave her a sympathetic smile. 'You wouldn't be in the family way yourself, now would you, my dear? I can always tell.'

'Well, it's like this . . .'

'There's no need to explain. I know the ways of the world, dear. It's hard on us women.'

'I'll be off when I can find myself a job and somewhere to live,' Josie said hastily.

'Yes, Mrs Wallace, that goes for us, too,' Sally added. 'We won't inconvenience you any longer than necessary.'

'Now, my dears, I don't want to hear that sort of

talk. I said it's a pleasure having you here and I meant it. I'd say you were heaven sent, in fact.'

'In what way?' Sally eyed her curiously.

'It's just that Mr Lawrence has been unsettled recently. Until not long ago he seemed set to marry Miss Appleton and save the farm from bankruptcy, but so far nothing has come of it. I know from Mrs Hart, the housekeeper at Fleet Hall, that Miss Cecily is not happy. She thought that Mr Lawrence was going to propose on her birthday, but for some reason, best known to himself, he did not. Although with her looks and the inheritance she'll come into, not to mention a huge dowry, she could have any man she chose.'

Sally digested this in silence, but Josie was hanging on Mrs Wallace's every word.

'Good Lord, it sounds like the plot of a penny-dreadful,' Josie said in an awed tone.

'Best forget I said anything. I'll show you the bedchamber and you can decide who goes where.' Mrs Wallace turned to Sally with a genuine smile. 'Although you might like the one I chose for you when you were going to stay last time.'

'I would indeed, and I still feel guilty for running off like that.'

'You had your reasons, Miss Suggs. I'm just glad you've returned. I think you might have the answer to our problems.' Mrs Wallace walked off before Sally had the chance to question her.

'I really shouldn't be here,' Josie said in a whisper.

'I'm not your family, Sal. I should be out there looking for work.'

'Don't worry about that now. You've got to look after yourself and the baby. If that means staying here for a while, then just accept it. At least we have a roof over our heads for the present.'

'Come on, young ladies,' Mrs Wallace called from the end of the passageway. 'Take a look at this room. I think it will do for the little ones, with your room next to it, Josie.'

'I'm not their mum,' Josie said sulkily. 'Just because I'm in the family way don't mean I want to look after all and sundry. That's your job, Sal.'

Sally gave her a gentle shove. 'Now's a good time to practise. I've got to sort out a future for Flower. Gideon is waiting for me downstairs.'

'Oh, go on then. Do what you have to do. I can cope here.' Josie strutted off to join Mrs Wallace. 'Well, love. Where are you going to put me?'

Chapter Thirteen

Cecily was in the drawing room at Fleet Hall when Stafford ushered Sally and Gideon into the room. It had been a hard decision, but Sally knew now that she had very little alternative but to sell Flower to Miss Appleton, and it had to be done quickly or not at all.

Cecily stared at Sally's smoke-blackened clothes in horror. 'Good heavens, what happened to you, Miss Suggs?'

'Someone set fire to her home, Cessy. She and her father have lost everything.'

'Everything?' Cecily sank down on one of the damask-covered chairs in the morning parlour. 'How simply dreadful. How will you manage now?'

'We might have lost our home and possessions,' Sally said guardedly. 'But that doesn't mean that I'll accept anything less than what you offered before. I won't let her go for less than she's worth.'

'I don't talk money,' Cecily said haughtily. 'Whatever my father offered you still stands, and for goodness' sake, please change out of those awful clothes. The smell of charring is making me feel ill.'

'Sally just told you that she lost everything in the fire, Cessy.' Gideon walked over to the window and stood with his back to them.

Sally stared at him in surprise. Gideon had always seemed to be so in tune with Miss Appleton, but today there was a note of impatience in his voice.

'There's no need to snap at me, Gideon,' Cecily said crossly.

'I'm sorry, Miss Appleton,' Sally said hastily. 'I know it must seem very strange to someone like you, but these clothes really are all I have.'

Cecily rose swiftly to her feet. 'I can't allow that. Come with me, Sally. I think the time for being formal is past. You'll wait here, I assume, Gideon?'

'Yes, of course I will.'

'It's good of you to grace my home with your presence,' Cecily said icily. 'We see so little of you these days.'

'I have a living to earn, Cessy. I'm not a landed gentleman.'

'Well, you have land, but you don't choose to stay at home to ensure that it's run efficiently.' Cecily tossed her head. 'Papa thinks you're wasting your time in London when you should be at least attempting to run the farm.'

'I'm a veterinary surgeon, Cessy. I'm not a farmer.'

'That is becoming patently obvious,' Cecily said acidly. 'Come Sally. We'll go to my room and select some suitable garments for you.'

Sally shot a questioning glance in Gideon's direction, but he merely shrugged and turned away. Sally had the uncomfortable feeling that her presence had caused this apparent rift between Gideon and Miss Appleton, but anything she might say would only make matters worse. She could do nothing other than follow Cecily to her room on the first floor, which was, as Sally had expected, quite the most sumptuous bedroom she had ever seen. Not only was it large, light and airy, but it was also warm and welcoming. A coal fire blazed in the grate beneath an elegantly carved mantelshelf. A huge four-poster bed was draped with pink and gold brocade curtains, which also matched those that framed the tall windows. Sally's feet sank into the thick pile of the huge carpet woven with pink and gold flowers on a pale cream background, and the highly polished rosewood furniture was both dainty and practical.

Seemingly oblivious to the luxury of her surroundings, Cecily crossed the floor and flung open double doors which led into a large dressing room lined with cupboards and shelves. She proceeded to open doors and drawers, pulling out garment after garment, including underwear, stockings and even shoes.

'Stop!' Sally said, holding up her hands. 'Please stop, Miss Appleton. I would be very grateful for a change of clothing, but I can't take all this. I've nowhere to put anything for a start, and secondly, these are all far too grand for a person like me.'

Cecily stared at her in genuine astonishment. 'What do you mean? These are all last season's clothes. I wouldn't be seen dead in them. Let's get one thing straight, Miss Suggs. I don't like you – I never have – but I'm prepared to be nice to you for Gideon's sake.'

'I'm a rag-and-bone man's daughter and you are a beautiful and wealthy woman. What possible threat could I be to someone like you?

'Men are strange creatures. Just remember not to cross me, because I will win.'

'I don't want your cast-offs, Miss Appleton.' Sally replaced a cotton lawn blouse that she had been admiring. 'I have to work to earn my living, and the only thing I know is the trade I was born to, but I don't need silk dresses and finery such as this.'

'I don't care what you want,' Cecily said, shrugging. 'Just change out of those awful garments. I'll send for Marsden, she'll know how to dispose of them.'

'They'll be all right if they're washed,' Sally protested. 'I'll take them to the public washhouse when I return to London.'

'Public washhouse?' Cecily repeated the words as if speaking a foreign language.

'It's where poor people go to wash their clothes, and take a bath. A rich lady like you can't begin to imagine how the poor live.' Sally was tempted to walk away, but the sickly smell of charring was making her feel ill too.

'Take what you like.' Cecily walked to the mantelshelf and tugged at an embroidered bell pull. 'Marsden will tidy up when you've done.' She sat down gracefully on a chaise longue, and waited while Sally exchanged her soiled clothes for the garments that she had selected. 'I suppose you'd better take a warm shawl,' she added when Sally had finished buttoning the simple but elegant white blouse.

'I will return the garments when I'm in a position to do so,' Sally said guardedly.

'Come in,' Cecily called out in answer to a tap on the door.

A neatly dressed servant entered the room. 'You rang, Miss Appleton.'

'Yes, Marsden. Kindly find a warm woollen shawl for Miss Suggs. Then you may tidy up.'

'Yes, madam.' Marsden shot a wary glance in Sally's direction, but she selected two shawls, both much finer and more expensive than Sally had ever had in her possession.

Cecily rose from her seat. 'We'll join Gideon downstairs and watch what you say in front of him.'

'Might I suggest you brush your hair before you're seen by others, miss?' Marsden bowed her head, avoiding her mistress's gaze.

'That was very impertinent, Marsden,' Cecily said

coldly. 'However, you have a point. You may use my hairbrush, Sally. Marsden will wash it when you've finished. I don't want soot in my hair at dinner this evening.' She left the room without giving Sally the chance to argue.

Marsden moved swiftly to the dressing table and picked up a silver-backed hairbrush. 'If you'd take a seat, I'll do my best with your hair, miss.'

Sally sat down, watching Marsden in the mirror as the maid worked dexterously on Sally's tangled curls. 'Why did you risk being reprimanded in order to tidy my hair?'

Marsden shrugged. 'It's all round the servants' quarters than you've had a bit of bad luck, miss. Not only that but you're taking care of little motherless nippers. You're one of us.'

'I'm flattered that you think so.'

With an expert flick of her fingers, Marsden twisted Sally's curls into a demure chignon at the back of her head, which she fastened with long hairpins. 'The mistress won't miss a couple of these,' she said, chuckling. 'There, you look a treat.' Marsden stood back admiring her work. 'But you still smell of smoke.' She picked up a scent bottle and drew out the stopper, which she dabbed behind Sally's ears. 'That's better, now you smell like a lady.'

Sally rose to her feet. 'My poor father won't recognise me. He's taken our losses very hard.'

Marsden shook her head. 'He's lucky to have you to look after him. There's many who are not so fortunate. Can you remember the way to the morning parlour, miss? I can take you there, if not.'

'I think so,' Sally said, laughing.

'Well, good luck, miss.'

'Thank you, Miss Marsden. I think I'll need it.' Sally hesitated as she was about to leave the room. 'I almost forgot my old clothes.'

Marsden made a neat bundle of the garments. 'If you'll allow me, I'll leave these with Stafford and you can collect them on the way out.'

Sally could see that arguing was futile. 'Thank you, you're very kind.'

When Sally entered the morning parlour, she was surprised to find Sir Gregory in conversation with Gideon, but there was no sign of Cecily.

Sir Gregory rose to his feet. 'What an improvement,' he said jovially. 'Last time we met you were togged out like a stable boy. You've been hiding your light under a bushel, Miss Suggs. You must have gentlemen falling at your feet.'

'Only if they trip over their bootlaces, sir.'

'Witty as well as modest. I like you, Miss Suggs.' Sir Gregory moved away, standing with his back to the fire. 'And I admire a beauty, but I don't take advantage of someone else's misfortune. I wasn't born a gentleman, but I try to act like one.'

'What is your offer, sir?' Gideon gave Sally an encouraging smile. 'Miss Suggs has been through a terrible ordeal, as I explained to you earlier.'

'Yes, of course.' Sir Gregory's smile faded and he met Sally's anxious gaze with a serious face. 'I know how much the Andalusian means to you, Miss Suggs.'

'I'm prepared to put my feelings aside, sir. We are just about destitute and it's a matter of extreme urgency.'

'We've been talking about that too. Please take a seat, and listen to what I have to say.'

Sally's knees were trembling with exhaustion and anticipation and she sank down on an upright chair. 'I'm listening.'

'I will purchase the animal because my daughter wants it, but Gideon knows Cecily as I do, and she has wild enthusiasms for certain things, and just as quickly she loses interest in them.'

'That was what I was most afraid of,' Sally said, looking to Gideon for support. 'You knew that all along, didn't you?'

'Yes, I did, which is why I raised the subject with Sir Gregory. I'm afraid I've offended Cessy, but I had to speak out.'

'And I understood,' Sir Gregory added, chuckling. 'I've had twenty-one years' experience of my beautiful daughter's foibles, which is why I will pay you a fair price, with the option of purchasing the animal back cheaply when Cessy tires of her.'

'It's a fair offer, Sally,' Gideon said earnestly. 'What do you say?'

Sir Gregory held up his hand. 'Just a minute, Lawrence. There is a proviso, of course.'

'What is it, sir?'

'My daughter was expecting a proposal of marriage from you, Lawrence. The ball was an ideal opportunity for you both to announce your engagement.'

Sally shot a sideways glance at Gideon, fully expecting him to apologise and explain, but Gideon's expression was anything but penitent.

'There was never such an understanding, Sir Gregory.'

'That's not what my daughter thinks. I wouldn't normally consider someone like you as my son-in-law, but there's the matter of the adjoining land, which will complete my estate. Marry my daughter and your farm will be secure. Refuse to comply with my proposal and both you and Miss Suggs will suffer the consequences.'

'That's blackmail, Sir Gregory,' Sally said angrily.

'It's business, Miss Suggs.' He turned to Gideon. 'You have toyed with my daughter's feelings, sir. Act like a gentleman and do the right thing.'

'Cecily and I have known each other for many years, Sir Gregory. We've always been good friends but that's all. Marriage between us was never mentioned.'

'I heard what you just said, Gideon.' Cecily entered the room, her eyes brimming with unshed tears. 'He's lying, Papa. Gideon led me to believe that we would be married one day.'

'Cecily, I'll handle this,' Sir Gregory said icily.

Sally had never felt more embarrassed or uncomfortable. She shifted from one foot to the other, trying desperately to think of a way to diffuse the situation.

'We've always had an understanding, Gideon.' Cecily's voice broke on a sob. 'Our engagement was to have been the highlight of the ball, but you walked away. How could you treat me like that?'

'Cessy, I'm truly sorry if you misinterpreted anything I might have said in the past, but there was never a promise of marriage.'

'Maybe not in so many words,' Cessy cried angrily. 'But you've ruined my reputation.'

'I've done no such thing, Cessy.'

'That's enough.' Sir Gregory took a step towards Gideon, his hands clenched at his sides. 'You've led my girl a merry dance, sir. You'll pay for what you've done. No one insults my daughter and gets away with it.'

'That's not fair.' Sally could keep silent no longer. 'Give him the chance to defend himself, sir.'

'It's her fault, Papa.' Cecily produced a lace-edged handkerchief from her pocket and held it to her eyes. 'She's turned his head with dressing up in breeches and her trick riding. I've tried to be nice to her. I even gave her some of my old clothes. She was dressed in rags and she smelled awful when she arrived.'

Sir Gregory moved swiftly to his daughter's side. He wrapped his arms around her. 'There, there, my pet. Don't take on. He's not worthy of you anyway.' He glared at Gideon over the top of Cecily's fair head. 'You'll leave here and I don't want to see your face again. Take that slut with you and her horse. I'm done with you, Lawrence, and your farm. I'll have your land, with or without your permission.'

'You can't do that, Sir Gregory. Hill Farm has been in my family for generations, long before you became owner of Fleet Hall.'

'And soon you'll be bankrupt and then I'll get the land for almost nothing. I'll have the added pleasure of evicting you and your friends, Lawrence. You haven't heard the last of this, but if you ever come near my daughter again, I'll have you horsewhipped.'

Gideon took Sally by the arm. 'Come on, Sally. We're leaving.'

'I knew it,' Cecily sobbed. 'She's taken my place in your heart. You're sorry for her and that's the truth.'

'I'm sorry for you, Cessy,' Gideon said softly. 'I never meant to hurt you, please believe me. Don't blame Sally, she is an innocent bystander in all this.'

A fresh bout of sobbing made Cecily's answer inaudible and Gideon hurried Sally from the room. 'I'm sorry, Sally. All this is my fault.'

'It was an impossible bargain,' Sally said angrily.

'Sir Gregory will stop at nothing to get my land. He intends to purchase every acre he can lay his hands on, including Hill Farm.'

'But he was using his daughter like a chess piece.

What manner of man bargains for land with his daughter's happiness?'

'Someone like Sir Gregory, I should imagine.' Gideon's lips curved in a wry smile. 'I'm just sorry that you've been dragged into this, Sally. Heaven knows you have enough problems.'

Sally pulled a face. 'I'm amazed that Miss Appleton didn't tear these clothes off my back. I expect she'll send Miss Marsden to collect them.'

'Cessy isn't mean. She's spoiled and wilful, but she's not spiteful.'

They came to a halt at the front entrance and Stafford stepped forward, proffering Gideon's hat and gloves. Sally wondered if the butler's stony expression was one of disapproval, or merely the face of a professional manservant. It was hard to imagine him smiling, let alone laughing, or going through any human emotions.

Stafford handed her the bundle of clothes. 'I believe these belong to you, miss.'

'Thank you, Stafford.' Sally took them from him, not knowing what else to do, and she was certain that he winked at her. Whatever the truth, she was glad to step outside into the fresh air. A shivering stable boy was walking their horses, and he brought them to the bottom of the stone steps to allow Sally and Gideon to mount.

The pale winter sun was reflected on the still waters of the ornamental lake, and a cold wind tugged at Sally's shawl as they rode off towards Hill Farm.

'I'm sorry for causing you so much bother.' Sally studied Gideon's strong profile. 'I know you're very fond of Miss Appleton.'

'Fond, yes, and we've been good friends for a long time, but that doesn't mean I want to spend the rest of my life with her. I know the gossips had us paired off, but I thought Cessy had more sense.'

'Have you considered the fact that maybe she might be in love with you?'

'Cessy enjoys attention more than anything. I'm not sure she's capable of loving another person more than she loves herself. If that sounds harsh it's only because I know her so well.'

'She was very upset.'

'She was crying because she couldn't have her own way, and her father had no right to use you and your misfortune as a means to make me propose marriage to Cessy. In fact, she's worth much more than that. She could have her pick of much better men than me.'

'At least she can be miserable in comfort,' Sally said wryly. 'I'm not sure what I can do now, especially with Pa being in such a state. He barely recognised me this morning when I took him a cup of tea in bed.'

'You know you're more than welcome to stay on at Hill Farm for as long as you like. I have to return to London on Monday, but you don't have to accompany me.'

She sighed, shaking her head. 'Nothing has

changed, Gideon. I'll never be able to afford to keep Flower in London.'

'Don't do anything rash, Sally. I'll keep Flower here as long as I have the farm.'

'Thank you, Gideon. I'll never be able to repay your kindness.'

They rode on in silence for a while but her father's confusion and inability to understand what had happened was uppermost in Sally's mind.

'A penny for them, as they say.'

She turned to Gideon with a smile. 'Sorry, I'm not being very good company.'

'You were miles away. Is there anything I can do to help?'

'Would it be possible for me to leave Pa here for a while, just until he recovers from the shock of losing everything? I might be able to earn enough money working for Kelly to rent rooms in London?'

'Is that what you want? Would you be happy working for Kelly?'

'Happiness doesn't come into it,' Sally said slowly. 'I have to find work and the rag-and-bone trade is what I know best. I don't want to go back to skivvying for ungrateful people like the Grindles.'

'I'd help you with money, but I only have my salary from the college and every spare penny goes into the farm.'

'And yet you've allowed us to stay with you, asking nothing in return.'

'It's the least I can do. I wouldn't want to see you and your father living on the streets.'

'I hope it won't come to that.'

'I might be able to help in another way,' Gideon said thoughtfully. 'There's an empty cottage on my land. I remember one of our farm labourers lived there when I was very young. He and his wife brought up ten children in that cottage, although heaven knows where they all slept. But if you find work in London, perhaps Josie could stay there with Ted and the two little boys until you can find them something better. What do you say to that?'

'I think it sounds like a splendid idea. It would help Josie and I wouldn't have to worry about Pa and the little ones.'

'It's not too far from here. We'll have a look and see what state it's in, although it hasn't been lived in for years. Let's hope the roof doesn't leak.' Gideon urged his horse to a canter and Flower seemed only too eager to keep up.

The labourer's cottage stood in a clearing surrounded by a mixture of deciduous and evergreen trees. A brook gurgled along happily at the rear of a small garden bounded by a picket fence, and the roof, which seemed to have worried Gideon, appeared to be intact. They dismounted and tethered their horses to a nearby tree.

'It looks like something out of a fairy tale.' Sally followed Gideon up the path to a front door, which was protected by a rickety wooden porch. The door creaked on rusty hinges as he opened it.

'You couldn't leave a house unlocked in London,' Sally said, smiling. 'You'd have at least five families moving in before the embers in the fire grew cold.'

'We never need to lock our doors round here.' Gideon led the way into the front parlour, which was festooned with cobwebs and cockroaches scuttled for cover. A door on the far side of the room led into a reasonably large kitchen with a rusty range and a stone sink. Upstairs there were three bedrooms, all dusty and draped with cobwebs, but Sally could see that with a little hard work the property would be ready for occupation.

'It's perfect,' Sally said eagerly. 'But, of course, it's up to Josie whether or not she thinks she can cope on her own.'

'I'm sure we can find enough furniture to make it reasonably comfortable.' Gideon glanced at the iron bedsteads. 'Mrs Wallace will be only too pleased to help.'

'It would be a weight off my mind if Pa was here.' Sally went to look out of the bedroom window. 'It's so peaceful. He'll have a chance to recover from the shock of the fire, and he won't have to worry about Mrs Maggs any more. He's convinced that she wants him to marry her, even though she has her sights set on Frank Jarvis.'

'I sympathise with him,' Gideon said with feeling. 'I hate to think I've led Cessy on unintentionally.'

'She's obviously very fond of you, and it would secure Hill Farm for the future.' Sally eyed him warily. 'I dare say that many men in your position would think it a very good proposition.'

'If you've seen enough of the cottage we'll go home, and you can discuss matters with Josie and your father.'

Sally nodded. 'Yes, of course. I think they would be very comfortable here, but it all depends on Josie. I can't leave Pa on his own, and then there are the boys. Someone has to take care of them.'

Chapter Fourteen

'No, Sally, that's not a good idea.' Josie stood her ground, shaking her head. 'I'm sorry, love. I like your pa and the nippers, but I ain't no housekeeper. I wouldn't know where to start.'

Sally stared at her aghast. 'But I thought you'd jump at the chance of a proper home, especially with the baby on the way.'

'I've got months to go, and I need to find work. I ain't no country girl, Sal. I can't imagine me living in a cottage in the woods. I'd miss London.'

'I didn't know that,' Sally said warily. 'I just thought you'd be glad of having somewhere safe to live.'

Josie gurgled with laughter. 'Since when have I ever wanted to live quietly? You know me, Sal. I like having a good time, and I ain't about to bury meself in the country.'

'What will you do?'

'It'll be nice to stay here on the farm for a couple of days, but I'm going to ask Gideon if he'll take me to London on Monday. More to the point, will you come with me?'

'I haven't much choice. I can't stay here and live on Gideon's charity. I'll have to take Pa and the boys with me.'

'What about Flower?'

'Gideon will allow me to stable her at the farm until I can make proper plans. I'm going to accept Kelly's offer. At least I know what I'm doing on Pa's old round.'

'Where does Kelly live?'

'I don't know.' Sally frowned, staring out of the bedroom window. 'He's been around ever since I can remember and yet I have no idea where he lives. But I do know where he keeps his cart and stables his horse.'

'Well, that's a start,' Josie said cheerfully.

'I'd better go and find Gideon before he tells Pa about the cottage and raises his hopes.' Sally climbed off her bed and hurried downstairs to the farm kitchen, where she found Gideon seated at the table with her father.

'Might I have a word with you in private, Gideon?'

He raised his head, meeting her meaningful look with a smile. 'Of course.' He rose to his feet. 'If you'll excuse me, Ted, we'll continue this conversation later.'

Mrs Wallace abandoned the pan she had been stirring on the range and she moved to Ted's side. 'How about a nice cup of tea, my dear?'

Ted gazed at her, frowning. 'You ain't Mrs Maggs. Who are you, lady?'

'Pa, this is Mrs Wallace,' Sally said hastily. 'She's been very kind to us.'

'I don't doubt it, but these widow-women are always looking for a likely husband.' Ted's stage whisper echoed around the kitchen.

'Mrs Wallace has a husband, Pa. His name is Arthur.'

'Don't mind me, dear,' Mrs Wallace said, chuckling. 'I understand that the poor gentleman has had a nasty shock and it's shaken him up.' She leaned over Ted, raising her voice as if he were hard of hearing. 'You'll be better soon, my dear. And you've no need to worry – I'm spoken for.'

'Are you?' Ted stared at her in surprise.

'Yes, dear. You were chatting away with my Arthur last night over supper.'

'Was I? My memory isn't too good these days.'

Sally did not wait to hear the rest of the conversation. She followed Gideon into the back parlour. 'You didn't mention the cottage to Pa, did you?'

'No. I was about to though. Have you changed your mind?'

'No, I haven't, but Josie wants to return to London. I'm afraid she didn't relish the idea of being left to look after Pa and the boys.'

'What about you, Sally? Are you determined to work for Kelly?'

'It's the only sensible thing to do.' She sighed, shaking her head. 'I'm truly grateful to you for all you've done for us, and I do hope that I haven't come between you and Miss Appleton.'

He laid his hand briefly on her arm, removing it quickly as he turned his head away to stare at the log fire blazing merrily up the chimney. 'No, of course not. It was Cessy's mistake, although I must accept some of the blame. I've always enjoyed her company, and I thought she felt the same. We used to joke about getting married one day, but it was never meant seriously.'

'But you knew that the gossips had you paired off from the start. Surely you could have let her down in a kinder fashion?'

'Yes, you're right. It's been troubling me ever since the scene at Fleet Hall. In fact, I'd already decided to go there tomorrow before church. Although she might refuse to see me.'

'I hope she won't, for her sake.'

'I'm returning to London on Monday morning. Do you want to come with me?'

'Yes, please, and that goes for Josie as well. I'd better warn Pa that we're leaving.'

'I'm still more than happy to have Ted to stay for as long as he likes, and that goes for the little lads, too. They've had a wonderful time and Mrs Wallace seems to enjoy mothering them.'

'That's more than kind, and is it still all right to keep Flower here?'

'Of course it is. I know what she means to you.' Gideon smiled. 'That's settled then. Tomorrow I'll go to Fleet Hall and make my peace with Cessy, and I'll leave you to talk to your pa.'

On Monday morning Sally and Josie returned to London with Gideon. They parted company outside the Veterinary College.

'Where will you go?' Sally asked urgently. 'We mustn't lose contact.'

'I haven't got much choice, Sal. I'll try Ma's lodging house in Paradise Row, although, if I know her she'll be sleeping off the excesses of last night. Anyway, I should have some duds there if she hasn't sold them to buy gin.'

'How long is it since you last saw her?'

'A couple of years or so. Anyway, the old soak probably doesn't remember she's got a daughter. Not that she was ever much of a mother to me, but I got nowhere else to go.'

'Good luck, Josie.' Sally gave her a hug. 'I don't know where I'll be staying, but you can always leave a message here, with Gideon, if you want to see me. I expect I'll be going to Highgate quite often, at least while Pa is staying at the farm.'

Josie put her head on one side, grinning. 'Gideon has you exactly where he wants you, at least for the time being.'

'Don't talk nonsense. He's been very kind, but I think he'll make a match with Miss Appleton.'

'You do?'

'He went to see her yesterday and he returned in a much better mood. If that doesn't bode well for their future relationship, I don't know what does.'

'And you're quite all right about that?'

'Stop trying to pair me off with Gideon Lawrence,' Sally said, chuckling. 'Anyway, I can't stand round chatting, I have to try and catch Kelly before he goes out on his round. Goodbye, Josie.'

'Goodbye, Sal. Keep in touch.' Josie sauntered off in the direction of Paradise Row.

Sally experienced a twinge of envy. Just days ago she had lived in that street, and now she had no address and, more importantly, nowhere to sleep tonight. She had lost all her personal possessions and she had yet to find Kelly. She headed for the stables where he kept his horses. It was still early morning, as they had left Highgate well before dawn in order that Gideon could begin work at the usual time, but the factory workers would have been at their benches for almost an hour, and now it was the clerks and office staff who hurried to their places of employment. They jostled each other as they walked with their heads down against the cold February wind, spiked with icy rain, but Sally was used to such behaviour. Having grown up in this area she had learned how to barge her way through crowds, elbowing them out of the way if necessary.

It was every man and woman for themselves on the streets of Pentonville.

As luck would have it she arrived just as Kelly was driving out of the yard, which was situated in between the marble works and the coal yard, flanked by the Regent's Canal. Kelly had Jim seated beside him and the boy's face lit up when he spotted Sally. He waved excitedly and Kelly reined in his horse. 'Sally, this is a pleasant surprise.'

'Is your offer still open, Kelly?'

'Of course it is, mavourneen.' He handed the reins to Jim and leaped to the ground. 'What changed your mind?'

'Where are the little 'uns?' Jim demanded suspiciously.

'They're safe and well,' Sally said, smiling up at him. 'They're staying on the farm with my pa for the time being. Mrs Wallace is a lovely lady and she's spoiling the boys.' She turned to Kelly. 'Has their dad been looking for them?'

'No, he's probably drunk himself into a stupor. If he misses them it's only for the pennies they brought in by begging.'

'We're better off without him,' Jim added quickly. 'I'm doing well, ain't I, Kelly?'

'You are, indeed.' Kelly's smile faded as he gave Sally a searching look. 'What about you, mavourneen? I'm happy to take you on, but have you anywhere to lay your head?'

'No, but I could sleep in the stable.'

'That won't be necessary. There's a room to rent in the house where I live. It's cheap and clean, and I'd be there to keep an eye on you.'

'Me, too,' Jim said, puffing out his chest. 'I'm a man now, Sally. I earn a good wage and soon I'll be able to look after the little 'uns.'

'That's settled, then. Hop up beside Jim and you can do your pa's old round today, Sally. I'll take the other cart and we'll meet up at Rags Roper's place at four o'clock. Does that suit you?'

Sally nodded. 'Yes, thanks Kelly.' She tossed the bundle containing the clothes that Cecily had given her onto the cart before climbing up to sit beside Jim. 'You can drive, Jim. Show me how well you handle the reins.' She looked down at Kelly and received a nod of silent approval. 'Drive on.'

It was a relief to be doing something productive, and Sally found Jim both enthusiastic and competent. His young voice echoed round the streets as he called out for 'Any old rags and bones?' while energetically ringing the hand bell that had belonged to Sally's father. Old and new customers flocked round the cart, throwing in objects of no value to them, although they would fetch a reasonable amount when sold in bulk to the right dealer. The only problem, as far as Sally could make out, was that the person in question was the crooked scrap dealer, Rags Roper. However, Kelly would be in charge of bargaining for the best price and she could just sit back and watch. The days when she had had to speak up for her father were over, and for that she was thankful. It had hurt her to see Pa brought so low by the fire that had destroyed their home and possessions, but Mrs Wallace was a good woman. She would treat Pa kindly, and in time Sally hoped to be able to bring him back to London where he belonged, and Flower was safe. Sally knew that, sooner or later, she would have to face the problem all over again, but for now she was concentrating on the job in hand, and beginning to enjoy herself.

At midday they stopped close to Ned's coffee stall and Sally treated Jim to a ham roll and a hard-boiled egg, and a cheese roll and a cup of tea for herself. Jim opted for ginger beer, purchased from another seller a little further down the street. Then it was back to work for the rest of the afternoon followed by a visit to the yard where they began to sort the contents of the cart. Kelly appeared soon after and he was visibly impressed. They worked together to sort both loads before setting off once more to Rags Roper's yard behind the Imperial Gas Works.

Rags sat on a stool in the corner, a hunk of bread in one hand, using the other to pick bits of cheese from his long shaggy beard. He peered at them with beady dark eyes, putting Sally in mind of a big black spider waiting for the next fly to become enmeshed in its silken web.

'So you've joined forces, have you?' Rags said, leering at Sally. 'I always knew that Kelly would get his hands on you one day.'

'We lost everything in a fire.' Sally glared at him, determined not to let him see that she was nervous. 'Kelly is helping me while Pa is recovering from the shock.'

'I heard you was selling that horse you're so fond of.' Rags narrowed his eyes so that they almost disappeared beneath his heavy brow. 'Is she still on the market? I could give you a good price for her.'

'Leave the girl alone, Rags.' Kelly hefted a bag of white rags onto the dirt floor. 'We've got ten of these, twenty coloured. You can see the pile of scrap metal, but I'll take it to your rival, Sid Irons, if you don't want it.'

Rags popped the last crumb of cheese into his mouth before sliding off the stool. He loped over to the cart and peered inside. 'I'll take it off your hands. You won't get a better offer from old Irons.' He shot a sideways glance at Jim, who was helping Sally to finish unloading the sacks of cloth. 'Your dad has been telling everyone in the pub that you kids ran away and left him on his own. He makes it sound so sad that he gets free drinks all evening. Does he know where you are?'

'I don't care what he does,' Jim said angrily. 'I ain't going back to him. I'm looking after the nippers.'

'Maybe he'll have something to say about that when I tell him you're working for Kelly.'

Rags uttered a strangled cry as Kelly grabbed him by the throat. 'Leave the boy alone. If you so much as breathe a word of his whereabouts to Fred Cotton, I'll make sure you go out of business. A word from me in the right places and no one will buy anything off you ever again.' He released Rags, who staggered backwards; unable to regain his balance he fell, landing on a pile of sacks.

'You'll be sorry you said that, Kelly. Don't threaten me. I've got friends who could make you disappear from the face of the earth.' He pointed at Sally. 'That goes for her, too, and the lad. You'vc chosen the wrong man to cross.'

Kelly faced him angrily. 'Do you want my trade or not? I can pack this lot up and take it to Lenny Gregg in Poplar. He'll give me a good deal.'

Rags shambled back to his seat in the corner. 'How much d'you want?'

'How much are you offering?'

Sally and Jim exchanged wary glances, but the price Rags offered was a fair one and Kelly accepted, although not until he had made a show of extreme reluctance. Sally wanted to laugh, but she knew better. Rags Roper was not a man to offend, and she was relieved when business was finally concluded and they were driving away from the stench of the gasworks.

When the horses were fed and watered and had

enjoyed a much-needed rub down after their day's hard work, they left the stables. Sally stood beside Jim on the pavement while Kelly locked up.

Sally had been too busy all day to think about where she would spend the night, but now the question was uppermost in her mind. 'Where do you live, Kelly?'

He turned to her with a wide smile. 'It's not too far from here, in fact it's quite close.'

It was dark now as the winter night had closed in on them, but Jim seemed quite at home and he sped off along Great College Street, with Sally and Kelly following him at a more leisurely pace. Jim turned into a narrow street lined with tall eighteenth-century houses, some of which had fallen into disrepair, while others looked quite respectable. Sally fully expected Jim to disappear into one of the more run-down dwellings, but he stopped outside a four-storey town house with a freshly painted front door and railings.

'You have rooms here, Kelly?'

'I do.' Kelly mounted the steps and unlocked the front door. 'Come in. I'm sure we can squeeze you in somewhere.'

Jim slipped past him and Kelly ushered Sally inside. She hesitated in the entrance hall, which was dimly lit by the street lamp outside.

'After you, mavourneen.' Kelly strolled over to a door at the foot of a staircase that curved up into the darkness. He selected another key from the bunch he held in his hand and opened the door. Jim struck a match and went round the room lighting candles stuck in glass bottles and small chamber candlesticks

'This is where you live?' Sally gazed round the large room that must once have been an elegant reception room. Time and constant use had had their effect, but it was still a well-proportioned space. The furniture was worn and shabby, but the sofa and chairs looked inviting after a hard day's work. Kelly lit the fire and, as the flames licked round the coal and kindling, the room took on a homely atmosphere, although it was obviously a masculine domain.

'I've got me own room,' Jim said proudly. 'It's the first time I've had a bed all to meself, although I suppose that will change when the little 'uns come to stay.'

Sally turned to Kelly, her eyebrows raised. 'Do you intend to look after all three of them?'

'They can't stay on the farm for ever, and Jim misses his brothers.' Kelly shrugged off his greatcoat and flung it over the back of a chair. 'Make yourself at home, mavourneen.

'I wasn't expecting this,' Sally said dazedly.

'You thought I'd be living in a cheap lodging house or a damp cellar?' Kelly's blue eyes lit with a disarming smile. 'Admit it, Sally.'

'It's exactly what I thought. How can you afford such luxury?'

'I work hard, mavourneen. It helps that I own the property.'

She stared at him in amazement. 'You own the whole house?'

'Yes, he does,' Jim said proudly. 'We got a kitchen, too.'

'I don't know what to say.' Sally sank down on the sofa. 'I misjudged you, Kelly.'

He threw more coal on the fire and the kindling crackled and spat sparks up the chimney. 'I suppose I ought to feel offended by that, but I've been in the trade since I was a boy like Jim.'

'But the house,' Sally said faintly. 'Pa worked hard all his life and he could never have afforded to rent a house like this, let alone to purchase one.'

'I doubt if I could either, but you see I inherited it from my great aunt. Aunt Kathleen left Ireland when she was a child and she married well, but she had no children of her own. I was her only living relative after my parents died within months of each other.'

'You're very lucky,' Sally said earnestly. 'I'd be happy to rent a room off you.'

'We'll talk about money later. Let's get something to eat first. I'm starving and Jim is always hungry. Isn't that right, my boy?'

'Yes, sir.' Jim grabbed a chamber candlestick and crossed the room to open a door. The aroma of cooking made Sally's mouth water. 'Come and take a look, Sally.'

Sally jumped to her feet and followed Jim into a kitchen. The pine table in the centre of the large room was surrounded by four chairs. On one wall, beneath a tall window, was a stone sink, and opposite stood a large dresser. The room was heated by a large black-leaded range, on the top of which Sally spotted a saucepan simmering gently on the hob.

'Kelly knows how to cook,' Jim said proudly. 'He makes a big pot of stew and we have it for supper most evenings.'

'I think he's saying it's time to eat.' Kelly went over to the range and lifted the lid on the pan. 'Perfect. My mother taught me how to cook, and I'm forever grateful to her. She even showed me how to bank up the fire so that it didn't burn to nothing. Fetch three bowls and cutlery, Jim. We have a guest for supper.'

Kelly served the stew and Sally ate hungrily. 'This is so good,' she said appreciatively. 'I've never tasted anything like it. We couldn't cook anything much at home.'

'This is Irish stew.' Kelly ladled another helping onto Jim's empty plate. 'It's mutton, potatoes, onions, carrots and a pinch of love, just like Ma used to make it.'

'It's the best meal I've ever had.' Sally sighed happily as she finished her meal, but she shook her head when Kelly offered her more. 'No, thank you, Kelly. I couldn't eat another mouthful.'

'I can,' Jim said eagerly.

'You'll finish what's on your plate,' Kelly said, chuckling. 'You'll eat me out of house and home.'

'He's a growing boy.' Sally sat back in her chair, eyeing Kelly curiously. 'How many people live in this house? And more importantly, are you sure you have a room that I can afford?'

'I like my privacy so I only let out the top floor and the attic. I have four tenants in all.'

'Am I likely to know any of them?' Sally asked, trying to sound casual.

'I doubt it.' Kelly rose from his seat. 'I'll show you your room, but if you don't wish to stay here I won't be offended. It's your decision, mavourneen.'

Chapter Fifteen

Sally awakened next morning and for a few seconds she could not remember where she was, and then it came to her that she had slept in Kelly's spare room. Daylight streamed through a chink in the curtains and she swung her legs over the side of the bed, thinking that she must have overslept. When she drew back the curtains she found herself looking down into a wilderness of a garden, which, even in the depths of winter was obviously very overgrown and must have been left untended for many seasons. There was a pitcher and basin on the washstand, both of which were thick with dust, and there was neither soap nor towel, although this did not surprise her. She would hardly expect a man like Kelly to be aware of the niceties of entertaining a guest, but then her status in the house had yet to be decided. Kelly had been evasive when she had asked him about the rent, and she had been too tired to press the point. She dressed quickly without having had the benefit of a wash, and she tied her hair back with a scrap of ribbon she found in the bundle that she had brought from Fleet Hall.

She opened her bedroom door and hesitated on the landing, listening for sounds of movement in the house, but it was suspiciously quiet. She was on her way downstairs when she heard heavy footsteps behind her and she stopped, turning her head to look up.

'Out of me way, young lady.' A burly man wearing a jacket that seemed to have been made for a much smaller person barged past her.

'Excuse me, sir,' Sally said crossly. 'You nearly had me over.'

'I'm late.' He clattered down the stairs ahead of her and slammed out of the house.

Shaking her head, Sally made her way to the kitchen, which was warm and inviting after the chilly bedroom and entrance hall. The kettle was still quite hot and she placed it back on the hob while she explored the cupboards. She found a poke of tea, but there was neither milk nor sugar. The crock that might have contained bread was empty apart from some mouldy crumbs, and there did not seem to be any food in the larder. She made a pot of tea and was about to fill a cup when the door burst open and Jim erupted into the room.

'You're up. That's good. I've got the cart outside, Sally.'

'There's no milk, Jim. For my tea,' she added, seeing his puzzled expression.

'I don't drink that stuff. Come on, Sally. We've got work to do.'

Reluctantly Sally abandoned the tea. 'All right, we can stop at a coffee stall later. Aren't you hungry?'

Jim raced on ahead and opened the front door. 'I can always manage to eat something. Will you buy me a cheese roll?' He sprinted over to the cart and leaped up onto the driver's seat.

Sally climbed up, edging him out of the way. 'I'll take the reins today, Jim. I know exactly where I'm going, and we'll beat Kelly at his own game.'

'I like that,' Jim said, chuckling. 'He'll be mad as fire.'

Sally flicked the whip above the horse's ears. 'Walk on, boy. I've got to earn my keep.' She concentrated on the road ahead. 'I saw one of the other tenants this morning, Jim. He was a big man, wearing a jacket and trousers that were too small for him. Who is he?'

'That's old Isaac Worthington – he works at the railway station. I dunno what he does, but he's an odd 'un. You never know what he's going to say or do. I keep away from him.'

'Who else lives in the house?'

Jim sat back in his seat, frowning. 'There's Dolly, who sells fish and she smells of it too, then there's Meg who works in the pub down the road, and a new man – not sure what he's called, but he used to work at Astley's.'

'I thought of working there once, like my mother,' Sally said, sighing. 'But it wasn't to be.'

Jim stood up in the well of the cart, ringing the hand bell. 'Any old rag-and-bone?'

A maidservant hailed them and Sally drew the horse to a halt. She put all thoughts of Astley's from her mind as trade improved and they were kept busy all day, loading the cart with all manner of discarded items. At the end of the day Kelly was pleased with their haul, and Sally had the satisfaction of noting that she and Jim had collected as much as Kelly himself, if not more.

That evening, after supper, Jim had gone to bed early, leaving Sally and Kelly still seated at the kitchen table, drinking tea while discussing the takings that day.

'At this rate we'll be able to buy another horse and cart by the end of the year.' Kelly counted out the money that Rags Roper had parted with so reluctantly.

'You're joking.' Sally sat back in her chair, eyeing the neat stacks of coins, both copper and silver.

'Perhaps, but we're doing very well. Although it's early days.'

'We haven't discussed the rent for my room, Kelly. That's if I choose to stay.'

He looked up, eyeing her speculatively. 'Are you having second thoughts?'

'It's my pa. I can't just leave him with Gideon's

housekeeper, and then there are Jim's brothers. I know he wants them to come here, but who will look after them in the day when we're out on our rounds? I don't think working with you is a solution to my problems.'

'What else could you do that pays so well?' Kelly passed half the day's takings across the table to Sally. 'That's your share. You are comfortable here, aren't you?'

'Yes, and thanks for the money, but that's not the point.'

'If it's your father you're worried about – Ted is welcome here, mavourneen. There is a room he could have and we could find room for Jim's brothers. Many kids that age are sent out to work, but in my opinion they'd do better to attend the ragged school.'

'You're right, but that would leave them roaming round to get into trouble after school.'

'Perhaps your pa would keep an eye on them until we return from work.'

'You make it sound so easy, but there's one thing you've forgotten. Where do I stable Flower? I can't impose on Gideon's good nature for ever.'

'You could leave her in the country for the time being. Your veterinary gentleman seems keen to keep her on his farm. I suspect it's a ploy to persuade you to visit him, but maybe I have a suspicious mind.'

Sally rose to her feet. 'Don't people in your world do things without expecting something in return, Kelly?' She picked up the dirty plates and took them to the sink. 'I'll wash these and then I'm off to bed. It's been a long day.'

'Leave them. Jim can see to that in the morning.' Kelly stood up and stretched. 'I'm going to the stable to check on the horses before I turn in. Think about what I said, Sally. I'm sure we could work something out between us that would suit everybody, including your pa.' He strolled out of the kitchen.

Sally was exhausted and tempted to follow Kelly's instructions, but leaving the dishes for Jim seemed unfair. She used the hot water in the kettle and had the washing up done and left to drain. She went to refill the kettle from a pail kept under the sink, but she realised that it was empty, and the pump was out in the back yard. She decided to brave the cold.

It was very dark in the small yard and the wind rustled in the tangle of brambles and overgrown bushes in the small garden. She filled the bucket at the pump, and was carrying it carefully back to the house when the door opened and a man rushed out. She sidestepped, spilling half the water.

He held up a lantern, staring at her with an apologetic grin. 'I'm sorry, miss. I was in a hurry to get to the privy.'

'That's all right,' Sally murmured, but he had disappeared into the privy at the end of the garden. With a resigned sigh, Sally went back to the pump and refilled the bucket. It was a struggle to open the door without further spillage, but the stranger came to her rescue and held it open.

'Thank you.' Sally put the bucket down while she flexed her cold fingers. 'I'm Sally Suggs. Are you a tenant here?'

'Luke Bridges. I've just moved in.'

'Are you the gentleman who works at Astley's? Young Jim told me about you. I expect you've seen him rushing around.'

'That'll be the boy who showed me to my room. Yes, I work for Astley's, but I'm not sure I'll be there much longer.'

'Why is that? Don't answer if it's too personal,' Sally added hastily. 'I'm always interested when Astley's is mentioned.'

'Here, let me carry that bucket for you.' Luke lifted the heavy pail with ease. 'Where do you want it?'

'The kitchen, please.' Sally led the way, her curiosity aroused. Luke Bridges was a young man in his prime, not very tall – about medium height, with light brown hair. His twinkling amber eyes were the most attractive feature in a pleasant open face, and Sally liked him instantly.

He put the bucket down by the sink in the kitchen and was about to leave when Sally stopped him. 'There's tea in the pot, if you'd like a cup, Mr Bridges.'

He hesitated. 'I would, if it's no trouble. But I'm supposed to keep to my room on the top floor. This is Kelly's private part of the house.'

'Do you know Kelly well?'

'Not really. This lodging house was recommended by Orrin Vasey.'

Sally stiffened at the mention of Vasey's name. 'Is he a friend of yours?'

'Vasey? No, he does business for Astley's, mainly finding new talent for the shows. It's quite hard.'

Sally filled two clean cups with tea and handed one to Luke. 'Yes, it must be. My mother was a star at Astley's.'

'Would I have heard of her?'

'I think everyone in the business knew Emily Tranter. She kept her maiden name for professional reasons.'

'She was a brilliant horsewoman. I saw her several times when I was a child.' Luke paused, gazing at Sally over the rim of his cup. 'Didn't she have a terrible accident?'

'Yes, she did. A fall from Gaia crippled her, and I'm afraid she died a couple of years later.'

'I'm sorry. It was a great loss to the public and an even greater one for you and her family.'

Sally looked away. His sympathy seemed genuine enough, but the mention of Vasey's name made her suspicious. 'I mustn't keep you, Mr Bridges. I'm sure you want to get some rest.'

He put his cup down. 'Thank you for the tea. It was most welcome. I'll say goodnight, Miss Suggs.' He left the room, passing Kelly in the doorway.

Kelly closed the door. 'What did he want?'

'Nothing. We bumped into each other in the yard

when I was fetching water, and he carried the heavy bucket for me.'

'So you rewarded him with a cup of tea,' Kelly said with a wry smile.

'Is there anything wrong with that?'

'No, mavourneen. Just be careful who you get friendly with, that's all.'

'He told me that Vasey recommended you to him, if that's what you're worried about.'

Kelly laughed. 'Me? I don't worry about anything, you know that. But you told me that Vasey wanted to buy Flower, and Bridges just happens to work for Astley's. I don't believe in coincidences, Sally. Neither should you.'

'Flower is safe in the country at the moment.'

His smile faded. 'Just remember this, Sally. Your Andalusian is a very valuable animal. I've done some asking around and I was told that the Spanish have banned exports of that breed, so the price of one like Flower has gone sky-high.'

'You're making me nervous, Kelly. Maybe I shouldn't have left her at the farm.'

'Don't do anything for now. We'll try to find a way, but be wary of strangers. The gangs in London are ruled by vicious thugs who will stop at nothing when large sums of money are concerned.'

'Now I'm really worried, Kelly. I think I'll visit Hill Farm on Sunday to make sure that Flower is safe, and I can check up on Pa at the same time.'

* * *

Busy as she was, Sally had not forgotten Josie, and she decided to alter her route the next day to include Paradise Row. Jim was worried that he might come across his father, but Sally reassured him. Even so, he was not very happy when Sally left him to look after the cart while she went into the house where Josie's mother had a room.

'I promise I'll be as quick as possible,' Sally said reassuringly.

'I'll drive off if I see him coming.' Jim pulled his cap down over his brow so that his small face was half hidden.

'I told you that he won't be up yet. You know that, Jim. I'll be two shakes of a lamb's tail and then we'll drive on.'

Jim seemed to shrink into the greatcoat that Sally had purchased for him in the second-hand shop. Sally glanced up and down the street, but there were the usual people hanging around in doorways and small children playing in the gutter, while the older boys were being rounded up by their mothers. No doubt they would be sent out to work selling matches or bootlaces, or cleaning shoes for gentlemen who were on their way to do business in the city.

The front door was unlocked and Sally let herself in. She knew that Josie's mother rented a room in the attic, which she shared with anyone who was willing to help with the rent or to buy a bottle of gin. The smell in the building was something that Sally had chosen to forget, but it assailed her nostrils now, making her gag. She pressed on, climbing the bare treads of the stairs and avoiding those that were cracked or splintered. Some of the balusters were missing, exposing a dizzying drop to the ground floor below. However, she reached the fifth floor without any mishap and she knocked on Mrs Bates's door. She had not really expected any response, and it was a shock when the door was wrenched open to reveal Josie, still wearing her nightgown, with her chestnut hair in a wild tangle.

'Josie, are you all right?'

'What are you doing here?' Josie stared at her blankly.

'You look terrible.' Sally edged into the room and instantly wished that she had remained on the landing. The stench of unwashed bodies, vomit and stale alcohol was overpowering, and she rushed over to the window, but it was shut and someone had hammered nails into the wood to prevent it being opened.

A loud snore from a palliasse in the corner beneath the eaves made Sally turn her head. In the dimness she could just make out the shape of a body, which she assumed must be Josie's mother. The room was otherwise bare. The floorboards were filthy and cobwebs hung from the ceiling. An overflowing chamber pot had been left by the door, and beside it was a bucket containing dirty water. Sally turned to Josie with a gasp of horror.

'Why are you living like this?'

'I keep throwing up,' Josie said plaintively. 'I can't keep anything down, and Ma's no use. She's been drunk ever since I came here.'

'This is no place for you.' Sally looked round in desperation. 'Where are your clothes?'

'She took 'em while I was sleeping and the bitch sold 'em. I got nothing but what I'm wearing.'

'I can't believe that your own mother would treat you like this.'

Josie rolled her eyes. 'You've known me since we was nippers. It's always been the same, which is why I went into service.'

Sally held her at arm's length, taking in the filthy cotton nightgown, stained with vomit, and Josie's bare legs and feet. 'Did she take your shoes, too?'

'Everything, even me shift. This is all I got in the world. I was hoping my old clothes were still here, but that's a laugh. I should have known better.'

Sally took off her shawl and wrapped it around Josie's thin body. 'You're coming with me.'

'But I can't go out looking like this.'

'You can't stay here, that's for certain. I'll take you back to my lodgings. Jim's outside with the cart. I don't want to leave him for too long. The poor boy is scared stiff that his father might turn up.'

'He very well might,' Josie said in a low voice. 'He's been here, drinking with Ma. She'll let anyone in if they've got booze.'

'All the more reason to get away. Can you walk?'

'I'm a bit shaky, but I'd crawl if it gets me away from this place.'

'Good, then we'll go quietly so that we don't disturb anyone. We don't need any of your ma's neighbours telling her you went with me. Everybody knows everybody in Paradise Row.'

'I just hope I don't spew all over you,' Josie said plaintively.

'Just keep going,' Sally hooked one of Josie's arms around her shoulders and they made their way slowly down five flights of stairs to the ground floor.

Outside the cart was surrounded by children, all clamouring for a ride, while Jim fended them off by brandishing the whip, but they took one look at Josie and the younger ones fled, while the older youths backed away, eyeing her warily. Sally helped Josie onto the cart.

'Do you always have this effect on nippers?'

'Round here I do,' Josie said with a wry smile. 'They're not scared of me but they're terrified of my ma. She'll clout them round the ear for nothing, especially when she's sober.'

'The sooner we get away from here the better.' Sally climbed up beside Jim. 'Let's go. We'll take Josie back to the house and then we'll go on our round.'

'Kelly won't like it. He'll do better than us today.'

'Never mind Kelly. Josie needs help and we're going to see that she gets it. Drive on, Jim.' Sally stared straight ahead when they went past the ruins of her old home. The smell of charring still hung in the air, bringing back memories of that disastrous night, but she would not dwell on all that she had lost – there were more important things to concentrate on now. First and foremost was Josie and her baby, and then there was Kelly. He would grumble if their load was too small, but she was sure that he would understand. Kelly liked to be seen as being tough and unfeeling, but Sally suspected that the rogue he liked the world to see was not the real man. She had always written Kelly off as a ne'er-do-well, but she was slowly beginning to revise her opinion of him.

They stopped at a dolly shop where, despite protests from Josie, Sally purchased garments, including a cotton shift, a blouse and a linsey-woolsey skirt. She selected a warm woollen shawl, with only a few moth holes, and a pair of shoes that were not too down at heel. As an afterthought she plucked a flannel nightgown from the rack and added that to her purchases. The cost of her generosity used up nearly all the money that Kelly had shared with her from their rounds, but Sally decided that Josie's needs were greater than her own.

When they arrived at the house in Pratt Street, Jim walked the horse while Sally took Josie to Kelly's apartment. She helped her wash and dress and, having settled Josie on the sofa in the parlour, Sally made a pot of tea.

'I'm afraid there's no food in the larder, but I'll bring some home later.'

'I couldn't keep anything down, anyway,' Josie said, sighing. 'I'll be fine, Sal. Thank you.'

'I have to go now,' Sally said when she was satisfied that she could do nothing more to ensure Josie's comfort. 'You know where everything is, and you shouldn't be bothered by anyone because the tenants aren't allowed in Kelly's private rooms.'

'I didn't think he'd be so particular,' Josie said with a shadow of a smile. 'But this is all too much, Sal. I don't deserve all this fuss.'

'Nonsense, of course you do. You and I are both in the same boat, so to speak.'

'You're in the family way?' Josie's eyes opened wide.

'No,' Sally said, smiling. 'Not that, but we're both homeless and we need Kelly's help. I'm sure there's another room here that you could have for a cheap rent. I'll ask him when I see him later today.'

'You're too good to me, Sal.' Josie lay back against the cushions. 'I'll find a way to repay you, honest I will.'

Sally covered her with a rug she had found in one of the cupboards. 'Don't talk soft. You'd do the same for me if I was in trouble. Now get some rest and I'll see you later.' She left the house and climbed up on the cart beside Jim.

He shot her a sideways glance. 'You'll have to tell Kelly why we haven't done well today. I don't want to get into trouble.'

Sally took the reins from him. 'Kelly will understand.

We'll do our best, but first I have to call in at the Veterinary College. I need to ask Mr Lawrence if I can visit Pa on Sunday.'

'Can I come, too? I haven't seen the boys for ages.'

'Of course you can. We'll make a day of it.'

'Will Kelly mind?'

'It's none of his business, Jim. I work with Kelly – I'm not his slave.'

'I'm sorry, but the answer is no,' Kelly said firmly. 'Sunday is the only day when the horses have a chance to rest. I'm not having either of them pull the cart all the way to Highgate.'

'Are you thinking about the animals, or is it that you don't want me to visit Hill Farm?' Sally demanded angrily. 'I told you why I wanted to go there, and Jim wants to make sure his brothers are well and happy.'

Kelly continued to groom Sultan, the oldest of the two carthorses. 'No, Sally. I make it a rule that these boys have a day off. I'm not trying to prevent you seeing your father.'

'If I didn't know you better, I'd think it was Gideon who was the problem.'

'He's not my problem, although you might find yourself in trouble if you pursue that gentleman. It seems obvious that Miss Appleton has her sights set on him.'

'You've never met her,' Sally countered. 'You don't know anything about her.'

'I know enough, and you still can't take either of my horses.'

Sally looked round at the sound of footsteps and saw Luke Bridges standing on the pavement outside the stable.

'I couldn't help overhearing,' he said apologetically. 'Are you planning to travel far, Miss Suggs?'

'I want to spend the day in Highgate with my father.' Sally cast a withering glance in Kelly's direction.

'I might be able to help.' Luke eyed Kelly warily. 'I exercise horses for Astley's on Sunday when there is no performance. I'm going there now.'

'Do you think they'd let me take one of their valuable animals to Highgate?' Sally stared at him in amazement.

'If I accompanied you, then I can see no reason why they would object.'

Sally turned to Kelly. 'Do you hear that?'

'You must do as you please, Suggs. You will anyway, whatever I say.'

'You are being particularly difficult today, Kelly.' Sally turned to Luke with a wide smile. 'Thank you, Mr Bridges. It would be my pleasure.'

'What about me?' Jim had been filling the manger with hay, but he pushed past Kelly to stand beside Sally. 'You said I could see my brothers.'

'I did,' Sally said reluctantly. 'I don't know if Astley's will allow you to ride one of their horses, Jim.'

'But you promised.' Jim's bottom lip trembled and his eyes filled with tears.

'You may ride Emperor,' Kelly said reluctantly. 'But that's on condition that you keep an eye on him, Suggs.'

'Of course,' Sally said hastily. 'But you wouldn't let me ride Emperor.'

'Jim will take things slowly, and a nine-year-old child weighs next to nothing.' Kelly turned to Jim, giving him a stern look. 'When you get to the farm I want you to promise to give Emperor a good rub down and make sure that he's well cared for. Do you understand?'

'Yes, boss,' Jim said eagerly. 'I promise – cross me heart and hope to die.'

'And don't be late back, Suggs. Your friend, Josie, needs you and I'm not a nursemaid.'

Luke gave Sally a wary smile. 'I'll fetch the horses, it won't take long, and it will give you time to make your arrangements.' He strode off before Sally had a chance to speak.

She turned to Kelly. 'What was that all about? Surely you don't mind if I have a day off?'

'You're free to do as you please, Suggs.' Kelly reached for the curry comb and continued to groom Sultan.

'If you don't want me to bring my father and the boys here, just say so, Kelly. I can't read your mind.'

He turned back to look her in the eye. 'You have to let go of the past before you can face the future, Sally. Of course your dad and the little fellows can come here, but you have to move on. You're allowing your affection for Flower to rule your life.'

'Jim, go and clean yourself up if you're coming with me,' Sally said sharply. She waited until he was out of earshot before rounding on Kelly. 'I don't know what you mean. I'm not living in the past.'

He took her by the shoulders, giving her a gentle shake. 'Yes, you are, mavourneen. Your mother is with the angels and that horse is just an animal. She's the legacy your ma left you, and you should make use of that, but you can't build your life around a memory.'

'Are you telling me I should sell Flower to the highest bidder?'

'You must work that out for yourself, but when it comes to Mr Bridges, just remember he was sent here by Vasey. Is he interested in you and your talent as a rider, or has someone put him up to persuade you to part with Flower? Be careful, Sally. That's all I'm saying.'

'I think you're exaggerating,' Sally said crossly. 'You just want me to work for you because Pa was popular in this area and people trust me because of him.'

'Think what you like. I'm just speaking the truth.'

'Do you want to know what I think, Kelly? I think you are as bad as the rest of them. They all want something from me and you're no exception.' Sally walked off in the direction of the house. She would tell Pa what Kelly had said, but a cold shiver ran down her spine. She was assuming that her father had regained his senses, but what would she do if he was still the same as when she had last seen him? She went to warn Josie that Kelly was in a bad mood.

Chapter Sixteen

Gideon emerged from the farmhouse as they dismounted in the yard. The sheepdogs and Pippy bounded round them, licking Sally's hands as she bent down to make a fuss of them. Eddie and Benny almost bowled their big brother over in their eagerness to greet him.

'Gideon, this is Luke Bridges,' Sally said, trying not to laugh at the children's antics. 'Luke works at Astley's and he was kind enough to let me borrow one of their horses.'

Luke held out his hand. 'Pleased to meet you, Mr Lawrence. We have met before, but I don't suppose you remember me. I brought a group of our stable lads to the college where you were giving a lecture.'

'How do you do, Bridges?' Gideon eyed him thoughtfully. 'I remember the occasion, of course. Welcome to Hill Farm.' He beckoned to Bert, who was hovering in the background. 'Take the horses to the stable. You boys may go with him, but don't get in the way.'

Jim held on to Emperor. 'I'll see to my horse. I promised Kelly I'd look after him.'

'Good boy,' Gideon said with a nod of approval. 'Come to the house when you've done.'

'Mrs Wallace has been baking.' Eddie grabbed his brother's hand. 'She's made a currant cake and buns. She always cooks lovely grub, Jim, and we never go hungry. You should come and live here with us.'

'I've got man's work to do,' Jim said grandly.

'I've been riding Dobson,' Benny added. 'Him and Boney are the best of friends.'

'Off you go,' Sally said, giving each of them a brief hug. 'It's good to see you boys.' She watched them scamper off after Jim, who was leading Emperor towards the stables.

'Should I go with them?' Luke asked anxiously. 'I'm responsible for Astley's horses.'

'If you wish,' Gideon said casually. 'But Bert knows what he's doing, and Ted is there to keep an eye on him.'

'Thanks, but I'm responsible for the horses, so I'd better make sure they're all right.' Luke strode off, following the boys.

'How is Pa?' Sally asked eagerly. 'Has he recovered from the shock of the fire?'

'Not fully, I'm afraid, but he seems happiest when he's with the horses, and Arthur's been very good to him. He talks to Ted and they sit by the fire in the evening, smoking their pipes and reminiscing about the old days, when everything was much better and people were more polite. You know the sort of thing.'

'Yes, I do. Pa has seemed to live in the past since that terrible night. I should let him know that I'm here.'

'All in good time.' Gideon proffered his arm. 'Let's go inside, it's a bit blowy out here and it'll probably rain later. You can tell me all about your new friend over a cup of tea.'

Sally hesitated on the threshold, gazing at the well-ordered farmyard with geese and ducks waddling about amongst the hens, and the cockerel strutting amongst them with his tail feathers waving in the strong breeze. She had been born and bred in the city, but she felt at peace here in the country.

'Welcome, Sally.' Mrs Wallace enveloped her in a motherly hug. 'Come in out of the cold. I've a pot of tea brewing and the cakes are still warm from the oven. How are you, dear? You look a bit pale. Are you eating properly these days?'

Sally allowed herself to be led indoors. She felt an almost overwhelming desire to lean on Mrs Wallace's shoulder and be mothered, but she merely smiled and briefly returned the embrace. 'I'm quite well, thank you. But a cup of tea would be lovely and the boys have already told me about the cake and buns. They're obviously loving being here.'

'And I love having them, Sally. They've brightened up our lives and they keep us on our toes. We never know what they're going to get up to next, particularly little Benny. He's a young monkey, but he's also very sweet. I love both of them.'

Gideon laid his hand on her shoulder. 'Don't get too fond of them, Jane. You know they're only here temporarily.'

She shrugged and hurried over to the range. 'Well, I intend to enjoy every minute of being a mother – or perhaps I should say a grandmother – to those boys. Sit down, Sally dear, and I'll pour the tea.'

Gideon pulled up a chair for her and Sally sat down. The warmth of the welcome and the homely atmosphere were almost overwhelming. 'Thank you, Mrs Wallace.'

'It's Jane, my dear. We feel as though you're part of our little family, and your pa has settled in a treat. He's still a bit vague and he gets his words in a bit of a muddle, but otherwise he's doing very well.'

'I can't thank you enough for looking after him. I hope to take him back to London, if not today, then very soon. It all depends on whether he feels up to the journey.' Sally glanced at Gideon. 'And, of course, whether you're willing to allow him to stay here a bit longer, should he wish to do so.'

'Ted can remain here indefinitely, if that's what he wants,' Gideon said firmly. 'That goes for Flower, too.'

'How is Miss Appleton?' Sally gave him a searching

look. 'Has she got over the disappointment of failing to secure Flower for herself?'

Gideon chuckled. 'Cessy never gives up on anything.'

'Has she forgiven you for taking my side?'

'We declared a truce.'

'I'm glad.' Sally accepted a cup of tea from Mrs Wallace with a nod and a smile. 'I'd really like to see Flower. Is she getting enough exercise?'

'Ah, now! There's the thing.' Mrs Wallace glanced anxiously at Gideon. 'I beg your pardon, it's not my place to say.'

Sally looked from one to the other. 'What's going on?'

'Well, it's like this,' Gideon said awkwardly. 'I'm at the college all week and I wouldn't trust Bert to handle such a highly strung animal.'

'So who's been riding Flower?' Sally shook her head. 'Not Miss Appleton, surely?'

'Cessy is an excellent rider, Sally. She's not in your class, of course, but I'd trust her with any of my horses.'

'So she has her own way by default. I should have known this would happen.' Sally jumped to her feet. 'If she's ruined Flower's mouth I'll – well, I won't be responsible for my actions.' She ran from the kitchen, her bonnet flying as she raced across the yard to the stables, with Gideon following close behind her. He caught up with her as she was about to enter the building.

'Calm down, Sally. No harm has been done. I've examined Flower both before and after she's been ridden and she's absolutely fine. You have no need to worry on that score.'

Sally slipped past him, surprising Luke and Bert by her sudden appearance. 'Where is Flower? Where's my pa? He'll tell me the truth.'

Luke eyed her warily. 'Mr Suggs took the boys to see the donkey. He said he'd be back soon.'

Sally looked into each stall in turn and when she did not find Flower she rounded on Gideon. 'Where is she? Or need I ask?'

He held up his hands. 'Flower should be back here by now, but she spent last night at Fleet Hall, in the luxury of their stable block.'

'I trusted you, Gideon,' Sally said bitterly. 'I don't blame Pa because he barely knows what day it is, but you've let me down badly.'

'There was a sudden storm last evening. Cessy was caught in the downpour and she had to return home. She sent a stable boy with a note to say that Flower was being cared for by Jackson, and she would bring her back first thing this morning.'

'I can't believe that you allowed this to happen.'

'I'm sorry you've taken it this way, but I was doing what I thought was best for you and for Flower.'

'I'd better get on with my work,' Bert muttered and hurried away.

Luke cleared his throat noisily. 'Perhaps I should leave?'

'No, stay here. None of this is your fault,' Sally said hastily.

'I'll wait outside.' Luke took a step towards the doorway.

'I can see that this is awkward for you, Bridges.' Gideon patted him on the shoulder. 'If you return to the house, Mrs Wallace will look after you.'

Luke nodded wordlessly and hurried from the stable.

Sally glared at Gideon. 'It's almost midday and there's no sign of Flower. I'm going to ride over to Fleet Hall and get her.'

'Wait a minute.' Gideon barred her way. 'I'll come with you. I can handle Cessy.'

'Do what you like, but I'm going to fetch my horse. Cecily Appleton isn't going to get away with this.'

'She was doing me a favour, Sally.' Gideon caught her by the arm. 'Don't blame Cessy. Blame me, if you must. I know how much that animal means to you and I thought I was doing right by both of you.'

Kelly's words of warning came rushing back to her, and Sally bit her lip. Perhaps she was overreacting, but she was at a loss as to whom she could trust. It seemed that everyone she met had their sights set on owning Flower, by fair means or foul.

'Wait a minute.' Gideon stepped outside into the yard. 'She's returned. Cessy has brought Flower back.'

Sally shielded her eyes against the low winter sun, and some of her anger dissipated at the sight of her beloved horse. Flower seemed none the worse for her experience, and although it was difficult to admit, even to herself, Sally could see that Cecily knew exactly what she was doing when it came to handling a highly strung animal. Jackson himself had accompanied his mistress and he was leading a second horse. He dismounted and lifted Cecily from the saddle.

'Before you say anything,' Cecily shook out the folds of her tailored riding habit, 'I apologise for being late, but I was unexpectedly detained.'

'You had no right to exercise my horse without my permission,' Sally said stiffly.

'I put Flower's welfare first.' Gideon met Sally's angry gaze with a steady look. 'Perhaps you ought to thank Cecily. She didn't have to put herself out in this manner.'

'I am not in the wrong here,' Sally protested.

Cecily handed the reins to Gideon. 'Jackson will swop over the saddles if you give him a moment.'

Sally examined Flower's mouth and she ran her hand over the animal's sleek coat. 'She seems all right.'

'Gideon would not have allowed just anyone to exercise Flower.' Cecily slipped her hand through the crook of Sally's arm. 'We need to speak privately, I think. Come with me.'

'There really is no need, Cessy,' Gideon protested.

She held up her hand. 'Keep out of this, Gideon. This is between Sally and me.'

He retreated into the stable.

'What did you want to say?' Sally demanded. 'You didn't exercise Flower for my benefit, I know that.'

'No, I didn't do it for you. In fact, at one time I could have scratched your eyes out and enjoyed the pleasure, but now I realise I've behaved badly.'

'What brought this about?'

'I'm going to be honest with you, and I want you to be just as candid with me.'

'I can do that.'

'I love Gideon. I've always loved him since I was a child. I'm not interested in marrying a rich man because, one day, I'll inherit more than enough money to keep me in luxury for the rest of my life.'

'Lucky you.' Sally had a vision of Josie lying on the worn sofa in Kelly's parlour, wearing clothes from the dolly shop. Her prospects were so different from those of this beautiful woman who seemed to be asking her for help.

'I truly thought he was going to propose on my birthday, but you came along and ruined everything. I think he's in love with you, Sally, and it's breaking my heart.'

Sally stared at her in surprise. 'I'm sorry, but I think you're wrong. Gideon has been very kind to me, but there's nothing between us.'

'He's taken your father into his home and those scruffy little brats. Why do you think he did that, if it wasn't to earn your good opinion? Gideon is reserved when it comes to expressing emotion, but he would have been mine if you hadn't come along.'

'Why would anyone choose me above you? I mean that, Cecily. I assume I may call you that since we're being so honest with each other.'

'I don't know what he sees in you. Maybe he's sorry for you, I can't think of any other reason, but I'm asking you to leave him alone. I'll give you money to help you . . .'

Sally pulled free from Cecily's grasp. 'I don't want your money. It's not that I don't need it, but if you love him so much that you're prepared to open your heart to me, I feel for you. I'll take my family, including Flower, and we'll return to London.'

'You'll promise me that you won't see Gideon again?'

'I won't go out of my way to see him.'

'But if he tries to contact you?' Cecily said anxiously. 'He might, you know.'

'I'll tell him I'm not interested. I can't do any more than that. But you must also promise me something.'

'Anything, what is it?'

'That you will not try to take Flower from me again.'

Cecily's laughter echoed around the farm buildings. 'I promise.'

'We won't say anything about this to Gideon,' Sally said urgently. 'I'm sure you're wrong, but I don't want him to think that I'm one of those scheming women, who are only out for what they can get.'

'I agree entirely. You fulfil your part of the bargain and leave the rest to me.' Cecily tossed her golden curls and her eyes sparkled with excitement. 'We'd better not look too friendly or Gideon will become suspicious.'

'I agree.' Sally adopted a serious expression as she marched into the stable. 'That's sorted out. Miss Appleton and I have come to an understanding.'

Gideon's frown deepened as he glanced at Cecily, who was standing in the doorway. 'Thank you again, Cessy. I really appreciate what you've done.'

'It was no trouble,' Cecily said graciously. 'I enjoyed riding Flower, but she belongs to Sally, and that's how it should be. I have to go now, but will I see you at dinner tonight? I believe Papa challenged you to a game of billiards, which you'll win, of course. You always do.' Flashing him a brilliant smile, Cecily walked out into the pale sunshine.

'Why do you keep that poor woman dangling?' Sally stared at Gideon, who was looking confused, and she could bear it no longer. 'You must know how she feels about you.'

'I told you before that there's nothing romantic between us. Why won't you believe me?'

'Because, to be honest, you'd be mad to throw up an opportunity like that. Cecily cares for you, Gideon. I wasn't supposed to tell you outright, but she loves you, and whether you admit it or not, you've been encouraging her to think that you care for her, too.'

'I'm very fond of Cessy, but she's more like a sister. It's you I love, Sally. I think I fell for you that snowy night when we bumped into each other, and you scolded me for ruining your supper.'

Sally stared at him in astonishment. 'You love me?'

'Dammit, yes. I've done everything I can to demonstrate how much I care for you, but you seem to be living in another world to the rest of us. All you can think of is that horse.'

'That's not true. I worry about Pa, and the boys, and now Josie needs someone to take care of her. What am I supposed to do?'

Gideon's expression melted into a rueful smile. 'That's you all over, my darling. I've been afraid to say anything in case I spoke out of turn. I know you're fond of that ne'er-do-well, Kelly.'

'I am not fond of Kelly. I work with him because I have to earn my living, but most of the time I could kill him.'

'I wish I sparked off such emotion in you, Sally. The only time you come to me is when you need help. I just keep hoping you'll feel something deeper than friendship, but you always seem to have your emotions under control, so I don't know what you're thinking.'

'I had no idea that you felt like this.' Sally stared at him, seeing a shy and reserved man, who normally appeared to be in charge of every situation, but now he was exposing his raw feelings, and it was obviously painful for him. 'I'm sorry if I've caused you pain, Gideon. I am very fond of you. You're a good man.'

He uttered a bark of laughter, but there was no humour in the sound. 'That's not what any man in love wants to hear.'

'I'm truly sorry. I don't know what else to say.'

He moved closer so that she could feel the heat from his body, although he refrained from touching her. 'Think about it. If you marry me you'll have a loving home and a husband who adores you. Your father can live with us, and Josie can have the cottage with the boys, if that's what they all want. You can keep your horse and you can ride her every day. You need never work again.'

'But I don't love you, Gideon. It would be unfair to accept such a generous offer when I can't return the affection you obviously have for me. I have nothing to offer you, so why can't you feel that way for Cecily? If you marry her, your farm will be secure for ever, and she would make you a wonderful wife.'

He turned away. 'Unfortunately the heart doesn't work that way, Sally.'

'I'm sorry, Gideon. I don't know what else to say. I'd better leave now and I'll take Pa and the boys with me.'

'There's no need to do anything so rash. Nothing has changed.' Gideon turned back slowly, meeting her gaze with a hint of a smile, but she could see tears in his eyes. 'You don't have to go. We can still be friends and your father and the boys can remain here as long as they like.'

'I doubt if that would work. I think it's time for us to return to London.'

The stricken look in Gideon's eyes made Sally want to give him a hug, but she knew that to weaken in any way would be fatal. Gideon deserved a wife who could love him unreservedly. As to herself – she had yet to find her way – but the path was out there, somewhere.

Despite Sally's attempts to persuade him to return to London, Ted was adamant that he wanted to remain at the farm. The boys proved equally determined to continue enjoying the benefits of living on the farm, and Jim opted to stay with his brothers. Sally's heart ached as she said goodbye to them all, but she had to be practical and she had to earn her living and theirs.

Sally returned to London later that day, taking Flower with her. Luke took the borrowed horses to Astley's, while Sally settled Flower in Kelly's stable. Exhausted both mentally and physically, she joined Kelly in the kitchen.

'What's up with you?' Kelly gave her a knowing look. 'You've been very quiet since you came back from Highgate. Don't say nothing, because I know you too well, Sally Suggs.'

She sighed, turning away from the range with a pan of milk she had been warming for Josie. 'It was all a bit difficult today. I'll be fine tomorrow.'

Kelly pulled up a chair and sat down at the kitchen table. 'D'you want to talk about it?'

'Not really.'

'That means you had a falling out with Lawrence.' Kelly's blue eyes narrowed. 'If he's upset you, I'll have words with the veterinary gentleman.'

'No, he didn't say anything wrong – the very opposite in fact.'

'He declared his undying love for you, then?'

'Stop it, Kelly. You're not funny.' Sally poured the milk into a mug. 'I'll take this upstairs to Josie.'

'You can't get out of it that easily, mavourneen. I want to know what he's done to put that look on your face. You went off happily enough this morning, but now you look as if you've got the cares of the world on your shoulders.'

'It was hard leaving Pa there, but he seemed so settled and he still thinks that we live above the stables in Paradise Row. He can't remember the fire.'

'Maybe that's a good thing, and if Lawrence is happy to have him there to help with the horses, why not leave him a while longer?'

'I know, you're probably right. But Jim was desperate to stay with his brothers, and Mrs Wallace simply loves pampering them.'

'So what's the matter with that?'

'Their father might find out where they are. He could report them as being kidnapped.'

'I think the police have got Fred Cotton's measure by now. They'd probably sling him out.'

'I hope so. Maybe I'm worrying too much.' Sally poured hot milk into a mug. 'This will be cold if I don't take it upstairs right away.'

'Never mind that.' Kelly reached out and snatched the mug from her hand. 'Now, take a seat and tell me what's bothering you. Josie can wait for five minutes.' He pressed her down on the nearest chair. 'Tell me what that idiot said to take the roses from your cheeks.'

'You are so nosy, Kelly.' Sally tried to make a joke of it, but tears filled her eyes and she turned away. 'Cecily Appleton has been exercising Flower.'

'Is that all?'

'Not exactly. Flower wasn't there when I arrived, and when Cecily brought her back I was angry. Then Cecily took me aside and told me that she was in love with Gideon, but she thought he wanted me, not her.'

'A man of taste, and a philanderer as well. I almost admire him.'

'That would be typical of you. You never take anything seriously.'

'Try me. So what happened next?'

'I wasn't very tactful. I told Gideon that he ought to be nicer to Cecily and she would make him a wonderful wife. She's rich and beautiful and she loves him – what more could a man want?'

'He might want the woman he loves more than anything in the world, mavourneen. And judging by your expression, that is what he told you, only it's you that Lawrence wants and not the wealthy lady.'

'How did you know?'

'So I'm right. If he made advances to you that were unwelcome, just tell me and I'll go to Highgate and call him out – pistols at dawn.'

'You wouldn't,' Sally said, laughing.

'I'd do anything to make you smile again, mavourneen.' He held up his hand. 'I know – I'm to stop calling you that because it annoys you, and I will. I promise never to call you mavourneen again.'

'Do you know, I don't think I mind it after all, Kelly. It has a safe and friendly ring to it and I need a friend.'

'So that's why you decided to bring Flower with you?

Sally eyed him warily. 'What do you mean?'

'You'd rather risk losing her than having to deal with a love-struck farmer.'

'I wouldn't put it like that exactly.'

'But it's true nonetheless.'

'In a way, yes. But I didn't want to feel beholden to Gideon.'

'Is that so?' Kelly rose to his feet and picked up the mug of hot milk. 'You'd best take this up to Josie. There's a nice thick skin formed on top of the milk.'

'I hate that,' Sally said, rising slowly to take it from him. 'I'm not sure what I've told you, Kelly, but please ignore what I said. I'm just tired.'

'I remember every word you've ever said to me, Suggs. Now get away upstairs and take yourself to your bed before Josie makes any more demands on your attention. I think I'll have to stand at the end of the queue at this rate.'

'You'll always be at the head of any queue, Kelly. That's just who you are.'

'Really?' He leaned over and kissed her on the cheek. 'Now go to bed before I forget I'm a gentleman.'

'You always make me laugh, Kelly.'

'Isn't that the very devil? Will you never take me seriously?'

Chapter Seventeen

Josie recovered quickly thanks to the loving care given her by Sally, and the generosity of Kelly, who saw to it that there was always good food on the table. Sally had been struggling to keep up the round on her own, mainly because she was very successful at getting people to part with unwanted items that also had some street value. The difficulties arose when it came to sheer physical strength, and that was when Sally missed Jim. He might be a child of nine, but he had been brought up in a hard school and he was as strong as she was, if not stronger. Between them they had managed to heft the heavy articles onto the cart and unload them at the end of the day.

'I need to find work,' Josie said one fine spring morning when Sally was rushing her breakfast in order to get an early start. 'I could help you on the cart.'

Sally stopped what she was doing to stare at her friend. 'You? But you're in the family way. You can't lift heavy things.'

'Not on my own, but the two of us could manage.' Josie grinned broadly. 'And there's usually a hefty bloke around who'd be willing to assist. A little flattery goes a long way.'

'I suppose we could give it a try. At least you could help me for a few months yet. After all, you're not showing very much.'

'And if I got a job working anywhere they'd expect me to do the same as everyone else. If I couldn't keep up I'd get the sack, so I'd be out of work anyway.'

'You're right,' Sally said thoughtfully. 'Let's try it and see how we get on.'

'There's one condition.'

'What's that?'

'I want to ring the bell.'

Sally chuckled. 'All right, and you can call out, too. You've got a voice that could shatter glass.'

'Sticks and stones, Sal. Give me five minutes and I'll be ready for a day's work.' Josie hurried from the room, leaving Sally to wonder whether she had just made the greatest mistake of her life, or had begun a successful business partnership.

She was about to leave the house, having almost given up on Josie, when she met Luke in the entrance hall.

'Good morning, Miss Suggs.'

'Good morning, Luke, and it's Sally. There's no need for formality.'

'I was wondering if you'd be interested in putting Flower to good use.'

Sally eyed him suspiciously. 'What do you mean by that?'

'Nothing bad, I promise. It's just that she's a beautiful animal and you are obviously a very accomplished rider. You're wasting your talents.'

'What do you suggest I do?'

He lowered his voice, glancing over his shoulder, as if afraid of eavesdroppers. 'Vasey told me that you had been interested in working for Astley's.'

The mention of Vasey's name made Sally wary. 'I was, briefly.'

'Well, as I said when we first met, I look for talent for them and for circus owners. Would you consider doing one or two performances a week?'

'I haven't worked out an act, Luke. I've never done anything like that.'

'But you know what your mother did. Isn't that so?'

'Yes, of course. I watched her rehearse and I saw many of her performances. I also saw her fall and break her back.'

'We take risks every day. Will you at least think about it?'

Sally glanced up as Josie came downstairs at breakneck speed. 'I'll think about it, but now I have to go.'

'I'll speak to you again,' Luke said eagerly. 'Maybe this evening?'

'Yes, perhaps.' Sally beckoned to Josie. 'Come on. I've been waiting for you for ages. You'll have to do better.' She hurried from the house with Josie clattering along behind her.

'What did he want?'

'Nothing. He's got the idea I want to perform at Astley's with Flower.'

'Do you?'

Sally quickened her pace, heading for the stables. 'I used to, but I don't know now. I mean we've got a roof over our heads, but it isn't very practical to bring Pa here. I don't want to lodge with Kelly for ever.'

'You could marry him, and the house would be yours as well as his.'

'Josie Bates, you've got a one-track mind.'

'If you don't want him, maybe I'll marry him.'

Sally came to a halt outside the stable doors. She shot a sideways glance at Josie, thinking she was joking as usual, but then she realised that her friend was serious. Somehow the idea of Josie and Kelly as a couple did not appeal to her.

'Do you know how to tack up a horse, Josie?' Sally unlocked the door and stepped inside.

Josie's eyes widened in horror. 'Me? No, of course not. I'm scared of horses – big nasty things with yellow teeth and iron hoofs.'

'I can see you're going to be a great help.' Sally

sighed and went about the business of harnessing Sultan and getting him between the traces. It was going to be a long day.

However, once they had set off and were doing the rounds of the streets that Kelly had allocated to them, Josie proved surprisingly adept at calling out and encouraging people to part with their goods. She had the right sort of banter to make people laugh and she encouraged them to rush back into their houses or factories to sort out more 'rubbish' that she and Sally could take away.

At the end of the day, Kelly seemed surprised to see Sally and Josie together, but he was genuinely appreciative of their combined efforts to collect, sort and bag their spoils. Roper was also impressed, but in a different way, and he leered at Josie, making lewd remarks until she set him down with a sharp retort that made him retire to his corner, glowering at her beneath his shaggy eyebrows. However, when it came to paying them, Rags was surprisingly generous.

'As we've all done so well today, I'll treat you both to an eel pie and mash, with plenty of liquor,' Kelly said as they returned to their vehicles.

'That would be lovely.' Sally climbed onto the driver's seat.

Josie turned her head away. 'If you don't mind I'll go home and have some bread and milk.'

'Are you all right?' Sally asked anxiously.

'Yes, Sal. Just tired, that's all. But the thought of eel pie makes me feel sick.'

'You used to love it.'

'Don't talk about it, please.' Josie leaned back, closing her eyes. 'You take advantage of Kelly's offer. I'll have an early night.'

Kelly drew his cart alongside the one that Sally was driving. 'Is she all right, Suggs?'

'Yes, don't worry. Josie's a bit tired, but I'll hold you to your offer of pie and mash.'

'We'll go as soon as the horses are settled down for the night. Walk on, Emperor.'

Sally waited until Kelly had driven off before flicking the reins to encourage Sultan to follow. 'Are you sure you're all right, Josie. It hasn't been too much for you, has it?'

'No, never. I'm as tough as the next person, but it's been a long day. I'll get used to it, so don't worry about me.'

'Are you sure she's up to it, mavourneen?' Kelly set a plate of hot eel pie, creamy mashed potato and liquor laced with parsley in front of Sally. He sat opposite her, his own plate untouched. 'Josie's in a delicate condition, as my dear departed mammy would have said.'

'There's nothing delicate about Josie. She's tired, and that's natural, but she's worked really hard today. You must admit we did well.'

Kelly picked up his fork and stuck it into the golden crust. 'Yes, I have to agree, but do you think you can continue like that?'

'I don't see why not. Josie and I have to support our families, and that makes it necessary for us to work hard. After all, what alternatives are there for women like Josie and me? We work hard or we end up on the street or in the workhouse.'

'Or you marry a man who will love and protect you for the rest of your life.' Kelly speared a chunk of eel and popped it into his mouth.

'That only happens in fairy tales or the gothic novels that Ma used to read.'

'I thought you would be a romantic at heart, mavourneen.'

'I don't know about that, but this pie is delicious. Thank you Kelly.'

He laughed and shook his head.

They finished their meal and Sally was about to wrap her shawl round her shoulders when she spotted Luke walking past the window. She had a feeling that Kelly did not like Luke Bridges, and she said nothing, but she was curious. There seemed to be no obvious reason for Kelly's antipathy to his latest lodger, and he offered no explanation when Sally questioned him.

'I'll see you home,' Kelly said as they left the pie and eel shop. 'But I have to go out again.'

'Really? Have you got a lady friend, Kelly?'

'Would you care if I had?'

'Of course not. It's your affair, not mine.'

'You disappoint me, mavourneen. I thought you might be heartbroken.' He chuckled and brushed a stray strand of hair back from her forehead with a careless flick of his index finger. 'I'm just teasing you. It is business, as it happens.'

Sally shrugged. 'Business or pleasure, it's all the same to me, Kelly.'

They walked on in companionable silence and parted outside the house. Sally was surprised to find Luke waiting in the hall.

He glanced anxiously over her shoulder. 'Where's Kelly?'

'He went out again. Did you want to speak to him?'

'No, this concerns you. I saw you in the pie and eel shop with Kelly, but I know he wouldn't have welcomed the intrusion, so I walked past.'

'Kelly is my landlord and we work together. He isn't my keeper.'

'No, of course not. Might we speak in private?' Luke added as the front door opened and Dolly breezed in, accompanied by a strong smell of fried fish.

'Good evening, love,' she said, beaming at Sally. 'And to you, Luke, my boy. What have you two been up to?'

'Nothing.' Sally felt herself blushing at the inference. 'We just arrived home at the same time.'

'I believe you.' Dolly winked at Luke and headed for the stairs. 'Night, night.'

'She's all right when you get to know her,' Luke said hastily. 'She speaks without thinking.'

'It doesn't matter. What did you want to say to me?'

'I need an answer to the question I put to you this morning.'

'I'm still thinking about it, but I'm really not sure it's a good idea.'

'But you could do it. I really need you to agree.'

'Why me, Luke? There must be plenty of riders who would be more than willing to oblige.'

'Maybe, but you are your mother's daughter. You would draw in the crowds.'

Sally eyed him suspiciously. 'Did Orrin Vasey put you up to this? He wants to get his hands on Flower, as do many others.'

'Everyone in the business knows Vasey, but I have as little to do with him as possible. I get commission from Astley's for introducing new acts, but that's all.'

'I said I'd think about it,' Sally said tiredly. 'It's been a long day.'

'All right, but I need an answer tomorrow, or I'll have to look elsewhere. They pay well for the right performers.'

'Good night, Luke. I promise to let you know in the morning.' Sally headed for the stairs and the peace and quiet of her room.

She was exhausted, but the opportunity to earn good money and to put Flower through her paces in front of enthusiastic audiences was overwhelming. If she accepted Luke's offer she would be following in her mother's footsteps, and Pa would be proud of her. Moreover, she would have the opportunity to rent somewhere they could call home. She could offer Josie a safe place to have her baby and, if the Cotton boys still needed shelter, she would take them in as well. She drifted off to sleep with happy thoughts in her head.

Next morning she knew she must face reality and come to a decision. She found Kelly in the kitchen, drinking tea. 'You're up bright and early,' she said, making an effort to sound cheery.

'What's the matter with you, Suggs? You look as though you've been up half the night.'

Sally filled a cup with tea and took a seat at the table. 'What would you say if I decided to undertake a couple of performances a week at Astley's?'

Kelly's eyes narrowed and his smile faded. 'Who's been getting at you this time? Not Vasey, I think, so it must be Bridges.'

'It doesn't matter who asked me. I could earn enough money to provide a home for my father and myself. We wouldn't have to be dependent on you.' The moment the words left her lips she knew she had said the wrong thing.

Kelly jumped to his feet. 'Don't be a fool, Suggs. These men are after your horse, and they don't want to have her as a pet or even a circus performer – she has a valuable bloodline and that's what they're after. They can't get Andalusians for love nor money, and Flower would be the answer to their prayers. I knew that Bridges wasn't to be trusted – I had a feeling the moment we first met.'

Sally stared at him in amazement. 'How can you say such things? Flower is a beautiful creature. Anyone would be proud to own her. Miss Appleton was desperate to have Flower in her stables.'

Kelly stared at her as if she were speaking a foreign language. 'Haven't you understood anything I just said? Miss Appleton was probably the only one who really appreciated Flower, but the others just want to make money out of her.'

'But my mother performed at Astley's,' Sally said dazedly. 'She was a star performer.'

'And what happened to your mother, Sally?' Kelly leaned closer to her, his eyes dark with concern.

'That's cruel. You know she had a terrible accident, but that won't happen to me. I'm not as daring as she was.'

'They'll chew you up and spit you out,' Kelly said angrily. 'Can't you see? This is a ploy to get you in their power. I suspect Vasey is at the bottom of this and Bridges is merely a cat's paw. I'll soon sort him out.'

'What are you going to do?' Sally rose to her feet and followed him out of the kitchen. 'Please, Kelly. Leave this to me. I can handle my own affairs.'

He brushed off her restraining hand. 'Stay there, Suggs. I'll deal with this.' He strode along the passage that opened out into the entrance hall.

Sally hurried after him, but she was too late to utter a warning. Luke was standing at the foot of the stairs, shrugging on his overcoat. He looked up at the sound of footsteps, but his expression changed when he saw Kelly advancing on him purposefully.

'What's the matter?' Luke backed away, but Kelly had him by the collar and he marched him towards the front door.

'Your tenancy is ended, Bridges. Your property will be left on the porch for you to collect later.'

'You can't do this, Kelly. What's the reason for such behaviour?'

'It's my house and I don't want you in it. Leave Miss Suggs alone. She's not interested in your propositions.' Kelly opened the front door and gave Luke a shove that sent him stumbling down the steps to the pavement.

'You can't speak for Sally. I want to hear it from her lips,' Luke protested.

Sally pushed past Kelly. 'Just answer me one question, Mr Bridges.'

'Yes, of course, only keep that madman away from me.'

'Are you working with Orrin Vasey? Just say yes or no.'

'We're both employed by Astley's. I can't say any more, but that doesn't mean . . .'

Kelly cut him short by slamming the door. 'You see, Suggs. He couldn't deny it, and I've seen too much of the way his sort works to be taken in by him. I knew there was something wrong when I agreed to let him take a room, but I never connected him to you. Now I know better.'

'But that's supposition, Kelly. You still haven't got proof.'

'How much do you want?' Kelly laid his hand on her arm. 'Come back to the kitchen and have something to eat before we go out on our rounds. Don't be fooled by Bridges or Vasey; they don't want to show off Flower to the world – they want money, big money, Sally. Enjoy Flower for what she means to you, mavourneen. She's part of your past and hopefully part of your future, too.'

Sally gazed at him in surprise. 'I didn't know you were so deep-thinking, Kelly.'

'You don't really know me at all, mavourneen.' He slipped his arm around her shoulders. 'Let's have some breakfast and then we'll go out on our rounds.'

'I will, but first I'd better go and see if Josie's awake. I don't think she felt too well last night.' Sally headed for the stairs. She was concerned for her friend, but she needed time to think. Despite her reservations, she knew what Kelly said was true, and it was disturbing as well as frightening.

She found Josie awake and in the middle of getting dressed.

'What's the matter?' Josie asked anxiously. 'You look upset.'

Sally perched on the edge of the bed. Telling Josie what had just happened helped her to clarify her own feelings. 'I was furious at first,' she said, recalling Luke's outraged expression. 'But I think Kelly could be right. It's not just Orrin Vasey who was after

Flower, it was Harvey Grindle, Rags Roper and now Luke Bridges. At least Cecily Appleton wanted to have her for personal reasons. She didn't want to breed from her.'

'Were you tempted to take up Luke's offer? I mean, do you see yourself as a star at Astley's?'

Sally shook her head. 'It was a childhood dream, but I'll do anything I need to earn enough to support my father.'

'I suppose I'll have to start thinking about someone other than myself soon.' Josie attempted to do up the last button on her blouse and failed. 'I'll be as big as a house soon, but I'm starving. I don't suppose Kelly is downstairs cooking bacon and eggs, is he?'

'He is a very good cook, as it happens.'

'We never had the luxury of a range, but I am very efficient with the toasting fork. I can burn bread better than anyone in Paradise Row.'

Sally stood up, smiling. 'You are the best tonic, Josie. You always know what to say to make things better.'

Josie coiled her hair in a knot at the back of her head and secured it with several long hairpins. 'I've had enough practice, love. You should try living with my ma. If you don't see the funny side of things, you'd end up in Colney Hatch.'

Sally linked arms with her. 'Come on, let's get a good start to the day. Maybe I've had a lucky escape, or rather Flower has.'

'I think so, too. But where does that leave you,

Sal? Will you keep her in Kelly's stable, eating her head off?'

Sally turned to give her a steady look. 'What are you saying?'

'I don't know anything about horses, but if I was Flower I wouldn't want to be shut up in a stuffy stable for hours on end, with the occasional trot around Regent's Park. It must feel like prison.'

'I hadn't thought about it like that,' Sally said reluctantly. 'I've been thinking about what I want.'

'Of course you have, and that's natural. You've got your pa to consider and a living to earn.'

'I suppose you're right. I'll think about it, Josie. But we have to work today so we'd better get some food inside us.'

The early morning sun had been banished by heavy clouds and it rained steadily all day. The streets were awash with water from blocked drains and horse dung, rubbish and bits of straw combined to make stinking mud. People were reluctant to venture out on the streets with their unwanted items, and the factory doors were firmly closed. They finished early and, despite the steady drizzle, Sally decided to exercise Flower. Kelly shrugged and told her she was mad to go out and get soaked for the second time that day, and Josie was equally discouraging. Sally ignored their pleas to reconsider her decision and she took off her wet working clothes, exchanging them for the well-worn riding habit that she had worn to Fleet Hall.

She returned to the stables and tacked up Flower, in preparation for a ride to Regent's Park. Flower was eager to be off and Sally had to rein her in as they headed towards the bridge over the canal and the outer circle of the park. There was too much traffic to allow anything more energetic than a brief canter, but it was good to see trees and grass. Sheep grazed contentedly, although their once-white wool was now blackened with soot and streaked with rain. Sally longed to allow Flower the freedom to gallop, but they both had to make do with a brisk trot.

It was dark by the time they set off for home, and the rain had finally stopped. Sally's riding habit was soaked through, but the exercise had kept her warm, and she was looking forward to sharing supper with Kelly and Josie. As Flower obediently slowed to a walk and they crossed the bridge, they entered an unlit area. Sally was suddenly aware of a figure leaping out in front of them, and a man grabbed Flower's reins, snatching them from Sally's hand.

'Let go,' Sally cried angrily. She raised her crop, but her assailant seized it and dragged her from the saddle. She caught a whiff of his sour breath, laced with stale alcohol. 'Who are you?'

'You know me all right, Miss High and Mighty. You've taken my nippers from me, but now I'm in charge. I'm going to take the thing that you value most.' He gave Sally a vicious shove that sent her sprawling onto the muck and mud. 'See how you like it.'

She scrambled to her feet. 'Your boys are safe and well, Fred Cotton. They're living in the country with a loving family, who are kind to them. They don't want to come back to you and the vile way you treated them.'

'They belong to me, as this nag belonged to you. But no more, miss. She's going to someone who'll pay me a fortune for me services.'

'You'll go to prison for this, Cotton. If you steal my horse you'll never see your boys again.' Sally scrambled to her feet and lunged at Cotton, but he held her off with one hand.

'With the money I'm getting I'll be off to somewhere the cops will never find me.'

'You won't get that far.' Sally struggled with him, but he was too strong for her, and with one mighty swipe of his ham-like fist he caught her on the jaw. She stumbled and fell into a pit of oblivion.

Chapter Eighteen

Sally could hear disembodied voices floating somewhere above her, but she could neither see nor move.

'Ain't that Ted Suggs's girl?'

'She's a totter, just like her old man.'

'What's she doing here?'

'Do something, Pa. Fetch some water from the canal and splash her face.'

'Where are the coppers when you need them?'

'Look, Pa. She's coming round.'

Sally opened her eyes and found herself staring into the earnest face of a young girl.

'What happened?' Sally attempted to raise herself, but a sharp pain in her head caused her to fall back onto the wet cobblestones.

'Looks like you was robbed, love.' A man leaned over her, shaking his head.

'My horse.' Sally reached out to clutch his hand. 'He stole my horse.'

'It ain't uncommon hereabouts, love. Where's your pa these days? I haven't seen him on his rounds.'

A woman, who had been standing behind the young girl, stepped forward and helped Sally to a sitting position. 'You lot ain't got the sense you was born with. The girl's soaking wet and probably got a cracked skull.'

Sally raised her hand to her swollen face. 'I'm all right, missis. Just a bit sore. Did someone send for a constable?'

'Whoever done this to you is long gone, love. We'd best get you home before you catch your death of cold.' The woman looked up at the man. 'Help me get her to her feet.' She turned her attention back to Sally. 'Where d'you live now, dear? I heard that your place burned to the ground. Someone has got it in for you and yours, I'd say.'

Between them, with the young girl running on ahead to forewarn Kelly, the woman and her husband supported Sally one on either side. Their progress was slow but, by the time they reached the house, Sally was able to walk unaided. Josie opened the door, uttering a cry of distress when she saw Sally's dishevelled state and bruised face. Kelly was not far behind Josie, and, despite Sally's protests, he swept her up in his arms.

'Thanks for bringing her home, mate. I owe you and your missis a couple of drinks in the pub.'

'I dunno who attacked her, but she was out cold.' The man slipped his arm around his wife's shoulders. 'I'd keep an eye on her if I was you. Someone bears a grudge and she might not get away so easily next time.'

Josie threw her hands up in horror. 'Get her inside quick, Kelly. There's a madman on the loose.'

Kelly carried a protesting Sally into the house.

'Put me down,' she said crossly. 'I'm all right now.'

He dumped her unceremoniously on her feet and she staggered, reaching out to steady herself by clutching the newel post.

'Really?' Kelly shook his head. 'I don't believe you, Suggs.'

Sally slumped onto the bottom tread, holding her head in her hands. 'He took Flower,' she sobbed. 'I'll never see her again.'

'Don't take on so.' Josie threw herself down beside Sally, wrapping her arms around her. 'Kelly will find Flower. He has contacts everywhere.'

'I wouldn't say that, but I'll do everything in my power to bring her back to you, Suggs.' Kelly kneeled on the floor beside her. 'Don't despair. Just tell me who did this to you.'

Sally raised her head, wiping her eyes on her wet sleeve. 'It was Fred Cotton. He said he was going to get a lot of money for Flower. He did it in revenge because I took his boys to safety.'

'Is he holding Flower to ransom in return for his sons?' Josie asked gently.

'I don't think he wants them back. It's money he wants, and he's going to sell Flower to the highest bidder. Maybe he's been put up to it by Vasey.'

'Or Harvey Grindle,' Josie added. 'Or even Rags Roper.'

'I never trusted Luke Bridges. I wouldn't be surprised if he had a hand in this.' Kelly rose to his feet. 'Come on, Suggs. You can't sit around in those wet clothes. Let Josie help you to your room, and I'll make you a cup of cocoa. How about you, Josie. Can I interest you in a cup of Kelly's special?'

'Yes, please. I love cocoa.' Josie helped Sally to her feet. 'The sooner you're warm and dry, the better. Leave things to Kelly, he'll know what to do.'

'Fred Cotton might ill-treat Flower. He's a brute.'

'I can't argue with that, but it wouldn't profit him to harm Flower. She's much too valuable. You said that yourself, so be sensible and let us pamper you for a change. You've been looking after me, so now it's my turn.'

Next morning Sally awakened with a swollen jaw and a black eye. Kelly took one look at her and sent her back to bed, refusing to believe her when she said she felt well enough to work. Josie backed him up and offered to accompany Kelly on his round. He accepted this too rapidly to salve Sally's wounded pride, and she returned to her room in a rebellious mood.

Josie brought her a cup of tea and a bowl of

bread and milk. 'I didn't think you could manage to eat toast,' she said hastily. 'Don't look at it like that, Sal. I sprinkled it with sugar, so it will taste lovely.'

'It's baby food,' Sally protested. 'I might look a sight, but I feel fine. I want to go out and look for Flower.'

Josie perched on the edge of the bed. 'Listen to me, for once. You've had a nasty shock and you cracked your head on the ground. Kelly says you have to rest and I agree with him. We'll do everything we can to find Flower. Kelly's going to put the word out, so the best you can do is to stay in bed and get well.' She stood up. 'And eat your breakfast. You'll need all your strength if we're going to find Flower and get her back.'

Reluctantly Sally spooned the mushy mixture into her mouth and swallowed. 'See, I'm doing what I'm told.'

Josie hesitated in the doorway. 'Probably for the first time in your life, if I know you, Sal Suggs.' She winked and waved as she left the room.

Sally put the bowl on the small table beside her bed, convinced that one more mouthful would make her sick. She waited until Josie's footsteps died away before throwing back the covers and getting out of bed. A wave of dizziness made her sit down abruptly, but when it passed she rose more slowly and put on her clothes. She opened the door and listened for sounds of movement in the house.

Isaac Worthington would have left for his job at the railway station early that morning. Dolly and Meg both worked until late evening, and they would still be asleep, leaving Sally free to leave the house unseen. She put on her bonnet, tying the ribbons under her chin to hide the swelling and, having wrapped her shawl around her shoulders, she made her way slowly downstairs and out into the street.

It was a bright day with gusty winds tossing small white clouds across the sky, and no sign of rain. She hesitated for a moment. There was little or no chance that she could find Flower on her own, but Fred Cotton used to work at the Veterinary College, and someone there might have an idea where he would have taken Flower. When she thought about it logically and without a burst of pent-up emotion, she reasoned that neither Vasey nor Grindle would take Flower openly. Therefore Fred must have had a place in mind where Flower could pass unnoticed until the deal was done. She took a deep breath and set off for the college. Every bone in her body ached after the brutal assault, but she had a purpose now and she ignored the pain, stepping out as if nothing had happened.

Armstrong greeted her warmly, and if he noticed her facial injuries he was too polite to say anything. His expression hardened when she mentioned Fred Cotton's name, and he shook his head in answer to her questions.

'Fred left here in disgrace, miss. I wouldn't know how he finds the money to support his drinking habit, but suffice to say, I'm sure he's up to no good.'

'I just want to know where he might have hidden Flower,' Sally said in desperation. 'I know he plans to sell her, because he told me so. He can't have gone far because, if I remember correctly, he was on foot.'

'He can ride, miss. He used to get on a horse whenever he got a chance. Mind you, I wouldn't want him looking after any animal of mine.'

Sally stared at him in dismay. This was not what she had hoped to hear. 'So you have no idea where he might have hidden my horse?'

'No, miss. Like I said before, he could have taken her anywhere. You'd do best to report the theft to the proper authorities. Set the police on him. I always said he'd end up behind bars.'

'Who are you talking about, Armstrong?'

Sally spun round to see Gideon standing behind them. She had not planned to visit him; in fact she had hoped, as it was Friday, that he might already have gone to the country. She felt the blood rush to her cheeks and her injuries throbbed with pain.

'Miss Suggs was asking about Fred Cotton, Mr Lawrence. Seems he's stolen her horse.'

'Sally? What happened to you?' Gideon stared at her, taking in her bruised and swollen features. 'You'd better come with me. Thank you, Armstrong. Maybe I can help Miss Suggs.' He led Sally out of the stables and they crossed the courtyard to enter the main building.

Sally would have protested ordinarily, but she was desperate and there was just a chance that Gideon might be able to help. He did not speak until they were in his office with the door closed.

'Sit down, Sally. Tell me who did this to you.'

She sank down on a chair in front of his desk. 'Fred Cotton attacked me and stole Flower, that's the nub of it.'

'I gathered that, but how did it happen, and why would Cotton want your horse?' Gideon leaned against his desk, his face grim.

'I'd been exercising Flower in Regent's Park and Cotton caught me by surprise. He pulled me from the saddle, and when I tried to fight back he knocked me down. The next thing I knew I was being helped back to the lodging house by complete strangers.'

'I suppose you're still living with Kelly.' Gideon leaned towards her, his eyes snapping with anger. 'Your father has been asking for you, and the boys, too.'

'I'm sorry. I intended to come and see you, but I've been fully occupied working on Pa's old round.'

'With Kelly, I suppose.'

'This isn't about Kelly or me. I came here to find out if anyone knew of a place where Cotton might have taken Flower. It's no use telling the police unless I have something definite to go on. I expect horses get stolen every day.'

'You're right, of course. I'm sorry, Sally.' Gideon gave her a wry smile. 'As usual I'm putting my own feelings first.'

'I must seem very ungrateful. You've done so much for me and my pa, and you've taken the Cotton boys into your home without a word of complaint.'

Gideon held up his hand. 'You don't need to apologise. Everything I've done is because I care deeply about you, but I know that you don't feel the same, and I accept that. However, when it comes to the welfare of a horse, or any animal, that is my concern. Of course I'll help you to find Flower.'

Sally had to resist the urge to hug him, instead she smiled and patted him on the arm. 'Thank you, Gideon.'

He nodded and turned away, clearing his throat. 'Now, tell me who you think might have put Cotton up to this. He's not clever enough to think it out for himself.'

'There's a long list, starting with Orrin Vasey, then Harvey Grindle, Luke Bridges and Rags Roper. Vasey and Bridges both said they were representing Astley's and they told me there was a chance that I might be taken on as a performer, with Flower, of course.'

'It's possible that Astley's might be interested in you because of your mother's success, but Flower isn't a racehorse, so I'm not sure why Grindle would want her. As to Rags Roper, I don't know the fellow, but I seem to remember you mentioning his name.'

'Kelly thinks the only reason they want Flower is to breed from her. The main thing is that Cotton has her and I want her back before any harm comes to her.'

Gideon paced the floor. 'Let me think of all the places I've been called to when I was in practice.' He came to a sudden halt, turning to Sally with a triumphant smile. 'I was thinking along the wrong lines. Where would you least expect to find a stolen horse?'

'If I knew that I'd be there already.'

'In plain sight,' Gideon said triumphantly. 'If I know Cotton, he'll have distanced himself from the evidence, while keeping the person or persons who've paid him to steal Flower in ignorance until he gets his money.'

'What do you mean by "plain sight"?'

'Not too far from here there is a large plot of pastureland earmarked for building, although that might not happen for some time yet. If I'm correct, I'll bet that Cotton has left Flower there amongst the other grazing animals until it suits him to hand her over.'

'What are we waiting for?' Sally said eagerly, all her aches and pains forgotten.

'Are you well enough to come with me?'

'Most certainly. A few cuts and bruises won't hinder me when Flower's life is at stake.'

'All right, but you'd better wait here while I go and rearrange my tutorials, and I'll bring the chaise round to the front of the building. You might feel reasonably well, but you mustn't overexert yourself.'

'I won't, I promise,' Sally said meekly. She had half risen, when a wave of dizziness had almost overcome her, and it was a relief to sit down again, but she was not about to tell Gideon in case he refused to take her to find Flower.

'I'll meet you in front of the college in ten minutes,' Gideon said as he was about to leave the room. 'Are you all right to make your way there unaided?'

'Yes of course,' Sally said brightly. 'My injuries look worse than they are.' She was lying, of course. Her head ached miserably and her jaw felt twice the size, but the thought of seeing Flower again made the pain worthwhile. She waited until he had left the room and then she rose, more slowly this time, and made her way to the main entrance. She waited impatiently for Gideon to arrive with the chaise.

It seemed as if she had been waiting for hours, although it could not have been more than twenty minutes, when the vehicle pulled up in front of her and Gideon sprang to the ground to help her onto the seat.

'I'm sorry, it took longer than I anticipated.' He shot her an anxious glance. 'You're very pale, are you sure you're all right?'

'Yes, I am. Drive on, please.'

He flicked the whip and they were off, edging out into the busy street and heading towards Kentish Town. Sally's heart was pounding with excitement and anticipation. It would seem like a miracle if Gideon's theory was proved correct, and if Flower was returned to her she made a silent vow to take her somewhere safe, away from the avarice of unscrupulous men.

They were about to pass the end of Pratt Street when they almost ran into Kelly's cart. He stood up in the well, brandishing his whip.

'Why aren't you at home resting?' he demanded angrily. 'You ought to know better than to take someone who's suffered a head injury for a drive, Lawrence.'

Josie leaned forward anxiously. 'What d'you think you're doing, Sally?'

'Let us pass.' Gideon faced Kelly with an out-thrust of his chin. 'Sally came to me for help and that's what I'm doing.'

'Where are you going?'

Sally held up her hand. 'Move out of the way, Kelly. Gideon thinks he knows where I might find Flower. Please don't try to stop me.'

'There, you have your answer, Kelly. Now let us pass.' Gideon guided his horse around Kelly's cart. 'You can follow us if you're so concerned. Walk on.'

Sally heaved a sigh of relief as the horse broke into a trot and they were on their way again, but as she turned her head she saw that Kelly was following them.

'Ignore him,' Gideon said tersely. 'We'll either find Flower, or we won't. There's nothing Kelly can do to help or hinder us.'

'He'll grumble because his takings will be low.' Sally sighed. 'None of this would have happened if I'd stayed in the country.'

'Does that mean you've changed your mind? You

know how I feel about you, Sally. I'd marry you tomorrow if you'd stay with me in Highgate.'

She smiled, even though it hurt her cut lip and bruised cheek. 'I thought you might have given Cecily a second chance. Why would you want to tie yourself to a poor rag-and-bone man's daughter when you could spend the rest of your life in luxury with a beautiful heiress?'

'If you put it that way, it does make me look a little mad, but you know the answer, Sally. I haven't given up hope.'

Sally had no answer to this and she sat in silence while Gideon concentrated on the road ahead. They reached the pastureland and, as Gideon had said, there were sheep and cattle grazing contentedly. Sally stood up in the well of the chaise, shielding her eyes from the hazy morning sunlight as she looked for Flower – and then she saw her. Flower was tethered to a tree on the far side of the field. Sally leaped to the ground and raced across the hummocky grass, ignoring both Gideon and Kelly as they called out to her to slow down. When she reached Flower her fingers trembled as she struggled to untie the rope.

'I'm taking you somewhere safe,' Sally said through gritted teeth. 'I don't care how much the greedy men offer, I won't give you up.' She looked round, hoping to find the saddle but there was no sign of it. It was annoying, but Sally was not going to let a small detail like this stop her, and she used a fallen branch as a mounting block.

'Sally, you can't ride her bareback.' Gideon had come running across the field, but now he stopped, staring up at her with a worried frown.

'I'm taking her where I know she'll be safe. Don't try to stop me.' Sally flicked the reins and dug her heels into Flower's flanks. Whether it was due to the long night tied to a tree or the urgency in Sally's voice, Flower responded by breaking into a gallop. She took the hedge with an effortless jump, leaving Gideon and Kelly far behind. When Flower slowed down to a trot, Sally realised that they were heading in the direction of Highgate, and the vague idea that she had been mulling over since she had awakened that morning suddenly crystallised into what might well be the solution she had been looking for.

The sun was high in the sky as Sally rode through the gates of Fleet Hall. There was a definite hint of spring in the air. The birds seemed to think so, and they were busy nesting in the hedgerows, singing their hearts out as if to welcome Sally back to the countryside. She reined Flower in at the foot of the steps and handed the reins to a surprised gardener.

'I won't be long,' she said hastily. 'Don't let anyone take her from you.' Sally continued up the steps to hammer on the front door, which was opened by Stafford.

'I must see Miss Appleton, Stafford. Please tell her it's urgent.'

'Wait here, please, miss.' Stafford walked off at his usual irritatingly slow pace.

Sally went to the window to check that the man was still taking care of Flower. She had thought that Gideon at least might try to follow her, but there was no sign of either him or Kelly, and for that she was grateful. Now she was putting all her hopes on Cecily Appleton, and she did not have long to wait.

Stafford reappeared. 'Come this way, please, miss.'

Cecily was seated by the fire with a book open on her lap, although she did not appear to be very interested in the contents as she snapped it shut and rose to her feet. 'Sally. What brings you here so early in the morning?' Her smile faded. 'What happened to you?'

Sally glanced at Stafford, who bowed out of the room. She waited until the door closed. 'I was attacked by a man who stole Flower from me.'

'My dear, how awful. Please sit down. Shall I send for some tea, or maybe you'd prefer coffee. It's a little early for a glass of sherry, although you look as though you could do with something stronger.'

'I'm all right, really. It's painful but it looks worse than it is.'

'How may I be of help? What's happened to Flower? Have you got her back?'

'She's outside in the care of one of your outdoor servants. I found her in a field, tethered to a tree. I rode straight here – it's the only place I can think of where she'll be safe.'

'Safe from what, Sally?'

'There are four men in London who would do anything to get their hands on Flower. They want her for breeding purposes, not because she's a beautiful and intelligent animal. They will stop at nothing to get her.'

'Are you suggesting that I ought to renew my offer to purchase Flower from you?'

Sally shook her head. 'No, I have a much better idea.'

'I'm intrigued. I do love a mystery.' Cecily put her book on a side table and reached out to tug at the bell pull. 'I think I need a glass of sherry wine after all. Go on, Sally. Tell me your idea.'

'I want you to have Flower,' Sally said in desperation. 'If you would keep her here, and ride her whenever you want to, at least I would know that she was safe and well looked after.'

'You're giving her to me?'

'Yes, well, call it a permanent loan. The only condition I'd make is that you would allow me free access to her. I would be able to come and see her and ride her sometimes.'

'But if I bought her from you the money would help. I mean, I know your father is still living with Gideon, as are the Cotton children.'

'It would be so permanent if I sold Flower to you. This way I have access to her without causing problems to you or myself, but I know that she will be safe here.'

'Is Gideon aware of this?'

'He helped me to find Flower. She had been left in a field, tethered to a tree, and it was then I knew I had to do something drastic. I suppose I panicked at the thought that Cotton might return at any minute and I wanted to get as far away as possible. I'm afraid I left Gideon without a word.'

Cecily chuckled. 'I would love to have seen his face. Gideon likes to be in control of any given situation.'

'He's been very good to me and my family, but even he doesn't quite understand my feelings for Flower, and the need to protect her from men who just want to use her to make money.'

'I understand your feelings perfectly. I would be the same.'

'Will you look after Flower for me?'

Chapter Nineteen

They toasted their arrangement in sherry, and then Cecily insisted on accompanying Sally to the stable where Jackson was instructed to take special care of Flower.

'There are unscrupulous people who want to use her for breeding purposes only,' Sally said urgently. 'I don't think they would come here, but they took her by force and I found her more by luck than anything else.'

Jackson met her anguished gaze and looked away, as if embarrassed by her injuries. 'I understand, miss.'

'You must warn the rest of the outdoor servants, Jackson,' Cecily said firmly. 'Flower is part of our establishment now, although Miss Suggs still owns her, and she is free to take Flower out as and when she pleases.'

'Yes, Miss Appleton.' Jackson led Flower away.

'You mustn't worry,' Cecily said calmly. 'I think you've done the right thing, Sally.'

'Have I?' Sally shook her head. 'It feels as though I've deserted her, but I can't see any other way.'

'Believe it or not, I do understand. Papa bought me a pony when I was a baby and I could ride before I could walk. I loved that little animal and I was heartbroken when she died. I'd grown up with her and, even when I was too big to ride her, she used to follow me round like a pet dog.'

Sally brushed a tear from her cheek. 'It's silly, I suppose. She's an animal when all is said and done.'

'Come back to the house and we'll have luncheon. I have no commitments today. You can tell me all about being a rag-and-bone trader. I assume you're going back to that now?'

'I suppose so. I hadn't really thought about anything other than getting Flower to a place of safety.'

Cecily started walking towards the house. 'But you went to Gideon for help.'

Sally fell into step beside her. 'It must look like that, but I went to the college to ask Armstrong, the head groom, if he knew where I might find Fred Cotton. Gideon happened to come along. He saw the state I was in and offered to help.'

'If I were a suspicious woman, I'd think you had planned it in order to gain his attention.'

'You would be wrong, Cecily. I've kept my word.'

'I'm a fair person, Sally. I like to think I'm a

generous woman, but if someone crosses me I can be quite ruthless, I assure you.'

Sally came to a halt. 'I count Gideon as one of my most trusted friends, but that's all.'

'Is that the honest truth?'

'Yes, it is. I can't say fairer than that.'

Cecily held out her hand. 'Then we can be friends, Sally. You're welcome here any time you choose, and Jackson will make Flower available to you.'

'Thank you.' Sally shook hands solemnly. 'If you don't mind I'll set off for the farm now. I want to see my father and the children before I return to London.'

'Of course. You did the right thing today. I hope all goes well for you.' Cecily glided off towards the house, leaving Sally to walk to Hill Farm.

Arthur Wallace was crossing the farmyard when Sally arrived, breathless and hot from the long walk.

'I wasn't expecting to see you today, Miss Suggs. Have you come all the way from London on foot?'

'Not exactly, Mr Wallace. I've just left my horse at Fleet Hall. Is my father around?'

'He'll be in the kitchen with Jane, and the boys will be having their dinner.'

'I hope you don't mind if I stay for an hour or two.'

'Of course not, miss. You're always welcome here. Jane will be pleased to see you – she misses a woman's company. Go on in.'

Sally bent down to pat the two sheepdogs, but

they remained outside as she entered the kitchen. Mrs Wallace was serving up a steamed pudding, glistening with hot jam, and the aroma of custard filled the room. She looked up and smiled.

'Miss Sally, this is a nice surprise. Look who's come to see you, Ted.' Mrs Wallace wagged a finger at Eddie and Benny, who were about to climb down from their chairs to greet Sally. 'You boys can stay seated until you've finished your meal.'

Pippy, who had seemingly adopted Benny, left his side to welcome Sally. She made a fuss of the little dog before moving on to where her father was sitting.

'How are you, Pa?' Sally kissed his wrinkled cheek. 'Are you keeping well?'

'Sally? Is it you?'

'Yes, I'm here.'

'Is anything wrong?' Ted's voice quavered. 'Are you all right?'

'She looks good to me,' Jim said with a cheeky grin. 'What happened to your face, Sal?'

'It's Miss Suggs to you, and you don't ask personal questions,' Mrs Wallace said sharply. 'Eat up boys and then you can leave the table, but not until every scrap is gone.'

Sally laughed. 'I don't think that will be difficult. The pudding smells delicious.'

'What am I thinking of?' Mrs Wallace wiped her hands on her apron. 'You must be starving. Have you come all the way from London on your own? Is Mr Lawrence with you?'

Sally was about to answer when the door opened and Gideon strode into the kitchen. He tossed his hat and gloves onto a chair and shrugged off his greatcoat.

'So you came here after all, Sally. Arthur told me you'd just arrived.'

'This is nice,' Mrs Wallace said, beaming. 'I'll put the kettle on.'

'Where is Flower?' Gideon took Sally aside. 'Why did you run off like that?'

'I'm sorry. I just had to get away from Cotton and all those people who want to take Flower from me.'

'But I was helping you, and I suppose Kelly was, too, in his own way. We were worried about you.'

'Where is Kelly? He didn't come here, did he?'

'I expect he went back to work. I realised you'd ridden off towards Highgate, so I came straight here.'

'Why don't you sit down and have something to eat, Mr Lawrence?' Mrs Wallace bustled over to the table and began clearing the plates. 'You boys can go out and finish your chores.'

'But we want to stay and talk to Sally,' Jim protested.

'I'll come and find you later,' Sally promised. 'Do as Mrs Wallace says, there's a good chap.'

'I have work to do, too.' Ted rose shakily to his feet. 'I help Arthur with the horses. It's like old times, Sal. Come to the stables and see.'

'I will, Pa. You go first and I'll follow on.'

'Don't forget, Sal.' Ted shambled out of the kitchen, leaving the door to swing shut.

'He's still very vague.' Sally shook her head. 'I don't think he'll ever recover from the shock of the fire.'

Mrs Wallace handed her a cup of tea. 'He's an old man, dear. He's happy enough, especially when he's working in the stable. Arthur says that Ted knows more about horses than anyone he's ever known. Excepting you, of course, Mr Lawrence.'

Gideon took a seat next to Sally. 'I think Ted's knowledge is more practical than mine. I could probably learn a thing or two from him.'

'There's some soup left in the pot,' Mrs Wallace said hopefully. 'Would either of you like some?'

'That would be excellent.' Gideon turned to Sally. 'You must be hungry, I know I am.'

She nodded. 'Some soup would be more than welcome.'

Gideon sat back in his seat, eyeing her curiously. 'Now that's settled, tell me what you've done with Flower. I didn't see her in the stable.'

'I've given her to Miss Appleton. We came to an arrangement so that I can see Flower whenever I want to. In return she will be looked after and cared for and she'll be safe from men like Cotton.'

'You've given her away?' Gideon stared at her in surprise.

'Not exactly, I still own Flower.'

'But Cecily has your permission to ride or show Flower, if she pleases.'

'It suits us both.'

Mrs Wallace placed a bowl of soup in front of Sally. 'You look as if you need feeding up, my dear.'

'But what will you do now, Sally?' Gideon reached out to take his plate from Mrs Wallace.

'I suppose I'll continue with my round. There's nothing else I can do. I dreamed of being a star performer at Astley's like my mother, but that's not going to happen.'

Gideon eyed her speculatively. 'Have you thought about teaching others to ride, and by that I mean the finer points of dressage?'

'No. It had never occurred to me, but,' she added with a wry smile, 'there are not too many people who can afford such a luxury in Paradise Row.'

'You know very well what I mean,' Gideon said, laughing. 'There is the very prestigious school for young ladies that Cecily attended, and it's not far from here. I'm sure that she would recommend you to the headmistress.'

'I'm not sure if I could fit something like that in with doing my rounds with Josie.'

Mrs Wallace, who had apparently been concentrating on washing the dishes at the sink, turned her head. 'The cottage is still empty, Miss Sally. It's big enough for all of you.'

Gideon pushed his plate away, unfinished. 'There you are then, Sally. That's the answer. Leave London and you can have the cottage rent free. I'd be glad to have someone living there, and Ted can still help in the stables. The boys could go to the local school.'

'Are you planning to adopt them?'

'No, but Fred Cotton isn't a fit father, and they don't want to go back to him. Young Benny cries if anyone even mentions his dad. If you took on the cottage you would be close to Fleet Hall and you could see Flower every day, if you so wished.'

Sally met his intense gaze with an attempt at a smile. 'It's a thought, Gideon, but I'm not sure. I grew up in Paradise Row and I'm used to city living. I'd have to think about it.'

'Nasty, dirty place. I don't know why anyone would want to live in London.' Mrs Wallace picked up a bucket of scraps. 'I'll just go and feed these to the chickens.' She hurried from the kitchen, leaving Sally and Gideon facing each other in tense silence.

'I wouldn't impose on you, if that's what you're afraid of,' Gideon said hastily. 'I know you don't feel the same as I do.'

'I appreciate the offer of the cottage, and I'm very grateful to you for looking after Pa, but I don't want to let Kelly down.'

'Will you at least give due consideration to my offer?'

'I will, and now I really should get back to London. Might I borrow a horse? I don't think I can walk all the way to Pratt Street.'

'I'll take you in the chaise. I only came here to

make sure that you and Flower were safe. But please think about taking the cottage.'

'I will, I promise, but, I have to speak to Kelly first. I owe him that.'

'Just answer me one thing, Sally.'

She eyed him warily. 'What is it?'

'Have you any deep feelings for Kelly?'

'I don't know, and that's the truth. At the moment I'm just relieved to have Flower safe, and that goes for Pa, too. Just earning enough to pay my way is hard enough without even thinking of anything vaguely romantic.'

'If you're so undecided it should be an easy decision. Your father must surely come first.'

'He does, of course.' Sally rose to her feet. 'If I did decide to take up your offer of the cottage, I would want to pay rent. I don't want to be beholden to anyone, even you, Gideon.'

He nodded. 'I understand. Sit down and finish your meal, I'll get the chaise ready to leave when we've eaten.'

'All right,' Sally said reluctantly. 'But I must say goodbye to the boys before we go.'

Surprisingly, Kelly had little to say when Sally told him that she had left Flower with Miss Appleton, and he was noncommittal when she asked him what he thought about Gideon's offer of the cottage. She had expected a different reaction and she was oddly disappointed by his seeming lack of interest.

Josie was dismayed at first, and she was quick to point out the disadvantages of country living, but after a day or two she began to change her mind. Sally was mystified at first by this sudden about-face, and then she discovered the truth.

Josie had taken to going out after supper, she said to clear her head and the exercise helped her to sleep, but on the third evening Sally was growing suspicious. She had not intentionally followed Josie on her walk, but she had found a child's rag doll caught up in a bundle of coloured material, and she happened to remember the house where it came from. A stuck-up maid had dumped the bundle in the cart, telling them to move on because they were lowering the tone of the neighbourhood. Sally and Josie had joked about it as they sorted the coloureds from the white material, but when Sally found the doll she had kept it aside without telling anyone. Some poor little girl was probably pining for her dolly, and it was possible that the mean-mouthed maidservant had taken it out of spite.

With the rag dog concealed beneath her shawl, Sally set off for the well-to-do houses in Oakley Square. She was so intent on her purpose that she almost walked past a couple, who were huddled together in a shop doorway, their arms around each other, kissing passionately, but the woman's shawl slipped to reveal a mop of copper curls and Sally recognised her instantly. She came to a sudden halt. 'Josie?'

Josie broke away from the man's grasp. 'Sally. What are you doing here? Why did you follow me?'

'I didn't. I was returning this doll to the house it came from.' Sally held the rag doll for Josie to see, but as the man stepped into the light of the street lamp, Sally realised that it was Ned Smith. 'I thought you'd finished with him.'

'What business is it of yours?' Ned demanded angrily. 'This is between me and Josie.'

'What about your poor wife? Doesn't she have a say in this?' Sally glared at him, ready to do battle for Josie and her unborn child. 'Have you told him, Josie?'

'Yes, of course.' Josie retreated to the shelter of Ned's brawny arms. 'We're going to leave London and find somewhere we can start again.'

Sally fixed Ned with a challenging look. 'Is this true? Are you deserting your wife?'

'She left me weeks ago. She run off with her fancy man, taking the nippers with her. I ain't heard from her since.'

'But you're still married to her. Who's to say that you won't desert Josie if you should tire of her?'

'You can't say that,' Josie protested. 'Why would he do that?'

'He's done it once, he could do it again.'

'That's all you know.' Ned took a step towards Sally, grinning broadly. 'I never married her, and that's the truth. She was me common-law wife, if you want to put it that way. I love Josie, and that's the truth. I'll look after her and the nipper.'

'You see.' Josie gave him a loving glance. 'We was meant to be together, Sally.'

'Well, I hope you'll be very happy. There's nothing more I can say.'

'You could wish us luck,' Josie said anxiously. 'We're leaving first thing in the morning. I was going to write you a note to explain, but seeing as how you've stumbled on the truth, I won't have to.' Josie left Ned's protective embrace and she held her hands out to Sally. 'You aren't disappointed in me, are you?'

Sally wrapped her in a hug. 'Of course not, silly. You're my dear friend and I'm glad if you've found someone you can love and trust.' Sally released her, facing Ned with a frown. 'But you'd better treat her well, Ned Smith.'

'I will, I promise. I got family in Chelmsford and we're going there tomorrow. They've got a good business going and me cousin is always asking me to join him. I got the muscle and he's got the brains so we should do even better together.'

'I wish you both the best of luck,' Sally said earnestly.

'I'm sorry if I've let you down.' Josie looked away, as if unable to meet Sally's gaze. 'I don't know how you'll manage the round on your own.'

'Don't worry about that. Just look after yourself and that baby.' Sally swallowed hard as her throat constricted. She would miss Josie and it really was the end of an era. Her last contact with her old life in Paradise Row was going away.

Josie slid her arms around Ned's waist. 'If it's a girl we'll call her Sally.'

This last remark brought genuine tears to Sally's eyes, but she managed a smile as she waved to them and hurried on her way. If she stopped a moment longer she knew she would break down and cry. Josie had never stopped loving Ned, that had been obvious from the start, and now they were together. Sally could only hope that his philandering days were over and he would settle down in Chelmsford and provide a good home for Josie and her child.

Sally kept going until she reached the street where the child lived, but she had not the heart to knock on the door. A lengthy explanation might be required, and, knowing how suspicious people could be of totters, they might even think she had stolen the rag doll in the first place. Sally knocked on the door and left the doll on the step. She hurried away into the darkness, heading for home.

Kelly opened the door. 'Where've you been, Suggs? I was beginning to think something had happened to you.'

'I found a rag doll in one of the bundles and I thought it must have been thrown out by accident, so I returned it to the house?'

He chuckled, shaking his head. 'You can't be everyone's guardian angel, Suggs. I'll make you a cup of my special cocoa. You look exhausted.' He gave her a searching look. 'And you've been crying unless I'm very much mistaken.'

His sympathy made her eyes well with tears again. She could take his teasing, but kindness always made her vulnerable. 'It's the cold wind,' she said, hurrying past him as she made her way to the kitchen.

'Maybe Josie would like a cup?' Kelly went to the range and unhooked a saucepan.

'She's not here.' Sally sank down on a chair at the table. 'I was on my way to Oakley Square when I came across her with Ned Smith.'

Kelly measured milk into the pan. 'The fellow who cheated on his wife and then abandoned Josie? He's no good for her.'

'I thought that, but he seems genuinely in love with her. His common-law wife has left him, so he's free to marry Josie. That seems to be what they both want.'

Kelly took the hot milk from the hob. 'And you're all right with that?'

'It's not up to me, Kelly. I'd like to think that Josie would live happily ever after, but that only happens in fairy tales.'

He laughed and poured the milk onto the cocoa powder, adding a generous amount of sugar. 'You're too young to be so cynical, mavourneen.' He passed the cup to her and pulled up a chair. 'I suppose this means that Josie will no longer be working with you?'

'They're leaving for Chelmsford first thing

tomorrow morning. Apparently Ned has family there and they've offered him work.'

Kelly sat down, facing Sally, his expression suddenly serious. 'As a matter of fact, this couldn't have come at a better time.'

'What do you mean?' Sally eyed him over the rim of the cup. The hot steam of the cocoa, redolent with the aroma of chocolate, was soothing and made her think of home.

'I've had enough of the rag-and-bone business, Sal. I've been involved in it since I was a boy, simply because that's what my father did when we came over from Ireland during the great famine. But I've been prudent, believe it or not, and I've saved money.'

Sally took a sip of the cocoa. 'What are you trying to tell me?'

'I've sold the house. I didn't tell you before because I wanted to be certain. These sort of deals can fall through until everything is signed and sealed. I only rent the stables, but I've put the carts up for sale, and I plan to take the horses with me.'

'What will you do next? I can't imagine you doing nothing.'

'Certainly not. I've bought a run-down farm not too far from where your friend Gideon lives. It must be my Irish blood, but land and horses are my passion. I intend to start a stud farm. I'm prepared to start in a small way, living mainly off the land, and building a business gradually.'

Sally jumped to her feet. 'You want my Andalusian. You're just the same as all the rest of them.'

'Sit down, please,' Kelly said wearily. 'I do not want Flower. She is yours and always will be, even though you've more or less given her away. I have plans which I hope will come off, but I won't bore you with them.'

Sally pushed her cup away. 'No, please. I am very interested. You know how much I love horses. In fact, I was considering Gideon's idea of teaching dressage at a girls' school near Highgate. Miss Appleton attended there as a pupil.'

'Your friend Gideon always seems to be poking his nose in, not necessarily where it's wanted.'

'Don't say things like that, Kelly. Gideon has been very kind to my father and to Fred Cotton's little boys.'

'He certainly knows how to get round you, Suggs. He's hoping you'll change your mind and accept his offer of marriage. He did propose, didn't he?'

Sally jumped to her feet. 'It's none of your business. Even if he did ask me to marry him, I'm still here, aren't I? I haven't let you down. In fact, it's you who are about to leave me homeless and without work. I can't afford to buy back Pa's cart, and I haven't got a horse anyway.'

'Be reasonable, Suggs. I have no intention of abandoning you, or your dad, come to that.'

Reluctantly, Sally sat down again, but inwardly she was fuming. 'You must have been planning this for months. Why didn't you say anything before?'

'I didn't say anything because nothing was settled. I saw no point in telling you if the whole business was going to fall through. Also, there was Josie to consider, and you've been so wrapped up in trying to protect your horse that I doubt if you would have listened to me.'

'You make me sound like a selfish monster.'

He reached across the table to lay his hand on hers. 'Nonsense, Suggs. Don't put words into my mouth. I'm telling you now because I value your opinion, and I was hoping that you might consider coming into business with me.'

She withdrew her hand as if his touch burned her skin. 'What do you mean? How could I be of help to you?'

Chapter Twenty

'I value your opinion on horseflesh, and the farmhouse is large – much too big for a bachelor like me. I'm offering you a home and an interest in my business from the beginning.'

Sally eyed him suspiciously. 'Are you offering to share, or do you simply want an unpaid housekeeper?'

'That's a bit harsh, Suggs. That never occurred to me, but you've been living in my house for the past couple of months quite amicably. I don't see why things need to change.'

'Kelly, are you really so dense? I lodge here and we work together. What would it look like if I came to live with you on your farm?'

'You've never cared for what others think before.'

She rose to her feet. 'That's where you're wrong. Anyway, thanks for the cocoa. I'm going to my room now.'

'I've probably put it badly, Suggs. I didn't mean to place you in a difficult position.' Kelly held out his hand. 'Sit down, please. Let's talk this over like sensible adults.'

She shook her head. 'No, you've made your position quite clear, and now I know exactly what I have to do. I'll go to Hill Farm in the morning. I'll tell Gideon that I'm going to take the cottage.' She was about to leave the room when Kelly called her back.

'Wait a minute, Suggs. There's no call to be miffed. I'm a clumsy fellow when it comes to expressing emotions, but what I had in mind was totally above board and honourable. Let me drive you to Hill Farm tomorrow, but first I'd like to show you the property I've purchased. Even if you don't want to join me, I'd value your opinion on making improvements to the stable block.'

His smile was disarming and Sally felt herself wavering. She nodded. 'All right, I'll come with you, but I'm telling you now that I intend to take up Gideon's offer of the cottage on his land.'

'You might change your mind when you see Kelly's Folly. I believe in starting small, but in ten years' time I'll have the biggest and best stud farm in the whole of the country.'

Sally had to curb the sudden desire to laugh. Kelly, who was usually in control of his emotions and cynical in his outlook on life, suddenly looked like a small boy enthusing over a new toy.

She managed a tight little smile. 'Goodnight, Kelly. I'll see you in the morning, bright and early.' She left the kitchen before he had a chance to respond and made her way to her bedroom.

That night she lay in her bed, staring at the pattern on the ceiling where the street light filtered through moth holes in the curtains. The sounds of the city were never silenced and the drumming of horses' hoofs and the rumble of wheels rarely ceased for more than a few minutes. The noise from the railway station went on until late, ceasing for a few hours until the early morning trains started up with loud hoots on the whistles and the bursts of steam emitted from the engines. It felt to Sally as though London never slept. The shouts and laughter of the drunks pouring out of the public houses had barely died away when the clatter of booted feet sounded like distant thunder. This grew progressively louder as men and women made their sleepy way to take up work in the factories and warehouses along the banks of the canal.

Kelly's sudden announcement had both startled and stunned her. Somehow she had never imagined him as anything other than a rag-and-bone man. His admission that he had other ambitions had come as a complete surprise, and she did not know whether to be flattered or insulted by the way he had assumed that she would be glad to follow him in his new enterprise. She had been tempted to refuse when he had offered to show her his new home, but curiosity had got the better of her. She closed her eyes in an attempt to visualise the run-down farmhouse and drifted off to sleep.

'Well? What do you think, Suggs?' Kelly reined in Sultan outside the farmhouse, having taken Sally on a tour of the surrounding land and the stables, some of which were virtually derelict.

'It doesn't look too bad from the outside,' Sally said slowly. 'It's quite large.'

Kelly climbed down from the driver's seat and looped the reins over a fence post. 'Let's take a look inside. I've only been here once before and it was almost dark then, so I didn't see too much.' He held out his hand to assist Sally to alight.

The yard was eerily silent, especially when compared to the lively atmosphere at Hill Farm, but Sally could imagine the difference a few chickens and a couple of farm dogs would make. Kelly unlocked the door and ushered her inside.

The kitchen was huge with a low, oak-beamed ceiling and small casement windows, although despite this it was surprisingly light and airy. Moreover, it was very clean. Sally had expected to fight her way through cobwebs and litter, but the flagstone floor had been swept recently, unless she was mistaken, and the range, though dusty, had been black-leaded. The brass rails and handles were a little dull, but would polish up with minimum effort. The large pine table in the centre of the room had been scrubbed snowy-white, and the benches on either side were neatly aligned and spotless. Sally had been expecting the worst and she was suitably impressed.

'What do you think?' Kelly asked eagerly.

'I'm agreeably surprised,' Sally admitted reluctantly. It would have been satisfying to condemn Kelly's choice out of hand, but that was unfair. She could see how much this meant to him. 'It's a splendid kitchen. What about the rest of the house?'

There were several much smaller rooms leading off the kitchen, including a scullery with a stone sink and a pump, which Sally secretly thought was wonderfully modern and labour-saving. There would be no need for forays outside in bad weather to fetch water. Kelly had already gone on to fling open the door to a broom cupboard, now empty, and another one lined with shelves and a marble slab. Having exhausted the working part of the house, they went on to explore a small parlour. There was a decent-sized fireplace and a window overlooking what would probably be a jungle of a back garden in summer, but was now a mass of twisted brambles and ivy, long grass and trees in need of pruning. There were two more much smaller rooms, one of which Kelly announced would be his office, and the other he did not seem to have a use for. Sally thought it would make an excellent sewing room, but that would hardly be of interest to Kelly. She closed the door without comment.

Upstairs there were four good-sized bedrooms, a smaller one and a box room. There was a narrow staircase leading to the attics, but Kelly shrugged and said he would explore those later. There was quite enough to do if he was to live here in any degree of comfort.

'But you'll need someone to keep house for you,' Sally said as they returned to the yard outside.

'I don't see why. I can look after myself. Unless you want to apply for the position of housekeeper, mavourneen,' he said with a mischievous grin.

'I think not, Kelly. But I will help you in any way I can. I haven't forgotten what you've done for me during the past months. Shall we take another look at the stables? They seem to be the most important part of your plan.'

'Yes, of course. It was the large stable block and paddock that made me buy the property in the first place.

'Then the sooner you get some bloodstock, the better. Maybe you should speak to Harvey Grindle,' she added, chuckling.

'It's funny you should mention him,' Kelly said, tucking her hand in the crook of his arm as they walked towards the stable block. 'I did call on old Harvey, mainly to warn him to keep away from you.' Kelly held up his hand as Sally opened her mouth to protest. 'Someone had to stand up for you, but that's not the point. He has two surprisingly well-bred animals, which he's treated abominably. The man knows nothing about horseflesh, or how to treat people, if it comes to that. I threatened to report him to the authorities, but I could see that he was growing tired of the whole business.'

'So what did you do?'

'I offered to buy his horses, and to my astonishment he accepted. It seems that he has developed another interest in life and it has nothing to do with horse racing. He was only too glad to let me take them off his hands.'

'Thank goodness I wasn't fool enough to let him take Flower off me. What is his new interest?'

'Hot-air ballooning?'

'I don't believe it.'

Kelly chuckled and patted her hand. 'It's true, I promise. He's used the money to buy shares in a hot-air balloon and he hopes to fly it across the Channel.'

'I don't care if he flies away to the moon. At least his horses will be well cared for. When are you getting them?'

'So you are interested in my business?'

'Of course I am, Kelly, especially when horses are concerned. Are the poor things being cared for at the moment?'

'They are indeed. In fact I enlisted the help of your friend the veterinary. The horses are at present in the stables at the college, being given a thorough examination and any treatment necessary.'

'Kelly, why didn't you tell me all this yesterday?' Sally met his amused gaze with a frown. 'You only told me half of your plans.'

'Would your answer have been any different had I told you everything?'

'It might, had I known that you were going to rescue poor creatures like the ones I saw being beaten and overworked in Hyde Park. Grindle should be reported to the Royal Society for the Prevention of Cruelty to Animals. I was sorely tempted to do so myself.'

'Well, he's out of the business now, mavourneen. When Lawrence says the horses are fit enough to come here, perhaps you'd like to give me a hand.'

'Of course I will. I'd be delighted, and if I can help to get the stables ready, I'll do anything I can.'

They spent the next hour concentrating on the disused stable block. Sally was able to make suggestions for improvements to the existing layout and Kelly seemed happy to agree.

'But all this will take money,' Sally said as they walked slowly back to the cart. 'I would imagine more than you could have made from the sale of your house in Pratt Street.'

'There's no keeping anything secret from you, is there Suggs?'

'Don't change the subject. Did you rob a bank?'

Kelly laughed. 'No, you can rest easy, Suggs. I didn't rob anyone, but I did do a certain transaction for Rags Roper, for which I was paid handsomely.'

'Then it must have been illegal.'

'I didn't ask too many questions.'

'But you didn't commit a crime?'

'Stop worrying, mavourneen. You might say I did a favour for a friend.'

'Rags Roper isn't anybody's friend. I hope whatever you did was worth it, Kelly.'

'I'd say that it was,' Kelly stopped and turned to gaze around his property. 'I think almost anything would make this worthwhile, and it's up to me to make a success of it.'

'Rags won't expect you to work for him again, will he?'

'No, I made that very clear.' Kelly walked on, heading for the cart and the patiently waiting horse.

'I hope you're right.'

He gave her a quizzical look. 'Does that mean you care about me, just a little, mavourneen?'

'We're friends, Kelly.'

He held his hand to his heart. 'And there was me thinking that you were worried about my safety. I'm cut to the quick, Suggs.'

'I never know whether you're serious or play-acting.' Sally shook her head. 'Are you going to be a gentleman and drive me to Hill Farm? Or do I have to walk?'

'I need to talk to Lawrence, if he's there. I want to know when my purchases from Grindle will be fit enough to bring them home.'

Sally laughed. 'You'd do better to fix the leaking roof first, Kelly. And you'll need to stock up on hay and straw.'

'Of course. You are the practical one, Suggs. I'll rely on your sound common sense.'

They had reached the cart and Kelly lifted Sally effortlessly onto the driver's seat. He unhooked the reins and climbed up beside her. 'Hill Farm it is.'

As they approached the farmyard, Sally let out a cry of delight. 'There's Flower. Look Kelly.' She pointed to the horse that Bert was leading towards the stables.

Flower whinnied loudly, refusing to move, and Sally leaped to the ground, barely waiting for the cart to come to a halt. She wrapped her arms around the horse's neck and Flower rubbed her head against Sally's shoulder.

'She's pleased to see you, miss.' Bert clung onto the reins despite Flower's antics.

'Yes, and I'm delighted to see her, too.' Sally stroked Flower's muzzle, crooning softly to her as if she were a baby.'

'Miss Appleton's in the house.' Bert shifted from one foot to the other, eyeing Sally warily. 'Can I take the horse now, miss?'

Sally moved away reluctantly. 'Yes, you have your job to do, Bert. Is Mr Lawrence at home?'

'Yes, miss.'

Kelly tossed a coin to Bert. 'Take care of my horse, there's a good lad. I won't be long, but he needs a drink.

Bert caught the money in one hand. He grinned. 'Yes, sir.'

'Come on Suggs,' Kelly said, taking her by the hand. 'Let's go inside. You can see your old nag any time you like now.'

'You can insult Flower all you like, but I'll ignore your taunts. I know very well that you'd give your right arm to have her as a brood mare.' She shot him a sideways glance. 'That wasn't your deal with Rags Roper, was it? You didn't promise to get Flower for him?'

'Certainly not. You must have a poor opinion of me. I wouldn't trust Roper with any living creature. He's been known to bite the head off a rat.'

'No!' Sally said, horrified. 'That's disgusting.'

'Well, maybe it's a rumour, but I wouldn't put it past him.' Kelly squeezed her fingers. 'I promise you that I'm done with Roper. I'm leaving my old life behind and starting anew. I want you to believe that, Suggs.'

'I think you mean it, but I'm not sure it's possible.' She opened the farmhouse door and stepped inside.

Mrs Wallace was heading towards the parlour with a tea tray clutched in her hands. She stopped and stared at Sally, her face breaking into a smile. 'Miss Sally. This is a lovely surprise.' Her smile faded as she looked over Sally's shoulder and saw Kelly. 'And you've brought a guest, too.'

'Mr Kelly has come to see Mr Lawrence,' Sally said hastily. 'He's bought a farm not far from here.'

Mrs Wallace's relief was obvious and she managed a smile. 'Really? That would be the old Parker place.

It's been empty for a while now, since Mr Parker passed away. A funny old soul he was, to be sure.'

'Shall I take the tray, Mrs Wallace?' Sally held her hands out. 'I'm sure Mr Lawrence will want to see us both.'

'I ought to announce you first,' Mrs Wallace said warily. 'But I'm sure you and the gentleman would like some tea.'

Kelly stepped forward. 'That would be very kind, ma'am.' He glanced round the room. 'You have a splendid kitchen. I might have to ask your advice on setting mine up, when I move into the farmhouse.'

'Yes, sir. I'd be delighted.' Mrs Wallace's flushed face deepened to a crimson hue. 'I'll put the kettle on and make a fresh brew, sir.'

'Come with me, Kelly.' Sally placed the tea tray in Kelly's hands and headed for the parlour, but as she opened the door without bothering to knock, she came to a sudden halt.

Gideon and Cecily moved apart swiftly, but not before Sally had seen them kissing.

'I'm sorry. I didn't think . . .'

'It's all right, Sally.' Gideon straightened his necktie. 'We were just discussing . . .' he paused, glancing nervously at Cecily. 'The weather,' he added lamely.

Cecily gave him a withering look. 'So this is your gentleman friend, the rag-and-bone man, Sally?' Cecily moved towards Kelly, holding out her hand. 'I'm delighted to meet you, sir.'

Kelly placed the tea tray on a table and, taking Cecily's hand, he raised her hand to his lips. 'I've heard so much about you, Miss Appleton. The pleasure is all mine.'

Sally stared at him in disbelief. This was a side of Kelly she had not seen before, and she wanted to giggle, but before she could say anything, Gideon drew her aside.

'It's not what it looks like, Sally.'

She shrugged. 'It's none of my business, Gideon.'

Cecily broke away from Kelly. 'What are you talking about? Is there a reason for this visit, Sally?'

'I'm glad you're here, Cecily. Kelly has sold his house in London and that made me realise I had to do something for myself and Pa, so I've decided to accept Gideon's offer of the cottage.'

'Oh! I see.' Cecily slumped down on the sofa, frowning and clasping her hands tightly in her lap.

'Gideon also suggested that I might find work at your old school, teaching girls the finer points of dressage. What do you think?'

'Well, I don't know if they need anyone, but I suppose you could apply to the headmistress. Are you sure you want to leave London?'

'Yes, quite sure.'

'I suppose you would want to use Flower for your demonstrations?'

'Yes, that's right. You did say I could ride her whenever I wished.'

'I'm beginning to regret my generosity,' Cecily said

crossly. 'It seems to me that I would be taking care of your horse without having any of the benefits you promised.'

Sally sent a desperate look to Kelly, who was standing by the door. He stepped forward. 'If the arrangement doesn't suit, you are welcome to stable Flower with me, Sally.'

'What is this?' Cecily was suddenly alert. 'I thought you lived in London, Mr Kelly. You're a rag-and-bone man by trade, are you not?'

Cecily's tone was condescending, and Sally was about to protest that it was a perfectly respectable business, but Kelly did not seem bothered.

'I've bought the old Parker place,' he said smoothly. 'I intend to start up a stud farm. Gideon has my first two horses under his supervision at the college, which is why I came here today. How are they doing, Lawrence?'

'Surprisingly well.' Gideon spoke quickly, as if relieved to have a change of subject. 'Considering the treatment that Grindle handed out, they have suffered nothing more than strained tendons and the results of a poor diet. I'd say another few days of care and attention and you can take them home.'

'Splendid. You must let me have the bill.'

Gideon shook his head. 'There's no charge. My students were only too happy to have such fine specimens to care for and they've learned a great deal. It was ignorance rather than cruelty that caused the horses' suffering, but I hope you have better knowledge of animals than Grindle. It's fortunate that he had not had them gelded, otherwise they would have been no use to you.'

'I'm aware of that. My father bred horses,' Kelly said calmly. 'My family were prosperous until the great famine, and our business suffered, although we were the lucky ones – we could afford to get away.'

'All this is very interesting,' Cecily said impatiently. 'But where does it leave me? I've been very forbearing with you, Sally, but if you're planning to rent Gideon's cottage, I see no reason why I should look after your horse.'

'Come now, Cessy, that's a bit harsh.' Gideon went to sit beside her on the sofa. 'You were telling me earlier how much you enjoy riding Flower. Heaven knows there are very few pure-bred Andalusians in Highgate.'

'Which is why she's so much in demand.' Sally was not about to be outfaced by Cecily Appleton, who seemed to have succeeded in getting Gideon exactly where she wanted. 'Kelly has offered to stable Flower so I can take her off your hands, Miss Appleton. I'm very grateful for everything you've done for me and my horse.'

Cecily had the grace to blush and shake her head. 'Really, it's no trouble. She's an adorable animal, and I do love riding her.'

Gideon patted Cecily's hand. 'I'm sure that Sally will let you ride her horse whenever you wish to, Cessy.'

'I don't want to press you, but is it still all right for me to rent the cottage?' Sally asked anxiously. 'I can look after my father and the boys, too.'

'Mrs Wallace might have something to say about that,' Gideon said, smiling. 'She's taken to the children like a mother hen. However, the cottage is yours, Sally. It will be good to have a tenant to keep it in good order, otherwise it will fall into disrepair. I can't afford to take on extra farm workers, so I have no need for it at the moment.'

'Thank you, Gideon.' Sally stifled a sigh of relief. One look at Cecily's stormy expression was enough to make Sally wary. Cecily had staked her claim and she was not about to relinquish her hold. Even so, Sally was confused. Gideon had professed to love her, but that had not prevented him from embracing Cecily. His true feelings were something of a puzzle, but Sally had the promise of the cottage, which would make a comfortable home for herself and Pa, and Flower would be safe with Kelly.

'I think perhaps we should be on our way, Suggs,' Kelly said firmly.

'Yes, of course.' Sally managed a smile. 'Thank you both.'

'You can move into the cottage whenever you want to, Sally.' Gideon rose to his feet. 'If there is anything you need, just ask Mrs Wallace. I'm sure the attics are stuffed with items of furniture that we no longer need.'

'Thank you. I'll remember that.' Sally hurried from the room with Kelly close on her heels.

Mrs Wallace looked up expectantly as they passed through the kitchen. 'Well? Are you going to take the cottage, Sally, dear?'

'Yes, I am. Gideon said we can move in as soon as we like.'

Mrs Wallace clapped her hands and her eyes shone. 'How lovely. Your pa will be so pleased. He's missed you, although he doesn't say too much. But, what about the little ones? Will they stay here?'

Sally's heart went out to her. 'Yes, of course, if that's what you all want. I think Gideon is quite happy to have them here, and they seem very fond of you.'

'Oh, what a relief. I was afraid they might be sent back to their pa, or that you would want to have them at the cottage.' Mrs Wallace gave her a watery smile. 'I love them like my own. They're little monkeys, but they've brightened our lives. Mr Lawrence wants them to attend the village school and he's going to speak to the schoolmaster.'

'That's wonderful, Mrs Wallace.' Sally gave her a hug. 'I'll be very grateful for some help in putting the cottage to rights before I take Pa there.'

'Quite right, dear. Your dear pa needs to do things slowly, and he can't abide change. He's used to us now, so we'll do it gradually. Maybe some of his memory will return when he's living with you again.'

'I do hope so.' Sally glanced at Kelly, who was

waiting for her by the door. 'What now? Are we going back to the farm?'

'No, I need to return to London, Suggs. I have to give notice to my tenants, and I'll need to arrange for a carter to bring my belongings to Highgate.'

Mrs Wallace laid her hand on Sally's shoulder. 'You could stay here while we get the cottage ready. We could do it together, dear. It would be my pleasure to help.'

Sally turned back to Kelly. 'There's no real reason for me to return to Pratt Street today, is there, Kelly? Josie will have left for Chelmsford with Ned.'

'If that fellow doesn't stand by her, I'll borrow a shotgun from Arthur and march Ned Smith to the church myself,' Kelly said with feeling.

'If you ever have a daughter, I pity the young men who pay court to her,' Mrs Wallace said, laughing.

'I'd have to be married to have a daughter. What do you think, Suggs? Shall we have a boy first, or a girl?' Kelly blew her a kiss as he let himself out into the yard.

'Well, I never did.' Mrs Wallace gazed at Sally in amazement. 'Unless I'm very much mistaken, that was a proposal of marriage.'

Chapter Twenty-One

Mrs Wallace was as good as her word and she ransacked the attics. With Sally's help and well-meaning, but not always very useful, assistance from Jim and his brothers, they resurrected enough furniture to make the cottage habitable. The iron bedsteads had been left in the cottage, being too heavy and cumbersome to move, but they found trunks filled with bedding and a pile of mattresses stuffed with cotton and horsehair in the farmhouse attic rooms. When all the furniture was piled up in the entrance hall, Arthur Wallace brought a farm cart round to the front door and Bert was summoned to help them load.

That night Sally slept in the spare room at the farm, but she was up early on Sunday morning. After a quick breakfast, she walked to the cottage and began unpacking and arranging the furniture.

The fact that everything was old and worn, and that nothing matched, did not bother her in the slightest. This, for the foreseeable future, was going to be their home, and she wanted to make it as welcoming and comfortable as possible. Her father had watched all the activity yesterday with a puzzled look on his face, and even though he had been told several times, he still failed to comprehend exactly what was going on. Sally gave up in the end, and she decided to take Mrs Wallace's advice. She would take Pa to see the cottage when it was fully furnished. Even then she realised that he might not settle in immediately, but she was prepared to let him grow accustomed to the change, albeit in his own time.

Mr and Mrs Wallace attended morning service at the village church, accompanied by Bert and Jim, but Eddie and Benny begged to be allowed to stay and help Sally in the cottage. They were allowed to do so, but only if they promised to attend Sunday school that afternoon. Eddie confided in Sally that Mr Wallace usually fell asleep by the fire after eating a roast dinner, and Mrs Wallace usually put her feet up after washing the dishes, leaving him and his brother to do as they pleased. Jane and Arthur Wallace were so kind to the boys and Sally did not want to undermine their authority, but she had to struggle to keep a straight face. The Cotton brothers knew exactly how to manipulate their foster parents and needed no encouragement from anyone, least of all herself. While she was working hard to make the cottage habitable, her father occupied himself in the stable, cleaning tack and pottering about contentedly amongst the work horses. Of Gideon there was no sign, but when Sally went to the farmhouse to borrow some dusters, she was told that he had ridden over to Fleet Hall.

Sally returned to the cottage even more confused than she had been previously. Gideon had declared his love for her, and yet he seemed to have changed his mind and had now set his sights on improving his relationship with Cecily. He had agreed that she might rent the cottage, but he had not shown any further interest, nor had he offered to help. Sally shrugged her shoulders and set to work to turn the neglected dwelling into a home. She congratulated herself on keeping a distance between herself and Gideon, despite the fact that she had been attracted to him in the beginning. She could do without the complication of a broken heart.

Later that day, after the boys returned from Sunday school, they were allowed to go fishing in the trout stream with Bert. Sally had a visit from Mrs Wallace, who came armed with a mop and bucket and a large bar of carbolic soap, and they set about cleaning the kitchen, even though to Sally's eyes it was already spotless. However, it did not meet up to Jane Wallace's standards, and she refused to leave until everything shone and the whole cottage reeked of carbolic, with just a hint of beeswax and lavender. A fire was lit in the range and another in the front parlour, and after Mrs Wallace left to make supper, Sally ventured out into the garden. She discovered a clump of primroses under the overgrown hedge, and she picked enough to fill a small cup, which she set on the rather rickety tea table in the parlour.

The boys returned just as dusk was falling and Jim proudly presented her with two large trout. 'We got some for the missis and the old man,' he said, grinning.

'If you mean Mr Wallace, you should say so. They've been very good to you and your brothers, Jim.' Sally took the trout from him and laid them on the kitchen table. 'Thank you. I'll have these for my supper.'

Jim hesitated in the doorway, shifting from one foot to the other. 'Can I ask you something, miss?'

'Yes, of course. What is it, Jim?'

'I don't want to go to the village school. I'm nearly ten.'

'But you should learn to read and write. You might even enjoy school.'

He shook his head. 'Nah! It's not for the likes of me. I can read a bit – at least I can write me name, but I want to work with horses. D'you think your man would let me work for him?'

'Do you mean Kelly?'

'Yes, miss.'

'He's not my man,' Sally said sharply. 'Mr Kelly is just a friend.'

'Well, I seen him ride up as I come over the stile. He's outside tying up his horse. Will you ask him, please, miss?'

Sally hurried to the window, thinking that Jim must be mistaken, but even in the dim light there was no mistaking Kelly's tall figure as he tethered his horse to the apple tree and came striding towards the door.

'Go home, Jim. I'll speak to him, but really it will be up to Mr and Mrs Wallace and Mr Lawrence. They've been looking after you and your brothers.'

'But you'll put a good word in for me, won't you, miss?'

She met his pleading gaze with a smile. 'Of course I will, but you'll have to accept what they decide.'

'And you'll speak to Mr Kelly?'

'Why would Miss Suggs want to do that, Jim?' Kelly stood in the open doorway. He stepped inside, taking off his hat.

Sally shooed Jim outside into the garden. 'Off you go. Leave it to me, Jim.'

'Ta, miss.' He scampered off into the gathering gloom, and Sally closed the door behind him.

'What are you doing back here, Kelly?'

'I've given my tenants the bad news, and they weren't too pleased, but they'll soon find alternative accommodation. Beside which, Dolly never paid her rent on time, and Meg was going to move out anyway.'

Sally went to the range and placed the kettle on

the hob. 'That doesn't explain why you're here. Would you like a cup of tea?'

'Only if you're making one for yourself.' Kelly pulled up a chair and sat down, stretching his long legs in front of him.

Sally lit several candles, strategically placed around the room, and busied herself making the tea. She shot him a curious glance. 'You still haven't said why you're here.'

'I planned to spend the night at the farm, but when I got there I realised it was a bad idea.'

'You haven't got any furniture, let alone a bed.' Sally laughed. 'You weren't thinking straight, Kelly. You need someone to look after you.'

'Are you offering?'

'Certainly not. I've got better things to do than to act as a nursemaid to a thirty-year-old child.'

'I am twenty-eight, but I don't mind if you fuss over me. I might even enjoy a little pampering.'

Sally placed a cup of tea on the table in front of him. 'That's as far as I'll go.' She sat down opposite him. 'You really are keen to move to the Parker farm, aren't you?'

'I suppose it reminds me of my childhood home. I was very young when we left Ireland, but I still have many memories, and they were all happy ones.'

'And you think you can recapture them by starting up a stud farm.'

'I have to earn a living somehow and horses have been a great part of my life.'

'How did you become a rag-and-bone man, Kelly? I've often wondered.'

'My father invested his money, and he dabbled in stocks and shares. He bought the horse and cart with what he had left, and started up the round that I continue to this day. Unfortunately his health failed, and he died when I was sixteen. My mother passed away within weeks of losing him – they were a devoted couple. If I found that kind of happiness I would count myself very lucky.'

Sally thought for a moment that he was being his usual flippant self, but meeting his serious gaze she knew that he was speaking from the heart.

'Your parents were very fortunate,' she said softly. 'Pa adored my mother, and he still grieves for her.'

'Will he live here with you?'

'I hope so. I know he likes being mothered by Mrs Wallace, but he hasn't recovered from the fire. I don't know what more I can do for him.'

'Ted was good to me when I was starting out on my own. The only assets I had were the house and the horse and cart. Your pa encouraged me when I was down, and he showed me a few tricks of the trade that my father never knew. I think I can return the favour now.'

'In what way?' Sally sipped her tea, eyeing Kelly curiously. She was beginning to like this new, thoughtful person who seemed to have replaced the Kelly she had always known.

'I'll need plenty of help in the stables, especially

someone with Ted's knowledge and experience. I would pay him well for his services.'

'That's nice of you, Kelly. But I doubt if Pa could manage the long walk every day.'

'I found an old dog cart in one of the outbuildings. I'm putting Sultan out to pasture, but Emperor still has a few good years in him. He would be at Ted's disposal, or yours if you needed to travel anywhere other than on horseback.'

'It sounds too good to be true. We've been rivals for as long as I can remember, Kelly. Now you're offering to share virtually everything with me and my pa.'

Kelly glanced out of the window. 'It's starting to rain. I need to stable my horse.'

'There's a barn where the hay is stored. It's on the far side of the cottage, and it seems as though they've used it as a stable at some stage. I had a look earlier.'

Kelly rose to his feet. 'Does that mean you're offering me a bed for the night, too?'

'I made up the spare room in case Pa wanted to sleep here, although I'm risking my reputation if I allow you to stay. As it happens I can offer you fresh trout for supper. The boys caught them this afternoon.'

'I have a bottle of wine in my saddle bag. It was supposed to be a present for your pa, but I think our need is greater. There are three of Mrs Maggs's finest pies in there, also.'

'You planned this all along, didn't you?' Sally said suspiciously.

He smiled and opened the door. His response was lost in a gust of wind and a spattering of rain. He returned minutes later, bringing with him his saddle, which he placed on a chair by the door. 'I'll have Emperor settled by the time you unpack the food and set the table,' he said conversationally. 'He'll be warm and comfortable in the barn. At least it's waterproof and well stocked with straw as well as hay.'

Half an hour later Sally and Kelly were seated once again at the table with what seemed like a feast set before them. Kelly opened the wine and poured it into teacups.

'You'll need to invest in some glasses, mavourneen. It's an insult to fine wine to serve it this way.'

'I wouldn't know about that,' Sally said, helping herself to a pie. 'I'll have to save one for Pa. He loves Mrs Maggs's pies, even though he was terrified she wanted to marry him.'

'He need not have worried. When she marries Frank Jarvis, they're going to live above her shop, although she intends to continue baking, which will be a relief to everyone who lives in Paradise Row and the surrounding area.'

Sally took a mouthful of wine. 'Why did you come here this evening, Kelly? You could have stayed in your house and been much more comfortable.'

'But I wouldn't have had supper with you, mavourneen.' Kelly raised his cup in a toast. 'Here's to our future partnership.'

'In business.' Sally was already feeling the effects of the rich red wine, and words seemed to pop into her mouth. 'Just business, Kelly. You do know that, don't you?'

'Of course, mavourneen.' He topped up her drink. 'We will have the best stud farm in the whole country.'

'If you say so, but I want your word that you won't try to take Flower from me. I don't want her to end up as a brood mare.'

Kelly covered her hand with his. 'I give you my word. All decisions about her are yours and yours alone.'

Sally smiled as he leaned towards her and she closed her eyes, half expecting him to kiss her on the lips, but a knock on the door made them draw apart. Before she had a chance to rise from her chair the door opened and Gideon entered the kitchen, taking in the scene with a scowl on his face.

'Jim told me that you'd turned up unexpectedly, Kelly. Just what do you think you're doing?'

Kelly sat back in his seat. 'Just what business is it of yours, Lawrence? Sally and I were just finishing our meal.'

'This cottage is my property,' Gideon said stiffly. 'That makes me responsible for Sally's safety.'

Sally rose rather unsteadily to her feet. 'We were discussing business matters, Gideon.'

'That's not what it looks like.' Gideon crossed the floor and picked up the wine bottle. 'Was it your plan to get Sally inebriated, Kelly? You are no gentleman, sir.'

The room seemed to revolve around her and Sally sat down suddenly. 'Don't be ridiculous, Gideon,' she said crossly.

'Where is your horse?' Gideon demanded. 'Jim said you rode here.'

'He's in the barn for the night.' Sally threw up her hands. 'What has that got to do with you, anyway?'

'I suppose that means you're staying here, Kelly? Sally's reputation will be ruined if this gets around.'

Kelly stood up, facing Gideon with an aggressive set to his jaw. 'You are not the lord of the manor, Lawrence. You seem to think that you have authority over everyone, when in fact you are a failed farmer and you don't even follow your profession as a veterinary surgeon. You are a schoolmaster who can bully his students even though they are grown men. Don't try the same tactic with me because it won't work. You weren't invited here this evening so I'm asking you politely to leave.'

'Just a minute, Kelly. This is my home now, so I say who stays and who goes.' Sally attempted to stand and then thought better of it. The wine must have been stronger than she had thought. 'You may go now, Gideon. I am perfectly capable of looking after myself and Kelly is a gentleman.'

Gideon uttered a derisive snort. 'He doesn't know the meaning of the word. I'm going, but if I tell your father that Kelly is spending the night in your cottage, he'll be furious. If it sets his recovery back, it will be your fault.'

Kelly followed him to the door. 'Don't try to browbeat Sally in my presence, Lawrence. She is perfectly capable of making her own decisions. I suggest you concentrate on your heiress – she seems more than amenable when it comes to you, although the Lord knows what the attraction is.'

Gideon fisted his hands. 'I ought to knock you down for that, Kelly.'

'Stop it, both of you.' Sally stood up, clutching the edge of the table. Suddenly she felt quite unwell, as if she were floating.

'Out,' Kelly said as he opened the door. He gave Gideon a shove that caught him off balance and he staggered outside into the rain and darkness. Kelly slammed the door, turning just in time to catch Sally as her legs gave way beneath her.

'I don't seem to be able to walk, Kelly,' she said dazedly.

'It must have been the meat pie.' He lifted her off her feet and carried her upstairs to her room, where he laid her on the bed. 'You'll have to learn to hold your drink, mavourneen,' he said as he unlaced her boots and slid them off, allowing them to fall to the floor.

'No, really, I'm quite all right,' Sally said sleepily.

'I'll just have a quick nap and then I'll come downstairs and make a pot of coffee.'

'Yes, of course you will.' Kelly pulled the coverlet up to her chin and blew out the candle as he left the room.

It was morning when Sally awakened with a headache and a dry mouth. At first she could not remember why she was lying in bed, fully dressed, and then the memory of the previous evening came back to her. She felt the blood rush to her cheeks. Had Kelly put her to bed? Someone had removed her boots and laid them neatly on the floor, and she did not think that Mrs Wallace would have come to the cottage to oblige. She raised herself carefully to a sitting position and the memory of the previous evening came rushing back. She must have been mad to allow Kelly to spend the night in her spare room. No wonder Gideon had frowned on the arrangement, although he had no right to act as if he owned her, as well as the cottage. She got up slowly, vowing never to touch another drop of wine as long as she lived, but after a wash in cold water and having changed her clothes, she was beginning to feel more like her old self. She opened her bedroom door and listened, hoping that Kelly might have left for his own property, but she could hear movement downstairs. There was nothing for it but to face him – after all, it was his fault. He should not have encouraged her to drink.

The heady aroma of tea and toast greeted her as she entered the kitchen, and an oddly domestic scene met her eyes. She laughed in spite of the pain in her head.

Kelly was standing at the stone sink in the scullery with his sleeves rolled up and his hands plunged into hot water as he washed the dishes from last night's supper. He glanced at her over his shoulder. 'Good morning, Suggs. How are you feeling today?'

'I'm never going to drink wine again.'

He chuckled. 'How many times have I said that myself? You'll be better if you eat something. I know from experience.'

Sally realised that she was hungry as well as thirsty. She took a seat at the table and poured tea into a cup, adding a dash of milk. 'Where did you get milk, Kelly?'

'I walked over to the dairy and Mrs Wallace was kind enough to fill a jug for me.'

Sally clasped her head in her hands. 'Oh dear. Now everyone will know that you stayed here last night.'

'Mrs Wallace doesn't seem like the gossipy type to me. She was very understanding.'

'Which is more than I can say for Gideon. He was really stupid.'

Kelly dried his hands on a towel. 'He was jealous, Suggs. You must know that the poor fellow is in love with you.'

'How can you say that? You saw him kissing Cecily Appleton.'

'Or was she kissing him?' Kelly sat down at the table and reached for the teapot. 'The Lord only knows why a rich and beautiful young woman would want to tie herself to someone like him, but there you are.'

Sally buttered a slice of toast and ate in silence while Kelly drank his tea. She looked up and found him watching her with an inscrutable expression. 'Why are you staring at me?'

A familiar self-mocking smile curved his lips. 'If I tell you the truth you'll laugh or tell me I'm lying.'

'You make me sound horrible.'

'Not at all. For the most part I deserve your censure, but if you must know, I was thinking how pretty you are.'

She was about to reply when she saw the twinkle in his blue eyes and she laughed. 'I'm not going to fall for that one, Kelly. But thank you, anyway. I can tell you I feel far from attractive this morning, but a breath of fresh air will do me no end of good.'

'You're going for a walk in the country? It's not like Paradise Row, mavourneen. There are all sorts of terrors hiding behind trees and in the undergrowth.'

'Now you are talking nonsense. As a matter of fact, I'm going to the stables to tack up Flower and I thought I'd ride over to Fleet Hall.'

'You're going to challenge Miss Appleton to a duel?'

'I'm going to ask her to introduce me to the

headmistress of her old school. I need to start earning money, or I won't be able to get by.'

'You know that I will pay you a wage, Sally. There's no need to go begging for work. I thought we had an agreement.'

'We do, but there isn't anything for me to do at the moment. From what I saw of the stables at your place, they will need a lot of work done to make them habitable. There's really nothing I can help with until you start up in business. I have to earn my own living, which is why I'm going to find paid work. You understand that, don't you?'

'Suggs, you don't have to put yourself through this. There's one simple way that we can go ahead.'

She put her head on one side, regarding him curiously. 'What's that?'

'Marry me, Sally. That way we can start up the stud farm from scratch without raising eyebrows, and you'll have a decent home of your own.'

Sally pushed back her chair and stood up. 'That must go down in history as the most unemotional, unromantic proposal ever.'

He rose to his feet, holding out his hand. 'I'm sorry, Suggs. I didn't mean it to sound that way. I'm truly fond of you and I think we'd deal well together.'

'We've had this conversation before and I said no then. I'm saying no now, Kelly. When I marry it will be for love, and love alone.' She took her shawl and bonnet from the row of pegs on the wall. 'I'm going now. Lock up when you leave.'

'Wait a minute, Suggs. Let's talk this over.'

'No, Kelly. There's no point. I'm going to Fleet Hall and that's that.'

Chapter Twenty-Two

Cecily was just finishing her breakfast when Sally was ushered into the grand dining room. It seemed ridiculous for one person to be seated at the foot of a table that would seat more than twenty people, but Cecily was used to living in such a grand style. Sally tried to visualise the elegant Miss Appleton having a meal in the kitchen at Hill Farm, or in the oak-panelled dining room, which was reserved for special occasions, like weddings, christenings and funerals. Somehow it was impossible to imagine Cecily as the wife of a veterinary surgeon. Cecily had been brought up to be a lady of leisure, and at that she excelled.

'To what do I owe this visit?' Cecily demanded coldly.

'I'll come straight to the point, Miss Appleton. I need to find paid work, as I told you when we last met, and I'd be most grateful if you would put in a good word for me at your old school.'

Cecily dabbed her lips on a pristine white linen table napkin. 'I suppose I could.' She rose gracefully from her chair. 'There is one condition.'

'Yes, what is it?'

'That you see as little of Gideon as possible. I know you're living in the cottage on his estate, and I don't want you to get too friendly with Jane Wallace. She's a gossip and I don't want our business talked about in the village.'

'I'm sure she's very loyal to Gideon,' Sally said stonily.

'The villagers are all the same. They're jealous of anyone who has more than they do. Oh, I know they give lip service to my papa and to me, but behind our backs they say dreadful things. They don't respect Papa because he made his money in trade. They're all frightful snobs.'

Sally was genuinely shocked. 'I find that hard to believe. Your servants all seem very respectful.'

'To our faces, but I really don't trust any of them.'

'I'm sorry, but I wouldn't allow anyone to speak ill of you or your papa, and neither would Gideon.' Sally realised instantly that she had made a mistake by mentioning Gideon's name. Cecily's pleased expression was replaced by a frown.

'You think you know him so well, don't you? No one knows him better than I do and I intend to marry him, so I'm warning you to keep away.'

Sally bit back a sharp retort. 'There really is no call to speak to me like that. I am not looking for a husband, and if I were I doubt if I would pick Gideon, much as I like him.'

'Why not? He's a gentleman even though he was born into a farming family. He's well-educated and well-respected.'

'So why would he choose a rag-and-bone man's daughter instead of a beautiful heiress?'

'Because he thinks he's in love with you, you stupid girl.' Cecily's eyes narrowed and her lips tightened into a straight line. 'You are the cause of our difficulties, and I want you gone.'

'Does that mean you won't help me to find work?'

'I was going to oblige, but when I think about it I would be foolish to encourage you to remain in this area. No, I won't put you forward to my old school. In fact, I'd go as far as to say I would advise my old headmistress not to take you on. I doubt if she would anyway. Your fancy riding tricks would be of little use to young ladies, unless they were to put on spangles and join the circus. Have you considered that option?'

'I'm sorry for wasting your time,' Sally said with as much dignity as she could muster. 'You won't be seeing me again because I will do my utmost not to cross your path. Goodbye, Miss Appleton. I can't say it's been a pleasure knowing you.'

'Keep away from here and leave Gideon alone. You're well suited to that Irish tinker – you'd better marry him.'

Sally came to a sudden halt. 'Finn Kelly is not a tinker. He's more of a gentleman than some who claim that privilege. As for Gideon, I think he's too good for you.' Sally marched out of the room, ignoring the insults that Cecily hurled at her. If that was how a lady carried on, Sally was glad that she had been raised in Paradise Row. The people who dwelled there might not have had much in the way of material things, but they did not pretend to be better than they were. Sally shot a wary glance at Stafford, but he was standing to attention by the open front door, his expression carefully controlled.

'Goodbye, Stafford. You won't be seeing me again.'

'I wish you well in your new venture, miss.'

Sally hesitated on the top step, gazing at Stafford in surprise. He was not one to make personal remarks. 'What have you heard, Stafford?'

'Mr Kelly has bought the old Parker place, and it's said he plans to start a stud farm.'

'My goodness, word gets round quickly.'

'So it's true?'

Sally could see no reason to lie. 'Yes, it is, and I'm going to help him.'

'There's something you ought to know, miss.' Stafford glanced round, as if expecting someone to be eavesdropping. 'A gentleman was here the other day. He came to see Miss Appleton.'

'Is that unusual?'

'It is when the person in question has a certain reputation.'

'I don't understand. Why would one of Miss Appleton's visitors concern me?'

'Are you familiar with the name Vasey?'

'Do you mean Orrin Vasey?'

'The same. Jackson tells me that he's a horse dealer who operates in the guise of a scout for Astley's and a number of well-known circuses, but it's the horseflesh he's really after.'

'Yes, I know about him. I came across him in London. He pretended to be interested in me as a performer at Astley's, but really all he wanted was my horse.'

'Exactly, miss. Jackson seems to think that he's still trying to get his hands on your animal. I don't know what he said to Miss Appleton, but if I were you I'd be very wary. He asked me to warn you, miss.'

'Thank you, and please thank Jackson for his concern. I'll keep Flower safe, no matter what.'

'Good luck, miss.' Stafford stood aside to allow her to pass.

Kelly was preparing to leave when Sally arrived back at the cottage. He gave her a searching look. 'What's wrong? What did that woman say to you?'

'I must put Flower in the barn first.' Sally paused, frowning. 'But I wouldn't hear if anyone tried to take her. It's not a secure place.'

'What has she said to make you nervous? I've never seen you like this, Suggs.'

'She didn't say anything about Flower, although

she was unhelpful to say the least. It was Stafford, her butler, who told me that Orrin Vasey had been to see Cecily.'

'Did he, now? There's only one thing he's after and it isn't Miss Appleton. Did Stafford know what passed between them?'

Sally shook her head. 'No, but Jackson, Cecily's head groom, told Stafford to warn me. It seems that Vasey is well known even here in Highgate. Jackson is certain that Vasey is still intent on getting Flower.'

'That won't happen, Suggs. Flower will be the first occupant of my stables when they're ready, but for now I suggest we ask Arthur Wallace to keep her in the farm stable. Bert is always there and I'll pay him to keep a special watch on Flower. Besides which, the farm dogs would let everyone know if there were prowlers.'

'But why should they look after Flower? I don't like to ask Gideon for more favours.'

'To be fair to the fellow, he cares just as much for animals as he does for people. He wouldn't want to place Flower in danger.'

'Cecily told me to keep away from him. I think she could be dangerous if crossed, Kelly. I'm not interested in Gideon, at least not in the way she imagines, but if she feels threatened she might side with Vasey. Who knows what he said to her?'

Kelly glanced up at the darkening sky. 'Go inside, mavourneen. Make yourself a cup of tea and stop worrying. I'll alert Arthur and Bert, and if necessary

I'll go back to London and have a man-to-man chat with Gideon. Miss Appleton needs to learn a few lessons in manners, if you ask me.'

'But Flower is my responsibility, not yours. I should take her to the stable.'

'Are you telling me I'm not a good enough rider?'

Kelly's comical expression had the usual effect of making Sally laugh. 'No, of course not.'

'Then do as I say. Flower will be safe with me.'

Reluctantly, Sally went indoors, but she could not resist looking out of the window to watch Kelly vault effortlessly onto the saddle and ride off in the direction of the farm.

Over the next few weeks, with Flower safely installed in the Hill Farm stable, Sally and Mrs Wallace worked together to make Kelly's new home habitable. They arranged the furniture that Kelly had sent down from the house in Pratt Street, laid rugs and hung curtains. Once fires were lit and the kitchen stocked with pots and pans, crockery and cutlery, there was little else they could do, and they left the men to work on the outbuildings. Sally would have liked to have a say in the refurbishment of the stable block, but she did not want to interfere. After all, this was Kelly's project, and even if they were to work together she must respect his right to make the major decisions about the property.

Sally's next task was to persuade her father to move in with her. He was very comfortable at the farmhouse, but she wanted to look after him herself. It took a few days, but eventually Ted moved into the cottage. Kelly was as good as his word, and he allowed them to keep the dog cart in the barn where Sultan was now stabled. Ted drove off every morning after breakfast to help Kelly in his new venture, although Sally suspected that her father was more of a hindrance when it came to physical work. Ted was convinced that his advice was crucial to the success of Kelly's business, and Sally was not going to tell him any different. When he was not at Kelly's stables, Ted pottered round the garden, and although he had never previously had the opportunity to grow anything, he developed a passion for gardening. Encouraged by Arthur Wallace, Ted cleared the weeds in the vegetable bed and planted seeds. His memory still failed him at times, but even so, Sally was relieved to see him so happy. Every time a green shoot sprouted was like a miracle to Ted, and Sally shared his excitement.

Each day, after she had done her chores, Sally set off for Hill Farm to spend time grooming Flower and cleaning out her stall. It seemed unfair to put extra work on Bert, although the boy was very willing and quite happy to do anything to make Flower comfortable. Jim, Eddie and Benny had all started lessons at the village school, but Jim raced home at the end of the day to help Bert, who was his idol.

Sally was careful to avoid the farm when she knew that Gideon would be at home, and she had not had any further encounters with Cecily, nor had Orrin Vasey put in an appearance. As the weeks went by, a routine developed, and Sally was beginning to enjoy country life. It was summer now, and Kelly was as good as his word. He paid Sally a regular wage, for which she kept his house clean and tidy. He and the men he hired worked tirelessly to rebuild and extend the stables, ready to start up the stud farm in earnest. Living in a male-dominated world, Sally really missed Josie, but she had not had a word from her since Josie had gone to live with Ned Smith. Sally could only hope that they were happy together and that Josie was keeping well during her pregnancy. She had briefly considered returning to Paradise Row to see if Josie's mother knew of her daughter's whereabouts, but after her last encounter with Mrs Bates, Sally doubted if she would get any sense out of her.

One evening in late June, Sally had given her father his supper and he had retired to bed early, having worn himself out at the stables. She went outside to empty a bucket of water when she heard the click of the garden gate. She froze, wishing that she had Pippy with her – a guard dog was something she needed now. It was a moonless night and the darkness wrapped itself around the garden like a cloak. She snatched up the broom that was propped against the outside wall and she raised it above her head.

'Who's there?'

'Sally, is that you?' A familiar female voice shattered the silence.

'Josie?' Sally dropped her weapon and took a step forward as Josie rushed into her arms. 'What are you doing here? Where's Ned?'

Josie burst into tears, leaning against Sally so that they were both in danger of overbalancing. 'He's in prison, Sal. They've locked him up.'

'Why? What did he do?' Sally held her at arm's length. 'Are you all right? Anyway, come inside and sit down.'

Josie picked up the bundle she had dropped to the ground when she saw Sally, and they entered the kitchen together. Sally closed the door and led Josie to a chair.

'Sit down and tell me everything.'

Josie subsided awkwardly onto the seat. 'I've walked all the way from Pratt Street. I went to Kelly's house and there was strangers living there, so I come all the way to Highgate and that nice Mrs Wallace told me where to find you.'

'Kelly's bought a farm not far from here, but that's by the bye. Tell me about you. How far gone are you now?' Sally stared at Josie's distended belly.

'Seven or eight months. I'm not too sure. The little devil don't half kick.'

'But you're keeping well?'

'Pretty fair, but I get very tired. It don't help that Ned got hisself in a bit of bother with the police, and now he's in Coldbath Fields Prison.'

'What did he do?'

'He stole a few potatoes and a loaf of bread. We was starving, Sal. He lost his job at the gasworks and he couldn't find anything else. I was working until a month ago when I had a funny turn and they give me the sack.'

'What sort of funny turn? Did you see a doctor?'

'Come off it, love. You know the likes of us can't afford to see a pill-peddler. I was feeling tired so I bought a bottle of elixir from a street doctor, but it made me worse and I passed out on top of a tray of cakes at the bakery where I was working. They sent me home covered in jam and sugar.'

Sally tried not to laugh. 'But you weren't hurt and the baby is all right.'

'Yes, but now I got no money and nowhere to live. I was wondering if you would put me up for a night or two. Until I get back on me feet?'

'Of course I will. You can stay here for as long as you like, Josie. You know you were offered the cottage once, and that still stands. Pa is living with me now, but there's a spare room and I just need to make up the bed.'

'I'll do it, I ain't a cripple, Sal.'

Sally glanced down at Josie's swollen feet and the uppers coming apart from the soles of her worn-out boots. 'You sit there and rest. I'll make a pot of tea and there's some stew left from supper. It's still quite warm if you'd like some.'

'Not half,' Josie said eagerly. 'Is that bread going begging? I ain't eaten since yesterday.'

'Take a seat at the table and start eating. No wonder you look thin and pale, despite the bulge in your belly. You need feeding up, my girl.'

Josie raised herself with an effort and waddled over to the table. She took a seat and grabbed a slice of bread, stuffing it into her mouth, chewing and swallowing as if she had not eaten for days. Sally set about filling a bowl with stew and making the tea. When she had served Josie, she went upstairs to take sheets and blankets from the chest on the landing. The back bedroom was small but certainly large enough to make Josie comfortable. Sally lit a candle and placed it on the washstand in the corner of the room before making up the bed. She fetched a clean nightgown from her own room and laid it on the coverlet. From the state of Josie's bundle, it was obvious that she possessed very few clothes, and they were all probably in need of a wash. Josie herself, who had always been very particular about her appearance and cleanliness, also looked as though a bath would benefit her – but that would wait until tomorrow.

Sally drew the curtains and went downstairs to see if Josie wanted anything else to eat. She found her slumped over the empty bowl, snoring loudly. With a great deal of effort, Sally managed to get Josie upstairs to her bedroom, where Josie collapsed, fully dressed, on the bed. After removing Josie's boots, Sally covered her with a patchwork quilt, extinguished the candle and closed the door softly behind her. She went downstairs to tidy the kitchen and made herself a cup of tea. It would be good to have Josie's company and the prospect of a baby in the cottage was both daunting and thrilling, but it also meant two more mouths to feed.

Her fears were put into words next day when Kelly arrived at the cottage with a wicker basket filled with eggs, which he placed on the kitchen table.

'Some of them might be addled. I've no idea how long these were in the coop, but they haven't hatched, so I assume they're edible.'

'You're no countryman, that's obvious,' Sally said, chuckling. 'But the eggs are a godsend, Kelly. I was wondering how I was going to feed Josie. She arrived last night in a terrible state.'

'Don't tell me she's been abandoned already.'

'No, she hasn't. Don't be horrible, Kelly. Ned was out of work and they were starving. He stole some food and got caught. He's serving time in Coldbath Fields Prison, and she had nowhere to go.'

'I thought she had a mother living in Paradise Row.'

'If you'd met Mrs Bates, you'd know that she's the last person Josie would turn to. She's my friend, Kelly, and this is my home. She can stay here as long as she likes and the baby is due in a few weeks.'

'Then let her live here and you can come and keep house for me. I inherited the chickens, but I don't know what to do with them. I can cook, of course, but I'm not much of a hand at making myself comfortable.'

Sally cut him short. 'If you want a live-in housekeeper, you can hire someone much better suited to the position than me. But I would be happy to work longer hours.'

'That's splendid, and I can ask for free advice when it comes to the finishing touches of the stable block.'

'That doesn't fall into the domain of a housekeeper. I charge more for acting as an expert on horse welfare.'

'Suggs, you're a woman after my own heart. We were meant for each other.'

Sally turned away. 'Don't start that again. I'm not in the mood.'

'Has Gideon been pestering you?' Kelly's voice had an edge to it.

'No, I've managed to avoid him, which is difficult as he's my landlord, and I have to go to the farm if I want advice from Jane.' Sally added, smiling, 'She really is a sweet lady, but I think she favours me above Cecily Appleton when it comes to prospective brides for Gideon.'

'He's a lucky fellow. He has women falling at his feet for no apparent reason.'

'I'm not one of them, Kelly.'

He pulled up a chair and sat down at the table. 'Take a seat, Sally. There's something I must tell you and I don't want anyone else to hear.'

She went to sit beside him. 'What is it? If you call me Sally it must be serious.'

'The fellows who work for me are all local men, most of them small farmers, taking on extra work to supplement their incomes.'

'So, what has that to do with us?'

He gave her a lazy smile. 'I like the term "us", Suggs.'

'Stop teasing me and tell me what they've said.'

'We know that Hill Farm isn't doing too well. Apparently Gideon Lawrence is on the verge of bankruptcy. Every penny he earns at the college goes into the upkeep of the farm. He's left too much to Wallace, who is a good worker but he knows nothing about balancing the books, and that's where Gideon has fallen short.'

'Are you saying he's neglected the farm?'

'He might be good at his job, but he's no businessman, neither is he a farmer. I suspect that Sir Gregory might have had a hand in ruining Lawrence's chances of success. He wants the land and he was even prepared to see his only daughter marrying below her station in life so that he could add to his acres.'

'Cecily loves Gideon. She would marry him tomorrow if he asked her.'

'Then the man's a fool. He needs someone to give him a good talking-to.'

'Don't look at me.' Sally sprang to her feet. 'I've been warned not to go near him, and I'm not in a position to go against Cecily Appleton. Heaven knows how far she might go if she thinks I'm making sheep's eyes at Gideon.'

'What a charming turn of phrase you have, mavourneen,' Kelly said, laughing. 'I wasn't suggesting that you try to charm Lawrence, which would serve no useful purpose. Besides which, you have beautiful eyes. When you're angry with me, as you are now, they go darker like a peat bog, but when you laugh they're the colour of fine French brandy, with golden lights.'

'I don't know whether to kiss you or to slap your face, Kelly. I don't imagine any woman would be flattered by having their eyes likened to a peat bog, and I'm not too sure about the French brandy.'

He caught her by the hand, his eyes dancing with mischief. 'I would enjoy a kiss, or even a slap.' He raised her hand to his lips. 'I was merely suggesting that you let Lawrence know, in no uncertain terms, that there is no hope for him as far as you're concerned.'

Sally snatched her hand away. 'I've tried that, Kelly. I've told him that I'm not interested in him now, and never will be. I'm not Cupid – I can't fire an arrow into his heart and make him love Cecily.'

'Maybe he's loved her all along, but he's grown so used to her company that it's simply become part of his very existence. Sometimes you can know someone for years and take them for granted, and it's only when that relationship is threatened that you realise you can't live without that person.' Kelly rose slowly to his feet, his gaze never wavering from Sally's face. 'Do you understand what I'm saying, mavourneen?'

Sally wanted to look away, but she was mesmerised by the intensity of his feelings, and she realised that Kelly was referring to himself. The man she had always thought to be flippant and self-serving was laying his own heart bare and waiting for her to respond.

She swallowed hard, desperately seeking the right words, when the kitchen door opened and Josie swanned into the room.

'Oh, dear! Have I interrupted something?'

Chapter Twenty-Three

Sally broke away from Kelly's grasp. She knew she was blushing furiously and she could not look at Josie, who would see through any attempts to make light of the situation.

'Of course you have, Josie,' Kelly said with a wry smile. 'I was about to go down on one knee and propose to Sally, but you've ruined the moment.'

Josie's hands flew to cover her mouth and she giggled. 'You are such a tease, Kelly. As if Sally would marry a man like you. Sal can aim higher than a rag-and-bone man.'

'My pa was a rag-and-bone man,' Sally said sharply. 'I was a rag-and-bone woman, if it comes to that.'

'Hoity-toity,' Josie said, grinning. 'I didn't mean it, Kelly. It's just that I seem to have walked in on a scene from a melodrama at the Royal Grecian Theatre.'

Kelly shrugged and headed for the door. 'I'm no actor, Josie. By the way, it's good to see you looking so well.'

It was Josie's turn to blush and she crossed her arms protectively over her belly. 'You're just saying that. I know I look a mess. Sally was a saint last evening when she took me in. I don't deserve such a good friend.'

'I'm glad you appreciate her.' Kelly opened the back door. 'I have to get back to the stables. I'll see you tomorrow morning then, Suggs.'

'Yes, of course, and thank you for the eggs,' Sally said hastily. 'I'll return the basket tomorrow.'

Kelly smiled and stepped outside. Josie barely waited until the door closed on him. 'Did I interrupt a proposal, Sal? I'm sorry if I did.'

'No, he wasn't asking me to marry him. We were discussing Gideon and Cecily as it happens.'

'What about them? What have I missed? Do sit down and tell me everything, Sal.'

'I'll make you some breakfast first. Kelly was kind enough to bring us a basket of eggs, so you can have some scrambled, boiled, poached or whatever you fancy.'

'Scrambled, please. I haven't had an egg since I left the house in Pratt Street. Ned and I were really hard up all the time, and we were starving when he stole that food. He'd been giving me the best of what we had. He's a good man, Sal. He didn't deserve a prison sentence.'

Sally fetched a bowl from the dresser and began cracking eggs into it. 'How long did he get?'

'Six months, and most of that will probably be on the treadmill. He told me not to visit him for fear of catching some horrible disease. I would go, but I have to think of the baby.'

'Of course you do.' Sally added a pinch of salt and began to beat the eggs with a fork. 'I'm so sorry, Josie. You didn't deserve that, either of you, but you can stay here for as long as you like. I've been doing some work keeping Kelly's house tidy, but I'm going to increase my hours.'

Josie's face fell. 'I'm sorry, Sal. Is it because of me? I can still pay me way. I was skivvying at the pub down the road from where we was living. At least I was until Ned got a stretch. I'd like to see the magistrate who sent him down in similar circumstances. I bet he'd nick a pie or two if he was desperate. I was lucky to get the job in the bakery after that.'

'You're too near your time to even think about working,' Sally said firmly. 'I have Pa to support as well as myself, you're welcome to share what we have.'

'You're a good friend, Sal. I don't deserve you.'

Sally laughed. 'Don't speak too soon. You can help me to keep this place clean. Pa tramples mud in from the garden and trails it everywhere. Then there's always washing to do, and ironing. I think there's enough to keep us both out of mischief.'

* * *

Next day Sally accompanied her father to Kelly's farm as usual, but this time she would work there all day. She had discovered in the beginning that Kelly was a tidy man, unlike her father, and there was not a great deal to do in the house, but there was plenty to keep her occupied in the farmyard. She had to consult Jane Wallace when it came to looking after the chickens, but as the days went by Sally developed a rapport with the hens. She found it oddly satisfying to call and have them running to greet her, clucking and vying for attention. One thing that Sally had not expected was the provision of a cooked midday meal for Kelly and the labourers that he had hired. Once again, she had to ask Jane for help, but after a few lessons Sally discovered that she enjoyed preparing and cooking food. It was just another challenge to overcome, but she was enjoying the work and the freedom from anxiety. The extra money would help to support her family, and Flower was being cared for at Hill Farm.

Josie was keeping well, and although she did not complain, Sally knew that her friend found country living dull. Josie did her best to carry out the chores that she and Sally had agreed upon, but after a couple of weeks it was obvious to Sally that Josie was becoming fretful. Her pregnancy was not giving her any problems, but she was growing larger by the day and it was obvious that she was missing Ned, who was not due for release until the autumn. Accordingly to Josie's calculations, the baby was due at the end of July, but judging by Josie's size, Sally thought it might come earlier.

After great deal of hard work, Kelly's stables were ready for occupation. Grindle's horses were thriving with good care, and Kelly made several visits to Tattersalls, with a view to purchasing another stallion. A special stall had been made ready for Flower, and Sally was eager to have her beloved horse where she could take care of her. When the day came to collect Flower from Hill Farm, Sally was up early, dressed and preparing to leave when Jim burst into the kitchen.

'You got to come. There's something going on at the farm, and Mrs Wallace is in a real state. I never seen her so put out. Mr Wallace has sent Bert to London to fetch Mr Lawrence and it's a proper to-do.'

Sally did not wait to pick up her bonnet. Bareheaded she ran from the cottage, following Jim, who sprinted on ahead like a young greyhound. It was a fine summer morning, with the promise of growing heat during the day, but the dew was still spangling the grassy banks and a gentle breeze fanned Sally's hot cheeks. She arrived at the farm breathless and anxious as to what she might find.

In the kitchen Jane Wallace was collapsed on a chair, fanning herself with a tea plate. She jumped to her feet when she saw Sally. 'Oh, you've come. Thank the Lord. We're in terrible trouble, my dear.'

Sally hurried over to her. 'Whatever is the matter? Jim didn't know what was wrong.'

'It's her high and mightiness – Miss Appleton. She came here first thing this morning with a strange-looking man, and she insisted on taking Flower. She said that she would make it right with Mr Lawrence.'

Sally felt a sudden cold chill. 'What did this man look like?' She asked the question, but she already knew the answer.

'Funny looking. Big curly moustache and pointed beard – like a billy goat. He scared me, I can tell you. I sent Jim to find my Arthur, and he sent Bert to fetch Mr Lawrence.'

'But did they take Flower? Gideon would never have let them, had he been here.'

'Miss Appleton was very firm. She said she was Mr Lawrence's fiancée, and she had his permission to act on his behalf.'

'They're engaged?' Sally could hardly believe her ears. 'She actually said that?'

'I know. I didn't believe her either, but that man obviously did, or else he wanted to believe it. I wouldn't trust him any further than I could throw him.'

'Orrin Vasey,' Sally said bitterly. 'I can't believe that Cecily Appleton would fall for his lies.'

'Who's he?'

'A man who'll stop at nothing to get what he wants. He's been trying to get his hands on my horse for months.' Sally ran to the door. 'How long ago was this, Jane?'

'About half an hour. They came in Miss Appleton's chaise and tied your horse to it as they drove away.'

'I must do something.' Sally thought quickly. 'I need to borrow a horse. Will your husband mind if I take one from the stable?'

'He's taken the cart to the market. There's only your old horse out to pasture with Dobson.'

'Then may I borrow a saddle? Boney will get me to Fleet Hall quicker than if I go on foot.'

'I'll fetch what you need, miss,' Jim said eagerly. He ran from the kitchen without waiting for an answer.

'I'll wait for you in the long meadow,' Sally called after him. She turned to Mrs Wallace. 'Will you tell Gideon that I've gone to get my horse back from his fiancée?'

'Oh, dear Lord. What a to-do!' Mrs Wallace sank back on her chair, covering her head with her apron.

Sally left the farmhouse and ran all the way to the meadow where Boney and Dobson were at pasture. Boney came in answer to her call and he rubbed his head affectionately against her shoulder. Dobson ambled over to join them, braying excitedly as Jim came into view, carrying the tack for two animals.

'I'm coming with you, miss.' Jim said firmly. 'I ain't allowing you to go there on your own. That man what come here might kidnap you as well as Flower.'

Sally did not waste time arguing. She opened the gate and went into the field to tack up Boney and Dobson.

* * *

Sally and Jim rode into the stable yard at Fleet Hall, causing a stir of interest and some amusement amongst the grooms and young boys. Jackson emerged from his office and strode across the cobbled yard to meet them.

'Miss Suggs? That's not your usual mount.' His lips quivered as if he was trying not to laugh.

'You know very well why I'm riding a carthorse, Mr Jackson,' Sally said crossly. 'Where is Flower? What have they done with her?'

Jackson's surprised expression seemed genuine. He shook his head. 'I'm sorry, miss. I don't know what you mean.'

'She stole Sally's horse,' Jim said bluntly. 'Miss Appleton took Flower from under our noses.'

'That's right,' Sally added. 'It was Miss Appleton and Orrin Vasey. You warned me about him.'

A frown creased Jackson's brow. 'Yes, I know of him only too well, miss. Everyone who knows anything about horses will have come across that fellow's name at some time. But he isn't here, and neither is Flower.'

'Miss Appleton was driving a chaise,' Sally said anxiously. 'Did she bring it back to the coach house?'

Jackson shook his head. 'No, miss. I'm sorry, I can't help. Maybe if you enquire at the house, Stafford might be able to help you.'

Dobson curled back his top lip and brayed loudly, as if commenting on Jackson's inability to help, and the resident horses stuck their heads out of their stalls, joining in the chorus.

'It's all right, Mr Jackson. We're leaving.' Sally beckoned to Jim. 'Come on, we're wasting time here.'

Jim urged Dobson to a trot, leading the way out of the stable yard with Boney lumbering along at a slower pace. Jim turned his head to give Sally a questioning look. 'Will we stop at the big house? I never been here before. It ain't half grand.'

Sally was trying to decide when Jim called out, pointing to a cloud of dust by the gatehouse. 'Someone's coming, miss.'

'Walk on, Boney,' Sally said urgently. But Boney's response was slow and measured, as if he were pulling the cart on their old round. By now the chaise was tooling along the tree-lined avenue and Sally could just make out Cecily Appleton's elegant figure as she handled the reins with the skill of a coachman. Of Orrin Vasey there was no sign, nor Flower.

Incensed, Sally drew Boney to a halt, blocking the way to the stables so that Cecily had to bring the horse to a halt.

'What are you doing here, Miss Suggs?' Cecily demanded angrily. 'Get out of my way.'

'What have you done with my horse? We're not moving an inch until you tell me where I might find Flower?'

'You've seen the last of her. Gideon has sold her to a dealer.'

'You're lying. Gideon is in London. Mrs Wallace told me so. You are the one who took Orrin Vasey to Hill Farm. You lied to Mrs Wallace and you stole my horse.'

'How dare you speak to me in that tone?' Cecily snatched up the whip and wielded it over Boney's head. 'I won't ask you again. Get out of my way.'

'Not until you tell me where Vasey has taken Flower. You had no right to involve that man, or to take it upon yourself to sell my property.'

'The Andalusian belongs to Vasey now. He has a bill of sale, signed by me on behalf of my fiancé.'

'You aren't engaged to Gideon, and I don't believe he would give you permission to sell something that belonged to someone else.'

'You don't know him as I do. I will marry Gideon and you have seen the last of that horse. You will find somewhere else to live and take your father and that trollop with you. I want you out of our lives forever.'

'Oy, you can't talk to Miss Suggs like that,' Jim cried angrily.

Cecily raised the whip as if intending to strike out, but Jim manoeuvred Dobson closer to the chaise and he reached up to snatch the whip from her hand.

'You common street urchin,' Cecily said through clenched teeth. 'I'll report you to Mr Wallace. He'll beat you black and blue for that.'

'No, he won't.' Sally brushed a strand of hair back from her hot forehead. 'You are the one at fault here, Cecily. I wonder what Gideon will say when I tell him what you've done.'

'As if he'd believe you.' Cecily flicked the reins and her horse started forward in the direction of the stables. 'Get out of my way or I'll run you down.'

Despite his advancing years, Boney had been raised in the busy London streets and he moved away instinctively. Cecily shouted at her horse and flapped the reins as the chaise moved off at speed.

Jim wiped his brow. 'That was a close 'un. I thought the bitch was going to run us down.'

Sally let this pass. She knew she ought to have corrected Jim for his language, but she was in no mood to be proper. 'I have to go to London, Jim. That's where Vasey lives, and that's where he'll have taken Flower.'

'Well, you won't get far on Boney,' Jim said, grinning. 'And Dobson is even slower. You'd do better to walk.'

'No, I'm going to Kelly's stable and borrowing one of his horses. I want you to tell Josie what's happened, but don't say anything if you see my pa. I don't want him to worry.'

Jim grinned broadly. 'You can trust me, miss.' He wheeled Dobson round and the donkey ambled off along the carriage sweep. Sally was anxious and eager to hurry, but the old horse was doing his best and she tried hard to be patient.

It was early afternoon when Sally rode into the courtyard at the Veterinary College. Armstrong recognised the horse she had been riding. He said that he remembered the state it had been in due to

Harvey Grindle's ignorance, and he was delighted to see the difference that Kelly's care and attention had made. Sally left him to take care of the horse while she went in search of Gideon. As luck would have it she found him in his office. The student he had been coaching was just about to leave and Sally waited, trying not to show her impatience.

When she challenged Gideon he denied all knowledge of Cecily's intentions.

'Honestly, Sally. I never discussed Flower with her, and I certainly would not have sanctioned selling her to that dishonest dealer. I wouldn't trust him to look after a snake, let alone a valuable animal like Flower. And nor would Cecily.'

Sally eyed him warily. 'Cecily said that you and she are engaged. Is it true?'

'No, it isn't. We've been getting along better recently, but only because she thinks that you and Kelly are a match. I've never spoken of marriage.'

'She thinks differently, Gideon. You need to be very frank with her if it's not your intention. Although from your point of view it would make sense to marry her. I know your farm is in trouble financially.'

'I suppose Kelly told you that.'

'It's common knowledge in the village. I think that Sir Gregory might have something to do with your troubles. He wants your land and he's prepared to sell his own daughter in marriage to get his own way.'

'Great heavens, Sally. You make him sound like some medieval monarch.'

'I think that's what he is, in his own mind, at least. And some of it has obviously rubbed off on Cecily. She threatened to have us thrown out of our cottage if I came to you for help.'

Gideon took a deep breath. 'The cottage belongs to me, and Cecily had no right to say such things. I don't know what's got into her. She used to be such a sweet girl, and good company, too.'

'She's in love with you, Gideon, and she's desperate. She sees me as the threat, even though I've told her that there was nothing between us.'

'I wish things were different, Sally.' Gideon gave her a searching look. 'Are you living with Kelly? That's what Cecily told me.'

'No. That's not true. I work for him as his housekeeper. I go home every night to the cottage, which Cecily wants to take away from me.'

'I'm sorry, but it won't happen. I'll have to have a serious talk with her.' He eyed Sally curiously. 'Why did you come to me? I don't know what I can do to help.'

'I thought you might know where I can find Orrin Vasey. He took Flower and I know he intends to sell her to the highest bidder. I need to get to him before he can do any more harm.'

'I don't know where he resides, but Armstrong might have an idea. Wait here, Sally. I'll go and ask him. Vasey has quite a reputation, so it shouldn't be too hard to track him down.'

'I left young Jim in the stable with Dobson,' Sally

said hastily. 'Don't laugh, Gideon. He insisted on accompanying me and he had no other means of transport.'

'I'm sure you made a quaint pair. You must have had heads turning,' Gideon said, chuckling. 'But, don't worry. I'll see that they're all taken care of. I expect Jim is starving as usual. Armstrong will see that he's fed. What about you?'

'I couldn't eat a thing. All I want is to get Flower back. Please hurry.'

'I will. Try to keep calm. I'll be as quick as I can.'

Sally tried to sit down quietly by the window, staring down at the busy street, but after a few minutes she jumped up and began to pace the floor. What would Vasey do next? She came to a sudden halt. The answer evaded her, but one thing was obvious – Vasey would not take a valuable animal like Flower to his home in London. He might stable her somewhere on the outskirts, or he might take her straight to Tattersalls.

She was about to go in search of Gideon when he walked into the office.

'No luck, I'm afraid. The last Armstrong had heard of him, Vasey was living in Albert Street, but it's unlikely he would have taken Flower there. Unless, of course, he has a stable somewhere in the area.'

'I think I know where he might be. If I were Vasey, I'd want to get the horse off my hands as soon as possible. There's a sale at Tattersalls today. Kelly will be there, but he doesn't know what's happened.'

Gideon frowned. 'Tattersalls moved to Knightsbridge Green last year. We'll have to get a cab.'

They arrived at Tattersalls after the sale had started, but Gideon was well known amongst the dealers, and, using the pretence that he wanted to check on a certain animal's health, he was granted permission to go to the stalls where the horses were awaiting their turn in the auction ring. Sally went with him, ignoring the raised eyebrows of the stablemen and boys. She was used to dealing with men on equal terms, and she stared them down until they turned away. Hardly daring to breathe, Sally followed Gideon from stall to stall, but there was no sign of Flower. Gideon had a word with one of the auctioneers, but he denied all knowledge of a dapple-grey Andalusian mare. He would have no good reason to lie and Sally experienced a wave of despair. If Vasey had not brought Flower here, the dire truth was that she could be anywhere.

They went into the area where the horses were paraded before prospective buyers, but although Sally scanned the rows of bidders, she could see neither Vasey nor Kelly.

'He's not here, Sally,' Gideon said in a low voice. 'It looks as if we were wrong. I have to get back to the college because I have a lecture in half an hour. I'm sorry.'

Sally nodded dully. 'You're right. There's no point in waiting around. Vasey has been too clever for us.'

'And Kelly has either got what he came for, or maybe he went to a private sale.'

'That's it, Gideon. Not about Kelly, but Vasey must have been working for a buyer who was prepared to purchase a rare breed, whatever the cost, and whether or not the animal was stolen.'

Sally followed Gideon out of the building and stood beside him while he attempted to flag down a hansom cab. 'You really do need to put Cecily straight, or else marry the woman.'

He shot her a sideways glance. 'Is there really no hope for us, Sally?'

'Do you even have to ask that question? I like you, and I'm fond of you. You've been a wonderful friend, but I don't love you, Gideon.'

He grabbed her by the arm. 'Look over there, Sally. On the far side of the road.'

'What am I supposed to see?' Sally followed his gaze, but she saw nothing out of the way on the crowded pavement.

'That man in the check suit, with the scarlet waistcoat and top hat. Do you recognise him?'

'His taste in clothes is awful, but I can't see his face. He's looking the other way.'

'Wait until he turns round. If I'm not mistaken, that's Fred Cotton.'

'No,' Sally gasped. 'It can't be. That fellow looks clean, well-dressed and sober.'

'I'd know him anywhere. I'm the one who had to sack him from his job at the college. He had a way with horses and an eye for a thoroughbred.'

'And he's known to Rags Roper, who mixes with every crook in London. Do you think there could be a connection?'

'It's possible.'

'I'm going to talk to him. He should be in prison for what he did to me. He stole Flower once before; who's to say he isn't at the bottom of this now? I never found out who put him up to it.' Sally was about to step off the pavement, but Gideon held her back.

'Don't be a fool, Sally. Keep out of sight. I'll have a word with him. I don't think he'll realise that there's a connection.'

Sally's first reaction was to summon a constable and have Cotton arrested, but it would be his word against hers, and the smart, if over-dressed version of himself he portrayed now, did not fit in with the brutal attacker who had kidnapped Flower. She melted into the crowd outside Tattersalls and watched as Gideon strolled across the road. She wished she could hear what was being said, but she knew that if Cotton were to associate her with Gideon he would say nothing.

She hung back, hidden amongst a group of men who were discussing horseflesh in loud voices, accompanied by guffaws of laughter when one of them cracked a joke, the meaning of which went right over Sally's head. She managed to catch a glimpse of Gideon talking to Cotton, but she was in danger of being squashed when other men joined the group, having emerged from the auction with their own tales to tell. Sally pushed past them and was dismayed to see Cotton striding away, while Gideon attempted to cross the street, dodging in between the horse-drawn vehicles, carts and riders on horseback. She moved some way along the pavement and raised her hand to alert him to where she was standing, but the sight that met her eyes made her freeze.

There directly opposite her was Kelly, and his dark head was bent towards a young and extremely pretty young woman, who was looking up at him with a smile on her face. She was obviously not a stranger to Kelly, and there was an intimacy in the way they were talking that made Sally catch her breath. They appeared to be saying goodbye as the girl stood on tiptoe to plant a kiss on Kelly's cheek, and he laid his hands on her shoulders, drawing her to him in a hug that went to Sally's heart like a dagger.

'What's the matter?' Gideon said as he joined her. 'You look as if you've seen a ghost.'

Chapter Twenty-Four

Sally looked again, but both the girl and Kelly had disappeared into the crowd.

'I'm all right,' Sally said weakly. 'What did Cotton say?' It was easier to demand the bad news than to admit she might have just seen something infinitely worse. The young woman obviously played a part in Kelly's life that he had never mentioned. Maybe she was the reason he had come to London, and the auction at Tattersalls had been a cover for a romantic assignment.

'He didn't tell me anything useful,' Gideon said in a low voice. 'Just the usual line of how hard done by he's been all his life, but now his luck has magically changed. He was boasting that his business associate was paying for him to go to New York, so I asked him point blank if it was Vasey. He gave me that cocky insolent grin and he said that London was getting too hot for him, just like it did for you and your pa.'

'So it was him who set fire to the stable. Didn't he know that his boys were sleeping there?'

'I asked him if he was taking his children with him and he shrugged. His exact words were – "you tell her she can keep them little millstones" – he laughed and walked away. I think you have your answer, Sally. It's the first time I've seen him sober, so he knew what he was saying.'

'He's a dreadful man and the boys are better off without him, but I suppose we'd better get back to the college now. Jim will be wondering where I am, and there doesn't seem to be anything more I can do here.'

Gideon gave her a searching look. 'That's not like you, Sally. You can't just give up.' He raised his hand and a cab wove its way towards them, pulling in at the kerb.

Sally climbed in and sat down, forcing herself to put Kelly and the young girl from her mind. She would think about that later. It was Kelly's business anyway. 'Did you find out how Cotton had come into money?'

'The Veterinary College, cabby.' Gideon sat down beside her, closing the wooden doors that protected them from the worst of the dung and detritus on the roads. 'Cotton said he was working for a businessman. He wouldn't say any more, but I could tell from his smug grin that whatever he was doing was illegal.'

'Do you think he could be working for Vasey? I'm sure that's who paid him to steal Flower when I was lodging in Pratt Street.'

'I couldn't say with any certainty. It's possible, but we'll never pin him down. At least, not while he's sober.'

Sally leaned back against the stale-smelling squabs. 'I hate to admit it, Gideon, but I don't know what to do next.'

'Maybe Kelly will have some ideas,' Gideon said reluctantly. 'I don't like the man, but he knows a thing or two about horses, and I expect he's learned a lot more recently. In the horse-breeding world there must be some really wealthy men who would do anything to get their hands on a mare like Flower.'

'I suppose so. But if I could find Vasey it would be so much quicker.'

'Always supposing that he would talk to you. He's hardly going to admit his part in a crime.' Gideon patted Sally's hand as it lay in her lap. 'Take encouragement from the fact that Flower is a very valuable animal, and no one in their right mind would harm her.'

'Yes, you're right. I must be positive.'

'That's the spirit. I haven't any more lectures after the one I've already missed. My colleague Peterson will have taken it for me, although I'll never hear the last of it. I'll ride to Highgate with you and I'll go and see Cecily. It's just possible that Vasey might have boasted about the person who wanted to get their hands on Flower, and you can ask Kelly if he knows any wealthy patrons of the racecourse who would give their eye teeth for a little mare like Flower.'

Sally nodded. 'Yes, you're right. I'll do that. Kelly doesn't know that Flower has been stolen. At least I know he cares about horses, probably even more than he does about humans.'

'Has he done something to upset you?'

'No, of course not. I'm just tired and hungry, and I'm disappointed that we haven't found Flower. But I think you're right. There's someone with a great deal of money behind this. Cotton and Vasey are just middlemen.'

Kelly caught up with them on the road to Highgate. He drew his horse to a sedate trot. 'What are you doing with one of my animals? And why is Jim riding a donkey? What is this?' He glanced at Gideon, giving him the briefest of nods.

'Gideon has been helping us to look for Vasey, who bought Flower from Miss Appleton this morning, even though she had no right to make such a decision.'

Kelly pushed his hat to the back of his head. 'Can we stop a moment so that you can tell me exactly what's happened?'

'We'll ride on,' Gideon said, beckoning to Jim. 'The sooner I talk to Cecily the better.' He tipped his hat to Kelly and rode on with Jim, urging Dobson to a trot.

'Well now. Perhaps you can tell me everything, Suggs.'

Sally met his earnest gaze with an impatient toss of her head. 'Who was that girl you kissed outside Tattersalls?' She had not meant to blurt it out but the question was uppermost in her mind.

Kelly threw back his head and laughed. 'Were you spying on me, mavourneen? I'm flattered.'

'No, I was not. You are an arrogant idiot if you think that. I had to go to Gideon for help because I wanted to know where Vasey lived, but no one at the college seemed to know. I thought that if Vasey were to sell Flower he'd take her straight to Tattersalls. That's why we were there, but that doesn't explain what you were doing there in the company of a pretty young girl. You obviously know her very well.'

Kelly's smile faded. 'Are you jealous, Suggs?'

'No, I am not. Why can't you answer a straight question?'

'Because it's ridiculous. The young lady you saw me saying goodbye to is my cousin, Consuela Riordan.'

'Your cousin? I didn't think you had any close family.'

'I'd hardly call California close, but my father's brother immigrated to America during the famine, where he met his wife, who is Spanish, which explains my niece's name. Anyway, Patrick did well and made a lot of money. Consuela is engaged to be married and she came to London to purchase her wedding gown. She wants to look like the queen, so she said.'

'Oh!' Sally looked away. 'Well, she's very pretty.'

'She is, and she's a sweet girl.'

'I'm sure she is,' Sally said awkwardly. 'I should move on.' A slight nudge of her heels and the horse obeyed instantly.

Kelly rode alongside her. 'I've invited Consuela to stay at the farm for a few days while she's waiting for her gowns to be made. You'll be able to get to know her.'

'Is that all you can say?' Sally shot him an angry glance. 'Flower has been sold without my permission and I don't know where she is, and all you can think about is entertaining your cousin.'

'That doesn't sound like you, Suggs. Of course I'll do what I can to help you, but it will take time.'

'You're in the world of horse breeders, Kelly. Can you think of anyone who would be wealthy enough to pay Vasey the price he might demand?'

'Not offhand, but I'll do my very best to find out. In the meantime, there's very little you can do.'

'I know, and that's what makes it so hard. I might never see Flower again.' Sally bit back tears of anguish and sheer frustration.

They rode on in silence until they reached the outskirts of Highgate. 'Don't despair, Suggs.' Kelly reached out to pat Sally on the shoulder. 'I think I have a plan.'

'Really? Or are you just saying that to cheer me up?'

'You know me well enough to realise that I never

say anything I don't mean. I promised Consuela I would pick her and her maid up tomorrow morning, and bring them to the farm. If you would care to accompany me, I'll leave you to entertain my cousin, while I do some detective work of my own.'

'Do you think you can find out who purchased Flower?'

'I have my sources, but I don't want to say too much at the moment.'

'What about Vasey? If we could find him, he could tell us.'

'Vasey will have gone to earth, like the sly fox he is. He must have worked hard to convince Miss Appleton to hand Flower over to him, however much money passed hands.'

'She won't tell me anything. We started off as friends, more or less, but now she hates me.'

'She's afraid that you'll take the stalwart veterinary surgeon away from her, Suggs. Can you blame her?'

'Yes, I can. I told her that I don't want Gideon. Why won't she believe me?'

Kelly gave her a straight look. 'Why, indeed?'

'Now you're laughing at me.'

'If I'm smiling it's because of what you just said about Lawrence.' Kelly wheeled his horse around. 'This is where I leave you, Suggs. Go home and try to rest. I'll bring the carriage to your door first thing tomorrow. That's if you agree to my suggestion.'

'Yes, of course I do. I'll be ready. Thank you, Kelly.'

'Wait until we have Flower back in our stables, Sally. Then you can thank me properly.' He tipped his hat and rode off, leaving Sally to make her way to the cottage where she knew she could face a barrage of questions from her father and Josie.

Consuela Riordan and her maid, Lucy, were staying at Brown's Hotel in Albemarle Street, and they were waiting in the foyer dressed and ready to leave.

Consuela rushed forward to hug Kelly. 'You're on time, that's good. Dada always says you can judge a man by his punctuality.' She turned to Sally, her dark eyes sparkling with curiosity. 'I don't know you, do I?'

'This is Sally Suggs, Consuela,' Kelly said smoothly. 'She's a good friend and a business partner.'

'A good friend,' Consuela repeated, chuckling. 'I may read into that whatever takes my fancy, I suppose.' She held out her hand. 'How do you do, Sally? I hope we too will be good friends during my stay in London, although I fear it's going to be much too short to really get to know you.'

Sally shook her hand. 'I'm pleased to meet you, Miss Riordan.'

'It's Consuela. I hate formality, and I'll call you Sally, if that's all right with you?'

'Well, now that's settled,' Kelly said smoothly. 'I suggest you ladies go shopping, or whatever you do for entertainment in Mayfair, while I go on a mission of my own.'

'No, Kelly. Are you really going to desert us?' Consuela said, pouting. 'You've only just arrived.'

'Sally will explain everything.' Kelly made a move towards the door. 'I'll be back in time to take you to luncheon, or we can set off for Highgate and stop at an inn on the way.'

'A village inn sounds so quaint,' Consuela said eagerly. 'This is my first time in England and I want to experience everything before I return to California and settle down to dull domesticity.' She turned to her maid. 'What was it you wanted to ask my cousin, Lucy?'

The maid, who reminded Sally of nervous little mouse, stared down at the tips of her boots peeping out beneath her skirt. 'I have relations in London. I would like to stay with them, if you don't mind, sir.'

Kelly shrugged. 'It has nothing to do with me. If Miss Riordan doesn't object, you may do as you please.'

Lucy looked up at Consuela and her plain face was transformed by a smile of delight. 'It is all right, isn't it?'

'Of course it is. I have your aunt's address in Camden. We'll pick you up from there on my return to London for my final fittings.' Consuela turned to Sally with a sigh. 'You know how tedious these things are.'

'Not really,' Sally said hastily. 'But I can see it must be a bit of a chore.'

'I'll meet you back here in two hours' time.' Kelly nodded to the doorman, who let him out into the busy street.

'Well, then,' Consuela said airily. 'You may go with that young man who's been waiting patiently for you, Lucy. I hope you have a good time with your English family.'

'Thank you, miss.' Lucy hurried to the door, blushing rosily when the doorman opened it for her. She scuttled outside and Sally saw a tall young man envelop her in a warm embrace.

'That doesn't look like someone's aunt,' Sally said, chuckling.

'I had to make up a tale to satisfy my cousin. Men can be so old-fashioned. Lucy met Edwin on board the ship. It was so romantic.' She grabbed Sally by the hand and dragged her into the oak-panelled parlour. 'I want to hear all about you. Never mind what Kelly says. I can sense a romance a mile off.' She sat down on a velvet upholstered sofa, patting the seat beside her. 'Would you like some tea or coffee? Perhaps something to eat.' She summoned a waiter with an imperious wave of her hand.

Sally did as she was bid. 'Some coffee would be nice.'

'Coffee and some of those delicious little pastries, please, Wilton.' Consuela gave him a brilliant smile, which the elderly waiter acknowledged with a slight nod of his head before walking away. Consuela waited until he was out of earshot and her smile faded. 'Can I trust you, Sally?

'Yes, of course. Is anything the matter?'

'Everything,' Consuela said dramatically. 'I couldn't

say anything in front of Lucy, because she's been told to keep an eye on me, which is why I encouraged her romance. It takes her mind off being my duenna.'

'Whatever do you mean?' Sally sank down beside her, taking hold of Consuela's hand. 'You can trust me.'

The mask of gaiety had slipped away, leaving Consuela pale and trembling. 'I was only allowed to come to London on the understanding that I was being fitted for my wedding gown. Dada likes to show off the wealth he made in the gold rush.'

'He discovered a gold mine?'

'No, he sold drink to the miners and opened a bar. Now he owns a chain of bars and hotels, and he wants me to marry a man who owns a rival hotel business.'

'If you don't want this match, why didn't you tell your pa?'

'I did, Sally. And I begged Mama to make him change his mind, but she told me I must do my duty. Then I had to listen all over again to the hardships Dada had suffered during the voyage from Ireland and the privations when he first arrived. Coming to London was my only way of escape.'

'But what will happen when you return to California?'

'I don't want to, that's the whole point. I want to persuade Finn to allow me to stay in London. I can earn my own living.'

Sally eyed her warily. 'What can you do?'

'I don't know until I try. There must be something. Perhaps I could be a governess and I might marry the widowed father of my young charges.'

Sally laughed. 'I'm sorry, but you've been reading too many penny-dreadfuls.'

'What are they?'

'Romantic stories, Consuela. Kelly might be willing to help you. I can't speak for him.'

'You could have a word with him, Sally.'

'I'll try, but I'm not sure he'll listen to me.'

Consuela gave her a hug. 'You're a darling girl, I can see why Finn thinks so highly of you.'

'He thinks I'm a little crazy,' Sally said ruefully. 'I will do my best for you, Consuela.' Sally paused while the waiter returned with the coffee and a plate of dainty pastries.

Consuela gave him a brilliant smile. 'Thank you, Wilton. You're okay.'

Wilton's raised left eyebrow was the only sign that he was unsure how to take this, but he bowed out of the parlour.

'What did I say?' Consuela turned to Sally with a puzzled frown.

'What is okay? I don't think he had heard that expression.'

'It means all right. We all say it.'

'Okay,' Sally said, chuckling.

'You are a little crazy.' Consuela poured the coffee. 'Now tell me about yourself, Sally. I'm sure we're going to get along splendidly.'

'I hope so, too.' Sally found herself telling Consuela everything that had happened since the fire in Paradise Row. If she faltered, Consuela prompted her eagerly, stopping her occasionally when she wanted a more detailed account. Her reactions were suitably enthusiastic or sympathetic, depending on which part of the narrative Sally had reached. They drank coffee and ate the delicate pastries, and Consuela answered Sally's question about life in California.

Time passed so quickly that Sally was quite startled when Kelly strode into the parlour at noon. 'Well? Did you find anything that might lead us to Flower?'

'Yes, Finn,' Consuela added hastily. 'I know all about it, so please put us out of our misery.'

Kelly sat down on a chair that looked too spindly to hold the weight of a fully grown man. 'It's good to see you two getting on so well, but I'll come straight to the point.'

'Please tell me who has bought Flower?' Sally clasped her hands together, hardly daring to breathe.

'I have a friend who works for Weatherbys, and he told me that Sir Bertram Eustace of Follyfield Park had been looking for an Andalusian mare to mate with his prize stallion. It may be a false lead, but I think it's worth following up.'

'Where is Follyfield Park?' Sally asked eagerly.

'It's near Hatfield. Quite a way from here.'

'Then we must go there immediately.'

'Yes, indeed.' Consuela clapped her hands excitedly. 'It's just the sort of adventure I was hoping for.'

Kelly frowned. 'We won't make it today, although we could break our journey halfway.'

'Then that's what we must do.' Sally jumped to her feet. 'We must leave now.'

'That's all very well,' Kelly said seriously. 'But what will you do when we get to Follyfield? You need to have a plan of some sort. We can't just walk in and demand to inspect Sir Bertram's stables.'

'I don't know.' Sally paced the room. 'We'll think of something, Kelly. I just need to know who has Flower and if she's being treated well. I'll work out how to get her back later.'

'I agree.' Consuela rose to her feet. 'What are we waiting for?'

That night they put up in a country inn, and set off again early next morning. It was late afternoon when Kelly drew the horses to a halt.

Sally tapped him on the shoulder. 'Where are we, Kelly? Why have we stopped here, in the middle of nowhere?'

Kelly turned his head. 'The signpost we just passed said two miles to Follyfield.'

'We could go on to the village and make enquiries there,' Sally said wearily. 'You know what it's like in a small community. Everyone knows everyone else's business.'

'Are we to sleep in a field, cousin?' Consuela asked crossly. 'I'm stiff and tired and I want something to eat.'

'You wanted to come with us, Consuela,' Kelly said sharply. 'Sally needs some answers, but we can't drive up to his front door and accuse Sir Bertram of buying a stolen Andalusian. If he has her, then he purchased her in good faith.'

'What are you going to do, Kelly?' Sally followed his glance in the direction of a farmhouse, nestling snugly amongst a stand of trees. A narrow lane ran between a field where cows grazed peacefully and another where ripening corn rippled gently in a light breeze.

'I'm going to walk to the farmhouse and ask for directions to Follyfield Park.' Kelly handed the reins to Sally. 'I'll see if they know anything. You two wait here.'

'But I'm hungry and thirsty,' Consuela said wistfully. 'Maybe they'll give us something to eat, if we ask nicely.'

'First things first.' Kelly leaped to the ground and strode off, heading down the lane towards the farmhouse.

'I hope he gets some good news,' Sally said wearily. 'The longer Flower is in the hands of a breeder, the less likely are my chances of getting her back.'

Consuela leaned back in her seat, frowning thoughtfully. 'If this Sir Bertram has purchased Flower, we will have to persuade him to part with her. I don't think it will be easy. After all, he must have paid a lot of money for her.'

'I know,' Sally said softly. 'That's what worries me. I suppose I could bear being parted from her, if I knew she was loved and well cared for, but it would still break my heart.'

'We both face heartbreak,' Consuela said dramatically. 'I would rather die than marry Newton.' She brightened suddenly. 'I have an idea, Sally.'

'What is it? Tell me, because I, too, am desperate.'

'It won't rescue your horse, but it will get us into Sir Bertram's home.'

'Go on,' Sally said eagerly. 'Tell me.'

'Well, I will pretend to be an heiress, which I will be one day, so that's not a lie. You will be my maidservant, and Kelly will be our coachman. We have some sort of accident outside the gates of Follyfield Park, and Sir Bertram will have to invite us into his house. I am very good at acting and will pretend to have hurt myself in some way that doesn't mar my looks.'

Sally stifled a giggle. 'You are quite conceited, aren't you?'

'Yes, I suppose so. But you have to admit that I am very pretty. Maybe not beautiful, but everyone tells me that I am also quite charming.'

'All right,' Sally said, laughing. 'So what then?'

'I don't know, but I'm sure we'll think of something. We'll be inside the mansion, and if the carriage needs repair we will have to stay for a day or two.

It will give you time to see your horse and work out a way to get her back. I can't think of everything.'

Sally's smile faded. 'It's worth a try, Consuela. But we have to get Kelly to agree, and it's his carriage.'

'I'm sure we can be persuasive, Sally. We're women, aren't we? We usually get our own way.'

Sally shrugged. 'I'm not sure about that. You're running away from an arranged marriage and I'm penniless. Even if we do as you suggest, and should Sir Bertram be a reasonable man, I would have to find the money to recompense him for the loss of the animal he thought he owned.'

'Oh, well. That's a mere detail. I have plenty of money, or at least, Papa has a lot of money. I can usually wind him around my little finger. He will pay.'

'I doubt that, but we have to start somewhere.' Sally shielded her eyes against the setting sun. 'Look! Kelly is coming this way. I do hope he has good news.' She waited impatiently until he reached the carriage. 'What did they say?'

'They didn't know anything about Sir Bertram, apart from the fact that he breeds horses. The farmer suggested that we try the village inn. I did tell you not to get your hopes up, Suggs. I'm afraid this is going to turn out to be a wild-goose chase.'

'Don't say that, Kelly.' Sally leaned forward as he took his position on the driver's seat. 'Consuela has had an idea. I think it might work.'

Chapter Twenty-Five

'No, absolutely not. That's the silliest idea I ever heard. We'll stay at the village inn tonight, and tomorrow I'm taking you both to Highgate where we will try to think of a better plan of action.'

'But Kelly, won't you reconsider?' Sally said urgently. 'If Consuela and I get into Follyfield we can find out if Flower is there without alerting Sir Bertram.'

'Yes,' Consuela added, clinging on to the side of the vehicle as Kelly urged the horses to a trot. 'I expect Sir Bertram is an old gentleman, whose only interest is horse racing. I plan to charm him into giving Sally back her horse.'

'No, you won't, Consuela. I'm responsible for you while you're in my company, and I won't allow you to do anything rash. You can't go round crashing vehicles – this is Hertfordshire, not the Wild West.'

'I still think it's a good idea,' Consuela said sulkily.

'Maybe he'll change his mind after a good dinner and a bottle of claret,' Sally said in a low voice.

'I heard that, Suggs, and for your information nothing in this world will make me go along with my cousin's idiotic plan.'

After dinner that evening, Sally and Consuela retired to their room at the inn, leaving Kelly to finish off the bottle of claret and enjoy a cigar.

'I really thought he'd change his mind,' Sally said sadly. 'A good meal and a glass or two of wine should have made him more receptive, but it didn't.'

Consuela slipped off her gown and sat on edge of the bed to take off her dainty shoes. 'Don't worry, Sally. I have another plan, only this time it doesn't include Finn or his horse and carriage.'

'Really?' Sally stared at her in surprise. 'What is it this time?'

'We can do it on our own. We'll get up early and walk to the gates of Follyfield Park. I'll pretend to have sprained my ankle. I'll fall down in a faint and we'll be taken into the house.'

Sally eyed her curiously. 'All right, but what then?'

'What do you mean? We'll be on the inside and then we'll decide what to do.'

'But Consuela, they will probably send us back here in a carriage, if we're lucky. If not it could be very embarrassing, and defeat the whole purpose of coming all this way.'

'I wanted an adventure, and this surpasses all my expectations. Don't worry, Sally. It will work, I promise.' Consuela pulled the coverlet up to her chin and closed her eyes. 'We have to get up very early.'

It was obvious from Consuela's steady breathing that she had fallen asleep almost as soon as she laid her dark head on the pillow, but it was not the same for Sally. She undressed slowly and lay down beside the sleeping Consuela, but it was some time before she managed to drift off into an uneasy slumber.

'Wake up, Sally. Wake up.'

In her dream Flower had turned into a person and she was shaking her violently. 'Leave me alone,' Sally murmured.

'Come on. We have to go soon or it will be too late. Get up, Sally.'

Sally opened her eyes. 'What's the matter?'

'We're going to save Flower. My plan will work, you'll see. Now, do I have to douse you in cold water, or are you getting up?'

Consuela was clutching the pitcher from the washstand, and Sally had no doubt that she would carry out her threat. Sally raised herself from the warm bed and dressed hastily. Consuela's plan did not seem any more feasible in the light of day, but Sally was desperate. This might be her last chance to save Flower from becoming a brood mare. They crept downstairs, having seen no one other than a sleepy maidservant, who unlocked the door for them.

'We're going for a walk before breakfast,' Sally said casually. 'If Mr Kelly asks for Miss Suggs and Miss Riordan, please tell him we'll be back soon.'

'That was rash,' Consuela hissed as they stepped out into the early morning sunshine. 'Now Kelly will know what we're up to.'

Sally shot her a sideways glance. 'Don't you think he'll have worked it out for himself? Kelly is not a fool. He'll realise what we're doing the minute he finds out that we've left the inn, so we'd better hurry.'

'I hope it's not too far to Follyfield Park,' Consuela said breathlessly as she tried to keep pace with Sally.

'This was your idea in the first place.'

'If you keep walking so quickly I won't be acting when I fall down in a faint.'

'Stop grumbling, Consuela. This is your chance for the big adventure you wanted so much.'

'Hmm.' Consuela fell silent, or perhaps she was too breathless to talk; in any event, Sally was glad of the respite.

The massive wrought-iron gates of Follyfield Park were open when Sally and Consuela finally reached their destination. A tradesman's cart was lumbering along the tree-lined avenue, leaving clouds of dust in its wake. Consuela followed it, breaking into a run so that Sally had to quicken her pace in order to keep up. It was only when they neared the

Georgian mansion with its white colonnade and elegant façade that Sally began to panic inwardly. The plan, which had seemed unlikely to succeed now seemed doomed, but they had come this far and there was no turning back.

'I'll have to stop,' Consuela gasped. 'I have a pain in my side. I think I'm going to die.'

'It's a stitch,' Sally said impatiently. 'Don't they have those in California?' She staggered as Consuela collapsed against her, groaning and clutching her side.

'Grip your thumbs hard,' Sally said in desperation. 'That's what Ma always made me do when I was riding and had a stitch.' She turned her head at the sound of horse's hoofs coming towards them at a gallop, but before she had a chance to drag Consuela out of the way, a horse emerged from the cloud of dust. The rider reacted quickly, but as Sally tried to protect Consuela she suffered a glancing blow that sent her crashing to the ground.

Sally opened her eyes to whiteness and a cool waft of scented air. She blinked, but as she attempted to move her head she experienced a sharp pain that made her wince.

'Sally, are you all right?' Consuela's voice seemed to come from somewhere far away.

'Oh, dear. I think she's broken her head,' Consuela said, sobbing. 'It's all my fault. I've killed her.'

'Nonsense. She's got a headache and I suspect she's a bit concussed.'

Sally opened her eyes again, and Consuela's anxious face came into focus, together with that of a young and extremely handsome man, whose blond hair flopped over his brow. His blue eyes were filled with concern.

'How are you feeling, Miss Suggs?' His voice was cultured and he sounded genuinely worried.

Sally drifted back to the whiteness and realised dimly that she was staring up at a high ceiling with ornate plasterwork, and surely there were chubby little cherubs flying overhead. Perhaps she was dying, as Consuela had feared.

'Speak to me, Sally.' Consuela stroked Sally's cheek. 'The doctor is coming and Kelly has been sent for. He'll be so angry with me.'

'It was an accident, Miss Riordan,' the stranger said calmly.

Sally closed her eyes. 'Where am I, and who are you?'

'That's a good sign.' There was a smile in the stranger's voice. 'You've had a nasty blow to the head, Miss Suggs. You're in Follyfield Park.'

'And this is Sir Bertram,' Consuela said hastily. 'You remember the name, Sally?'

'I think so.' Sally closed her eyes. If she kept looking at them, the little angels would come down from the ceiling and take her up to heaven. She would be with Ma again. She was vaguely aware of voices, and something cool was pressed against her brow, but she kept drifting off to sleep. Time ceased to mean anything, and she felt as though she were floating on a soft cloud. Someone lifted her gently and held a cold glass to her lips. She drank thirstily, but the liquid was bitter and she drifted off to sleep.

'Suggs, can you hear me?' Sally recognised Kelly's voice. She would know him anywhere and, although her eyelids were heavy, she managed to open them enough to see his face hovering above her.

'You're here,' she whispered. 'Don't let the angels take me, Kelly.'

'The only person who'll be taking you anywhere is me, Suggs. But you have to get well first.' Kelly held her hand.

'They're on the ceiling, Kelly,' she said weakly. 'They're flying around above me.'

'Don't worry, sir. It's a case of mild concussion. The young lady doesn't know what she's saying.' Another voice broke into Sally's consciousness, making her tighten her grip on Kelly's hand.

'For god's sake, man. I don't need a medical man to tell me what's wrong. She can see those damned cherubs.'

'I never liked them. They used to scare me when I was a child.' The voice that seemed to belong to Sir Bertram held a hint of laughter. Sally wanted to speak to him, but she was floating far away again.

'She will get well, won't she, doctor?' Consuela sounded as if she was crying again.

Sally wanted to comfort her, but she was too tired.

'Can she be moved to somewhere quieter, doctor?'

'Rest is what she needs, Mr Kelly.'

'The blue bedchamber is probably the best place. Miss Riordan can have the adjacent room.'

'Thank you, Sir Bertram. I won't leave her side. It's all my fault.'

More sobbing from Consuela and Sally struggled to open her eyes. She wanted to comfort her friend, but suddenly she was being lifted in the air and now she really was floating.

'Don't worry, Suggs. I'm sending the angels back where they came from. You'll be more comfortable where I'm taking you. Consuela is coming, too.'

It was dark when Sally opened her eyes, but there were candles set at strategic positions around the room, and she was lying in a canopied bed with crisp cotton sheets. Her fingers played with the silk coverlet. She peered nervously at the ceiling, but the angels had flown away. She was safe and she realised that Kelly was in the chair at her bedside.

'Kelly.'

He was instantly alert and he leaned forward. 'Suggs, you've come round at last.'

'My head hurts, Kelly.'

'You have had an accident, but thank God, you're on the mend.'

'I can't remember. Everything's a blur. Where am I?'

'You're in the blue bedchamber at Follyfield Park.

You've been in and out of consciousness since you were knocked down by Sir Bertram's horse this morning.'

'Where's Flower?' Sally attempted to sit up, but fell back against the down-filled pillows.

'I believe she's here in the stables, but this isn't the time to worry about a horse. We have to get you back on your feet.'

Sheer relief flooded over Sally in a rush of warmth, bringing tears to her eyes. 'I'm sorry, Kelly.'

He stroked her tangled hair back from her forehead. 'What are you sorry for?'

'We shouldn't have come here without telling you.'

'Don't worry about that. You have to rest and keep quiet for a day or two.'

'Where's Consuela?'

'She was exhausted. I told her to get some sleep.'

'Is Sir Bertram angry with us?'

'D'you know, he's a really decent chap, Suggs. He's very concerned about you and he's been a most generous host. When you're better we'll raise the subject of buying back Flower, but I'm not saying anything until you're on the mend.'

'Thank you, Kelly.' Sally managed a smile even though it hurt her bruised face. 'I'm hungry. Do you think I could have something to eat?'

The doctor called next day and he advised Sally to remain in bed for the rest of the week, but she had other ideas. Her head ached and she had a black eye, but she was feeling much better. She waited until the doctor left before attempting to rise from the luxury of the feather bed, but the door flew open and Consuela rushed into the room.

'You must stay in bed, Sally. The doctor said so.'

'I feel much better. It was just a bump on the head.'

'The doctor said you must rest and you mustn't get excited. Please be sensible.'

Sally raised herself to a sitting position. 'Have you been to the stables, Consuela? Is Flower there?'

'That's what I came to tell you.' Consuela perched on the edge of the bed, meeting Sally's anxious gaze with a wide smile. 'I've just come from there. I went down to breakfast early, but Sir Bertram was already there. He said he was going to exercise a new horse he'd just purchased, and I asked if I could see the stables.'

'Yes, that's very interesting, but you haven't answered my question.'

'I'm just getting there. I've never seen Flower, of course, but Sir Bertram's new horse is an Andalusian dapple-grey mare, and when I whispered her name she looked at me with those beautiful brown eyes and I'm sure I saw a tear in the corner of one of them.'

'Don't say things like that or you'll make me cry.'

'I'm sorry, but I was so excited that I had to come upstairs and tell you. I didn't like to ask any questions because I don't know all the details, so I left it to you and Finn.'

'I must get up. I have to see Flower for myself. I can't lie around in bed all day.'

Consuela stood up, eyeing her with a worried frown. 'I wasn't supposed to upset you. Finn will be cross with me.'

'I can handle your cousin. Help me to get dressed, Consuela. I still feel a bit giddy.'

'Oh dear.' Consuela glanced at the door, as if wondering whether to make a hasty retreat, but Sally was already on her feet and she grasped Consuela's hand.

'I have to tell Sir Bertram everything before he introduces Flower to one of his stallions. You understand what I'm saying, don't you?'

Consuela chuckled. 'I've been around horses all my life, Sally. I think I know how things work.'

'Good. I'm glad I don't have to go into more detail, but you have to admit it's urgent.'

'I'm getting on so well with Sir Bertram,' Consuela said, sighing. 'But if you tell him we tricked our way into his home, he won't speak to me again.'

'You're engaged to be married.' Sally reached for her chemise and slipped it over her head. 'Remember?'

'I know, but I told you that it was arranged by Papa. I don't love Newton, and I think I could easily fall for a man like Sir Bertram.'

Sally picked up her stays. 'Lace me up tightly. I need something to keep me upright.'

Consuela obliged, tightening the strings until Sally could hardly breathe. 'You're being mean now, Sally.'

'That's tight enough.' Sally held up her hand. 'Did you tell our host that you came to London to have your wedding dress made?'

'I'm not a fool.' Consuela slipped Sally's plain cotton gown over her head. 'I really like him, Sally, and I think he likes me, too.'

'This is complicated enough without you adding to our problems, Consuela. What does Kelly say?'

Consuela's olive skin paled alarmingly. 'He doesn't know. Please don't tell him. I'm sure he'll be on Papa's side.'

Sally ran her hand through her tumbled curls. 'If you'll do something with my hair, I promise to speak to Kelly. He's a reasonable man – most of the time, anyway.'

Kelly pushed his chair back from the dining table and stood up. 'Sally! You should be resting in bed.'

'Finish your meal, Kelly,' Sally said calmly. 'I'm feeling much better.'

'You'd better sit down and have some breakfast as you're here, and then you must rest.'

Sally was in no position to argue. If she were being honest she would have to admit that she felt a little weak, but she refused to give in to her injuries. 'I'd like some coffee, if it's still hot.'

'You must eat as well,' Consuela said anxiously.

'I wish you would both stop fussing.' Sally reached

for the coffee pot and filled a cup, hoping that Kelly had not seen that her hand was shaking.

If he had noticed, Kelly said nothing. He went to the sideboard, lifted the cover of a silver serving dish and spooned buttered eggs onto a plate. He placed it on the table in front of Sally.

'Try to eat something. You need to keep your strength up.'

She smiled. 'You sound like Pa.'

'Then I hope you'll do as I say, Suggs.' Kelly resumed his seat. 'I think it's time we told Sir Bertram why we came to Follyfield Park.'

'Is that necessary?' Consuela looked from one to the other. 'I mean, it really was an accident. We didn't plan for Sally to get hurt.'

'Of course not,' Kelly said agreeably. 'But we need to put our case to him and offer to buy her back. We can't expect him to give her up without recompense.'

Sally was about to respond when the door opened and Sir Bertram walked into the dining room.

'Miss Suggs, it's good to see you up and about. How are you feeling?'

'Much better, thank you, sir.'

'Don't let me interrupt your breakfast.' Sir Bertram was about to retreat when Kelly stood up.

'Don't go, Sir Bertram. We have a matter to discuss with you.'

Consuela bowed her head. 'It was all my idea, sir. I'm at fault, not Sally.'

Sir Bertram pulled up a chair and sat down. 'I'm intrigued. What have you done that is so terrible, Miss Riordan?'

Sally was quick to hear the cajoling note in Sir Bertram's voice, but Consuela was not to blame for any of this. She cleared her throat. 'Consuela was only trying to help me, Sir Bertram.'

Kelly resumed his seat. 'Perhaps I should explain?'

'No, Kelly,' Sally said firmly. 'Flower is my property, or she was until Orrin Vasey managed to persuade Miss Appleton to sell her.'

'Vasey?' Sir Bertram was suddenly alert. 'That's the man who sold me the Andalusian mare. Are you telling me that the animal was not his to sell?'

Sally nodded emphatically. 'Flower is my horse, Sir Bertram. She is a foal out of Gaia, who belonged to my mother. I can't prove any of this because the registration papers were burned when our home was razed to the ground.'

'Gaia was a famous Andalusian,' Sir Bertram said thoughtfully. 'She was Emily Tranter's horse. I saw them perform several times at Astley's Amphitheatre. Your mother was a brilliant horsewoman, Miss Suggs.'

'Yes, she was.' Sally managed a smile even though unshed tears were burning her eyes. 'And Flower is all that I have left of her. Vasey was desperate to get his hands on her.'

'We came to Follyfield in the hope that the animal you purchased was Sally's horse.' Kelly leaned towards Sir Bertram, his expression serious for once. 'If you will allow her to see the Andalusian, she will know instantly if it is her horse.'

Sir Bertram sat back in his chair. 'What exactly are you proposing, Mr Kelly? You told me that you have started up a stud farm of your own. How do I know that this isn't a ruse to get a thoroughbred mare on the cheap?'

'Flower isn't a brood mare,' Sally said angrily. 'I might breed from her one day, but that isn't why I want to buy her back. I'll work for the rest of my life to pay you whatever you ask.'

Consuela leaped to her feet. 'Sally loves that horse, Sir Bertram. This isn't just a matter of money, can't you see that? Haven't you ever valued something more than life itself?'

Sir Bertram eyes lit with a smile. 'How passionate you are, Miss Riordan.'

'I know what heartbreak feels like.' Consuela clutched her hands to her bosom, her dark eyes magnified by tears. 'I am being forced into an alliance with a man I barely know. My life is in ruins, but I do not want Sally to suffer as I am suffering.'

Sally was startled by this sudden outburst. It was theatrical, but there was no doubting Consuela's sincerity. Her passionate words seemed to have had the desired effect on Sir Bertram, who rose to his feet, taking Consuela's hands in his.

'You poor girl. That's appalling, but it happens even in this country.'

Kelly also stood up. 'Why didn't you tell me this, Consuela? You let me think that all was well with you.'

Genuine tears were coursing down Consuela's cheeks. 'You would have sided with Papa.'

'Don't deny it, Kelly.' Sally raised herself from her seat with difficulty. 'You would have sent her home because you would have thought it your duty. When will you men learn that we women have hearts and minds of our own? We aren't chattels to be sold off or given away. I feel exactly the same about Flower. She's my horse and I will look after her for the rest of her life.'

Kelly and Sir Bertram stared at her as if she were speaking in a foreign language.

'We just try to protect the women we love,' Kelly said slowly. 'Of course you are your own person, Sally. I never thought of you in any other way.'

'What about Consuela?' Sally demanded. 'Will you send her back to California to face an arranged marriage?'

He shook his head. 'Consuela, you are a free woman as far as I'm concerned, and I'll tell my uncle that when I write to him. It's your choice. If you want to remain in England, you are welcome to stay with me for as long as you wish.'

Consuela wiped her eyes on a table napkin. 'I'm sorry, Sir Bertram. I haven't got a hanky.'

He produced a spotless white cotton handkerchief from his pocket and gave it to her. 'You are brave as well as beautiful, Miss Riordan. I'm proud to have you as my guest for as long as you wish. That goes for you too, Miss Suggs and Mr Kelly. I suggest we go to the stable and you can judge whether the horse I purchased is the one you so lovingly call Flower. Do you feel well enough to visit her now, Miss Suggs?'

Chapter Twenty-Six

The ecstatic welcome that Flower gave Sally was enough to prove their connection without resorting to official papers. Sir Bertram acknowledged this immediately.

'There's no doubt in my mind that the Andalusian is your horse, Miss Suggs.'

Sally leaned against Flower, rubbing her cheek against the horse's smooth neck. 'What do we do now, sir?'

'You'll have to name your price,' Kelly said slowly. 'But it will take me a while to raise the money.'

'We should make Miss Appleton pay. She was completely in the wrong.' Sally stroked Flower's muzzle.

'We'll repay you, Sir Bertram,' Kelly said firmly. 'That is if you're willing to part with Flower.'

Consuela grasped Sir Bertram's hand. 'You must

let Sally have her horse. It would be cruel to keep them apart. You can see how they love each other.'

Sir Bertram smiled down at her. 'You have a tender heart, Consuela. I may call you that, mayn't I? After all, I think we all know each other well enough now to drop the formalities.' He raised her hand to his lips. 'I agree that Flower should be with her original owner. I'll look elsewhere for a replacement.'

Sally breathed a sigh of relief. 'You are more than kind, Sir Bertram.'

'It would take a hard-hearted fellow to resist when faced with two such indomitable ladies. But perhaps this would be a good time for you to return to the house, Sally. The doctor did prescribe rest as the best cure for a head injury.'

'I'll see that she obeys his orders.' Kelly proffered his arm to Sally. 'Flower is safe and soon she'll be back in our stable. You can rest now.'

Sir Bertram turned to Consuela. 'Perhaps you'd like to see the rest of Follyfield? I could have one of my quieter horses saddled up for you. I think we still have a side-saddle somewhere in the tack room. My late mother was a keen horsewoman.'

'Sir Bertram, I was born and raised in California. I could ride a horse before I could walk and I don't need a side-saddle.'

Sally turned her head so that they would not see her smiling. Consuela was on her way to charming the wealthy owner of Follyfield Park into falling in love with her. Unless she was very much mistaken, there would be some use for Consuela's wedding dress after all. Miss Consuela Riordan knew her own mind and handsome, rich Sir Bertram did not stand a chance.

Four days later, the only outward sign of Sally's accident was the fading bruise around her eye. Enforced rest, good food and her reunion with Flower had all contributed to a speedy recovery, and Sir Bertram was an excellent host. Moreover it was becoming increasingly obvious that he had fallen in love with Consuela and the feeling was mutual.

'My uncle will blame me,' Kelly said ruefully as he waited with Sally while Sir Bertram and Consuela said their goodbyes.

'I don't see why.' Sally turned away, not wanting to embarrass Consuela, although she doubted if either of the love-struck pair was aware of their presence.

'I'm responsible for Consuela while she's in London. She came to purchase her wedding gown, but instead she appears to have picked a different husband.'

'Do you think Sir Bertram will propose?'

'After dinner last night, he asked my permission to pay court to my cousin.'

'So what did you say?'

'What could I say? I told him that I have no objection, but my uncle might feel differently. Consuela is under age and she needs her father's permission to marry. Besides which, they've only known each other for a few days. It could turn out to be a terrible mistake.'

'What has happened to you, Kelly? You never used to care a jot for convention, and you never took anything seriously.'

He met her amused gaze with a steady glance. 'You did, Suggs. I used to treat life like one long joke, but you've made me stop and think. I'm beginning to see people and situations differently. Maybe I'm turning into a responsible citizen.'

'Don't blame me, Kelly. If you've changed I'm sure I had no hand in it.'

'I wouldn't be too sure about that.' Kelly moved aside as one of Sir Bertram's grooms brought the carriage round to the front of the house, followed by a boy leading Flower. Kelly caught Sally by the hand as she was about to mount. 'Are you certain that you're well enough to ride? It's a long way to Highgate.'

'Of course I am. I haven't had a chance to exercise Flower for such a long time.'

He lifted her onto the saddle. 'You can do the first stage, but when we stop to give the horses a rest we'll see how you feel then.' He turned to Sir Bertram. 'Thank you, once again, for your hospitality, and for the return of Sally's horse. You'll get your money as soon as possible.'

'It's not important, Finn. I'm happy to see Sally and Flower reunited.'

'Bertram is going to visit us often,' Consuela said, beaming.

Sir Bertram bowed over her hand, holding her gaze with a tender smile. 'We could meet when you return to London. I have a town house in John Adam Street, not far from the opera house at Covent Garden, although to be honest I prefer the Gaiety Theatre.'

'I love the theatre,' Consuela was about to climb into the carriage, but she hesitated. 'You will come and visit me at Kelly's farm, won't you?'

'Nothing would keep me away.' Sir Bertram helped her into the vehicle, releasing her hand with obvious reluctance.

Sally leaned over in the saddle. 'Thank you for everything, Sir Bertram. I look forward to seeing you again very soon.'

'It's been my pleasure, Sally.'

She wheeled Flower around, encouraging her to a trot and then a canter. It was wonderful to feel the wind in her hair and the sun on her face. There was a slight hint of autumn in the air even though it was late summer, but the leaves on the horse-chestnut trees on the edge of the estate were drooping and beginning to turn brown. Sally had to wait for the gatekeeper to do his duty, and as she took a last look at Follyfield Park, she could not help thinking of Paradise Row. The stark contrast between the two made her realise how far she had come since the fire had changed their lives forever. She had accused Kelly of being a different person, but she realised suddenly that she, too, had changed. She knew now where she wanted to be and what she wanted to do with her life. She turned and waved to Kelly as he drove the carriage towards the gates and home.

It was early evening when Sally finally arrived at the cottage. It had been a long ride and she was exhausted, but the sight of her father weeding the flowerbed in the small front garden gladdened her heart. She dismounted and tethered Flower to the fence while she went to give her father a hug.

'You've been a long time at market, Sal,' he said, chuckling. 'I told your mother that you'd forget something and we'd have to send you out again.'

Sally's heart sank. 'Ma's not here any more, Pa.'

'No, my duck. She's gone to visit Aunt Poppy, or I think that's what she said. But that girl who's in the family way has been looking after me. I think we should keep her on, Sal. She's a good cook.'

'Yes, Pa. That's a good idea.' Sally kissed his whiskery cheek. 'I'll just take Flower to the stable and I'll give her a rub down.'

'That's right, love.' Ted went back to his weeding, humming tunelessly.

Sally walked Flower round to the barn where she was stabled and gave her a good rub down. Having made sure there was fresh water and feed freely available, Sally gave Flower a last pat before she went indoors. She found Josie seated by the range with her feet up on the brass rail, but she heaved herself off the chair when she saw Sally.

'You're home. Why was you away so long? I had to make up all sorts of fairy tales to tell your pa, although, bless him, I don't think he remembers anything for more than five minutes.'

Sally met her halfway and gave her a hug. 'You're looking well. I'm sorry if Pa has been difficult.'

'He's just confused and forgetful, but he's a love really. I just make sure he's well fed and he's happy enough. What happened to you? Did you get Flower back?'

Sally sank down at the kitchen table. 'Is there any tea in the pot? I've just ridden from Hatfield and I'm worn out.'

'Where did you get that black eye? Was it Vasey who clouted you?'

'No, it was an accident.' Sally held her hand out to take the cup and saucer from Josie. 'Sit down and I'll tell you. It's been quite a week.'

Josie listened open-mouthed, throwing in a question every now and then. 'My goodness,' she said when Sally paused for breath, 'I want to see this Spanish heiress. D'you think Sir Bertram really will come and visit?'

'She's only half Spanish, and yes, I'm sure he will. He was obviously besotted with Consuela, and she is very pretty, and lively.'

'So what about Miss Appleton? If she took the money for Flower she ought to give it back.'

'That's exactly what I think. It isn't up to Kelly to repay Sir Bertram. Flower is mine, and Miss Appleton should not have let Vasey talk her into selling a horse that belonged to someone else. I'll go see her tomorrow and tell her in no uncertain terms to give me the money.'

'You must be hungry,' Josie said, heaving herself to her feet. 'I've got a stew simmering on the range, and I made some bread this morning. Jane's been teaching me how to bake, and I even made some buns. I'm quite proud of meself.'

'I dare say I could manage a plateful, but we stopped at an inn and Kelly treated us to a meal.'

Josie shot her a sideways glance. 'You're getting very cosy with him, aren't you?'

'We work together, and he's a good friend, that's all. Don't look at me like that, Josie.'

'Hoity-toity,' Josie said, laughing.

Sally shrugged. 'Anyway, tomorrow morning I'm going to ride to Fleet Hall and have it out with Miss Appleton, and if she won't cooperate I'll speak to Gideon. As I see it, he's the only person she'll listen to, apart from her father, of course.'

Cecily was seated at a rosewood escritoire in the drawing room. She dismissed the housemaid with a wave of her hand. 'Well, what do you want, Miss Suggs?'

Sally stood her ground. 'You know very well why I've come here today.'

'Enlighten me.'

'You sold my horse to Orrin Vasey, without my permission.'

'As I recall, the animal in question had been abandoned by you and was in Mr Lawrence's care. I was acting on his behalf, and I don't have to justify my actions to you.'

Sally took a step towards Cecily, clenching her fists at her sides. 'If I go to Mr Lawrence, do you think he will agree with you?'

Cecily rose to her feet. 'You have done nothing but cause trouble ever since you came into our lives. I want nothing to do with you.'

'I'm not leaving until you give me the money you accepted from Vasey. We managed to rescue Flower from the person who was tricked into buying her, but he is entitled to a refund.'

'I don't deal with financial matters,' Cecily said stiffly.

'Then I'll go to your father and see what he says.'

'You will leave this house immediately, or I'll ring for Stafford and have you thrown out.'

'Do you think Gideon would approve of the way you're treating me? He's a good man and he'll be on my side.'

'Don't bring him into this.'

There was a note of panic in Cecily's voice and Sally knew she had the upper hand. 'Then give me the money and we'll say no more about it.'

'I can't,' Cecily said reluctantly. 'I gave it to

Gideon. He had to pay some urgent bills, or risk losing Hill Farm.'

'Why did you have to sell my horse? Surely you have money of your own.'

Cecily turned away. 'I have an allowance from my father, that's all. One day all this will be mine, but until then I am totally dependent upon him for everything.'

'Then I'm sorry for you. Maybe it would do you good to go out and earn money for yourself. Perhaps you would have more respect for other people's property if you had to work for what you have.' Sally left the room without waiting for a response.

She tipped the stable boy who was holding Flower's reins, and she used the low wall as a mounting block. She took a last look at Fleet Hall and suddenly it seemed to have lost its glamour. Instead of a fine country house she saw it as a prison, with Cecily trapped by wealth and position, a victim of her father's ambition and pride. As she rode away Sally could not help comparing the love and attention she had received from her own father, and she was genuinely sorry for Cecily.

There was one more call she had to make before she went to Kelly's place, and, as luck would have it, Gideon was at home. He was dressed for the road and was about to leave when Sally arrived at Hill Farm.

'Sally, this is a surprise. I thought you were in London with Kelly.' There was an icy note in his voice, but his expression was well controlled and unreadable.

Sally dismounted and tethered Flower to the gate post. 'I'm so glad I caught you. Can you spare me a few minutes?'

'Of course, what is it?'

She followed him into the kitchen where, as always, Mrs Wallace was busy preparing the midday meal for the workers.

'It's good to see you, Sally. I thought you'd gone to London.'

'I was in London, Mrs Wallace, and then we went to Hatfield.'

'Would you like a cup of tea, dear? The kettle's just boiled.'

'Thank you.'

'Sit down and tell me what's happened to make you come here on the off-chance of catching me at home.' Gideon pulled out a chair for her and took a seat opposite.

'I went to London with Kelly, that's true, but I was looking for Vasey. I was right, he'd got his hands on Flower at last, and I knew he would sell her to the highest bidder.'

Gideon's forehead creased into frown lines, and he met her gaze with a questioning look. 'What are you saying?'

'I've just come from Fleet Hall. Cecily confessed to selling Flower, but when I demanded the money, which should have come to me by rights, she told me that she'd given it to you. She wanted to help you out of a difficult situation.'

'It's true that she loaned me some money, but I'm sure it was hers to give.'

'Then you were deceived. She's just admitted her guilt.'

Gideon shook his head. 'Why would she do something like that? I wouldn't have asked it of her.'

'Because she's in love with you, Gideon. You've given her hope and then you've dashed it, but she would steal in order to help you. Doesn't that mean anything?'

'Are you saying I've led her on?'

'Yes, I suppose I am. Although I wouldn't have put it quite so baldly.'

'You have, sir,' Mrs Wallace said firmly. 'You've played fast and loose with that young woman's feelings, if I may be allowed to say so.'

Gideon looked from one to the other, his eyes wide with astonishment. 'I never meant to. On my honour, if I've done anything to hurt Cessy, it was unintentional.'

Mrs Wallace placed the teapot in front of Sally, adding cups and saucers and a jug of milk. 'You've had stars in your eyes ever since you met Sally. I'm saying this because I've looked after you since you were a boy. But you've overlooked the one person who's always loved you.'

'Thank you, Jane,' Gideon said with a wry smile. 'I think I get the point you're trying to make. I suppose I have treated Cessy badly, but I can't believe that she stole to help me out of difficulty.'

'I'd say it was heroic, except for the fact that I have to find the money to reimburse Sir Bertram Eustace, who was the person who purchased Flower from Vasey.'

'I haven't got the money now, Sally.' Gideon ran his hands through his already tousled sandy hair. 'There's only one way out – I'll have to sell Hill Farm.'

'Oh, no, sir.' Mrs Wallace threw up her hands, her eyes filling with tears. 'What will become of Arthur and me, and young Bert, too?'

'There is another way,' Sally said softly. She met Gideon's frantic gaze with a smile. 'You know the answer, Gideon. I don't have to tell you, do I?'

'She's right, sir,' Mrs Wallace said eagerly. 'But you'd best make up your mind quickly. Miss Cecily has many admirers. My friend Mrs Hart told me that the gentlemen practically queue up at the door.'

Sally laid her hand on Gideon's as it rested on the table. 'You were never in love with me, Gideon. It was just a passing fancy. I like you more than I can say, but that's all.'

He slid his hand away and stood up. 'I need some air. I have to think.' He hurried from the kitchen, allowing the door to slam of its own accord.

Sally and Mrs Wallace exchanged meaningful glances.

'Will he be all right?' Sally asked anxiously.

'I hope so, dear. But one thing I do know, and

that is he loves Hill Farm, and I think he'd do almost anything to keep it going.'

'I hope it works out well for him, but I'm afraid it doesn't help me. I now have to find the money to repay Sir Bertram, and it's obviously no use asking Gideon if it's already been spent.'

'I wish I could help.'

Sally patted her on the shoulder. 'Just look after him, Mrs Wallace. I think it best if I don't come round here too often.'

'I understand.' Mrs Wallace patted Sally on the shoulder. 'You're always welcome in my kitchen, but maybe it's best if you come when Mr Lawrence is away from home.'

Sally smiled, but there was nothing she could add, and she left the farmhouse with a feeling of sadness. She would miss Gideon, but she knew that his happiness and future security depended upon someone else, and the best thing she could do for him was to walk away.

She untethered Flower and rode off in the direction of the old Parker place.

* * *

It was hardly a surprise to find a carriage and pair in the yard, with a footman walking the horses, and the coachman leaning against the wall, smoking a clay pipe. He straightened up and tipped his hat when Sally dismounted, which she acknowledged with a smile. She tethered Flower to the fence and made her way across the yard to enter by the kitchen door. The sight that met her eyes was hardly welcoming. The flagstone floor was covered in muddy footprints and the table was littered with dirty crockery, empty bottles and butter pooling in an oily mess on a cracked plate. Wet garments had been slung over the backs of the chairs, and boots caked in mud had been abandoned where the wearers had discarded them.

'Kelly.' Sally opened the door and called his name again. The sound of her voice echoed throughout the house, but there was no response. The rest of the ground floor was equally untidy and it seemed as if the workers had been enjoying their master's hospitality in his absence. Sally marched out through the French windows in the sitting room and made her way to the stable block, where she found Kelly chatting to Sir Bertram and Consuela.

'Sally, how nice to see you,' Sir Bertram said, smiling. 'I came to ask Consuela if she would like to go for a carriage ride, but you would be most welcome to join us.'

'Yes, indeed,' Consuela said half-heartedly. 'That would be nice, Sally.'

'I'm afraid I have too much to do.' Sally smiled although inwardly she was furious. She met Kelly's quizzical gaze with a frown. 'Might I have a word?'

He shrugged. 'That sounds ominous. Will you

excuse us, Bertram?' He followed Sally out into the yard where the men were hard at work.

'Have you seen the state of the house?' Sally demanded angrily. 'It looks as though the farm labourers have turned it into a pigsty. Unless, of course, you and your guest had a party for the whole village last night.'

Kelly laid his hand on her shoulder. 'Yes, I know it's a mess. I've had words with the men and they're well aware they must make amends. I should have locked the house up before I left, but I won't make that mistake again.'

'No, I should hope not.'

'And you'll soon have it shipshape again.'

Sally stared at him aghast. 'Do you expect me to clean up the mess made by your employees? I've kept house for you, Kelly. I'm not a skivvy.'

'No, of course not, but . . .'

'No buts. I'm surprised at you for allowing this to happen.'

'Come on, Suggs. You're being unreasonable, and you're very late today. What happened?'

Incensed by his casual attitude, Sally glared at him. 'I was trying to get the money to repay Sir Bertram, while you were here having a party, by the look of things.'

'That's not fair. I had Consuela to look after. Anyway, did Miss Appleton cooperate?'

Sally stood, arms akimbo. 'It just shows what a besotted woman will do for an ungrateful man – she gave the money to Gideon because he had creditors on his heels. It's all gone, Kelly, and Flower still technically belongs to Sir Bertram.' She was about to walk away when Kelly caught her by the hand.

'Sally, I can see why you're upset, but I'm sure we can come to some amicable arrangement with Sir Bertram. He's been talking business already, and I think we might be able to help each other.'

'Where does that leave Flower and me?'

'That's what I meant. I don't see why we can't go on as we were . . .'

'So my place is in the kitchen clearing up the mess, while you talk horses to Sir Bertram with no certain outcome where Flower is concerned?'

'Not exactly, but with Consuela here perhaps we could both make an effort to make her feel at home.'

'I'm not your servant, Kelly.' Sally untied her apron and flung it at him. 'You can hire a scrub woman. I've had enough.' She marched off, ignoring Kelly's pleas for her to stop.

Chapter Twenty-Seven

That night, when all was quiet in the cottage, Sally had made up her mind. If Kelly had followed her and they had talked things over like sensible people, she might have changed her mind. But he had allowed her to walk away, and she was now without any means of supporting her family. Josie was looking after Pa, and Kelly would soon find another housekeeper. It seemed that she was no longer needed, except perhaps as a breadwinner, and there was little likelihood of finding a well-paid occupation locally. There was only one course of action left to her, and that was to return to London.

Sally had always toyed with the idea of performing at Astley's, and perhaps this last setback was the very thing she needed. She packed her mother's riding habit and a few essentials in two saddlebags and crept out of the cottage, heading for the stables. As always, Flower greeted her with soft whinnies and Sally was tempted to make a fuss of her, but a sense of urgency prevailed and she tacked up as quickly as her trembling hands would allow. Within the hour she was on her way to London.

The roads were deserted at first but the traffic increased gradually, and Sally broke the journey halfway to give Flower a rest while she used some of her precious money to purchase breakfast at a roadside inn. She had managed to save a little from the wages that Kelly paid her, although she had left a small amount for Josie, together with a note promising to send more money as soon as she found work. Sally had not mentioned anything about her intention of seeking employment at Astley's, in case she failed when the time came to test her ability as a horsewoman.

It was late morning when she eventually arrived at Astley's, where she found a queue of would-be performers extending along Westminster Bridge Road. However, she was not in the mood to wait in the pouring rain, and she had Flower to consider. Sally rode to the head of the queue and used her riding crop to rap on the door. As she had hoped, the door was flung open, but she found herself facing an irate man dressed in hunting pink and a battered top hat.

'What the hell d'you think you're doing? We ain't open yet.'

'I am Emily Tranter's daughter,' Sally announced

in a loud, clear voice. 'My mother was a star here, and I have come to take her place.'

'You've got a blooming cheek,' the man said gruffly. 'Better come inside before the crowd lynches you.' He stood aside to admit them, closing the door hastily as the would-be performers surged forward.

Sally dismounted. 'It's true what I said.'

He examined Flower in silence, running his hand over her muscular body with grim satisfaction. 'She's Gaia's foal, all right. I knew your ma. She was a lady and one of the best performers we've ever had.'

'So you'll give us a chance?'

'Why would a nice young person like you want to join this business? It ain't glamorous and the pay ain't brilliant.'

'I have my reasons, but I'm prepared to work hard. Ma taught me everything she knew but I haven't had a chance to use my skills yet. I want to show Flower off to her best advantage, and I need the work.'

He pushed his top hat to the back of his head, revealing a bald pate fringed with fluffy white hair, reminding Sally of a dandelion clock. His shrewd eyes narrowed as he looked her up and down, and then he nodded. 'I'll give you a go, but only for a week, you understand.'

'Thank you, sir.'

He extended a grimy hand. 'Jem Skipton, temporary manager. Can you be ready to perform this evening?'

Sally gulped and swallowed. She had not expected this. 'Yes, I think so. What would I have to do?'

'Oh, things,' he said vaguely. 'We're doing a Roman scene – you'll get a costume in wardrobe and the stage manager will put you in the picture. Make sure you wear pink tights, the audience likes to see a bit of leg.'

'Really? I thought they came to see the horses perform.'

Jem slapped her on the back. 'If it weren't for your accent I'd say you'd come up from the country, little girl. Just do what you're told and you'll be fine.' He patted Flower's neck. 'Nice piece of horse-flesh. Worth a small fortune. You need to sleep in the stable with her or you might find she's disappeared come morning.'

It was Sally's intention anyway, but now she was really nervous. She followed Jem's instructions and took Flower to the stables, where she found the grooms and stable boys sitting round, smoking, drinking beer and playing cards. No one seemed very interested in her or her horse, but one of the older men directed her to a stall, which was reasonably clean and well kept. It would not be the first time Sally had slept in a stable with Flower, but with the cacophony of noise going on all around her, she doubted if she would get much rest.

The next hour was spent grooming and feeding Flower, and cleaning the tack. When she was satisfied that she had done all she could, Sally went to wardrobe, where an overly plump woman with suspiciously bright red hair handed her a skimpy pink tunic and a pair of pink tights. Secretly horrified, Sally managed to smile and was about to thank the wardrobe mistress, but she turned away to chat to a tiny creature who was mending a costume.

Sally took the garments to the stall, which was to be her home for the coming week. Her stomach rumbled and she realised that she had not eaten since breakfast at the inn, but she caught a sudden waft of fried fish and she went to investigate. Mid-afternoon seemed to be a quiet time at the amphitheatre, with most of the stable boys and grooms falling asleep under the influence of alcohol, although some of the younger lads were larking around in the sawdust-covered ring. Sally followed the scent of food, but she came up short at the sight of Dolly, one of Kelly's lodgers, who was frying fish over a small spirit stove.

'Dolly?'

Dolly squinted at her through a haze of blue smoke from the pan of hot fat. 'That you, Sal?'

'Yes, it is. What are you doing here? Apart from cooking fish, that is?'

'I had to go somewhere when Kelly closed up shop, love. So I got a job here, feeding the ungrateful specimens what work for Astley's. Picky lot they are, too.'

'How much?' Sally said eagerly. 'I'm starving and I'm new here, so I don't know where to go for food.'

Dolly lifted two pieces of fish from the pan and

laid them on a none-too-clean plate. 'These are the last two and no one else seems interested, so you can have 'em for free. Just this once, mind.'

Sally was too hungry to argue and she sat cross-legged on the floor next to Dolly, burning her fingers as she broke the fish into bite-sized chunks.

'So why are you here, Sal?' Dolly leaned back against the wall and lit a cheroot, puffing smoke rings into the air. 'Where's Kelly these days?'

'We've gone our separate ways,' Sally said, swallowing a lump of hot fish.

'Funny,' Dolly mused. 'I thought as how you two would make a go of it.'

'What about you?' Sally asked, changing the subject hastily. 'I thought you had a gentleman friend.'

'I got several, but I don't let 'em take over me life. I likes me freedom too much. Take a tip from me, dear, keep yourself to yourself, especially here. Oh, and watch out for the bloke who plays Spartacus – you'll meet him tonight in the ring. He thinks he's a lady killer, but he's just after one thing, and then he goes on to the next woman.'

'Thank you, Dolly. I'll try to avoid him.'

Dolly scrambled to her feet. 'I got to go down the market to get fresh supplies. You should try my fried eel for supper. They're very popular, so you got to race off after the finale if you want some, or I'll have sold out. Good luck, Sal.'

* * *

As the afternoon wore on towards evening and the beginning of the performance, Sally was beginning to feel extremely nervous. The stage manager had come to give her instructions as to what was expected of her, and it sounded simple enough, but when she was waiting to go on it was a different matter altogether. However, Flower behaved as if she had been in the ring all her life. All Sally had to do was to look the part of a Roman slave, exposing an embarrassing amount of leg in the slightly baggy pink tights, which must have been made for someone much larger. The orchestra accompanied the performers loudly and with gusto, giving the acrobat who played Spartacus the opportunity to overact, playing to the gallery, to the obvious delight of the audience.

When her part of the show was over, Sally had the satisfaction of knowing that she had not disgraced herself, and one of the other girls stopped to congratulate her.

'You done well for a newcomer. We're all going to the pub after the show. You can come with us, if you like.'

'Thanks,' Sally said, smiling. 'Another time perhaps, but to be honest I'm worn out. I don't know how you do it, especially if you do two performances a day.'

'You get used to it, ducks.' The girl with the copper hair and green eyes held out her hand. 'I'm Emerald, by the way.'

'Sally Suggs.' Sally shook hands solemnly. 'That's a pretty name.'

'Me real name is Molly Jones, but Emerald sounds better, don't you think? It's me stage name, and one day I'm going to be the star of the show.' Emerald winked and sauntered off in the direction of the dressing room.

Sally made her way to Flower's stall. She was too exhausted to do anything, let alone think about food. She wrapped herself in a smelly horse blanket and lay down in the straw. If anyone tried to steal Flower they would have to step over her, and she kept her riding crop by her side, ready to fend off any intruder.

Each day was a challenge and Sally did her best to live up to her mother's reputation, but it was a strange life and the performers were a mixture of actors, circus folk, expert riders and even a few clowns. They were a polyglot crowd with a mixture of accents, customs and mercurial temperaments. Sally found an ally in Emerald, and Jem Skipton was as helpful as his position permitted, but Sally missed everyone at home. She scanned the audience every evening in the vague hope that Kelly might come looking for her, and one night she thought she saw him in the fourth row, but when she looked again the seat was empty, and she realised it was wishful thinking.

Sometimes, in the middle of the night when sleep

evaded her and her body ached from arduous rehearsals and the discomfort of sleeping on the floor, she wondered if all this was worth the sacrifice. She had expected Flower to take her rightful place as the successor to Gaia, but they were relegated to supporting the more experienced performers. The wages helped, but she sent most of her money home, entrusting it to one of the stable lads who visited his mother in Highgate every Sunday. Sally knew that he kept his word when he gave her badly spelled letters from Josie, some of the writing illegible with ink blots, but at the end of the first month there was good news. Josie had given birth to baby George, and both of them were doing well. Sally experienced a pang of heartache so severe that it made her cry. She missed her father and Josie, and she could even forgive Kelly for his cavalier treatment, but she could not admit defeat and return home.

Autumn turned into winter, the days were getting shorter and the nights were bitterly cold. Sally had to use some of her money to purchase warm clothing and a couple of blankets, as she was still sleeping on the stable floor. Most of the girls and other performers lived in digs close by, but Sally was determined to keep what was left of her wages to send home. Ned had been released from prison and was seeking work, which meant that Josie and the baby would eventually move into a home of their own. Sally was beginning to feel that Highgate, Hill Farm and Kelly's place were another life, and one which she greatly missed. However, as Emerald always said, no matter how the performers were feeling, they had to paint a smile on their faces and get on with the show. The audience were not interested in the lives of those whose sole purpose was to entertain them – they had paid good money and they were out to enjoy themselves.

As the weeks went by, Sally and Flower were given more prominence, and Flower lived up to her dam's reputation. Sally knew that she should be thrilled, but somehow the thought of being the star of the show had lost some of its lustre. Their performance was becoming automatic, although the applause made the hard work seem worthwhile, and Jem had given Sally a raise in her wages. But the biggest thrill so far was one evening when Sally spotted three familiar faces in the front row. She could hardly believe her eyes, but Gideon, Consuela and Sir Bertram were applauding enthusiastically, and after the finale they came backstage.

Consuela hugged Sally, despite the sharp spangles on Sally's costume. 'You were magnificent, Sally,' she said breathlessly. 'I've never seen such an exciting show.'

Sir Bertram kissed Sally's hand. 'You were splendid. You and your horse move as one.'

'Thank you both. That means a lot to me.' Sally turned to Gideon with a tentative smile. 'How are you? Is all well at Hill Farm? I can't believe you came to see me in the show.'

'I came with good news, Sally. I wanted you to be among the first to know.' Gideon grasped her hands in his. 'Hill Farm is saved.'

'You've asked Miss Appleton to marry you?'

'Yes, you were right all along. I should have listened to you in the first place.'

'Yes, you should,' she agreed, smiling. 'You are a stubborn man, Gideon Lawrence. But I'm very happy for you. I take it she accepted?'

'She did and we're to be married in the spring.'

Consuela edged him out of the way. 'Bertram and I are also to be married.'

'That's wonderful. I don't think I can take any more good news.' Sally brushed a tear from her cheek. 'You'll have to forgive me. I'm just delighted for you.'

Gideon eyed her critically. 'You're too thin, Sally. I think I can say that as an old friend. Do you get enough to eat?'

Sally laughed. 'You sound just like Mrs Wallace. I'm quite all right, thank you.'

'You must allow me to buy you dinner.' Sir Bertram slipped his arm around Consuela's waist. 'Where are you staying, Sally? You might like to change into something more comfortable.'

Sally was about to accept when she realised that she had nothing suitable to wear, and she did not want them to know that she slept in Flower's stall every night.

'That's very kind of you,' she said hastily. 'But I have to tend to Flower and we have a new show to rehearse tomorrow, so I really need to get an early night.'

Consuela drew her aside. 'I know this must be difficult for you, Sally, but I've wanted to come and see you for a long time. Are you really happy here?'

'Of course. It's what I always wanted to do.'

'Kelly was frantic with worry when you left so suddenly.'

'Was he?' Sally shrugged, turning away so that Consuela could not see the expression on her face. 'I haven't seen or heard from him since I left.'

'Sally, he's been here several times that I know of. He must have seen your performance a dozen times or more. When he's at home he drives the workmen like slaves in an attempt to finish the stable block, and he's had the farmhouse painted and decorated so that you would hardly recognise the place. Although,' she added modestly, 'I've helped him to choose the colours and the wallpaper, and new carpets. Anyway, he's spending every penny he has to make the place into a home.'

'For some lucky lady,' Sally said bitterly. 'I was just his rag-and-bone assistant and then his housekeeper.'

Consuela took her by the shoulders and gave her a hearty shake. 'You are both stupid. I wish I could bang your silly heads together.'

'I know you mean well, but things are better like this. I'm earning my own living and I can send money home for Pa and Josie.'

'What about Finn? He misses you so much, Sally.'

'Let him tell me that. I'm sorry, Consuela, but I have to go now and see to Flower.' Sally kissed Consuela's soft cheek. 'I'm so glad you're happy with Sir Bertram, and that your parents agree to the match.'

Consuela pulled a face. 'That's just it. Papa still wants me to marry Newton. He says I'm to return to California, but I won't go. I wrote him a long letter telling him that I'll be a proper English lady if he agrees to let me marry Bertie, but if I don't hear from Papa very soon we plan to go to some place in Scotland. Gretna Green, I believe it's called.'

'What does Kelly say to that?'

'I haven't told him yet because I know he'll try to stop me. That's another reason why I'm begging you to come home, Sally. Papa has made Kelly my guardian. It's the condition Papa imposed when I begged him to allow me to stay on in London, but I'm supposed to go home in time for Christmas, and that would mean leaving within the next couple of days.'

'So that's why you came here tonight?'

'Not entirely. I hate seeing Finn looking so down-hearted. He's thrown all his energy into setting up the stud farm and making the farmhouse into a beautiful home, but without you it all seems so empty.'

Sally shook her head. 'I'm sorry, Consuela. But Kelly will have to tell me that himself if he wants me to return. I'm tired of being treated like someone of no account. He thinks of me as a servant, not an equal. I find it almost impossible to believe that he's done all that for me.'

'So you won't help me.'

'Don't look like that, Consuela. You know I would if I could, but if I return to Highgate now it means that I've failed on all counts. I would be in the same sorry financial position as I was when I left. I have a father to support as well as myself.'

'But . . .' Consuela bit her lip. 'I can see it's no use trying to persuade you.'

'No, and I'm truly sorry I can't help, but you should speak to Kelly. He's all talk but beneath the bluster he's a kind-hearted man. He wouldn't want you to marry a man you didn't love.'

'Consuela, my darling. It's time we were going.' Sir Bertram approached them, smiling tenderly at his fiancée. 'Are you sure you won't join us for dinner, Sally?'

'Maybe another time, Sir Bertram.' Sally patted Consuela's hand. 'I wish you well, and remember what I said about Kelly.' She moved quickly to where Gideon was standing a little apart from them. 'I hope you'll be very happy with Cecily. You're a good man and you deserve a wonderful life.'

Gideon leaned over to brush her cheek with a kiss. 'You're an amazing woman, Sally. I can't tell you how much I admire your spirit and your courage.'

She smiled. 'But Cecily is the right one for you, even if it took you a long time to realise it.'

'You're right, but I'll always be your friend, and so will Cecily.'

'Maybe, but I wouldn't bet on that, Gideon.' Sally left him, forcing herself to walk slowly to the stables where Flower was waiting patiently to be settled down for the night.

A week passed, with the performers getting into the Christmas spirit. Matinees were fully booked, as were the evening performances, giving Sally little time to think about home. But in the early hours of the morning when sleep eluded her, she suffered agonies of homesickness. She missed her father and Josie, and she had not even seen the new baby. She missed everyone, and in her heart she knew it was Kelly she wanted and needed most of all. The question that was uppermost in her mind was why he had come so often to see the show, but had never tried to speak to her. Only he could answer that, and she found herself wishing that he would put pride behind him and come to see her. There would not be any performances on Christmas Day, and Sally was planning to go home, if only for a brief visit.

It was Tuesday afternoon, exactly a week before Christmas, when Sally was in the ring rehearsing a particularly difficult series of dressage movements at Jem's request, as he was thinking of giving them star billing. Flower had just executed a perfect piaffe, and Sally was leaning over to praise her when she heard a familiar voice calling her name.

She froze. 'Kelly?'

'I couldn't keep away any longer, Suggs.'

How long he had been standing there, with his arms full of red roses, Sally had no idea. She dismounted and handed the reins to the one stable lad whom she trusted to look after Flower. 'Take her to her stall and give her a good rub down, please.' She walked slowly across the ring to where Kelly was standing.

He held out the flowers. 'For you, Suggs. I know I should say something romantic and clever, but I'm suddenly dumbstruck, like a schoolboy.'

'I've never known you to be lost for words, Kelly.' Sally took the flowers, holding them tenderly as if they were as fragile as glass. 'Whatever happened to your usual blarney?'

'I'm sincere, probably for the first time in my life. I've been rehearsing speeches in my head all the way from home, but it's not complicated. I've missed you every minute of every day, and most nights when I couldn't sleep. I can't live without you, and you probably hate me for the way I neglected you, but I love you and I think I always have.'

Sally's knees gave way beneath her and she sank down on the sawdust, clutching the roses in her arms. 'If this is one of your jests, it's in very poor taste.'

Kelly leaped over the low wall that separated the auditorium from the ring, and he raised Sally to her feet, crushing the flowers in a passionate embrace. 'I never was more serious.'

'You're ruining my bouquet,' Sally said dazedly.

Kelly laughed and caressed her cheek. 'Is that all you can say? You kissed me back, Sally. You can't pretend that you didn't.'

'I did,' Sally murmured. 'Why did you wait so long to kiss me?'

His answer was a kiss that seemed to go on forever, causing her pulse to race and fire to course through her veins. The scent of him was so familiar that it went to her head like fine wine. His hands caressed her body and she felt herself melting into his embrace. Time stood still and it seemed as though they were the only two people on earth.

He drew away just far enough to look into her eyes with a tender smile. 'I love you, Sally. I want you to come home with me now. I'll never let you go again, and you won't recognise the place – I've done it all for you.'

'Just a minute, sir.' Jem Skipton strode into the ring, brandishing the whip he used in the show. 'You can't come here and take my star performer away. Leave her be, sir.'

'Come with me now, please, Sally. Let me show you what I've done for you – for us.'

'You have an agreement with me, Miss Suggs,' Jem roared. 'You can't walk out on me.'

Sally cradled her crushed roses like a baby. 'I will come to you, Kelly. But it's only fair if I finish the week off.'

'You don't owe this fellow anything, my love. Come with me now.'

'No, Kelly.' Sally shook her head. 'I can't do that, even though I want to more than anything else on earth, but Jem gave me a job when I was desperate and I've worked my way to star billing. I owed Ma that, and now I'm doing it, for her if for no one else.'

Kelly's mouth drooped at the corners and his eyes darkened. 'I love you, Sally. I adore you and I want you to come with me now. Is there nothing I can say to change your mind?'

She kissed him on the lips. 'I love you, too, Kelly. But I have to honour my commitment to everyone here. I'll come home on Sunday, the day before Christmas Eve.'

'I'll come for you then,' he said reluctantly.

'The roses are beautiful, Kelly. Thank you.'

He smiled ruefully. 'You have to thank Sir Bertram. He sent to Follyfield Park and his head gardener must have cut every bloom in the hothouse.'

'Can we get on with the rehearsal, Miss Suggs?' Jem demanded impatiently. 'That's if you've finished spooning with the Irish gentleman.'

'You're talking to my future wife, sir,' Kelly said with a triumphant smile. 'I've waited this long for her. I can wait for a few days longer.' He enveloped Sally in a kiss that gave much, and yet demanded more, and then he walked away with a swagger in his gait.

* * *

Every show was a huge success. Sally and Flower were undoubtedly the stars and the audience demanded encore after encore. On Saturday evening Sally was buoyed up with excitement as she rode into the ring, and when she saw her father seated in the front row, between Kelly and Josie, she was choked with emotion. As her gaze travelled along the row she realised that Ned Smith was holding his wife's hand, looking every inch the proud husband. Gideon was there with Cecily, and Consuela was seated next to Sir Bertram. Sally blew them a kiss and went into her routine.

At the end of the evening, Sally and Flower received a standing ovation, and when the audience began to disperse and Flower had been taken to her stall for a well-earned rub down, Sally went to join her family. She wrapped her arms around her father, tears of joy running down her cheeks.

'It's so good to see you, Pa.'

He hugged her until she was breathless. 'Your ma would be so proud of you, Sal. You are so like her. You have her touch of genius.'

Sally kissed his lined cheek. 'I'm so glad you enjoyed the show, Pa.'

'You'd better give Kelly a kiss, too, or he'll be getting jealous. You've got a good man there, Sal.'

Suddenly everyone was talking at once. Sally was caught up in the midst of hugs and congratulations. Cecily unbent enough to be gracious in her praise, but Sally noticed that she clutched Gideon's hand as if she expected him to run away at any minute.

'I had a letter from Papa,' Consuela confided happily. 'He gave permission for me to marry Bertie, if we promised to wait for him and Mama to arrive from America.'

'I'm so happy for you,' Sally said earnestly. She met Kelly's gaze and found herself blushing. 'Isn't that good news?'

He nodded. 'I have something to ask you, too, Sally. But it can wait until after dinner. We're all booked into Brown's Hotel tonight, including you.' He raised his hand as she was about to argue. 'Don't worry. I managed to get Flower into a livery stable close to the hotel for tonight. She'll be well cared for and safe.'

'I'll help you to get your things together,' Josie said eagerly. 'It will be so good to have you at home again. I can't wait for you to meet my baby boy. Jane is looking after little George tonight, but I miss him already.'

'I'm sure you do. I'm looking forward to seeing him.'

'And Ned and I want you to be his godmother, Sal. Will you do that for us?'

'I'd be proud to.' Sally linked arms with Josie. 'Come and see where I've been living these past few months.'

They walked arm in arm to the stable. 'This can't be where you've been sleeping?' Josie looked round, shaking her head. 'Oh, Sally. How awful.'

'It wasn't too bad. But Josie, I can't go to a smart hotel like Brown's. I haven't anything to wear.'

Josie smiled. 'Don't worry. Consuela's maid has a gown ready for you to change into when we get there. We've thought of everything, and tomorrow we'll travel home in style. There's Sir Bertram's landau and Miss Appleton's barouche.'

'I feel as if I'm in the middle of a dream.'

'Wait until after dinner. I have a feeling that Kelly has something important to ask you.'

Chapter Twenty-Eight

The ivory satin gown that Consuela had given Sally was so beautiful that it brought fresh tears to Sally's eyes. The décolleté neckline was enhanced with Valenciennes lace, as were the sleeves, and the bodice emphasised Sally's tiny waist, as did the wide skirt falling in silken folds over a crinoline cage. Lucy put Sally's hair up in a most becoming style, and Consuela went through her jewellery case to find a pearl necklace and earrings to complete the outfit.

When Sally entered the dining room, where a late supper had been laid out for their party, she knew that she looked her best by the stunned expression on Kelly's face. He held both her hands in his, gazing into her eyes.

'I can't wait until after dinner, Sally.' He went down on one knee. 'I love you more than life itself. Will you marry me, my darling girl?'

Tears of happiness filled Sally's eyes. 'Yes, Finn. I'll marry you.' She looked round in surprise as everyone cheered and clapped. She had quite forgotten that they were not alone, but Kelly ignored their audience and he stood up, sweeping her into a warm embrace.

'The sooner the better, Sally. I've waited far too long.'

Next day, after a blissfully comfortable night's sleep. Sally was up early and was about to get dressed when Consuela's maid came to her room, carrying a scarlet velvet hooded cloak trimmed with fur and a pair of matching gloves.

'These are a wedding present from Miss Consuela and Sir Bertram,' Lucy said excitedly. 'I'm so happy for you, miss.'

'I'm sorry your romance didn't blossom, Lucy.'

'Well, to tell you the truth, I met someone much nicer at Follyfield Park. I think I'm going to be very happy there.'

Sally gave her a hug. 'I'm so glad, Lucy.'

'And there's more, miss.' Lucy laid the cloak down and held up a pale blue wool merino morning gown. 'Miss Consuela chose this for you, too. We've had a lovely time picking out things we both think will suit you.'

'But I can't pay for all these expensive clothes,' Sally said sadly. 'They'll have to go back to the shop.'

Lucy shook her head. 'No, miss. They're all part of Sir Bertram and Miss Consuela's present to you. Sir Bertram says it's through you that he and Miss Consuela met and he cannot ever repay you.'

Sally slipped the gown over her head, waiting patiently while Lucy fastened the tiny fabric-covered buttons at the back of the bodice. Sally gazed at her reflection in the mirror. 'I look like a lady.'

'You are a lady, miss. Don't let anyone tell you different.'

Kelly was in the foyer talking to the doorman when Sally made her way downstairs. His eyes lit up when he saw her and he hurried to her side. 'Let's get away before the others appear,' he said with the eagerness of a small boy. 'My chaise is waiting outside and it looks as though it might snow later on. It's certainly cold enough.'

'I can't leave Flower at the livery stable.'

He chuckled. 'Well, you're not dressed for riding, darling girl. I've arranged for Bertram's footman to bring Flower back to the stud farm.'

'You should have told him to take her to the cottage. That's where I live, unless you've forgotten.'

He toyed with one of her dark curls that had escaped from the chignon at the back of her neck, the humorous smile that she had always loved twisting his mouth into a grin. 'Trust me, mavourneen, I have everything in hand. We'll go now, unless of course you want to stay for breakfast.'

'I'm not hungry, Kelly. But I wish you'd tell me what's going on.'

He hurried her to the door. 'Wait and see.'

Sure enough, as Kelly had predicted, small flakes of snow started to fall just as they reached the outskirts of Highgate, and as they approached the stud farm the scene took on a magical fairy-tale look. The snow was falling heavily now, coating the bare branches of deciduous trees and icing the fronds of the tall firs. As they approached the farmhouse, its silhouette softening by the misty whiteness, Sally gasped at the sight of a huge Christmas tree situated in the middle of the yard. It was bare of decoration except for a large silver star on the top, and the glistening crystals of snow on its branches. In the soft light, the old farmhouse looked like an illustration from a picture book – the paintwork had been refreshed, the windows cleaned, and the door was now bright blue with a shiny brass knocker.

Kelly guided the horse towards the stable block, above which in striking black and gold lettering a sign proclaimed, 'Kelly & Kelly – Stud Farm'.

'Kelly and Kelly,' Sally said, frowning. 'Does that mean what I think it means?'

'Of course it does.' Kelly leaned over to kiss her chilled lips. 'I always intended you to be my partner, whether or not you agreed to be my wife. Now I have the best of both worlds.' He climbed down, handing the reins to Jim, who had come running from the tack room accompanied by his brothers and Pippy.

'Don't forget we're having everyone to dinner on Christmas Day, Jim,' Kelly said, smiling.

'I won't, sir.' Jim hesitated as he was about to lead the horse towards the stable. 'Welcome home, miss,' he added with a cheeky grin. Pippy bounced up and down, barking excitedly.

'It's lovely to see you again, boys.' Sally held her arms out to Kelly and he lifted her to the ground. She hugged the children and bent down to pick up Pippy, who licked her face excitedly. With a last loving pat Sally handed her back to Benny. 'Has she been good?'

'Yes, miss,' Benny said shyly. 'She's the best dog in the world. You won't take her away from me, will you?'

Sally smiled. 'I think she wants to be your special dog, Benny. She's obviously very happy with you, but you must promise to bring her to see me very often.'

'I will, miss. Of course I will.' Benny hugged Pippy, chuckling at her antics as she tried to eat snowflakes.

'It's nearly Christmas, miss,' Eddie gave her a gap-tooth grin. 'Aunt Jane has got presents for us under the tree at home.'

'Yes, miss.' Jim grinned widely. 'We ain't never had presents at Christmas afore. I can hardly wait. Come on, you two. We got to get home or they'll be out looking for us.' The boys ran off in the direction of Hill Farm, tossing snowballs at each other and laughing as they skidded on the icy ground.

Sally watched them as they disappeared into the trees. 'I'm glad they've settled in so well. But what will happen if their father tries to make trouble?'

'My solicitor is drawing up adoption papers, Sally. Jane and Arthur Wallace are desperate to bring up the boys, and Ted Cotton is always in need of money.'

'I thought he'd gone to New York with Vasey.'

'They were both arrested at Southampton. There are enough charges, including arson, to keep Cotton in prison for several years, and Vasey too. Rags Roper decided to turn Queen's evidence against both of them in return for a pardon for his misdemeanours. When Cotton is released he'll agree to anything if the price is right.'

'That's so good. The Wallaces will make wonderful parents, and we must make sure that the boys always have the best Christmas ever.'

'We will, and that's a promise.' Kelly scooped her up in his arms and carried her into the house. 'Welcome to your new home, or at least it will be when we tie the knot the day after tomorrow.'

Sally gasped as he set her down on the newly scrubbed kitchen floor. 'But that's Christmas Day. We can't get married so soon.'

'Why ever not? What's to stop us?' Kelly brushed snowflakes from her hair. 'The vicar has agreed to conduct the ceremony.'

'Well, there are lots of other things. We haven't

invited anyone. I haven't got a gown. We haven't arranged a wedding breakfast.'

He took her in his arms, smiling. 'I'm not letting you get away this time, mavourneen. Consuela, Josie and Cecily have helped me to organise the best and most splendid celebration anyone round here has ever seen.'

'Cecily agreed to help?'

'I think she wants you off the list of eligible young ladies. She won't be happy until she's got Lawrence's ring on her finger, but she's been very generous. She might expect a ride on Flower occasionally, but she's allowed her servants to assist in the preparations.'

'I don't know what to say.' Sally was genuinely shocked, but also delighted. There was magic in the air at Christmas, and the snow had added the final touch.

'Come with me,' Kelly said, taking her by the hand. He led her through the oak-panelled hall she had come to know so well, but now it was carpeted with a warm red Turkey square and copper pots filled with holly were placed on the two wooden monks' benches. When Kelly opened the sitting-room door, Sally's hand flew to her mouth when she saw another huge Christmas tree, but this one was covered in brightly coloured glass balls, tinsel and red satin bows. The walls had been papered with a delicate flower pattern and new curtains draped the windows. The scent of beeswax polish mingled with that of the pine logs blazing up the chimney, and a vase of winter jasmine made a splash of colour on the tea table in the window.

'I hired a girl from the village to do the hard work, mavourneen,' Kelly said, chuckling. 'You will have far too much to do to bother about mundane tasks.' He led Sally to a kissing bough hanging from one of the wooden beams. He held her at arm's length, looking into her eyes with a tender smile. 'Josie has everything ready for you at the cottage, and you were right – there is still a lot to arrange so I won't see you tomorrow. I'm afraid I'll have to wait until I see you in the church on Christmas morning.'

'This has all happened so quickly. It feels as though I'm dreaming.'

He kissed her tenderly. 'If this is a dream, I never want it to end, mavourneen.'

When Sally awakened on Christmas morning she sat up in bed and stretched – she could hardly believe that it was her wedding day. She was about to reach for her wrap when the door opened and Josie walked in, cradling the sleeping baby in her arms.

'I hope he didn't disturb your night's sleep, Sal. George has got a good pair of lungs on him, just like his pa.' She sat on the edge of the bed. 'Isn't he beautiful?'

Sally stroked the baby's downy head with the tip of her finger. 'He's a fine boy, and you look happy, Josie.'

'I've never been so happy in me whole life. Ned's a good man and I'm glad we decided to stay here instead of going to live in Chelmsford. Ned really enjoys working for Kelly and he's been helping your pa to do the garden. I never thought he'd settle down, but he has.'

'That's wonderful, Josie. You deserve to be treated well, and you have a lovely baby.'

'And you have a wedding to prepare for, Sal,' Josie said, chuckling. 'I'll put George in his crib and I'll see to our breakfast. Ned's gone off to work at the stud farm, but we'll meet up later.'

'What are you planning?' Sally asked warily. 'It's just a quiet wedding in the village church, followed by a family meal, isn't it?'

Josie stood up and walked to the door. 'You don't have anything to worry about. It's all organised.' She left the room and Sally could hear her singing softly as she put George in the wooden crib that Ned had made for his son.

The rest of the morning passed in a haze of nervous expectation. Consuela and Sir Bertram had been invited to stay at Fleet Hall, and in an apparent burst of generosity, Sir Gregory had placed one of his coachmen and the landau at the bride's disposal. Consuela sent Lucy to help Sally get ready for the ceremony, and this allowed Josie to concentrate on her baby son. Even so, she still she managed to supervise Ted, who had struggled into his best suit, but was having difficulty with his tie, and his shoelaces kept coming undone.

Sally had no choice other than to wear the ivory satin gown given to her by Consuela and Sir Bertram. She had to admit that it made a perfect wedding dress, although she would have walked down the aisle in her riding habit if necessary. Her doubts about Finn Kelly had long since been swept away, and she knew that he was the only man she would ever love with all her heart and soul. Her brief infatuation with Gideon had faded into nothingness months ago, and she suspected that he had always loved Cecily, even though he had denied his feelings for a long time.

'I was certain that you and Kelly would make a match of it one day, love.' Ted rose from his seat at the table as Sally entered the kitchen. 'You look beautiful, just like your dear mother. She would have been so proud of you, Sal.'

Sally wrapped her arms around him and kissed his whiskery cheek. 'Thank you, Pa.'

'Are you nervous, Sally?' Josie asked anxiously. 'You don't need to be. Your pa is right, you look a picture.'

Sally turned to Lucy, who was holding her cloak and a posy of white camellias from the hothouse at Fleet Hall. 'Thanks to Lucy. I couldn't have done my hair like this for a start.'

Ted proffered his arm. 'I'm a proud man, Sal.'

* * *

The drive to the church through snowy lanes was something that Sally knew she would remember for the rest of her life. The village church was packed with family and well-wishers and the ceremony went off without a hitch. The bells rang out for Christmas Day and the wedding. It was too cold to linger outside, but Sally was surrounded by people, some of whom she barely knew, all wishing the happy couple health and happiness in their new life. Large flakes of snow had started to fall as they drove the short distance to the house, and Sir Gregory's coachman drew the carriage up as close to the front door as was possible. Kelly leaped to the ground and helped Sally to alight. He tipped the coachman and carried Sally over the threshold, setting her down on the floor beneath a huge bunch of mistletoe.

'Welcome home, Mrs Kelly.' He kissed her tenderly.

'Where are the others?' Sally asked when he finally gave her time to breathe. 'Is it just going to be us for the wedding breakfast?'

'Come this way, mavourneen.' Taking her by the hand, Kelly led her through the house to the large room that had once been the dairy, only now it was barely recognisable.

A log-burning stove had been fitted and the flag-stone floor was covered in brightly patterned rugs. A long table in the centre of the room was surrounded by gilded chairs with red plush seats. The white damask cloth was laid with sixteen place settings, crystal glasses and silver candelabra ablaze with lighted candles. Swags of holly and ivy were pinned to the wooden beams and the scent of hot rum punch, spices and lemons filled the air.

'Did you do all this, Kelly?' Sally looked round in astonishment. 'It's wonderful.'

'I was kept busy yesterday,' he said, chuckling. 'But I can't take credit for setting the table or providing the food.'

Outside there was the clatter of horses' hoofs, the muffled rumble of wheels and the sound of voices as the guests tumbled from their vehicles. Kelly flung open the double doors and a gust of wind covered the floor with a powdering of snow as the three Cotton boys rushed into the room, followed by Arthur and Jane Wallace together with Bert, who had been spruced up for the occasion. Kelly had barely closed the doors when Ned and Josie arrived together with Ted. Josie had George in her arms, but she took him through to the sitting room where she laid him on the sofa, wrapped in a blanket. She rushed back to give Sally a hug.

'We'll hear him if he cries. You don't mind having a baby at your wedding breakfast, do you?'

Sally kissed her cheek. 'Of course not. I'm glad you brought him.' She turned to her father and gave him a hug. 'Have some warm punch, Pa. It will keep out the cold.'

Ted smiled vaguely. 'That's what your mother used to say, Sal.'

She caressed his cheek with a gentle hand. 'She's here in spirit, Pa. I know she is.'

He wandered off to where one of the servants from the Hall had brought in a bowl of punch and a tray of cut-glass cups.

Shortly afterwards more carriages arrived, and Sir Gregory marched into the room followed by Cecily and Gideon. Another vehicle drew up and Consuela entered on the arm of Sir Bertram. The room was filled with loud conversation and laughter. Sally was quick to notice that Cecily clung to Gideon's arm and never let him out of her sight. When they came over to offer their congratulations, Gideon drew Sally aside.

'I want you to know that I'll always be there should you need me, Sally.'

'Thank you, but I hope that won't happen, and anyway you have Cecily now. She loves you as you deserve.'

He gave her a wry smile. 'My farm is safe, and I hope will go from generation to generation.'

'What are you talking about?' Cecily demanded sharply.

'We were congratulating ourselves on finding the perfect partners.' Sally gave her a sympathetic smile. 'I wish you all the happiness in the world, and thank you for all this, Cecily. I know it was at your doing and I want you to know that I really appreciate it. I hope we will be good friends as well as good neighbours.'

Cecily's lovely face lit up with a genuine smile.

'I hope so too, Sally.' She tucked her hand through the crook of Gideon's arm. 'I'd love a glass of champagne, darling. Papa only buys the very best.' She led him away to where Jackson was opening a magnum of Veuve Cliquot.

Consuela hurried to Sally's side. 'It was a beautiful ceremony, Sally. I hope my wedding will be as lovely. Bertie wants to have ours at Follyfield Park, but you and Kelly will come, won't you?'

'Of course we will,' Sally said, smiling. 'I wouldn't miss it for worlds.' She glanced at Jackson, who was hovering in the doorway as if he had an announcement to make. 'I think the meal is ready to be served.' She raised her voice. 'Shall we all take our seats and enjoy the wonderful wedding breakfast so kindly supplied by Sir Gregory?'

Sir Gregory puffed out his chest. 'It's my pleasure, ma'am. Champagne for everyone, Jackson.'

Jane Wallace was about to take her seat but she stood up, glaring at Sir Gregory. 'Not for the children, sir.'

'I don't know – give them cider, I suppose, or lemonade.' Sir Gregory moved to the head of the table and sat down, but Cecily hurried to his side.

'Not there, Papa. That is the bridegroom's place.'

Kelly held up his hand. 'Don't move, Sir Gregory. I'm happy to sit anywhere just as long as I have my wife at my side.'

A round of applause followed them as they moved to the opposite end of the festive table, and the rest of the party took their seats without any fuss. Jackson clicked his fingers and the servants from Fleet Hall appeared as if from nowhere, bringing the first course of mock turtle soup, which was followed by roast turkey with all the trimmings, and the meal was crowned with the entry of a Christmas pudding flamed in brandy, mince pies and a large sherry trifle.

The old dairy was filled with the sound of conversation and bursts of laughter, which grew more frequent as the champagne flowed freely. Jim and Bert were allowed cider, which left them rosy-cheeked and slightly tiddly, and the two younger boys drank lemonade.

Kelly rose to his feet. 'I want to thank Sally for agreeing to marry me. I count myself the luckiest man in the world to have won such a wonderful woman, but I don't want to bore you all with a long speech. We would both like to thank you all for coming and particularly Sir Gregory for his generosity in providing such a splendid feast.' Kelly paused while everyone clapped politely. 'And without further ado I suggest we should move to the drawing room, where I believe I can hear a young man crying for his mama, and as it's Christmas, there are presents under the tree for everyone.'

Sally rose to her feet. 'How did you manage that, Kelly?'

'I didn't. I must confess that I left it to Consuela and Josie.'

'You must have been very sure that I would accept your proposal of marriage, Kelly.'

He leaned down to plant a kiss on the tip of her nose. 'I lived in hope, mavourneen.'

She smiled. 'You have an answer for everything.' She was about to follow the rest of the party through to the drawing room, but Kelly caught her by the hand and raised it to his lips.

'I love you, Sally, and I have done for a very long time. I could never have imagined that one day you would be my wife, and I can't wait to show you how much I adore you.' He drew her gently to him and kissed her.

Sally slid her arms around his neck, responding with growing fervour. 'I love you, too, Finn Kelly. And everything you've done with the house is wonderful.'

'It's yours and mine, mavourneen. We will share everything from now on and for ever.'

Read on for a sneak peek at Dilly's brand-new book

The Reluctant Heiress

Coming Spring 2021!

Chapter One

East India Docks, London 1858

Katherine Martin stood on the upper deck of the steamship *Aldebaran*. She took a deep breath of the none-too-clean London air, tainted by the stench of the river mud and the manufactories on the banks of the Thames. It was a cold and rainy February day and the monochrome tones of her surroundings were a complete contrast to the heat, dust and vibrant colours of India, but it was home, and freedom from the terrors she and her parents had encountered at the start of the uprising. They were some of the fortunate ones whose loyal servants had helped them to escape from Delhi moments before the rebel army attacked. Kate recalled with a shudder the night when they had left the luxurious home of her uncle Edgar, who held a senior position in the

East India Company. It had been a long and terrifying journey, but somehow, and with the help and goodwill of many villagers along the way, they had arrived in Bombay. They had stayed at the home of Sir Robert Audley, Uncle Edgar's solicitor, and a letter of introduction to the manager of Uncle Edgar's bank had been enough to secure funds for their return to London, travelling first class, and the basic necessities of clothing.

'Don't just stand there, Kate. I've sent Fellowes to find a cab.' Sir Bartholomew Martin tapped the deck with his silver-headed malacca cane. He was not a patient man. How he had managed to hold on to the wretched stick throughout their hair-raising experiences was still a mystery to Kate. However, she was used to her father's bursts of ill-temper and she brushed past him, heading to where her mother was waiting at the top of the companionway.

'Are you all right, Mama?' Kate asked anxiously. 'You look very pale.'

'It's the half-light, my dear. I'll be fine when we get home. I long for a comfortable bed and a hot bath, and especially a change of clothes. I will put everything we've been forced to wear for all these weeks in the missionary barrel at the church.'

'I don't know,' Kate said, smiling. 'Having only two or three choices does make dressing much less of a chore.'

'You see the bright side of every situation, Kate.' Arabella Martin sighed and glanced anxiously at her husband. 'Your papa looks angry. What has upset him now?'

'He's just miffed because Fellowes is taking his time.' Kate kept a straight face with difficulty. Her father, who had been a magistrate in Delhi for three years, was used to having his orders obeyed instantly and without question.

'Perhaps our luggage has been lost,' Arabella said anxiously. 'Maybe that's why Fellowes is taking so long.'

'We only have three cases and a carpet bag. I'm sure I could carry most of them on my own.' Kate leaned over the side and waved. 'There he is now, and I think he's found a carriage. We'd best hurry or someone else might snatch it, and I want to get you home as soon as possible, Mama.'

'Come along, ladies. What are you waiting for?' Sir Bartholomew shooed them down the steps to the next deck as if he were herding sheep.

Fellowes, Sir Bartholomew's valet, was guarding the hackney carriage as if it were made of solid gold, but there was considerable competition for its services. The former passengers of the *Aldebaran* staggered around with a rolling gait, as if the ship's deck were still beneath their feet, as they sought desperately for transport to take them to the final destination.

'Get in, Arabella,' Sir Bartholomew said testily. 'You, too, Katherine. Don't dawdle.'

Kate faced him angrily. 'Can't you see that Mama is exhausted?'

'Don't use that tone to me, miss. You may be twenty-one, but you're under my jurisdiction until you marry. Then some other man will have the task of keeping you in order.'

Fellowes raised an expressive eyebrow as he helped Kate into the cab, barely allowing Arabella time to settle her voluminous skirts around her.

'Thank you, Fellowes,' Kate said loudly. 'You may sit next to me.'

'Fellowes will sit up with the driver.' Sir Bartholomew fixed his servant with a stern gaze.

'Of course, sir.' Fellowes closed the door.

Kate cast a worried glance at her mother, who had suffered from chronic malaise during their time in Delhi. The climate in India had not suited her, but perhaps now they were back in London her mother's health would improve. Kate sat back, gazing out of the window at the mean streets that surrounded the docks as the cabby urged his horse to a brisk trot. When they had left England three years previously, they had sailed from Southampton. Although they had lived in the centre of London at the time, Kate had never been this far into the East End. it was quite shocking to see such poverty, with barefoot children running wild. Feral dogs and cats were slinking around in the shadows, snarling and fighting over the tiniest scrap of food. Kate had seen poverty in India, although she had never been allowed to go out and explore on her own. She suspected that care had been taken to avoid the poorest quarters of the cities she had visited, but she was appalled now to see small, ragged children and the elderly begging on street corners in such terrible weather.

She closed her eyes to shut out the unpleasant sights, casting her mind back to happier times when life seemed to be a round of parties and balls at the barracks. Kate turned her head away from her parents as tears seeped through her closed eyelids. She was transported back to the candlelit ballroom where she had first met Subedar-Major Ashok Patel, who had been assigned to ensure that she and her family had everything they needed during their time in Delhi. He had bowed over her hand, and when their eyes met she knew that she had found her destiny. Ash had held her hand as if he would never let her go, and at that moment she would have been prepared to follow him to the end of time. His dark eyes, lit by glints of pure gold, had kept her captive and his handsome face still haunted her dreams. They had danced every dance that magical evening, although it was against all the rules, and had caused heads to turn. A young lady of her class was not supposed to mix with the natives, which was something that her mother had drummed into her even before they had arrived in India. The divisions were there for a reason and must be obeyed. Despite the fact that Subedar-Major Patel had earned his promotion by his gallant actions in skirmishes on the North-West Frontier, he was, Sir Bartholomew had said at length, not a suitable companion for any daughter of his. Kate had been forbidden to see Ash again. However, the old saying 'love laughs at locksmiths' had proved true and they had managed to meet in secret. Ash told her later that his commanding officer had also warned him of the consequences of such a liaison, but the objections of their elders hardly seemed to matter.

Over a period of several months Kate had spent as much time with Ash as possible. She discovered that he was an Anglo-Indian. His mother, the daughter of an English employee of the East India Company, had died in childbirth. Ashok's father, a captain in the cavalry, had been killed in action some years previously. His family were as much against mixed blood marriages as Ash's maternal grandparents, and Ash had been sent to boarding school. Kate remembered comparing him to a cuckoo in the nest, and when she had explained the metaphor they had both laughed at the ridiculousness of the social mores that were affecting them even then.

Kate leaned her head against the cold window glass; recalling the good times only intensified the agony of their parting. It was Ash who had risked everything to help them get away that terrible night, but he had insisted that it was his duty as a soldier to return to his unit. The tenderness of their last embrace still burned upon Kate's lips, and the salt tears that trickled down her cheeks now had the bitterness of gall. The long sea voyage had kept her in total ignorance of the progress of the rebellion and there was no way of knowing whether Ash was alive or dead. Kate was alone in her misery, for there was no one in whom she could confide. She knew she would get no sympathy from either of her parents.

The hackney carriage trundled onwards, rumbling over cobblestones, each turn of the wheel and every hoof beat taking Kate further away from the ship, which was her last connection with India and the man she loved. She shot a surreptitious glance at her parents, but her father was glaring into space and tapping his malacca cane impatiently on the floor of the cab, and her mother was lying back with her eyes closed. Kate dashed her tears away on the back of her hand and struggled to compose herself. Her heartbreak was hers to bear on her own, and she would have to find an alternative way of living her life. Marriage for her was out of the question. She could not imagine any man taking Ashok's place in her heart, but there must be something she could do that would give her a new purpose.

The carriage was slowing down and as she wiped the steamed-up glass she realised that they were pulling up outside her old home in Finsbury Square. Lights blazed from the windows on all floors and the front door opened to reveal a uniformed footman.

'Papa, we're home at last,' Kate said with a heartfelt sigh. 'Mama, wake up. We've arrived.'

Fellowes opened the cab door and Sir Bartholomew alighted first. He marched up the front steps, leaving Kate to help her mother from the carriage, while Fellowes paid the cabby. Henry, the footman who had served the family for many years, moved swiftly to assist them.

'You'll have to excuse the state of the house, my lady,' he said earnestly. 'We only got the letter informing us of your imminent arrival this morning. Mrs Marsh and the servants are in a real state.'

'Oh dear.' Arabella's eyes filled with tears. 'Well, never mind, Henry. All I want is my nice comfortable bed, a warm fire and a hot drink.'

'I'm sure we can arrange that, Mama,' Kate said softly. She tucked her mother's limp hand through the crook of her arm. 'We can manage, if you would help Fellowes with the luggage, please, Henry?'

'Of course, Miss Katherine.'

'You must be exhausted, Mama.'

'I am perfectly capable of walking up the steps into my own home.' Arabella teetered off, swaying slightly as she crossed the pavement and ascended the steps to the front door.

Kate followed her parents into the elegant five-storey house that had been her childhood home. She could hear her mother's querulous voice and the deeper responses from their housekeeper, Mrs Marsh. Housemaids were scurrying from room to room, their arms filled with holland covers. There was no sign of her father, and Kate felt safe in assuming that he had gone straight to his study.

'I have had a fire lit in your bedchamber, my lady.' Mrs Marsh turned to Kate with a pained expression. 'We only heard of your arrival this morning, Miss Katherine. I've had to hire maids and scrub women because we weren't prepared.'

'My mother is worn out,' Kate said firmly. 'We'll have to employ a new lady's maid as soon as possible, but in the meantime have you someone who could fill that position on a temporary basis?'

'There's my daughter, Jenny. She's only sixteen but she worked for Lady Dalrymple for a few months, so she knows how things should be done.' Mrs Marsh lowered her voice. 'She only left because Sir Horace was rather free with his attentions, if you know what I mean?'

'That must have been very disturbing for her. I do remember Jenny. She was a skinny little thing who was always singing.'

A reluctant smile deepened the creases on Mrs Marsh's lined face. 'That's my Jenny. A ray of sunshine, if you'll pardon the expression. Shall I send her up to my lady's room?'

'By all means, and she should take a pot of tea and some bread and butter. Cake would be nice, if you have any.'

'Leave it with me, Miss Katherine. What about yourself and Sir Bartholomew?'

'I expect my father will dine at his club, and I'll be happy with a light supper.'

'There's a fire in the morning parlour. I didn't know whether you'd get here today or tomorrow. We're all at sixes and sevens.'

Kate could see that Mrs Marsh was genuinely upset at the lack of preparations. 'That suits me very well. I'll be retiring to my room early – it's been a long journey and an equally tiring day.' She did not add that the emotional strain of leaving the man she loved and not knowing if he were alive or dead had affected her more than she would have thought possible.

'I'm sure we all understand, Miss Katherine. We've been reading about the terrible goings-on in that country in the newspapers. Thank the Lord you were all spared and have come home safe and sound.'

'Yes, indeed.' Kate realised that Mrs Marsh was eager to learn more of their escape, but she could not bring herself to talk about it now, or perhaps ever. Some things were best forgotten, if that were possible. 'I'd better let you get on, Mrs Marsh. It's good to be home.'

Mrs Marsh inclined her head and turned away slowly, but if she hoped that Kate would change her mind and pass on more information she was doomed to disappointment.

Kate set off towards the morning parlour. The house seemed too large, too echoing and too cold. She missed India and the privileged life she had led there: it was another world and a land of extremes. Until the uprising each day had been an adventure - now she had come back to reality. The smell of carbolic soap mingled with that of beeswax polish, and there was a hint of burning soot in the stuffy morning parlour.

An hour later, after a supper of soup followed by bread and cheese, eaten on her own, huddled by a desultory fire, Kate went upstairs to her bedroom. The curtains had not been drawn and she went over to the window, gazing down into the square. It was quite dark now and the trees in the residents' private garden had a fairy-like quality, shimmering in the gaslight. A few tender young leaves fluttered bravely against the chilly wind, and the first early tulips stood to attention like soldiers on parade in the well-kept flowerbeds. She drew the curtains and was relieved to find a nightgown laid out for her on the bed. She was about to undress when there was a timid knock on the door.

'Come in.'

A young woman, barely more than a girl, rushed into the room and came to a halt by the bed. 'Ma thought you might need a hand to get undressed, miss.'

'You've changed quite a bit since I last saw you, Jenny,' Kate said, smiling.

'So have you – that's if you don't mind me saying so, miss?'

'Not at all. We've both grown up a lot in three

years. I believe you are going to be my mother's maid, until she can find a replacement for Bennett.'

'Yes, miss. That's right. But I could be your maid, too, if you so wish.'

Kate thought of the beautiful Mira, who had been assigned to her in Delhi. Mira had anticipated Kate's needs, fulfilling her duties with serene dignity and grace. There could be no comparison, of course, but there was something about Jenny's eagerness and simple honesty that was both warming and refreshing.

'I think that would be a very good idea, Jenny. You may start by bringing me a jug of warm water so that I can wash off some of the city dirt before I go to bed. In India my maid used to float rose petals in the washbowl.'

Jenny wrinkled her nose. 'Funny habits them foreigners have. I wouldn't fancy washing my face with all them greenfly swishing around in the water, not to mention the odd bug.' She left the room, allowing the door to swing shut behind her.

Kate laughed for the first time since she had left Delhi, and then she began to cry. The tears that she had shed since parting with Ash were nothing compared to the heart-broken sobs that now shook her whole body. She collapsed on the bed, unable to control her pent-up emotions for a moment longer, but the storm of crying had passed by the time Jenny reappeared with the water. She set the jug down on the washstand and moved to the side of the bed.

'You're tired out, miss. Upsadaisy, now. Let's get

you washed and into your nightie. I was just the same as you after I come back from Lady Dalrymple's place. Run all the way, I did, and when I come home I didn't know if I was to get a clip round the ear or a cuddle. Got both, as it happened, but Ma never made me go back there.' Jenny helped Kate to her feet and undressed her, talking all the time so that there was no need for Kate to respond other than a nod every now and then.

When Kate was settled in bed, propped up by a soft bank of pillows, Jenny stood back with a nod of approval. 'That's better. I'll fetch you a nice hot cup of chocolate, shall I? I knows that Ma has some in because I was sent out special to fetch some when she got the letter to say you was arriving today. Your ma just drank a cup and she lay back in bed and was asleep afore I got to the door.' She left the room without waiting to see if her suggestion had been accepted.

Kate sighed and closed her eyes. Sometimes it was nice to be treated like a child again. Tomorrow she would organise herself and start a new life back in London. She would put all thoughts of Ash, India and the events she had witnessed from her mind. It would all be forgotten – it must be forgotten, or she would go mad with grief.

Look out for Dilly's next book

The Reluctant Heiress

Coming Spring 2021